W9-CDU-837

7661 0100 612 709

MAY the BEST MAN WIN

ZR ELLOR

ROARING BROOK PRESS
New York

Published by Roaring Brook Press
Roaring Brook Press is a division of Holtzbrinck
Publishing Holdings Limited Partnership
120 Broadway, New York, NY 10271 • fiercereads.com

Copyright © 2021 by Zabé Ellor
All rights reserved

Library of Congress Control Number: 2020919612
ISBN 978-1-250-62512-0

Our books may be purchased in bulk for promotional, educational,
or business use. Please contact your local bookseller or the Macmillan
Corporate and Premium Sales Department at (800) 221-7945 ext. 5442 or by
email at MacmillanSpecialMarkets@macmillan.com.

First edition, 2021 • Book design by Cassie Gonzales
Printed in the United States of America

1 3 5 7 9 10 8 6 4 2

To Aster and Kitty, two incredible friends

CHAPTER ONE: JEREMY

Three Weeks to Homecoming Kickoff

"Please try to look presidential, Jeremy. Keep your tongue in your mouth," Hannah Kim says from behind the camera lens. "This is for our senior class yearbook. Like, your grandkids will be cleaning this out of your attic when you die."

"At least it'll be easy for them to find my photo." I plant my hands against the cement and lift myself into a headstand. "Take it now! I'm making my serious face."

Behind me, Ben, vice president of the student government, cracks up. Debbie, our treasurer, grunts and rolls her eyes. The shutter clicks, and the Cresswell Academy Class of 2021 Student Government Association is immortalized. Posed on the sunbaked sidewalk before the flagpole, the sun scorches down on us from a flawless sky, turning the school lawns and hedges a saturated green. Late-summer humidity clings to my bare arms. My battered boat shoes kick at the air as Debbie makes a gagging sound.

"Really, Jeremy?" she asks me. Hannah waves us off to crowd the whole debate team into one shot. "Coach picked you as cheer co-captain, and you've already won SGA president. Naomi says you're even planning to run for Homecoming King. How much more attention do you need?"

"I thought it was funny!" Ben says, slapping me on the back. I wince, then cough to cover it. "Who says you need a stick up your ass to lead?"

His voice, deep and booming, echoes off the concrete and linoleum as we reenter the school by the gym doors. In the halls, lockers alternate in a bold, clashing medley of gold and blue—the Cresswell colors. Students eat lunch in tight knots and huddled bunches, curled against their lockers and sprawling out of classrooms. Tupperwares burst with curry and pasta. AP Physics students toss back thermoses of coffee and scrawl equations with their free hands. The administration lets us eat lunch wherever we choose, to study, socialize, or work on special projects. The local public schools have tighter rules, but Cresswell trusts its students to make good choices with their time.

Busy as they are, the other students slide out of Ben's way. He cuts a path for me and Debbie like an icebreaker ship, leading us back toward the student government meeting room. Discomfort builds low in my stomach as I watch Ben's broad shoulders plow forward.

I should be leading the way. *I* should be gliding through these halls like Ben—the muscular varsity quarterback, six foot two and sporting a five-o'clock shadow at 12:15 p.m. But three weeks on testosterone has done nothing but transform my throat into a slide whistle packed with gravel. Frozen in the amber of yearbook photos, I'll always look like a short-haired girl in too-big boy's clothes.

Hence the tongue waggling and headstands. I'm going to draw attention no matter what. I'd rather my fellow class-mates see me as a class clown and glory hog than just "a guy who switched genders senior year."

"Debbie! Jeremy!" Anna Kim, Hannah's little sister, waves at us from across the hall. She's surrounded by a horde of pink-clad freshman cheerleaders, swapping mouthwatering pumpkin cupcakes with their names scrawled across the top in rose frosting. Anna frowns at my outfit. "Jeremy, aren't you going to be in the cheer team picture?" She plucks at the string of faux pearls around her neck nervously.

"Yeah, Jeremy, aren't you supposed to be cheer captain?" Debbie says, fluttering her lashes and pulling out her own set of pearls. "We agreed we'd all wear pink today."

I flinch. The cheer team planned to wear pink and pearls for our yearbook photo. I bought the perfect outfit to immor-talize my place as captain, but an untimely acne breakout distracted me on my way out the door this morning, and I left it at home.

"My mom's bringing my outfit, don't worry," I say. "I found this adorable salmon dress shirt and a tie covered in silk rosettes." I don't mention that I went to six different stores to find the XXS size, and I bought the super-skinny tie online. Years of practice mean I know my way around the mall, but even I could barely find formal clothes that don't make me look like a kid playing dress-up in his dad's suit.

"Do you still have your grandma's pearls?" Debbie says. "Or did you hock them when you decided to be a dude?"

I didn't decide on any of this. "It's tacky to wear a tie and pearls at the same time, Debbie." Luckily, before she can respond, my phone buzzes in my back pocket. "Sorry, I think my mom's here."

"Come back dressed in pink or not at all!" Debbie says as I push through the crowd.

Mom's parked on the south side of the building, where the imperious brick façade gives way to the concrete and cinder block of the humanities hallway. Neatly manicured hedges and vast green fields sweep the campus grounds, filling the air with a cut-grass scent. Her Tesla—a gift to herself for making partner at her law firm—idles by a stack of hurdles abandoned by the track team. Even in yoga pants and a sweatshirt, her high ponytail and bleached grin are still flawless. She's the image of the polished, professional DC woman I once thought I'd grow up to be.

"Hey, sweetie," she says, and kisses me on my cheek. "I come bearing picture day outfits and one pumpkin spice mocha." I duck my head through the door and see a garment bag and two steaming Starbucks cups sitting in the front seat.

I exhale. Tension eases from my binder-compressed chest.

Mom and I have always been close—my dad was never around, and she left my stepdad when I was really young. The two of us have always been a team, the Harkiss girls against the world. But that ended when I transitioned, cut off like an electrical short. I'm not sure what we are now.

After taking a sip of my delicious mocha, I unzip the garment bag.

And the first thing I hear is the rattle of pearls.

Grandma's antique necklace is draped around the hanger. I remember her dry fingers as she clasped it on me for my twelfth birthday. *Real ladies wear pearls*, she used to say. The rest of the outfit is almost as bad: a pink blouse and cardigan. No skirt, but the dress pants she brought are for girls, fitted and small-pocketed, made to advertise all the curves I'm trying to hide.

"Mom," I say, breath coming short where my binder squeezes my lungs. "This isn't the outfit I packed. It's a girl's outfit."

Red creeps into her hairline. She knows she messed up. "Oh. Well. I don't know, Jeremy. It's just clothing. It doesn't come with a gender attached."

"But if people see me in those, they'll think I'm a girl." The Cresswell administration may be okay with me transitioning, but that doesn't mean I won't get misgendered. Names and pronouns get stuck in people's heads, with no malicious intent. But getting called "she" and "her" hurts, even when it's accidental.

What cis people don't get is that it's not the wrong clothes, the wrong name, the wrong pronoun. It's the strangling feeling, like you've been buried alive and are struggling to breathe, like you don't exist. That the most important part of you is invisible and, thus, unreal. If people don't see me as a boy, then they don't see me at all.

And my mom's the one I need to see me most.

"I'm sure no one will notice," she says. Like it's no big deal, a faux pas as small as showing up to a party in the same dress as the host.

You'll always be my daughter, she had said.

My fists tighten. My eyes sting bitterly, and I look away so she can't see me break. I want to yell, scream, cry. I want to shout so it will finally stick in her mind. Finally convince her to see me as I am. *I'm your son! Say I'm your son!*

But what if I yell and she says something that hurts worse than this stupid wardrobe malfunction? Grandma had ugly views on gender. She hated that Mom wasn't married when she had me, and made it clear that she didn't want me repeating my mother's "mistakes." I was supposed to be a good girl, in pearls and cardigans, no drinking, no smoking, no sex before marriage. Her beliefs still nip at my heels like her ancient, bad-tempered Chihuahua. Telling me every step I take away from being that perfect girl is one in the wrong direction.

Mom has to hear the echo of Grandma's voice, too. But I

don't want to ask about it—I don't want to know what lessons she can't shake.

Just because she's letting me transition doesn't mean she sees me as her son. And while she still gets final say on all my medical decisions, I'm too scared to threaten the fragile balance between us. I already fought one uphill battle getting here.

"Thanks," I murmur, zipping the bag shut so no one can see what's inside. "See you at home tonight." I turn and head back toward the school, my mocha forgotten on the roof of the car.

Students scurry into classrooms and off to the gym, sneakers squeaking and voices bouncing off the walls. I bow my head to hide my red face, weaving through a thicket of backpacks and sliding around the cherry vinaigrette splatter where some poor kid dropped their salad. Just one more body in a crowd.

A voice in the back of my head says that maybe I should be grateful. Blending in is the point, just like Principal Meehan suggested when we met to discuss how my transition would work at school.

There are a few other trans and nonbinary students at Cresswell, but since I'm the only one legally changing my name and gender, doing all the medical stuff, I get all the administrators' attention. My mom and I worked out a plan with Principal Meehan and the school counselor. My deadname was removed from all school documents. I have access to the boys' bathroom and locker rooms. My teachers were instructed to gender me correctly.

In return, I promised to behave. To be an example, to adhere to the Code of Conduct that has governed Cresswell students since the 1950s. Drafted back when the school still only admitted white, cisgender dudes, it says a lot about "honor" and "gentlemanly conduct" but nothing about gender transition. Cresswell hasn't historically been a progressive school, and relics of that past—like the spectacle of Homecoming itself—still litter the school's culture and calendars.

But history can only move forward. And I refuse to let my transition define me. This is my senior year. It should be my time to shine. To lead the cheer team and SGA. Be crowned on the Homecoming Court.

Since my freshman year, I've watched glittering seniors in formal wear sweep onto the football field during the Homecoming halftime, crowned by Principal Meehan as the crowd cheered them on. I've dreamed of ascending that same stage in glory, on my boyfriend's arm, all of Cresswell chanting my name. Only now it's the king's crown I'm after—and it still hovers before me, bright and shiny as a spotlight.

For cheer captain, I risked my neck as a flyer. For SGA president, I debated six other juniors and made an unforgettable speech promising free admission to football games. For

Homecoming Court, people just need to like you enough to vote. I want—I *need*—everyone to like me that much. To see me as one of Cresswell's golden sons, crowned in shimmering plastic.

"Excuse me, coming through," rumbles a familiar voice from behind a stack of boxes. Close. Too close. My head snaps up. I try to step sideways, but a clump of boys carrying lacrosse sticks block my path, and I stumble—

The boxes tumble from the boy's arms, cascading over me in a tide of glitter and craft feathers.

"Shit. Sorry," he says, kneeling to scrape up the mess. A tall, suntanned white boy, dark hair messy, a streak of blue paint down the firm line of his chin. "I can't see over these Homecoming Committee craft supplies—oh. Jeremy."

I freeze. The sound of my name in his mouth, rich and smooth and edged in nerves, hooks me like an anchor, dragging me back in time. But it also feels like the rush of something new. It's the first time he's said my name. And now I don't know what to say to him. Because the last time we spoke, I broke his heart.

"Hi," I squeak out, shuffling back as he tries to sweep up the mounds of glitter. My shirt's drenched in the stuff. "What's up?" There. That feels like what one guy says to another guy—when they're friendly acquaintances, not buds or bros or anything that matters.

He shrugs. But as I try to slide past him, he gives up on the glitter and puts a hand on my arm. "Hey. Are you okay?"

he asks. And then I remember my blotchy red face and the cursed garment bag I'm holding. His voice is genuine and warm. Concerned. And I hate it. Because who the hell gets concerned about the feelings of their exes, especially after how mean I was to him? He probably just sees me as a hysterical girl he needs to calm down.

Some people sink past the ears in sexism until it colors everything they see, but not Lukas, says the voice at the back of my mind. *Lukas cares about everyone, regardless of gender. He cares so much it hurts him.* And I only care about me.

"I'm fine," I say. "Super fine." I move to walk away and then hesitate. "Hey, you're leading Homecoming Committee this year, right?" I know he is. He's been on the committee since he was a freshman, working his way up the ladder. Lukas loves organizing complicated, flashy events. "Will you put my name down on the court ballot?"

Lukas sweeps the craft supplies back into the box and straightens up. For a moment he just stands there, like he's waiting for more. "Is that all you want to say to me? That you're running for Homecoming King?"

My heart flutters beneath my ribs, tight and squeezed low by the pressure of my binder. I shrug. "That, and you have paint on your chin."

"Where?" He brushes at his face with the back of his hand and then smirks at me. "I'd ask you to rub it off, but you can't reach that high."

"I'll wait until next time a linebacker flattens you on the

field," I say. "Should be easy to reach you then." And it's almost like old times. The way we used to flirt *before*.

"Jeremy," he says. "Seriously." His face goes stony, and the moment is over. Jaw set, lips narrowed. A face I recognize from the day it all ended. "Don't you want to talk about what happened?"

I pull on a light smile, but it's like I'm trying to catch helium in a fist. "I'd love to brag about all the hearts I've broken, but it'll take hours and I need to get to class."

"Still the same old you." Lukas rolls his eyes. "Irritating as hell."

I wink and blow him a kiss. He pivots and sweeps up the boxes before walking away from me without another word. Once he melts into the crowd, I let a small, bitter smile creep across my lips.

We're both so much better off as rivals than as a pair.

CHAPTER TWO: LUKAS

Carrying my helmet and pads, a bulging backpack, and a bag full of carpentry supplies from the morning's float building, I climb aboard the team bus with the grace of a beluga. "Sorry—hey, watch your face!" A sophomore linebacker nearly collides with a drill bit as his seatmate jokingly shoves him my way. "Settle down!" I swing my backpack up over the seat, nearly clobbering a teammate in the throat, and rest it on the backseat as I drop down beside Ben. Ancient, cracked pleather creaks below the combined weight of me and all my projects.

The bus belches exhaust as it pulls away from Cresswell. It rolls through the open windows, the last summer breezes shifting to black. Mixing with the tide of twenty different deodorants and the reek of one freshman asshole who's forgotten to wear any. Every bump on the road rattles through the shot suspension and nearly knocks all the crap from my grip.

"How'd the first Homecoming Committee meeting go?" Ben asks. "Did you blow your whole budget on glowsticks yet?"

I laugh. "We set a hard limit of two thousand dollars for glowstick-related activities. Laurie Perez suggested turning the whole dance into a rave. The alumni would die of embarrassment."

Cresswell Homecoming is the mother of all big deals. A weeklong festival celebrating our school's traditions and honoring our alumni. The students—as expected from rich kids in Montgomery County, Maryland—go all-out for an entire week. We create Comic-Con-worthy costumes for spirit days. Host canned food drives and build massive sculptures from the haul. Every class has a theme around which we design T-shirts, paint banners, construct parade floats, and stage original musical comedy sketches. It culminates with a football victory (sometimes our only win of the year), a dance, and the coronation of our Homecoming Court.

"Do you ever think you might be doing too much?" Ben asks, eyeing my hoard. "Three AP classes? Football? Homecoming Committee? You're allowed to say no to stuff."

"I like being useful," I say. And busy. Busy keeps my mind off things.

To the administration and Principal Meehan, Homecoming

is a chance to solicit donations from wealthy alumni—to shore up their connections with the prestigious colleges and corporations they're attached to. But, to me, right now, it's everything. The planning and the pageantry ground me, give my world a calm center that keeps my brain from skidding off track. I've volunteered on the committee for three years; now, as a senior, I'm leading almost a hundred student volunteers in planning the year's biggest event.

It's not what I should be focused on, but my family doesn't pay too much attention to how I spend my time. They couldn't care less about my grades or me getting into an elite college.

After all, I'm not the kid they expected to succeed.

"Dude," Ben says, "who are you asking to Homecoming?"

I shift uncomfortably in my seat. I've never needed to ask anyone to a dance. I haven't been single since middle school, back when I started dating the girl I thought would be the love of my life.

But she never existed, and I need to get her out of my thoughts. Jeremy and I are nothing to each other. The boy I collided with in the hallway felt like a stranger. He had nothing to say to me but a request I add his name to the Homecoming ballot. I tried not to think about the way things ended—strawberry milkshake sliding down the back of my neck on one of the worst days of my life.

I fish a pen from my bag and dig the point into my hand, sharp and cool, willing myself to stay focused. I shouldn't fixate on Jeremy's drama. Compared to losing my brother and my parents barely speaking, it's so pointlessly small. Like a jab from a thumbtack after being stabbed with knives.

But I feel like I'm buried in thumbtacks.

"How's your studying?" I ask Ben, nodding at the AP Bio textbook open on his lap.

"Okay. Did you know all dogs are genetically identical to wolves? Even Pomeranians and Chihuahuas?"

"I haven't started the reading," I lie. I've tried to start three times. Facts slip from my head when I take notes using the weird method Dr. Coryn requires. Typing them out on my laptop lets them stick.

"I want to get ahead on the material," Ben says. "That first test was the hardest I've ever taken."

"The test was rigged," Philip Cross, one of our linebackers, insists. His dad's a big military contractor, and he speaks in declarations when he isn't speaking commands. "Dr. Coryn wants us all to fail."

What an obnoxious shithole. But still, this one time, Philip is right. "I didn't understand a single question." I say. "Dr. Coryn isn't just bad at writing tests. She's bad at teaching."

Jeremy and Philip had been weirdly close until freshman year. When they drifted apart, I was so glad I never bothered to ask why. With them it was always *Philip and I lit a toilet on fire*, or *I caught a snake in the woods. Philip freaked out and wouldn't touch it, but he dared me to slide it in Mr. Price's briefcase and I did.* The joy in their eyes was unsettling. Making me feel shitty because I didn't want to do the same danger-ous crap.

Part of the puzzle clicks into place, too late. *The same embarrassment I felt when my brother and his friend Terry called me a girl for not eating dog shit on a dare.* Bro bonding. A sub-tle game of one-upmanship and bragging that occasionally breaks into fistfights. Something I both hate and suck at.

Jeremy would have grabbed the dog shit two-handed and forced it down my brother's throat. I smile at the thought, then guilt rushes through me. *Damn it, Jason. You had to die and take all the fun out of loathing you.*

Ben bites his lip. "Wish I could drop AP Bio. We can take an incomplete mark if we drop in the first six weeks of classes. But my parents would kill me." He turns to me. "Lukas, would you drop if—"

"Nope," I say. "I've never dropped a class, and I won't ruin my streak over one test." Dropping AP Bio would be like admitting I can't handle the hard work.

When we march onto the field at Rockville Prep, I know immediately it's a lost cause. The setting sun glints off their white helmets, each a head taller than the corresponding Cresswell player, and they're packed eighty-two deep in their end zone while our whole team can fit on one bus. We parade past each other, cleats chewing the freshly mowed grass, shaking hands. I stare down the massive defenders, ice-cold. They squeeze my fingers like they want to break them.

Cresswell wins the coin toss. Ben takes the snap and I'm off like dynamite, darting through green-and-white-uniformed mountains, bursting into free space downfield. My shoulders twist back, reaching for Ben's pass—and then a Rockville player plows into me.

I hit the ground with a jaw-jarring thud, teeth sinking into my spit-rich mouthguard. The ball hits my helmet and leaves my senses ringing.

"Again," Ben mutters as I pass him on my way back to the line. I give him a thumbs-up; he squeezes my shoulder. A signal. Trick them. Run the same play twice. Rockville won't expect that.

But they do.

We lose 27–9. Before Coach lets us board the bus home, he lines us up in the bleachers and lectures us on what we did wrong. I listen intently, jotting notes on the tiny pad I carry in my duffel bag while Ben shakes his head at me. No matter how many notes I take, improvement for our team is unlikely. When Coach finally gives us the okay and we head back to the bus, I pull out my phone and open the group chat for Homecoming Committee to check everything I've missed in the last two hours. My timer app spins in soothing circles, counting down to my goal. Two weeks, six days, twenty-one hours, and eleven minutes until the Homecoming game kicks off. Two weeks, six days, twenty-one hours, and eleven minutes to secure the crown I've spent three years chasing.

The junior class subcommittee went to get float-building supplies from Home Depot, but only brought a tiny Ford Focus and had to leave three people behind after they packed in the sheet wood. The sophomore class T-shirt design conceals a phallic shape, and they'll have to redesign from scratch. The senior musical sketch team wants me to allocate four thousand dollars for a giant TV screen to display backdrops during their show.

Lukas Rivers: Denied unless I can keep it after.

"What's up with you, Lukas?" Ben mutters beside me. "You were super distracted on the field. You would have dodged that last guy if you'd seen him. Instead, you got flattened." He gives me a long look. "Is it your brother?"

Early last May, two days before my eighteenth birthday, a drunk driver plowed through my brother's car while he was driving back to Cambridge after a job interview. He was gone by the time the hospital called us. When we heard, my dad froze solid and my mom started screaming. I just thought, stunned, *I don't know how to feel about this.*

Jason was the perfect son, the perfect grandson, the perfect student. But he sure as hell wasn't the perfect brother, and some small, shitty part of me was mad at him because we'd never have the chance to figure our relationship out.

"I'm fine," I tell Ben. That feels like the easiest thing to say. "Just wish things felt more settled at home. It's been four months. We should be back in a routine by now."

"And you live for your routines," he says, patting me on the back. "You sort your underwear by color and pattern. It's pretty weird."

I know he's joking, but his words still sting. Besides my parents, Jeremy is the only one I ever told about my diagnosis. He never called me weird. Well, he did, but for genuinely weird stuff, not autistic stuff. I shoot Ben an awkward smile and turn away. Being Jason's screwup brother was hard enough without people treating me like some broken, emotionless robot who could never measure up.

The bus drops us off back at school. A low, mocking clap greets me when I arrive at my car in Cresswell's senior parking lot.

"Heard you got your ass kicked," says Sol, a short, trans nonbinary sophomore who lords over the computer lab. They're always draped in comic-book T-shirts and forever spinning a Rubik's Cube. Our families live on the same street, so I've taken responsibility for driving them home most days after school. I don't always appreciate their sense of humor, but they pay for gas and volunteered to build the Homecoming website for free. I try not to think too hard about what they could be getting into, staying at school until eleven when it's a game night.

"Rockville outweighs us," I say as we slide in the car. The battered old Honda belonged to Jason, before he went to college. He kept it spotless, but it's since acquired a French-fry aroma and coffee stains on the upholstery. "Pope Pius is our Homecoming game. Forty skinny Irish Catholics. We can beat them."

"Nothing like beating the shit out of the pope," they say, grinning. "Don't tell my parents I said that."

I laugh, unsure if they mean it as a joke. *I barely talk to my own parents these days. Why would I talk to yours?* It has to be sarcasm. I laugh again, louder, and Sol looks at me oddly. *Stupid. I can't let people see me messing up the little things.* The stress doesn't help.

Cresswell's ivy-wrapped main hall towers over the school's ringing hedges. This late, most windows lie dark, though a few flickering lights mark where straggling students are still working. I pull away from the school; the empty senior courtyard flies past, benches and tables marked by generations of student graffiti. It feels more like home than the place I'm going. Safer. It works how I expect.

Driving through Cresswell's tall gates, where the blare and blaze of highway lights await us, feels like leaving a part of me behind. I know I shouldn't be this deeply attached to a school I'm leaving in a year, but it's the first place I've felt even an inch of control in my own weird skin. Not knowing what's next makes me feel a little like the *Titanic*, drifting unmoored toward that iceberg. A future I can't stop from coming and find harder to ignore with every college brochure that shows up in my mailbox.

"Can I ask you a weird question?" I glance at Sol. "Does it hurt?" I awkwardly sweep my hand across my chest. "You know—binding?"

"It depends on how long and how tight." Sol shrugs. "I can get through the whole school day, no problem. But once I accidentally fell asleep in my binder, and woke up feeling like the devil themself danced on my spine."

I nod. Part of me wants Jeremy to suffer, a little. A near-constant ache in the lower back feels like fit punishment for flinging that milkshake and breaking my heart. But it wouldn't be quite the same. I don't want him to hurt his transition as much as I want to know he's hurting like I am.

Still, I ask the next question before I can help myself.

"Would you look out for Jeremy for me?" I ask, even though I know it's a bad idea. "He said he might run for Homecoming King."

"Really?" Sol giggles. An orange-dyed plume of hair flops over their face. "A trans Homecoming King? He doesn't know what he's getting himself into. But I've got better things to do than babysit our student body president. My friends in

Warsaw pay fifty bucks for every hour of anime I upload on their server. If I really buckle down, I'll have twelve thousand dollars by the end of the year. That's car money."

"Not if Principal Meehan realizes what you're up to in the computer lab."

Sol laughs. "You wouldn't turn me in. I pay half your gas bill."

They have me there.

Part of me wonders why we don't hang out more, outside of these rides. But my world is football and Homecoming. Sol only has the computer lab and the GSA—a club with almost no budget and almost zero presence at school. They're fun to hang out with one-on-one, but they wouldn't exactly fit in with me and the people I know best.

All the people I know best, save one.

"Seriously," I say. "Jeremy probably needs a friend. And maybe . . . you could sniff out why he dumped me?" My ears burn with embarrassment. I don't dare look away from the road.

"It's still bothering you, dude? I thought you were over him."

I shrug. "I've already lost a lot this year. I just . . . At least with Jeremy, I have a shot at getting some closure."

There was never any explanation. No reason. No way to understand how I had screwed up so much. How messed up was I that I didn't know what I'd done? I've worked all my life to learn how to read people, how to treat others—social cues other people know naturally. I loved the person I dated.

Followed all the signals I could catch about how to be a good boyfriend: bought lattes on our month anniversaries, handed over my letter jacket at cold fall football games. And what mattered most came so naturally—listening on those long nights as he told me how strange and empty he felt. How distant from his own life. Holding him, stroking his hair, and telling him it would be okay.

But I missed something big. After a summer of silence, I found out Jeremy was trans along with the entire student body when he sent an email announcing his new name and pronouns. How else did I fail him?

How can I move on without answers?

"I'll talk to him," Sol says finally, and I relax.

My phone beeps in the cup holder. "Open that," I say, and tell them my passcode. "It might be a Homecoming Committee emergency."

"Just weekly grades going up online," they say. "Whoa. You got a negative score on your AP Bio test. I didn't know the system let you enter negative scores."

Shit. My stomach drops. One more loss. One more punch in the gut.

"Are you okay?" Sol says softly.

My tongue feels stone heavy. Sweat itches where my palms grip the wheel. I can't find the words to reassure them I'm fine.

"Didn't you give some of Dr. Coryn's students the answer keys to her tests last year?" I ask.

"Yeah, she hasn't updated her password in ages." Sol nods. "I generally charge a hundred bucks per key, but I'll give you the friends and family discount. I want an invite to a senior party. And a selfie of the two of us doing shots. The rest of the GSA will never believe I'm cool enough to pull that off."

After they're gone, I drive to the end of the cul-de-sac. The lights in my house are still on, glittering eyes looking out past weathered brick and the high, tight cedar fence that encloses our overgrown front lawn. *Shit.* I park at the end of the block and wait. It takes another half hour, but our windows finally go dark. Even the one in Jason's room.

Safe to go in, I think. But once I slip off my shoes and hang my jacket in the hall, a cough sounds from the darkened living room. A figure sits up on the couch. Dad, covered in a quilt, eyes red-rimmed and PJ shirt hanging loose on his shoulders. He's reaching for his glasses on the table. The only light comes from the lamp near his head, casting long shadows over his cheeks and sliding into every wrinkle on his brow.

"My back is hurting me," he says. And my brain's shit at parsing expressions and interactions, but even I know that's a lie. "Your mother and I need to buy a new mattress."

A framed photograph lies on the floor. I pick it up—decide I don't want to know why it fell off the wall—and set it back on the rough brick fireplace mantel. A family snapshot from four years ago. Scrawny eighth-grade me, my smile flashing thick braces. Grandparents gathered in a line of ancient sweaters and wispy white hair, all of them smiling. My parents, beaming proud beside Jason in his MIT sweatshirt at a fancy Boston restaurant. The whole family had gathered to see him off to college.

I haven't felt that warm since. Not around my family. My mom's parents died the year after we took that photo, only a few months apart, and arguments over whether to sell their house tore up that side of the family. Without Jason to fuss over, my dad's parents—who live just over in Virginia—stopped coming around as often.

I was the disappointing son, the disabled son. I've only seen my nana cry twice—once at Jason's funeral, and once the day my parents told her about my diagnosis. When he learned I'd be repeating fourth grade, my granddad said, "At least you have Jason," and even if my mom's family didn't say it out loud, I knew they meant the same with their cracks that I'd one day be bagging their groceries.

It doesn't matter that I've learned to hide most of my symptoms. It doesn't matter how good I am at football, or how many AP classes I take. Jason set a high bar; the cracks he left in my family run deep. I don't know how to pull them all together like he did.

"Thinking about college applications?" Dad says.

No questions about the game they missed tonight. I tell

myself it's for the best, even as their absence sucks at my attention like a missing tooth. *If they'd been there, you'd just have worried about your mom breaking down and your dad walking away from her. Yes, they used to watch every game, but your family has changed, and your routines will change, too.* I try lying to myself. *This is normal. This is fine.* It wasn't like Jason visited much the last couple of years, busy at MIT and all his engineering internships. Having him permanently gone shouldn't feel like such an anchor around my neck.

"Yeah. Pretty much. I've already made a schedule with the Ivy League deadlines, charted out the early decision timelines, cross-referenced all the essays for the in-state schools—"

"And you're retaking the SAT?"

"Next month." After Homecoming, when I've got some time to study. I know I can do better than a 760 math, and my 720 verbal is abysmal.

"Good. You don't need to go to MIT or Stanford. UMD is an okay school. Plenty of Maryland graduates go to Hopkins for graduate study or do the five-year masters and go into engineering—"

Stanford. A face pops into my head—Peter Mueller, last year's quarterback. UMD had been his dream school for years. But then he'd won Homecoming King, and colleges started urging him to apply. Stanford made him an offer he couldn't refuse.

Cresswell isn't just any school. It has deep roots in the DC area, powerful alumni. Eight members of Congress, two senators. Executives, lobbyists, tycoons. That's where the Homecoming budget comes from—the alumni maintain a vast private fund so the students can throw them a massive party every year. And they're happy to open doors for the members of the court, the stars of the show.

Peter Mueller, Stanford. His girlfriend, Carol Chen, Homecoming Queen, Caltech. Brandon Kyle and Erica Wyatt—Yale and Princeton, even though Brandon failed three classes his senior year. Every member of the court, every year I've attended Cresswell, has been handed alumni favor—glittering golden tickets to success alongside their crowns. If I can impress these people, get their attention by winning Homecoming King, I could get into a school families brag about.

"—as long as it's a solid program, with a good track record of alumni achievement, your mother and I will be fine with paying for it—"

"Don't give up on me yet," I say. *Like they didn't write me off as a failure at age eight.* My life is a juggling act of sports, studying, family, Homecoming Committee—but finally I have a way to please everyone at once. Homecoming King. I'm going to win, get into an elite college, and give my crumbling family something to care about again.

It's an answer to every problem but one: Jeremy.

The only obstacle between me and the crown.

CHAPTER THREE: JEREMY

Three Weeks to Homecoming Kickoff

It's not until I'm driving to school early on Monday morning that I finally tell someone about my run-in with Lukas.

"What happened?" my best friend, Naomi, asks from the passenger seat. Her dark brown curls frame her face, highlighting the rose blush on her perfectly moisturized, pale cheeks. I miss wearing a full face of makeup.

"I didn't know what to say to him," I admit, slamming on the brake as I fight through Bethesda traffic. The blue steel and concrete of town yields to the rolling green fields of NIH and Walter Reed in a flash, but we're still bumper-to-bumper. Some asshole is honking behind me. "I told him to put me on the Homecoming Court ballot."

"We're both officially in the race now? That's awesome!" Naomi looks up from her AP Bio textbook and grins. "Running together will be so much fun. I've been looking forward to it all summer."

I can't help feeling like she's missed the most important part of what I've said. "Naomi. I talked to Lukas. For the first time since we broke up."

"Oh." She finally closes her textbook. "Did you guys talk about it?"

It being our very public breakup. I made a joke the other day, but I can't help but feel like I owe him an apology. I just haven't figured out the script for how a guy apologizes to another guy. *Hey, bro, sorry I ripped your heart out and stomped on it at your most vulnerable moment. My bad. Wanna go lift?* Just speaking with Lukas about what we once were would feel pathetic. Embarrassing.

"No, I just . . . I knocked a box of craft glitter from his arms." When I shampooed last night, the shower water turned sparkly. "It was pretty brief and awkward. I don't know what I ever saw in him." *Soft brown eyes like a puppy. How he flushes when he laughs at something* really *funny.* "Everything we had was fake."

"Really?" Naomi says, giving me a hard look. "You don't have any feelings left for him at all?"

I make myself laugh. "Nope," I say, but I keep my eyes locked on the road. That part of my life is over. We were boyfriend and girlfriend. King and queen. A neatly woven pattern. And we tried so hard to fit the roles laid out for us that there was no room to step outside them. Lukas made that clear the first time I tried coming out to him.

A smile tugs at the edges of Naomi's lips. "Wow . . . Lukas Rivers and Jeremy Harkiss, single for the first time in years."

"Yeah," I say playfully, ignoring the pang in my chest. "That's what usually happens after a breakup." *There's also still something bothering him*, I think, remembering that look he gave me in the hall. But that's not my business anymore.

The day is blue-skied and sunny, green ivy crisp against red brick as we pull into Cresswell's senior parking lot. When we leave the comfort of the AC and step out, our shoes crunching in the gravel, humid Maryland September envelops us.

Washington, DC, and its suburbs are every bit as swamplike and disgusting as Middle America preaches. It has nothing to do with seventeen-year-old trans boys pissing in the right bathroom and everything to do with funneling the wealth of a continent through a single city. Montgomery County has more wealthy little shits than I can shake a stick at, and I should know. I'm one of them. Stuffed full of privilege in every way but the one that matters most.

We've come to school early, because both of us want first dibs on the oral presentation topics for AP Gov. Naomi wants to grab a public-health-related topic, since she's planning to go premed in college. I just want something meaty I can dig my teeth into and argue half to death. Acing AP Gov will be crucial for my Harvard application. I'm going to be a lawyer like my mom. I'm going to make a difference like she does, and Harvard is where she got her start.

"You know I'm proud of you, right?" Naomi says when we reach our lockers in the chemistry hall, rusty metal clanging as we force them open. Jeremy Harkiss and Naomi Guo have always had lockers right next to each other, pushing us into each other's lives long before we were actually friends. I couldn't stand friendships with other girls—*no, just girls*—when I was a freshman. The way they seemed to be comfortable in their skin left me itching and aching at the vast, uncrossable chasm that lay inside me. Hanging out with Philip Cross, owner of the world's only mixed-media bug-and-bullet collection, filled in that gap for a moment, but also packed it tight with poison. When I finally saw Philip's true colors, Naomi was there for me, and I'll always be grateful to her for that. "You've come so far since this summer. You've been so strong."

"Thanks."

Guilt festers in the bottom of my stomach. I wasn't really strong. I was a drain on everyone around me, especially Naomi. She was the only person I could talk to about my mom's transphobia and my breakup with Lukas. Even when she bombed the SAT this summer and had a nervous breakdown, somehow she came to me for consolation and ended up listening to me rant about my inability to find short-enough men's shirts.

I should have let her have the space she needed, but my own crises ate up all my compassion. She stopped sharing things with me after that, and I'm not sure how to get us back to the way we were.

But Naomi's smile when I picked her up this morning was genuine, so maybe she's already forgiven me.

"I made something for you," she says. "Well, I made it for us."

She pulls a bundle from her locker and unfurls a blue-and-gold banner that's as tall as me. *Jeremy and Naomi for HC Court*, written in cursive gold thread loops, wraps around a felt phoenix. No one's watching, so I hug her and squeal.

"It's beautiful, Naomi!"

"Thanks! I worked on it for weeks. Ben's been dying to tell you about it, but I swore him to secrecy." My student government VP is also Naomi's twin brother. "I really hoped you'd agree to run with me. And I'm so excited to get to be Homecoming Queen. Unquestioned, unopposed." She rubs her hands together, already anticipating. "I know it's shallow, but I'm excited for the chance to be the star."

"Still not over me winning Junior Prom Princess last year?"

"I'm not over you winning Little Miss Montgomery in eighth grade! It was all anyone could talk about at my own bat mitzvah."

We laugh together, but she's only half joking. We've been competing against each other for a long time. Most cheerleaders love the spotlight. A little push-and-shove comes naturally for us. But I already pushed Lukas out of my life in dramatic fashion, and I want something steadier with her now. Running together will be good for our friendship. With her planning skills and my knack for publicizing events, we'll make an unstoppable pair. What happened this summer is already far behind us.

"Well, no more pageants for me."

"Plenty allow boys into the competition. You just need a tuxedo."

Tuxes are so blah compared to flashy evening gowns. "I don't think so. If people find out I still do girl stuff—"

"It's not girl stuff. There's no such thing as girl stuff and boy stuff, only what people choose to do. Liking pageants doesn't make you less manly."

I roll my eyes. "I'm a male cheerleader, Naomi. But it's not about me. It's about how other people see me." Right now, my heart aches for people to look at me and see the boy I am. I can put pageants, ball gowns, and makeup on pause. I like those things, but they're not my soul. I can't hold my soul back any longer.

I won't turn into anyone else's stereotype of what a man should be. I'm not that trans guy who knew from age two his lifelong dream was playing pro baseball or growing a lumber-jack beard. I let myself cheer, since there's already a few boys on the team, and I give up things like skinny jeans. But I need to be careful. I need to signal to Cresswell I'm male enough, so people remember my pronouns and don't hesitate when they see my name on the king's ballot instead of the queen's. And when I'm out on the street, with assholes still honking from their cars as they blaze by, my health, life, and every-thing depend on people seeing me as I am. Walking the edge of a razor I didn't make for myself.

"I'm sorry," Naomi says. "I wasn't thinking about it that way."

"I'm going to be weird about gendered stuff for a while," I say. "That doesn't mean I'm being a jerk like a cis guy. I'm just figuring stuff out and trying to keep my head on straight."

"Or keep your head on *gay*." She winks, and a giggle escapes me, the tension in my guts loosening a little. Then she presses her hand to her mouth. "Wait, are straight people allowed to make jokes like that?"

"It's not like there's a whole queer shadow government dictating what straight people can and can't say. We've got better stuff to do, like deciding how we feel about *The L Word* reboot."

"We could watch that together!" Naomi suggests, wagging her brows.

I roll my eyes, laughing again. "I think the support I need is an all-night *John Wick* marathon in your basement."

"My parents won't let us do all night, but we could get away with watching one," she says thoughtfully. "Ben would probably join us. And we can plan what to do with the banner! We'll need a good place to display it. I've got a rotating schedule of locations worked out."

"Sounds like a plan." I tuck the banner into my locker and bang the crooked metal door shut. "I'm curious, though—if I'd decided not to run, what would you have done? Covered my name in fabric?"

She bites her lip. "I wouldn't have run alone. Exposing myself to the whole school when I know I'm not the person everyone wants? That's terrifying."

"I can't think of a better Homecoming Queen."

"Well, lots of people can. You."

Right. Naomi's running against my ghost.

All my life, I knew being a girl wasn't supposed to be fun or easy. I absorbed Grandma's barbs about how a *little lady* should behave, imitated my single mom, studied Naomi and Debbie, watched countless rom-coms (ignoring the collection of action comedies hidden under my bed like prison collateral). I taught myself *girl* like a foreign language. I thought that was normal. My grandmother had made girlhood into a list of rules to follow: clothing, posture, hygiene. *Scrub behind your ears, or all the other girls will whisper about how dirty you are.* I know about the patriarchy and the shit it forces girls to be. I know it's supposed to suck and hurt. But no one seemed to be hurting the same way I was.

Then Debbie introduced us to yaoi—really gay Japanese anime. Those androgynous pretty boys with big eyes and fancy suits had awakened something inside me. I watched everything I could pirate, switched to slash fanfic, and dove into gay romance novels. I started imagining I was the boys in those stories. Dreaming I was them. I told myself it was just a fetish, that I was a dumb straight girl who didn't respect gay people as anything but jerk-off fuel.

But I couldn't stop thinking about it. Because something in it clicked. It felt deeper and more real than anything I'd ever felt in my life.

Then Sol gave their speech on gender and pronouns at the

Cresswell Diversity Festival last spring, and I realized every-thing. All at once.

I don't have to be a girl. I can be a boy. I can be myself.

Lightning had struck my soul. Pure euphoria. Like I'd been living my life on Novocain and now the world came clear. I felt seen. Found. I'd been holding my breath for seventeen years, and if I could let myself exhale, I'd settle safely in place as a clueless teenage homosexual.

Things all happened rather quickly after that.

Outside Mr. Ewing's classroom, a sign-up list is stapled to the corkboard. I slide onto my tiptoes to read it, looking for a meaty topic—like the ethics of big agribusiness or the environmental impacts of the military.

What I don't expect is to see *Transgender Rights* as the first item on the list.

Naomi gives it an awkward look. "You don't have to take it, Jeremy. It's not like he added it because of you."

"He added it knowing I'd be in this class." My guts coil and knot. I hate this. But I can't imagine sitting silent through some cis kid's clumsy defense of my rights—or worse, some cis kid explaining why I, the coolest student at Cresswell, am somehow not human.

Because that's what all these talks devolve into. Who is and isn't human. I won't let anyone else speak over me.

"Oh, here's one on the ethics of requiring SAT scores for college applications," Naomi says. "I could talk for ages about why the SAT is a scam, but maybe I should do the one on medical data sharing, since it's relevant to me going premed in college . . ."

I grit my teeth so hard my jaw hurts and sign my name beside the trans rights presentation. I don't know what I'm going to say, but I know that it's going to flatten Mr. Ewing. Naomi's already blocked out three hours in her planner so we can practice our presentations without getting distracted by cheer practice or Homecoming prep. I couldn't ask for a better friend—especially with college admissions coming up and both of us putting the final polish on our applications.

But knowing she's on my side doesn't make any of this feel better.

"Jeremy?" Naomi says. "What do you think?"

"Of course," I say, so quickly it's obvious I wasn't listening.

She sighs. I look away, shame prickling where I've buzzed the hair down my neck. All my reflexes have rewired for fight or flight, survival. Friendship feels like a luxury.

"I'm going to the locker room," Naomi says, changing the subject. "Anna and the other freshman girls brought us bagels. I'll bring you some when I'm done."

I shrug, even though my heart feels wrung out. Out of everything I'd expected would change when I transitioned, I'd never imagined the tradition of locker room bagels would slip from my grasp. "I'm good. I had a yogurt before I left."

"Maybe the boys do something special, too?" Her eyes are wide and encouraging. She doesn't want to leave me, but hey, free bagels. "Mike would know."

Mike joined cheer junior year—either as a joke or to inspire a college essay. He can't keep rhythm, let alone organize bagels, but Coach likes him because he can hold up pyramids.

"Maybe," I say. "I'll ask. You go." I owe her this much. I'll let her go eat bagels, and I'll sit silently with my pent-up feelings until the bell rings.

"See you at lunch. I've got three binders full of campaign ideas." She squeezes my hand and runs off. I lean back against the bank of lockers and breathe a long, shaky sigh.

Students start filtering into the main building. Girls float in tight-knit groups, laughing over inside jokes, swapping coffees and snacks. Boys tower over lockers, sprawling across doorframes and their girlfriends. Eyes pick me out as I wander, alone. Marked. I wonder what they see when they look at me. A loser who has to argue for his basic right to exist?

I prop open my locker and pretend to mess with my textbooks to avoid the eyes. I think of hiding in my car until the first bell rings, but no. That'll only fuel the seething gray whorls of dysphoria inside me, the buzz of the world telling me what I can't be. My eyes find Naomi's banner. A crisp gust of wind blows through an open window. Outside, I spot the school flag snapping.

The flag. Towering above the senior courtyard. Visible to all.

I peer out the window and check the courtyard for watching teachers. Empty of everyone and everything but green grass and unoccupied picnic benches. Then I hoist Naomi's banner over my shoulder and set off downstairs.

CHAPTER FOUR: LUKAS

I wasn't always the future king of Cresswell.

When I was a kid, people were more likely to shove my head down a toilet than put a crown on it. I was the boy who cried in music class, who ate nothing without sriracha mayo on it for all of third grade, and who once bit a teacher for taking away my action figures. Other kids laughed at me. Adults whispered behind my back. My own brother ignored me on the playground.

Even at eighteen, as a technically legal adult, the memories rise uninvited, reminding me of how far I can fall. Jeremy and I met on the school bus in fifth grade, back when a seat was big enough to hide you from the world. "You're that kid who screamed and punched the gravel at recess," said the mud-streaked blond white kid who'd sat down beside me. Taking my hand. Sizing me up with big green eyes as I shied away from them.

"Leave me alone," I growled. "Everyone else does. You're supposed to be scared of me."

To make my point, I snapped my teeth in the air. I didn't even get a flinch.

"Nothing scares me."

And nothing did. Not speaking before crowds, joining new clubs, facing down hard-ass teachers. We grew up together. Survived middle school and conquered Cresswell arm in arm. Thanks to my extra year in fourth grade, I hit my growth spurt before every other kid in my year and walked onto the varsity football team as a freshman, which opened doors for me and my girlfriend—*not a girlfriend, never really, but then what word?*—to attend senior parties and hang out with the most popular upperclassmen. We were the golden couple. Our names intertwined. Our legend carved in the courtyard bricks. Now I stand alone.

I make myself meet Dr. Coryn's piercing glare, and the ghost of that overwhelmed kid inside me screams, *Run*, and the overwhelmed technical-adult wants to listen. *No. Running isn't the answer. Only success.*

"Lukas, if you want to pass AP Bio, you need to start taking notes." The white lab coat Dr. Coryn wears nearly camouflages her against the thick corkboard thumbtacked with collected papers and posters like a spray of feathers, like she's about to blend in to her work. "Not only do they help you study, they're five points of your weekly grade."

"I'd love to take notes," I say, and it's true. I came into

school early to ask Dr. Coryn for extra credit, but she's more interested in dividing the class into A's and F's than helping me succeed. "I do my note taking on my laptop."

"We use the Milschner method in this class, remember?" She hands me a paper folded in three columns labeled *points, concepts, reflections*. "First, while I'm speaking, we outline bullet points of my lecture. We divide the points into color-coded concepts in this column. Then we reflect on the lesson as part of our homework. You'll be required to do this in college."

No, I won't. This is pointless. "I can't learn that way. It doesn't stick in my mind. If you let me use my laptop—"

"If I let you use your laptop, you won't pay attention. Kids these days rely too much on technology instead of brainpower."

I'm trying to use my brain! This is how my brain works! Mom's offered a couple times to press the school for accommodations, but I never wanted anyone to see me taking extra time on a test or getting an aide to help me. I don't want to expose such a private part of myself for public scrutiny, and I don't want my friends to think I'm as weak and useless as my family does. I press a pen into the ball of my hand, grounding myself in pain. "Please. You don't understand—"

"My decision is final, Lukas. For once in your life, you and your classmates will have to do the work instead of expecting things to be handed to you."

I work harder than anyone ever sees.

After leaving Coryn's classroom, I duck into the bathroom. It's dark and reeking from freshman boys who can't aim. But I need the quiet. I lock myself into a tight-walled stall and bury my head in my hands as the world spins around me. I fish out a handful of rubber bands and lash them tight around my wrist, twisting until they bite skin, quieting the rush and flood into single, painful peace.

I can't drop the class. Winning Homecoming King is my ticket to a good school, but the rest of my application also needs to be strong. *Jason aced AP Bio.* He'd found a way to process his notes even with Coryn's weird rules. If he were here, he'd tell me just to suck it up and do it. *If you can be normal on the football field and at parties, you can make yourself normal when you study.* But it's not working.

If I can't force my brain into line, I've got only one tool left. I text Sol.

Lukas Rivers: Do you have Coryn's test answer keys?

Sol Reyes-Garcia: As soon as you're ready for them

I exhale. AP Bio will *not* be the death of me.

Once I've calmed down and stuffed the rubber band back into my bag, I step out of the bathroom and nearly slam into the only person who could make my day worse.

Unfortunately, I can't help the kick of excitement I get at seeing him. I don't know if it's a reflex that will ever go away.

Jeremy is coming down the stairwell leading from the government hallway. Sunlight filters through the wide windows, bouncing little rainbows off the fuzz wisps of his buzz cut. Royal-blue cloth drapes over his shoulder like a cloak. The building feels still and strangely quiet. It suddenly feels like we're the only two people here.

I wonder if he feels it, too.

"Excuse me," he says, trying to slide past me. I shift to block his way, and his eyes flash up. Green as the signal *go*. "*Move*, Lukas." And suddenly I'm hit by a wave of déjà vu— standing in a silent diner covered in strawberry milkshake.

"What are you doing?"

"I'm working on my Homecoming Court campaign. What's it look like I'm doing? Streaking through the halls?"

"You would," I point out. "If you thought you could get away with it. You love attention, good or bad. Listen—I just wanted you to hear this from me directly. I'm running for Homecoming King, too."

Jeremy steps backward. Like he's just been struck in the chest. His jaw drops—then smoothly slides back into his usual irreverent grin. But now I know I've found a crack in his armor. "Why? You'll lose to me in a landslide."

"Seriously?" I know he likes to pose and posture, but even he has to occasionally face the facts. "I'm the head of the Homecoming Committee. I'm the one everyone at Cresswell

associates with the dance; I'm the one who makes it happen."
And I need this win. For my future. For my family. "You're just
dicking around. Like you do with the feelings of everyone
around you. I want the crown. I have a plan to get it. And—
you know what?—people at this school still like me. That's
why I'm going to win."

"You think I was just fucking around with your feelings
for three years?" Danger flashes like ice chips on a road in
his deep green eyes. "No. I've already lost enough this year.
I'm not giving this up. You want the crown? Take it. May the
best man win."

He pushes past me just as a busload of freshmen surge up
the stairs, vanishing into a crowd of backpacks and body odor.

All through AP English Lit, I seethe. By the time I reach calculus, I've flipped it over in my head. So what if I have to run
against Jeremy? He's one opponent. No one else stands a serious chance. The only people running against me are weirdos
like Psychic Simon, who's had a vision of himself winning,
and the kid who vapes in gym class. Anyone can enter, but in
all Cresswell history, only the most popular seniors have won.
I'm one of the best players on the football team. Homecoming is my show. I just have to beat one person.

I grin over my parabolic integrations. Kicking his ass and
taking the crown will be the sweetest imaginable revenge.

I slide out of calculus ten minutes early—which will probably get me written up in the Academic Decathlon group chat as Fake Nerd of the Week (last week was Han He, who dropped chess club to start a YouTube channel.) But I have an excuse: an email inviting me down to Principal Meehan's office.

Her domain is wallpapered with inspirational quote posters and framed newspapers highlighting notable alumni, so many I'm shocked the county fire marshal hasn't made her take them down. I fish a handful of mints from the secretary's bowl, slide through Meehan's open door, and drop down on one of the too-small plastic chairs she's set up before her desk.

"Lukas!" she says warmly. "How go the Homecoming preparations?"

A short white woman with sharp suits and enough positive energy to ram a freight train through a wall, Ashleigh Meehan has a ten-thousand-dollar smile that nothing gets past. She's young for the principal of a famous private school like Cresswell, and she loves getting student groups involved in running events. But even the old principal who led the school in Jason's day invested heavily in Homecoming. Maintaining the alumni network is critical to Cresswell attracting new students and wealthy donors.

"I think there's an issue with the can sculptures," I say. My phone notifications have been building up since calculus started.

"I'll write you an excused absence until lunch," Meehan says. "That's the school's biggest charity drive."

I nod. "We also need to make a deposit on the bonfire food. Five hundred bucks up front." The bonfire on the Friday before Homecoming Week marks the traditional kickoff of the celebrations. I booked a local barbecue restaurant to serve food but didn't know they'd need money up front until they called me this morning.

Meehan pulls a debit card from an envelope and offers it to me. Cool plastic, shiny with foil. I run my thumb along the bumps of the number. "This is linked to the Homecoming budget in the alumni booster funds." Translation: it's the donors' money, not the school's. Alumni-sponsored events are funded separately from general school activities, thanks to some complicated tax law. "There's instructions taped to the back on how to activate it with a PIN."

I log into the bank site on my phone and type in the year I was born. Thirty thousand dollars wait in the account. "The alumni are seriously okay with you trusting me with this?" Last year Meehan was obsessive about tracking each individual purchase herself.

"Well, I wouldn't just give it to any student. But you're Lukas Rivers. I haven't heard a single complaint against you in four years. You're just like Jason—a model member of the Cresswell community."

"Wow. Thank you." I shiver as another responsibility sets down on my shoulders, but I tell myself it's not as heavy as it feels. A good chunk of that money is already earmarked to rent the gym and pay the custodians. I'm just responsible for the rest.

And I'm doing just as well as Jason once did. Good enough for a crown. Good enough for the Ivy League.

With the rest of the period clear, I can answer the emergency brewing in the Homecoming Committee group chat. Debbie, whose rich lobbyist parents don't care if they get a hundred emails about her skipping class, meets me in the alley outside the locker rooms. A pile of leaking tuna cans and the broken pieces of a plywood dragon's head spill across the asphalt. I wrinkle my nose as I get close and the sunbaked fish smell hits me.

"I knew we shouldn't have let the freshmen start building their canned food sculpture without our supervision," she says. "They wanted to see how much weight they could rest on a board before breaking it. And they decided they'd use the dragon head from the sophomore float."

I wipe tuna off the cracked dragon's head. The lower part of its face has come off, making it look strangely sheepish. The sophomore class theme this year is Flights of Fantasy. We seniors are Senior Superheroes, which is my idea, and I really love it.

"What made them think this was a good idea?"

She huffs. "Some of these kids brought in boxes of food instead of cans. I don't think their nannies ever taught them better."

We agree she'll go yell at the freshmen, and I'll break the bad news to the sophomore float subcommittee. Julie Chen nearly chews off her lower lip when I catch her by her locker at the lunch bell to show her the broken board. I offer duct tape and superglue, since her subcommittee has already exceeded their budget for supplies. We still have two weeks, four days, seven hours, and forty-three minutes until Homecoming kickoff. We can't get ahead of ourselves.

"Maybe you can cover it with cloth?" I suggest when she moves on to biting her nails. "Fill it with newspaper to make it 3D?"

"Painted wood is more rustic and aggressive. I don't want my dragon to look defective." She sighs. "Whatever. Maybe Jeremy and Naomi know where we can get some cheap cloth. Did you see what they did?"

All the hairs prickle on the back of my neck. "What?" I snap, too fast, and regret it. What if they did something super obvious, and I missed it? What if I look completely oblivious?

"Check out the senior courtyard. You should see it yourself. He really wants to be Homecoming King. It's impressive."

I'm impressive! I want to scream. But that'll get me nowhere. *Jeremy has already won over part of my own committee.* He's gaining ground. I need to start campaigning, hard.

My sneakers squeal as I push through the lunch crowds—"Sorry, excuse me. Sorry, man, Homecoming Committee business!"—and step out into the humid air of the senior courtyard.

The first thing I see is *Jeremy and Naomi for HC Court*.

The banner soars above the sun-parched lawn. Snapping tall from the flagpole, just below the American flag. Students take photos and whisper, impressed. Jeremy sits atop a picnic table, ringed by eager, awestruck faces. Even Ben sits by his side, staring up with a goofy grin as Jeremy waves his hands to make some grand point. *Some best friend you are.*

Jeremy and Naomi for HC Court. But Naomi is nowhere to be seen. This is Jeremy's show. Prime-time-worthy drama with the spotlight just on him.

He sees me staring and winks my way.

This summer, back when I was processing the news about his transition—which was at the bottom of the list of things I needed to process—I told myself it didn't matter. If we weren't speaking, did it matter if he was a girl or a boy? I'd just be using a different name and pronoun for the same person.

"How's your campaign going, Lukas?" he calls. I don't even recognize his voice. "Careful. You don't want to fall behind me. You'll never catch up."

CHAPTER FIVE: JEREMY

Is this what being high feels like? I want to preserve the look on Lukas's face forever. His mouth is still flopping open and shut like a stunned carp.

"How long have you been planning this?" he asks, brown eyes widening with shock as he drinks in the banner and moves toward the picnic table I'm sitting at.

"For a while," I say. "But our conversation this morning definitely inspired me to make the announcement official."

He glares at me. I shiver. Lukas doesn't make eye contact unless he means it, and his brown eyes hit me like a nail dug in deep. But I refuse to let him ruin my good mood.

I had stepped out into the red-bricked courtyard where seniors eat lunch to the sweet sound of applause.

The sun pierced down brightly, sparkling off quartz in the courtyard red brick, and the students sprawled lazily in T-shirts and shorts bordering on Code of Conduct violations.

But they leapt to their feet when I arrived, cheering and clapping beneath my snapping blue triumphant banner. Jin, captain of the lacrosse team, slapped me on the shoulder. "Up the flagpole! Sick moves, man!" My back stung from the blow, and the tight press of my binder on my diaphragm nearly made me vomit, but *whatever*. The lacrosse captain thinks I have sick moves. That's praise I can wear like a medal.

"Did you climb the pole?" a soccer player asked. I nodded—you need a special key to raise and lower the flag ever since the Class of 2003 stole it for a midnight game of manhunt. His face lit up. "Dude! Incredible!"

I drank in the heady praise and hoped no one saw the grass stains on my butt from the two times I fell midclimb.

"You actually sewed that thing?" asked a tall, broad-shouldered brown boy playing chess across the courtyard. I shook my head and shouted, "Naomi!" She deserves credit for her work, and I don't need anyone thinking *he sews, he must still be a girl*—but he just smiled and said, "Dude, would she teach me if I asked? I'm always wrecking my hems and my mom's stopped fixing them for me."

I croaked out a "yeah." Forcing my voice low. It came easier the second time, deep, resonant, and pretty. Maybe the testosterone was finally kicking in.

They recognized me as a boy—and that let me recognize myself. For the first time in my life, I could breathe—at least, metaphorically, considering how tightly my binder squeezes.

"Congrats on finally announcing your campaign," Ben said,

offering me a fist bump. I returned it. My hand shook a little. "But that's pretty ballsy way to do it, Harkiss. I mean—"

"I know what you mean, man." Thrill, thrill, thrill in my bones, like butterflies were about to swarm up and spill out of my mouth. Like I could have skipped around the courtyard. *Do boys do that? It feels gay. I am gay, screw it, I could get away with it.* The tightrope I've been walking on all year, the delicate dance of cherry-picking my every action to look male, slackened and lowered me back onto steady ground.

They saw me. I could breathe. I could be myself.

"You're a good pick for the court," Ben mused, waving me to the picnic table the football team eats draped around. I jumped up and perched on the tabletop. "Maybe I should talk to Lukas about dropping out of the running. I know he really wants it, but I'm not sure he can handle it right now, especially after losing Jason. His class schedule is almost as hard as mine, and I'm taking six AP classes."

My heart twinged. My thrill dimmed at the reminder Lukas was dealing with more than I could see. "Is he . . . handling it okay?" How does a boy ask another boy how a third boy is feeling?

"I don't know," said Max, the heaviest linebacker on the football team. "Lukas doesn't talk about his brother. I mean, he's so scary calm all the time."

Lukas is rarely calm. But he does get overwhelmed. When life gets chaotic, he sinks inside himself and blanks out all else. He needs someone he trusts to sit with him, give him warm tea, and hold his hand. But that's not my job anymore.

Lukas wouldn't want you there anyway. Lukas is nothing to you, remember? This is your moment. Enjoy it.

So I sat at the football team's picnic table to eat lunch. Debbie stuck up her nose and sniffed as she walked past me to eat alone. *No Naomi?* Part of me wanted to look for her, but I knew she wouldn't like the stunt I'd pulled with her banner. Besides, I wanted to enjoy being a guy with other guys for a while. I wanted to play along with Ben as he taught me the football team secret handshake and help Max rank the Fast and Furious movies in order of physical impossibility. I could work things out with Naomi later. And for those brief, precious moments before Lukas arrived in the courtyard, I basked in the warm glow of being folded into a group.

Now he's staring at me sitting with his friends, arms folded, jaws agape. I'd feel bad for him if he hadn't been so smug about his inevitable victory earlier. As is, I'm tempted to blow raspberries like a spoiled toddler. *Ha-ha. I win. You lose.*

But Lukas's presence—and Naomi's absence—are nowhere near my biggest problems right now.

"What the fuck is this shit?" The voice—sharp, indignant, pointed—cuts through me like a knife. Philip Cross, wearing heavy boots with his knee-length khakis, stomping across the courtyard from the flagpole green. "Messing with the flag? Who thinks that's okay?" He turns around and locks eyes on me in the center of the courtyard. "Let me guess. Is it the same egotistical bitch who thinks she can change what the whole school thinks of her with a shitty haircut and some new clothes?"

A hush falls over the courtyard. The part of my brain that still cowers screams, *Run!*

But another part of me, that's fought seventeen years to get out, is awake and screaming, *She. Her.* I want to scream that I'm anything but. To yell until I wear him down with sheer volume. This is the first time I've come face-to-face with Philip since transitioning. It must stick in his craw that his precious masculinity isn't as exclusive as he thought.

The hardest thing is, I know how he got this way. Back in middle school, Philip would invite me to hang out with his Boy Scout troop. We'd go hiking together, play in the woods, fish and canoe on the banks of the Potomac. Harmless kid stuff. But the older guys in his troop, the guys who also worked at the local bait shop and shooting range, saw the woods as their own little kingdom, complete with its own army and creed. The more time he spent around them, the more he became someone I didn't recognize. And, after how our friendship fell apart sophomore year, I want him to choke on me.

"It's a flag, Philip," I say. "Not some religious icon. I'll take it down if Meehan asks me to. But you don't get to order me around."

"Always knew you were a sissy liberal dumbass. Didn't know you'd go as far as disrespecting the troops."

"What's disrespectful is your daddy making a fortune every time they go to war." My mom had represented, pro bono, a group of disabled vets suing Philip's dad's company over charges their helmets didn't adequately prevent hearing damage. His lawyers squashed the suit. "Don't pretend you care about 'the troops.' You're just looking for an excuse to throw punches."

"Yikes," Ben says, not bothering to hold back his laughter, and a flush of power rolls through me.

But then Philip clambers onto the table. Grabs the front of my shirt and digs his sharp nose into my face. *Oh. Shit.* Philip loves nothing more than a good fight. I've seen the collection of antique firearms he and his dad keep, the six types of knives framed in shadow boxes in his bedroom. Before I even knew I was a guy, I was drawn to them. The part of me my grandma hated, the part I had no words to express to Lukas or my mom—Philip saw it, clear as glass, even if he didn't know what he saw.

He knew he could use it to hurt me. And I guess he enjoys it still.

"I'm not going to punch a girl."

That word cuts me like lightning. It sprints up my spine and grabs my limbs. The world flashes white.

Next thing I know, Lukas grabs my fist as I swing for Philip's face.

Raw with fury, I shout, "Call me that again, and I'll bite your fucking balls off!"

"No, you won't," Ben says, hands out like he's trying to calm a wild horse.

Gently but firmly, Lukas secures my wrists behind my back. His breath washes into my ears, a steady pattern worn into my memory over a hundred nights curled at his side. A pattern gone wrong. Ben and Max seize my shoulders. Pinning me while Philip laughs.

"He's not worth it." Max dodges as I jab my heel at his foot. "You'll be suspended, or worse. No one's worth a police record right before college applications. You'll hurt yourself more than him."

Not worth it. None of these cis guys know what it's like to have your soul cut out from beneath you with a word.

The blast of Meehan's whistle cuts the courtyard air. Our principal waves her arms as we all turn to look at her. I uncurl my fists. She promised she'd help me transition, that she'd support and defend me as needed. Philip is fucked.

"Mr. Cross?" she says. "What's going on here?"

"He misgendered me in front of the whole senior class." Everyone saw and heard him. There's no way he'll weasel out of punishment. Detention. A write-up. Meehan promised me and my mom I'd be safe to transition at school.

"Jeremy, let's take a walk," she says, rubbing her temples. I think we've given her a migraine, which I get. What I don't get is why she's only talking to me. My stomach drops.

"Didn't you hear?" I say. "Philip—"

"Jeremy," Lukas says, low and urgent. "Let it go. You can explain what's happening to Meehan in her office."

I glare at Lukas. Is he helping by telling me to leave with Meehan or trying to get me in trouble? He shoots me a look as I follow Meehan inside. It's the most we've connected since I dumped him, and for a heartbeat, I pretend he's still on my side.

It sucks how much I'd like to believe that, after everything.

I remember our first date. I was thirteen years old. We wore matching T-shirts from middle-school band, me in Converse, him in Nikes. We saw some dumb Kevin Hart movie and ate ice cream outside the theater. He wanted to hold my hand. Instead of just giving it over, I thumb-wrestled him and let him keep my thumb after he pinned it.

"My mom wants me to try out for cheerleading at Cresswell," I said as we sat together on a wrought-iron bench. "I'm going to do it. She was a cheerleader, and my grandma was a cheerleader. It's important to her." Important that I carry on the long, pom-pommed traditions of the Harkiss girls. Because even though my mom didn't get along with her mom, she'd gotten a lot from her.

"I thought we were both doing football!" he answered, indignant. Voice booming down my arm, already deep and carrying where we pressed together. "You're going to be the only girl on the team. It'll be feminist and stuff."

I wanted to do football. I liked the idea of knocking boys down, even though realistically I'd be thrown across the stadium. "Cheerleading's also feminist. I don't have to do boy things to be feminist." Plus, I liked pom-poms and being the center of attention, and the cheerleaders won more prizes than the varsity football players, who could never break 3-12.

"I don't know if I'm brave enough to try out without you. Jason goes to Cresswell. High school is just going to be more of people comparing me to him and calling me a weirdo." He pulled his hoodie low over his face. "I just want to be invisible. And football is the opposite of that."

"We don't have to be brave," I said. This was the second half of my grand plan. "We just have to be different. Smart. We can play by their rules, instead of being weirdos all the time. We can be popular, if we work together. We can be any sort of people we want." Such a vast chasm already lay between who I was and how people saw me. I felt it, even if I didn't know then what it meant. I thought I could use that for my own gain.

I didn't feel like much of a person, under the surface. So why not be, on the surface, someone people would like and admire?

"Together." His hand squeezed tighter on mine. I smiled, showing him how easy it was to be brave. I wasn't afraid. Maybe I should have been, but I wasn't. "Let's do it. Let's be super popular and be Homecoming King and Queen senior year. If anyone can do it, it's us." He'd kissed my cheek, then quickly pulled away. It had felt soft. And good.

We'd almost made it all the way. I traded T-shirts for pom-poms and Victoria's Secret. He worked his ass off joining clubs and mimicking senior jocks. We drew elaborate diagrams of Cresswell's hierarchy, tracing who liked who, who hated who, who sucked what dicks. Posing in my bedroom for him, I tried on bags full of mall-fresh outfits, fluffy skirts and skinny jeans, blouses and pearls and thigh-high gladiator sandals. *Battle armor.* Sort of.

It had crept into our lives. Lukas got us into senior parties after he made the varsity football team. Upperclassmen taught us to drink alcohol from water bottles during home games, how to play Spin the Bottle and Never Have I Ever in the basement of their parents' lake houses. I won my first election for student government, worked my way up to varsity cheer—and it didn't matter how uncomfortable I felt with the girly bits, because popularity meant little bits of power. Little bits of freedom. I dumped Philip for Naomi, surrounded myself with people who drove me forward instead of pulling me back. I built myself as a cheerleader from the ground up. Just like I'm building myself from the ground up as Jeremy.

But Lukas and I would have been nothing without each other.

CHAPTER SIX: JEREMY

I hate Principal Meehan's office. It's bright and sunny, walls slathered in bland motivational posters, the most prominent being *100 Quotes from History's Most Important Women*. Potted plants and old chess trophies line wall racks. It's a room trying too hard to convince me all's well.

I don't want alumni memorabilia and aphorisms. I want Philip punished. I want to feel safe.

"What Philip said out there wasn't true," I say, shifting awkwardly in a too-hard plastic chair. For once, I don't welcome being the center of attention, with her fair-but-strict gaze upon me. "He was trying to start a fight. Lukas, Max, and Ben will all back me up."

She nods. "I'm sure they will. I get students in here every month talking about something foolish Philip's done. I believe you."

"So what ... what will you do?" She's taller than me, with

her twisted updo giving her another two inches. I hate how small she makes me feel. "The rules we agreed on with my mom . . ."

She takes a long, drawn breath. Like she's thinking over something difficult. "You're familiar with the Code of Conduct, right?"

I nod, confused. Every freshman pledges at a special assembly to abide by it. "Treat our fellow Cresswellians as gentlemen," and "never raise a hand in anger," and "succeed or fail by my own merits, without plagiarism or deception." It ends in "so help me God" and there's always one freshman in the hall who yells "so help me Satan" and ducks low before the administration finds them.

That's a newer Cresswell tradition. One I started myself.

"It's outdated," Meehan says. "All that stuff about 'gentlemen' and 'honor'—well, both you and I know how ridiculous that is. But the Code doesn't cover written or verbal bullying. Only physical. Unless he physically harms you, Jeremy, I can't take action against another student."

All I can think is *this is my senior year* and *this is supposed to be my time to shine* and instead, I'm a target. Because I'm trans. This shouldn't be happening now. This shouldn't be happening in such a progressive school.

"But that . . . that's bullshit," I stammer. "Sorry, Principal Meehan, I just—"

"I don't like it any more than you do, but my hands are tied. I've tried to amend the Code, but the alumni association always threatens to withhold donations. They want Cresswell to remain what it was when they were students, and part of that is the administration doesn't rule by fiat. It's the students who set the standards for what is and isn't acceptable behavior. Amending the Code would require the support of the whole student body."

I tell myself to breathe. I'm not a victim. I'm not weak, not without allies. There has to be a way I can fix this. "If the student government can get enough support, can we update the Code?"

"Absolutely." She leans across her desk and meets my eyes. Hers are steely, purposeful, and I can't help but hope to soak up some fraction of her certainty. I'm not made small by this cinder-block-and-plastic enclave. I can rise above this, make this right. "Get the student body's support, and I'll be happy to sign off on an update to the Code. This is your school, Jeremy. I want it to work for you—and the whole student body."

In AP Gov, we discuss freedom of speech. Mr. Ewing asks, in ha-ha-I'm-so-funny tones, if hate speech should be protected by law. I sit in the back of the class, where the ancient AC unit wheezes like a boiling kettle, insides rioting, and say nothing.

My pediatrician said testosterone might make me feel

angrier, more aggressive. But I'm not exploding like the Hulk. There's no green monster fueling me. Just . . . me. Angry. Alive. Unleashed. *Toxic masculinity. Almost elemental.* These days, anger comes naturally to me, like weeds finding their place in a garden, twining up through my soul. A fire I've always carried, even before I knew what it meant. I bask in it now. Anything that hurts me, anything that stings, I can turn into anger and fling back. Who I become when I chase my happiness over everyone else's.

Under the desk, I text Ben.

Jeremy Harkiss: Hey, VP. I think student government should reform the Code of Conduct.

Jeremy Harkiss: I'm thinking we can set up an inbox where students can anonymously report incidents and put together a report for Meehan. I know a kid who can set it up for us.

Ben Guo: Sounds good. What does Debbie think?

Another message intrudes.

Naomi Guo: YOU ASSHOLE

My whole body clenches up. Fuck. Is she mad at me? Before I can text her back, Mr. Ewing spots the phone in my hand.

"No texting in class." He scoops up my phone. "You can have this back at the end of the day."

"Sir, what about my freedom of speech?"

He laughs and drops my phone in his desk drawer. It rattles shut with a metallic slam. I seethe until class ends.

Cresswell's final period is kept open every day for students to attend clubs or study halls. Until the big game, almost everyone will use it to prepare for Homecoming. I sneak off to the computer lab.

Sol's hideaway lies at the far back of the school. It's white concrete, walled with server towers, monitors flashing *Matrix*-esque walls of text. Low murmurs rise from students packed around computer terminals. The air smells of Cheetos and Gatorade. Loser food. I'm blessing these nerds with my presence.

"I've got a plan to fix everything wrong with Cresswell," I tell Sol. Their T-shirt portrays a comic-book illustration of a brown woman with billowing curls wearing an American-flag T-shirt and punching through a boulder. America Chavez, grinning with a confidence I can only dream of possessing. Their denim jacket swings free where it's tied about their waist, ready to be pulled back on the moment someone yells at them about the dress code. I wonder what it's like to be them—to be out of the closet and carefree—though maybe their life sucks, too. We queers are experts at hiding our feelings. "I need a web programmer to help me set up an anonymous bullying report system—"

"The Homecoming King needs my help?" They let out a bark of laughter before their face drops. "I only do favors for friends. Which you're not, considering how shitty you were to Lukas Rivers this summer."

Please. Handsome Lukas will have no shortage of girls lining up to take my place. "I had my reasons."

"Which were?"

Oh, no. I don't need my breakup to become fodder for the underclassmen's gossip machine. "Personal reasons. Didn't you just say we weren't friends?"

They laugh. The humming server tower behind them flashes rainbow lights. "Fair enough. But we could be. Come to a GSA meeting, and we'll talk about me setting up your anonymous inbox."

The GSA. A club too small for a page in the yearbook. They don't even dress well. Might as well brand *Losers* on their foreheads—and brand it on mine if I joined them.

I stare Sol down. Soft brown eyes framed by blue powder eye shadow, neatly blended against cool violet-peaking teak skin, punk eyeliner long and thick. We have nothing in common besides not being girls, and tons of people aren't girls. But everyone says they're Cresswell's foremost computer expert. I need their help reforming the Code of Conduct. I should probably try to get to know them.

"Why do you hang out here?" I ask, hopping onto a desk and glancing around. "It feels like hell. Where nerds burn alone for eternity."

"Hell is safer for queers than the Homecoming Court. Everyone knows Satan is asexual."

They're glib. Clearly, they enjoy it down here, though I can't imagine why. "How long have you been programming?"

"Since I went to computer camp after fifth grade. It's a useful skill. If you're good with a computer, people want you around. It's easier to master IT than social skills."

They're right. After all, I'm only here because I need a web programmer to set up my inbox. But *useful skills* can't be the only reason trans people like us are wanted. People should want us for us. Because we can win crowns. Because we're worth wanting. "Have you tried possessing a charming personality, Sol?"

They laugh, and scrawl their phone number on a piece of scrap paper. "GSA meets Tuesdays beneath the theater room. If you bring food, you should get enough to share, keeping in mind Connor is gluten-free. Text me if you get lost on the way."

That's tomorrow. I sigh. "I'll think about it," I say, but what I really mean is *no*. The last thing I need is to be hanging around people who remind me how fragile I am. And I won't bare my soul to a stranger in a computer lab.

"Thanks." I shove the paper with their number into the bottom of my bag. "I'll see if I can make it to a meeting." *I'd rather die.* Going feels like such a surrender. Like admitting it's my transness that defines me, instead of all the brilliant burning things I am. I want people to see me as a guy, not a trans guy. *Trans* seems to overpower any words that follow after. If being trans is what defines me, I feel like I might as well go hide under a rug. Because no one likes trans people.

"Open-door policy," they say, still smiling. I flee.

Clearly I need another programmer.

I head to my car and change for cheer practice, squirming about the backseat as I try to find an angle where I can pull off my pants. Meehan's cleared me to use the boys' locker room if I want, but I'm not ready for that. My mom has packed me new men's athletic wear from Target—loose, oversized black T-shirts and billowy navy-blue shorts. *Uniform for a fashion disaster.* I miss my rainbow spandex booty shorts with a passion, but at least she's given me clothing for the right gender this time. I don't know how to tell Mom that me being a boy doesn't mean I'm a straight boy.

Once I'm changed, I march into Mr. Ewing's AP Gov classroom and demand my phone back. As he turns it over, he adds, "I can't wait for your oral presentation next week!"

The thought of defending my right to exist before the class sets my stomach churning. I can't remember the last time I breathed fully. I smile, leave, and check my phone as I run to the field.

Fifty unread notifications. My stomach clenches a little, and I shove my phone into my pocket.

The varsity cheer team rings the gear shed. I catch my breath as I approach. *Good, we're still hauling out the equipment, I'm not late yet—*

Naomi's sob breaks across my ears like a slap.

My best friend sits with her head in her hands. Shaking with the force of her tears.

"Naomi?" My heart twists. Lurching downward, caught up by some sick gravity. The fear I'm already too late. I don't think about what boys should do versus what girls should. I push my way to Naomi's side and throw my arms around her shoulders.

She ducks away.

On the sidewalk before the cheer shed lies our banner— the one she spent weeks making—slashed up and covered in Sharpie. My name is crossed out, replaced with my deadname with *slut* and *fag* scrawled beneath it.

Well, comes my first thought, *Philip isn't wrong.*

Then comes the rest. The rush. The fear, wobbling in the pit of my stomach. The whole world seems to tremble, unstable and shaking.

I could lose everything, says the sudden stab of adrenaline as the bottom of my stomach drops away.

"Why did you hang it from the flagpole?" Naomi cries. "You put it right in front of him!"

"Wait a minute, you're blaming me?" I ask, taking a step back. "I'm the victim here, Naomi!" *Victim.* I hate that label, hate that feeling. Being a guy makes me feel powerful. Good, right, and clean. *Victim* makes me feel pathetic, weak, and itching to explode and prove myself stronger—exactly Philip's goal.

I hate how easy it is for me to understand him. Like the only difference between him and me is that no one's ever challenged his right to be a man.

"That banner was ours! This campaign was ours. You took our banner, you made it all about you—and you never even texted me back today when I asked you about it."

All those notifications. "Mr. Ewing took my phone in Government!"

"Whatever. You didn't even ask before putting it up." She folds her arms over her chest. "I don't just live to make you banners, Jeremy. To pick you up whenever you so much as stub your toe. You're not the only one who needs stuff from their friends. When I bombed the SAT? When my parents spent hours lecturing me for fucking up? When I came to you for, like, a crumb of sympathy, you couldn't stop talking about yourself for a *second*."

"It wasn't like that!" She makes it sound so small and petty. She doesn't understand my dysphoria—I *needed* that shirt to fit, damn it. I needed it.

I just never thought about what she needed.

"At some point, you run out of excuses. What they always add up to is me coming in at second place. To everything always being about you."

I don't know what to say. Because it's true. Everything has

been all about me lately. My transition, my need to protect my gender at all costs. My need for the spotlight, ever present, now laced with my need to control what people see when the light beams high upon me. I just never thought it would hurt so many people.

From over by the track, Coach blows her whistle. "Girls! And guys! It's practice time!"

"I'm sorry," I whisper. But it half catches in my throat, and it feels like too little too late.

"Don't talk to me," Naomi says, sniffling. She and the other cheerleaders march off in a pack that, in the world of last year, I would have been leading. Girls of every height, race, and body type, even a few boys, crossing the green in a pack with their noses lifted high.

I let my team walk away and leave me really and truly alone.

When I thought about coming out last year, I worried people would hate me if they knew I was trans. Now I can't escape the burning fear they hate me because I deserve it. That I deserve it.

I wanted to start senior year with a crown on my head. I'll be lucky if I'm not stuck eating lunch alone in my car.

CHAPTER SEVEN: LUKAS

I'm hiding out in a restaurant bathroom, texting Sol as, outside the stall, two men talk loudly at the urinal. Better my family think I'm taking a massive dump than catch me texting under the table.

Sol Reyes-Garcia: Your ex really doesn't like me. Is he this prickly around everyone?

Sol Reyes-Garcia: How the hell did he win the student government election last year with his attitude?

Lukas Rivers: People find him fascinating. Like a car crash or a particularly dramatic season of The Bachelor.

Lukas Rivers: He's hard to look away from.

I'm sure all of Cresswell is gossiping about Jeremy and Philip's almost-fight in the courtyard. Hopefully, what they remember most is me breaking it up before the first punch could fly. *Lukas Rivers, born leader, perfect Homecoming King.* Not a screwup. Not a mess.

But what I can't forget is the look on Jeremy's face when I told him to leave Philip behind and talk to Meehan. Betrayed and hurt. But I wasn't trying to hurt him.

Lukas Rivers: Keep working at it. Jeremy pushes people away for shits and giggles. But you're lucky—he doesn't know you well enough yet to sting where it hurts. You can still surprise him with friendship.

Ben's also sending me a string of nervous texts—Naomi is crying in their car as she drives them home.

Ben Guo: This sucks. He's her best friend.

Ben Guo: She spent the whole summer taking care of him as he went through this massive transition drama. She made this awesome banner for them, spent weeks designing posters and planning giveaways for their Homecoming Court campaign, and he treated it like nothing.

Lukas Rivers: Jeremy treats everything like it's nothing. He gets really into his own drama and forgets who he's hurting. Remember the matching dresses thing? Naomi's right to be mad.

Naomi spent weeks combing the internet for the perfect outfit for Sadie Hawkins, refused to show it to any of us before the dance. I drove Jeremy to the mall an hour before the dance and he ran out with the first green sheath he saw. By karma or freak coincidence, when we met at Cresswell, they were wearing the same dress. Naomi asked him to change and he offered to arm-wrestle her over the rights to the outfit.

Ben Guo: Well, Philip trashed the banner. She should be mad at him. Or both of them. I don't know. I just know that someone hurt my sister, and I fucking hate that.

I'm not equipped to settle sibling drama. Eighty percent of my interactions with Jason were just me trying to avoid his bullying. At school, I deal with drama by marching in and ordering everyone to get in line. Since that only works with my team and Homecoming Committee, I ignore the rest. But Ben sounds more desperate than I've heard in a long time.

I text Naomi.

Lukas Rivers: Are you okay?

No response. I sigh.

Friend drama is a better alternative to what I'm dealing with right now.

Riviera Steakhouse is an abomination of a restaurant that can't decide between lightweight Mediterranean cuisine or heavy slabs of Midwestern beef. But the teardrop chandeliers and gilded crimson wallpaper, the practically posh location just off the Tysons' Corner metro stop, all radiate success, so that's where my family will celebrate Mom's new job. Since I can't drink wine with my fifty-dollar filet mignon, I consider the dinner half wasted. It's hard to think of myself as a classy adult when I'm drinking Coke.

Plus, some awful, guilty part of me wants to be buzzed. Because Mom insisted my dad's parents join us, and the tension of grief thickens whenever one of my grandparents speaks. The last time we all gathered in one place was Jason's funeral. We don't know how to restart. The shape of my family feels like a pair of too-short pants. I think we might all feel the same way, but we don't know what to say about it. *He was only twenty-two. Now he's gone forever.* True words can only hurt worse.

Thankfully, Mom's best friend, Emily Harkiss, metro'd down from DC to join us, so there's plenty of conversation to fill the gaps.

"It's such a shame your dau—I mean, Jeremy couldn't make dinner," Mom says to Emily. My parents are mostly good about remembering Jeremy's new name and pronouns, though they haven't seen him since he transitioned. I tried explaining to my grandparents, but they didn't really get it, and so I awkwardly changed the subject. I guess it doesn't matter what they think, since Jeremy doesn't spend time with me anymore. Since, by the time I'm done beating his campaign, he'll never want to speak with me again.

"He didn't want to miss practice," Ms. Harkiss says, swirling her wineglass. "And he's very busy working on his campaign for Homecoming King." Jeremy was skipping the dinner—I mean, thank god—but I can't help wondering how much further ahead of me he's getting since he has an evening free. How many posters can he make? How many votes can he win? I always try to do what I should. And it feels like I'm competing with one hand tied behind my back.

"How long have you been planning to go back to work full-time?" my granddad asks Mom, his bushy white eyebrows pushing his forehead up into lines. They've never been close—he wanted my dad to marry some girl whose father he worked with, and I've heard him insinuate Mom's occasional smoking made me autistic. But his tone is neutral tonight. "Partner management director, eh? Sounds like a great opportunity."

"I've wanted to do it for years," Mom says. "Emily connected me with Poole Associates for part-time admin work back when Lukas started high school and Jason . . . mmmmh." She bites her lip.

Ms. Harkiss must have caught that note of strain, because she slides in as smoothly as a batter into home plate. "You were ten times better at sorting paperwork than Jeremy. My kid insisted on arranging everything by how cool he thought the case was, instead of by last name."

"You should have let him have his fun," my nana says, chuckling. "He sounds like such a clever boy." "Boy" turns golden on her lips. Something few people would say about a girl, because girls aren't expected to make trouble. The back of my neck prickles as Ms. Harkiss frowns and says, "Actually . . ."

We're headed toward a six-car pileup of gender roles, queerness, generations, and expectations, right on the Interstate of My Life. If I don't fix this situation, it will blossom into a six-car fire.

I lean out of my seat and wave the waiter over. My hand flops awkwardly on my wrist, and I'm painfully aware of how weird it must look. "We're ready to order!"

He hurries over. Thank god. I order steak and a crab dip appetizer because I need everyone to stuff something in their mouths and stop talking. "Homecoming Committee planning is going well," I say, taking over the conversation with today's story: the freshmen gathering boxed cake mix as part of the canned food drive, Meehan entrusting me with the debit card, my five unanswered calls to the caterer. "Besides, I'm also running for Homecoming King. I've got a great chance of winning. The boy who got it last year went to Stanford."

My granddad looks at me. I make myself meet his eyes,

bristly old brows arched and waiting. For a moment, I'm scared he'll laugh at me. Break down point by point why I'm not good enough for an elite school, every place I've failed, from being held back in fourth grade to me quitting middle school violin lessons in a tantrum to my dismal SAT score. He was the first in his family to go to college, aced his classes at Princeton, built a life on being the best of the best. I want to live up to his example. Show I'm good enough to carry my own weight and Jason's, too.

But instead of saying anything, he sighs and drops his gaze. My heart gives a little lurch, like it's crumpling into some new and smaller shape. How much have we lost if even college plans can't stir conversation?

Just get to Homecoming, I tell myself. *You're doing so well. Push across the finish line and claim your crown.* Early decisions will start flying in winter. In a few short months, I could hold an Ivy-League Yes in my hands.

I could make everyone happy again.

"What's your class theme?" Ms. Harkiss asks, and I turn the conversation back to Homecoming. The decorations. The lights. The giant model phoenix I'm going to build in the cafeteria. I fill the empty air with plans and dreams, weaving a picture of what I'm building, the celebration to end all celebrations, with myself crowned safe at the center.

Entrees arrive. Ms. Harkiss and my nana eat instead of bringing up sons and daughters. My mother orders a second bottle of wine, and my granddad says she's earned it, with all her hard work. I describe how our screen printer accidentally sent the first batch of freshman shirts to a school in California. We hold together. At least, until dessert.

"Well," Mom says, lifting her glass. "I'm excited to be celebrating with everyone tonight. This is an incredible opportunity—for me to stash away some money for my college-bound boy!"

I can't quite parse her tone, her too-still expression, but something is off. The wrong words, the wrong feel, for the moment. Or maybe the wrong is inside me. Every inch of me that's failed these people pushing me not to fail again. "Thanks, Mom," I say. It feels like the safest reply.

"Of course," she says, cheeks rosy from the glow of wine. "I'm proud of you, Jas—"

My grandparents freeze. So does my father. Ms. Harkiss drops her tiramisu-loaded fork on the floor.

"Lukas," Mom breathes. "I'm sorry. I—"

I don't think of the pain, or anything else I've lost. *Calm things down. Balance things out.* It's her perfect son she wants, and I can give her an approximation of that, at least.

"Mom! Ms. Harkiss!" I say, just loudly enough to fill my voice with false cheer. Like I didn't hear her. Like the last ten seconds never happened at all, and I'm just her helpful, proud son. "You two are celebrating! Why not stay and have another drink while I drive my grandparents home? Dad, you can take the other car back to the house, and I'll stop here on my way back to pick up Mom and Ms. Harkiss! I'll be designated driver!" Usually, after a night out they would just take an Uber home, but I'm not sure my mom's in a clear enough headspace to work it out. Better she knows she can rely on me.

"That's not necessary—" Ms. Harkiss starts.

My mom, who's turned beet red, cuts her off. Catches the lifeline I've thrown. "Thank you, Lukas. That would be great."

The only necessary thing now is making this right. When we dine here again, we'll be celebrating my admission to Harvard and all will go well.

I usher my grandparents quickly out to the car. They're as eager as I am to escape, I can sense it, but on the long drive back to their house in Alexandria, we do nothing but agree on how good the steaks were. It's easy. Safe. And I'm out of things to say.

When I lose the words to speak, it's entire. A clamp on my tongue. The link between knowledge and speech, exhausted and lying limp. I can't drag my brain from the rut, only hide behind a polite smile and nod, waiting for the knot to untie. I loathe being speechless. Without words, I'm the kid in elementary school everyone avoided on the bus.

I used to be the only speechless one in my family. But we've been running from things too painful to speak out loud, even before Jason died. *Mom's saving up college money. At least she believes good things can still happen to us.*

I need that crown, now more than ever. My head spins. Everything else drops away, this one idea anchoring me. *Win.*

Network with alumni. Get into good college. Fix my family. A siren's call idea, a lighthouse dragging me through the storm. I doubt the neurotypical kids at Cresswell would understand the strength of the lure. But they don't see the patterns I do; they don't chart out risk like me.

I know this'll work.

Only after I drop my grandparents off and sink into the glorious, still darkness of my car can I sweep my thoughts back to the safe haven of school, Homecoming, and the texts waiting on my phone.

Naomi Guo: Thanks for asking if I'm okay. I'll be fine. Could you withdraw my name from the Homecoming Queen ballot? I don't want to run alone.

I text back. At least in writing, my words come easily:

Lukas Rivers: I can, but I still think you should run. You're awesome and you deserve it.

She and Jeremy make a good pair, leading the cheer team. Jeremy brings the energy, and she brings discipline and planning skills. I could use more of that in my life.

Naomi Guo: What happens if we both win? And I'm crowned your queen? Do I become your girlfriend?

Naomi Guo: hahahaha

Lukas Rivers: Maybe? IDK how that works. I've been dating the same person for years. I feel like there's a whole bunch of rules I skipped learning about, all to be with someone who ran away the first chance he got.

Naomi Guo: Yeah, that sucks. You're a great friend, Lukas. Always there for everyone who needs you.

Naomi Guo: Hey, would you like to grab dinner after the game Friday? Just the two of us. It would be nice to hang out and talk and maybe . . . figure out who we are to each other without Jeremy in the middle?

I squint at my screen, trying to read between the lines. I *think* Naomi just asked me on a date.

Lukas Rivers: Did you just ask me on a date?

Naomi Guo: Yeah, I guess I did. If that's all okay with you?

Naomi wants to go out with me. It's a strange, prickly feeling, new and demanding. And it makes sense, academically. I'm her brother's best friend, and she's known me for years.

Who wouldn't have a crush on the Homecoming King? From an academic standpoint, it makes sense.

But do I want to date Naomi? Jeremy and I were together so long, I've never had to think about what I want in a relationship. Naomi's more laid-back than Jeremy, but that isn't hard. She's pretty, with her long brown-black hair and flawless pink-lip-gloss smile. She's always been part of my friend circle. She brought my family three rotisserie chickens after Jason died. I like being around her, but does that mean we should date? Remembering my relationship with Jeremy makes me want to scream, cry, punch the steering wheel—but picturing myself with Naomi feels empty. Like opening a box on Christmas only to find socks.

I need to get over Jeremy. What we had wasn't even real. Maybe I don't need to date someone who makes my heart do jumping jacks, or maybe that feeling will come in time. Naomi will be happy. Ben will be happy. Dating her will bring some sense of order, of normal, back into my life, and right now I need stability instead of feelings.

I'm not sure those are good enough reasons to say yes. But a puzzle piece snaps into place, and I find a reason that is.

Lukas Rivers: That sounds great. We'll run together, the two of us. We'll take the crown as a team . . . and see where things go from there.

I'm not sure how I feel about Naomi. But I can straighten

my feelings out later. This makes sense, for her, me, both of us. No senior girl stands a chance against her in this contest. What better way to cement my position as Homecoming King than with a Queen on my arm?

Three big red hearts come back.

Naomi Guo: I can't wait!!!

I've got this, I tell myself on the long, quiet drive back to the restaurant. *I make everyone happy, and everyone loves me back. That's how I win.* I'm even, in a strange way, giving Jeremy what he wants. Pushback. If he didn't want me to smile at the thought of beating him, he shouldn't have broken my heart.

I'm already beating him at his own game. Between Naomi and Sol, everyone around Jeremy is now on my side. And if part of me said yes to Naomi because her popularity will help me win, if some part of me knowingly encouraged Sol to befriend a loose cannon—well. If they get pissed at me for using them, I can deal with the fallout later.

I know it's not right, but I need this win like I need food and water.

CHAPTER EIGHT: JEREMY

Naomi didn't speak to me for all of practice. None of the team did, not even Anna, the sweet, tiny freshman we'd promoted to varsity only because she was small enough to throw. Naomi asked Debbie to drive her home and refused to make eye contact with me as they left practice together.

All day Tuesday, I felt the eyes creeping up me. Weighing me. Judging me. A few people in first period told me what Philip did was awful. But by the day's end, the tides of gossip had shifted against me. Three different people—including my calculus teacher—pulled me aside to say I was wrong to hang the banner without Naomi's permission. One girl called me an asshole to my face. I deserve it, of course, but I haven't heard of anyone saying the same to Philip. Yesterday I was "that trans kid," and now I'm that trans kid with a target on my back.

What if I was a cis guy? I try imagining who I might have been, though it makes me ache in every inch of my too-short body. Tall, strong, and powerful. Definitely still gay, but that cool, handsome sort of gay who stars on *Queer Eye* and leaves girls bemoaning his unavailability. Would Philip have dared pick on someone his own size?

I don't know. But when school started, I dug under my bed and fished out the hunting knife I bought back when Philip and I still hung out. Freshman year, it made me feel dangerous, edgy, part of Philip's tough little clique. Now it sits at the bottom of my locker. *Just in case,* I tell myself. *Philip's so much bigger and stronger than me. Just in case.*

I started this year—I ran for Homecoming King—hoping like hell I could have the senior experience I really needed. That I could snatch a few moments for myself, build four years' worth of teen boy high school experience out of one. A year, a crown, defined by *boy* and not whatever adjectives came before it.

I just want to be normal. But Sol was right. *Normal* has never been an option for me.

I need support. I need allies. For more than winning the crown.

The GSA meeting room is located in the basement beneath the theater wing, in a room still half occupied by the costumes from Cresswell's 2006 production of *Cats.* Plastic fur stiff with years gathers dust on old hangers. The rainbow banners on the cracked plaster walls haven't seen sunlight since before I was born. Ms. Daniels, the club sponsor, lies asleep in the corner, head atop a pile of ungraded reports on *The Scarlet Letter.*

"Hi, Jeremy!" Sol chirps as I enter. They've dyed their hair candy red and swapped their usual T-shirts for a knee-length black dress with fluffy petticoats. "Guys, check it out. I got us a new member! A popular one!"

"Oh my god!" Anna sits bolt upright, nearly knocking a prop kettle from *Beauty and the Beast* off a desk. "Jeremy?"

My jaw drops. "You're gay? But you're a cheerleader!"

"You're *also* a cheerleader," Hannah Kim points out. I know her from several classes. The GSA president, yearbook photographer, head lesbian on campus, and Anna's big sister. A collection of rainbow barrettes fills her messy black hair.

"I'm a male cheerleader," I point out. "Ergo, gay."

"And trans," Sol inserts. "Obviously."

No shit. Even here, that detail's attached to my name, invalidating everything around it. My gayness feels comfortable, natural. But being trans itches at some part of me, at least in this moment. *What's so obvious about me?* My pediatrician says transitioning is a journey I need to take one step at a time, but I don't want to be on the boy train. I want to feel like I've arrived.

"Could you not . . . rub it in?" I say. My identity feels like an axe hanging over my neck.

"Sorry," Sol says, and I can tell they earnestly mean it. "I just like having someone else around to talk trans stuff with. Aside from you, I only have Kaytie and Quince." I've never seen them as relaxed as they are in this room, surrounded by other queer people. And, as if they've given me a permission slip, my own tangled nerves start unwinding.

I have no idea who Kaytie and Quince are. I thought Sol

and I were the only ones. And I only knew Sol was trans because of the long lecture they gave Naomi and me last year when she told them, "There's a place on the cheer team for every Cresswell girl!" Still, Meehan isn't handing out access to the right bathrooms and locker rooms to any other Cresswell kid but me. Teachers haven't been ordered to respect anyone else's gender but mine. Because my mom went to the administration and *pushed*. Not every parent does. It's not fair that trans kids have to stand up to their own families before they get the care they need.

"Why aren't they here?" I ask, looking around, and I vaguely recognize the other faces in the room. I feel a twinge of worry for kids I may have passed a dozen times in the hallways but never met.

Sol shrugs. "I mean, they don't often come to meetings because their parents suck. But they're freshman transes, and they're, like, annoyingly in love."

"Aren't we not supposed to use trans as a noun?" I say. "Like those Republicans who scream about 'the transgendereds' corrupting their kids." There's something hilarious about how they say it. Like gender itself can rise up and beat you over the head until it bends you backward. Which isn't that far from the truth.

"Cis people aren't. Connor can't."

Connor West sits on the far side of the room. He's tall and skinny, hazel eyes, a shy smile, and cis. He's staring at himself in the window, the fuckhead. Probably enjoying how pretty he is.

I wonder what it would be like to date him and feel dizzy with hope. *Actually dating an actual gay guy.* I'd feel so real in his arms. The trans label wouldn't burn at me. My body wouldn't itch and ache so bad if I knew someone else wanted it.

It would be proof beyond proof that someone saw me deeply enough as a guy to overlook how I got there.

"Don't worry," Connor says. "I don't think about trans issues enough for it to come up."

Ouch. It's an elbow jab to the heart of my crush on him.

"Connor," Hannah says, and her usually patient voice is rough with irritation. "You can't just say stuff like—I mean, I know we've talked—"

"It's okay," I say, and take a deep breath. If he doesn't know about trans stuff, I can teach him. He can teach me about secret gay shit. We can find common ground once everyone in this club worships me.

Because that's what needs to happen. I'm going to turn on my dazzling cheerleader charm and win them to my side. We've got just over two weeks until Homecoming. It's not enough time to make close friends, but it's also not enough time for me to inevitably disappoint and alienate them. *I hope.* Just because Naomi's not standing beside me doesn't mean I'm giving up.

When I'm crowned Homecoming King, that's the part of me Cresswell will remember. Me in a crown. Me as a man, all adjectives and modifiers and history aside.

"What about you?" I ask the sisters. "Are you cis?"

"Rude!" Anna says. "You can't just ask people if they're cis."

"Gender is personal," Hannah continues. "Presentation and pronouns are public facing. We think we're cis, but we're not sure. We're still exploring."

If gender is personal, then why does mine feel as visible as a bug's guts on a truck windshield? "I thought I was the only trans kid at school!"

"You're the only one medically transitioning," Sol says. "That makes you the most visible. And the luckiest. Quince's parents have threatened to pull him out of school if he doesn't stop asking for puberty blockers. He's only fourteen, and he's petrified because, if he can't get treatment, he'll be forever trapped with the wrong skeleton."

Dysphoria crawls in me, tightening like an unreachable itch in the small of my back, a place I can't reach to soothe. A redness, a wrongness. *Me. Always too short, hands too stubby, never graceful and pretty like Connor or Lukas.* Mom's promised I can get top surgery before I go to college, so at least I can get my chest fixed. But looking in the mirror and still not seeing Jeremy—just that ugly version of the girl I was, hair chopped flat and makeup missing—makes the pit of my stomach drop and my ears scream at all the pain and emptiness.

So, I do what I can. Flash out tough and pointed ambition to wash away my feelings. "Is the club planning anything for Homecoming?" *Like supporting a candidate in the court elections? I need to get this back on track. Shove off toward the place I want to be going.*

"We might," Hannah says. "Our central leadership structure

is only a formality for the school administration's sake. Meeting agendas are decided by vote, after collaborative discussion, and I keep the notes. If we want to do something for Homecoming, we'll decide it together."

"But we never have in the past," Connor says. "People yelled at us when we put up posters to advertise. We don't like being too visible. Our goal is to take care of each other until we graduate."

How disappointing to hear from my new crush. *Running. Hiding.* Just like society expects. "The safest way to be queer is hide in a basement? This is the twenty-first century."

Sol shrugs. "Bigotry doesn't have an expiration date."

Jesus, this is depressing. And not at all how I want my life story to go.

"What if I told you we could change everything?" I say, grabbing a pink silk scarf from a costume box and dramatically tossing it back over my shoulder. "Cresswell pretends to be all progressive and shit, but you guys still act scared."

More shrugs and nods. Like they've accepted the status quo. Sol winces, their eyes wide behind thick makeup. *A dozen queer kids at Cresswell, afraid to claim themselves. Hundreds of millions silenced around the world.*

Now I know why Sol is so eager to claim me as trans. They're sick of being alone. Of pushing back alone against the homophobic school hierarchy. Their mysterious computer-god persona is a front thrown up by a lonely kid who wants to protect themself.

I understand wanting to protect yourself. That's why I have all my anger, for better or worse.

"Jeremy," Hannah says gently. "This is our place. It's not much, but it's safe. If we get loud, people like Philip try to shut us down."

"Then we kick his ass," I say. The GSA flinches, and I can't help thinking of the knife I hid in my locker. *I don't actually want to hurt anyone.* "I mean, metaphorically. With homosexual good feelings. I know the Cresswell hierarchy. I can make things happen within it. If we work together, we can pull off something spectacular by Homecoming. We can show this school we're here, we're queer, and we're fucking in charge."

"By what?" Sol says. A note of skepticism creeps back into their voice. "By helping you become Homecoming King?"

"You and I should run together. So *all* of us can put someone queer on the Homecoming Court." I give them my best, most dazzling smile. "Cresswell shouldn't just tolerate us. Fuck their tolerance. They should be forced to cheer while we shine in front of them." Connor's eyes light up. The sisters lean in close. "How much shit have queer people put up with just to get to *tolerance*? When I came out to my mom ... All I did was tell her the truth, and she looked at me like I'd just killed her daughter."

The guilt had hit me like a truck. I was a boy, but she'd always seen me as a good girl. Killing good girls was neither encouraged nor allowed. Mom had apologized for how she'd responded after I broke down and finally confessed how her reaction nearly tore me apart, but I still fear she might one day say she wishes I'd never transitioned.

Because the world values our lies over our truths, our silence over our voices, our deaths over our lives.

"Our story is supposed to be about suffering," I tell the GSA. "I propose we shine."

Sol grins, grabbing a plastic crown from the bin labeled *Macbeth* and dropping it atop their curls. "Call me the first nonbinary Homecoming Monarch."

It's settled. I have them on my side.

I'd expected this year to be different, but familiarly so. I'd believed I could slide back into my comfortable slot atop Cresswell's hierarchy. A peg of a new shape. *I'm not even a new shape yet. My hips and ass are still fucking massive.* But my transition has kicked off a cascade of changes, and I don't know where it'll land me or Cresswell.

All I know for sure is that the changes aren't over yet.

By the time the bell rings at the day's end, our plans are set. Anna and I walk to cheer practice together. She asks me not to tell the rest of the team that she's queer, and I promise not to. It's the right thing to do, and anyway, none of the other cheerleaders are speaking to me.

We practice our step routines. I take my place at the end of our line and let the sound of my teammates' footsteps rise around me, matching the pace and flow of my steps to theirs. My body knows this, moving as a unit, an unbreakable line. We lock in sync, steps and claps and words blending. I can pretend I'm part of something where I don't have a body, where I fit as part of a greater, genderless whole.

But when Coach shuts off the music, the girls flow back together, a knot of bright-colored spandex and bobbing ponytails. I'm standing on the outside. Anna shoots me the smallest look of pity before joining them. Neither Debbie nor Naomi looks my way. *Of course Debbie would take Naomi's side.* We've never been close, and ever since I transitioned, even the civility she'd normally offer a fellow cheerleader has evaporated. Plus, I'm clearly the one in the wrong.

I square my shoulders and march across the field to the watercooler Ben and his friends have surrounded. Football players in full padding hulk around, pressing their lips to a ratty, chewed-up tap. To Ben's credit, he's drinking from a separate water bottle. The last thing our 0-3 team needs this season is mono. "Hi, VP. I got us a computer programmer for our student government project. We should start on that soon."

"Sounds good," Ben says. "Tomorrow at lunch?"

I nod.

"Bitch," Philip mutters as he walks past me. His fingers graze my shirt collar, hook my sports bra strap, and snap it.

"Are you trying to practice your SAT words?" I demand, refusing to acknowledge the sting. "Pretty sure that one isn't on it."

"Always with the jokes." He grins, smug as a beauty queen just handed her sash. "If you were really a man, you'd fight me."

"Go on," Ben says to Philip, cracking his knuckles. I jump up on the bench, behind him. Just because I can't have his broad shoulders doesn't mean I can't use them to stand between me and danger. "What was that you were telling Jeremy?"

"Just that . . ." Philip pauses. Takes another look at Ben's fists. "I'd settle this the old-fashioned way, for the honor of the flag and all, but I won't hit a . . . a short guy."

"Like they said on the *Titanic*," I cut in, safe behind Ben. "Short guys and children first. We can still make this work, Philip." From my place on the bench, I vault atop Ben's shoulders. He stagger-steps forward but doesn't fall, neatly grabbing hold of my legs. For once, I'm grateful to be wearing ugly men's cheer sweatpants instead of the girls' short skirt.

"Fight! Fight! Fight!" Max and a few of the younger players peel away from the cooler, shouting and hooting. "Piggyback fight! Piggyback fight!" One offers me a half-full bucket, and I hoist it over my head as Ben totters toward Philip.

"You wouldn't." Philip throws up his hands, taking a huffy breath. "Oh my god, we're all seniors. Stop acting like little kids."

Behind us, one of the younger players shouts, "Water fight!" lobbing his water bottle at another boy. The contents splash out, and that player grabs a towel, soaks it in the ice bin, and chases the boy with the bottle down. A boy on the bench squeals as he's drenched from both sides. Two more dash to a storage shed and uncoil a hose. Laughter, shouts, and splashes ring up and down the field. Is this what it feels like to be one of the guys?

"Afraid to take me on an even footing?" I ask, laughing at Philip. Ben charges forward, and Philip takes a hasty step back. I raise the bucket to upend it over his head, but the weight of the water sloshes me forward. Ben's feet go out from under him and my stomach lurches as we drop. I fling the bucket at Philip and catch a brief glance of his shocked face before tumbling down with an *oof*.

"Get your knee out of my armpit," Ben mumbles, dazed and rolling over.

"Get your face out of my crotch," I say, untangling myself. Thank god for his helmet and padding—and my own indomitable cheer training. The other players laugh, good-natured, in on the joke as we stand. Definitely worth a black and blue tailbone tomorrow.

"That's fucking freezing," Philip gripes, shivering theatrically. I roll my eyes. I got most of the water on me, and I'm not even cold.

"Aren't I supposed to be the dramatic one?" I say. "Follow your own advice. Take it like a man."

His face reddens where the water drips down his cheeks. His fists tighten. Reflexively, I take a half step backward. The shudder running down my spine isn't from the clinging water.

I'd forgotten that Philip, like me, can't stand other people joking about his masculinity.

"Want up?" Max says to Philip, jerking a thumb at his shoulders. "Come on. We can take 'em. Let's grab the hose. Round two." I think Max is trying to distract him, pull Philip away from his furious stride in my direction, but he brushes Max off.

"Keep it up, Jeremy," Philip says. "We've all seen how you treat your friends. Sooner or later, you won't have anyone left to hide behind—and then we'll see what it takes to make a real man."

I shiver, and not just from the icy water soaking through my shorts and socks. *He's just messing with me*, I tell myself. But Philip knows me, in the way only a former friend can. All my faults and failings, stored up in his head.

Thirty minutes later, the football coach blows his whistle, ending practice. Lukas jogs to the sideline where cheer practice ended moments before. His black hair slides free as he removes his helmet, damp with sweat and humid Maryland air. The testosterone-tinted urge to be touched surges within me, but it's more than my sex drive crying out. I want Lukas to speak to me in that secret language we invented as kids, to build me pillow forts and curl up inside to watch scary movies. I want his eyes to light with awe as I leap off bridges into rivers and climb trees to rescue cats. That look of his always made me feel seen.

So seen that I've wondered if his eyes picked out the self I worked so hard to hide. So seen that once or twice I fantasized it was Jeremy, the boy, he loved, instead of the girl I'd faked and ultimately failed to be.

I remember how his hair felt on my cheek; the smile in his eyes is familiar, too. I've loved that smile, I've missed that smile—and my mutinous flash of joy dims as Lukas and that smile walk past me to embrace Naomi.

For a heartbeat, I don't understand. I don't want to understand. But then Naomi kisses his cheek, and my world becomes backlit with fire.

He's straight. Very, very straight. He's not mine anymore.

Those hopes flutter up and die as his big, gentle hand cradles Naomi's curls. He likes girls. Pretty girls. Just like he told me when I tried to come out. *You'll always be my girl.* But I'm not. And I never was, not like how Naomi can be. Now I'm the one losing to her, with my guts feeling clawed out and my shriveled heart beating *why?* It stings, like a rock stuck in my shoe digs to the blistering truth: that I might have made Naomi feel this bad every time I beat her, and I didn't care until she finally won. How selfish; what a bad friend I've been.

Maybe I'm doomed to wind up with no one at all.

Being chased down by the Philips of the world.

Self-loathing and despair bubble up into something caustic inside me. "Congrats," I say, slowly clapping. "On your new relationship. Be sure to buy fresh condoms, Lukas. Those flavored ones I got you have expired by now."

"Oh my god," Naomi says, turning away from his arms. "Seriously, Jeremy? Are you twelve?"

"Hopefully a twelve-year-old wouldn't know where to buy flavored condoms." Bitterness is thick on my tongue, rising out of me like poisoned smog to join the swampy air. "Seriously, Naomi? Lukas? We're best friends. He should be off-limits. I said I was sorry about yesterday. Are you doing this just to piss me off? Because it's working."

"Jesus." She laughs, and there's smog in her throat, too. "Not everything's about you, Jeremy. *I'm* not all about you. If you want the best friend code to apply, you should start acting like one. In the meantime, Lukas is allowed to date whoever he wants. You told me you two were one hundred percent over."

"Ignore him, Naomi," Lukas says, voice cold and flat. A sign I'm not worth the effort it takes him to signal emotion. "Just like he ignored you this summer when you needed him."

"I was dealing with my own stuff," I shout. "Don't talk about me like I'm not here." God, I hate it. Makes me feel like I'm too small, too femme, too young to matter.

"You want me to talk to you?" Lukas asks, taking a step toward me. His cleats tear into the field grass. "Fine. I'll tell you to your face: You've been treating everyone who cares about you like garbage. Your best friend. Me. You didn't just dump me, Jeremy. You threw me away like we were nothing on the worst day of my life, and you didn't even tell me why." His nostrils flare. He jabs his hands firmly into his pockets.

It's the closest he's ever come to yelling at me, and it makes the back of my neck flush hot.

I didn't realize he didn't know why I dumped him.

We had all gathered at the diner that afternoon. Together, we had whisked Lukas away from his family's house, packed tight with elderly relatives and grief thick as their clashing perfumes. Lukas had been moving on autopilot—offering food to his grandmother, making excuses for his father's absence, pulling his mom away from the wine and holding her up as she fell apart at random intervals in front of their guests. In the course of one night, the weight of the world had fallen on his shoulders, and he would barely stop hoisting it long enough to breathe. No one could read him the way I can, but all our friends still sensed this was Lukas fracturing.

I sat beside him, trying to project calm, quiet strength, his anchor in a storm. But all I could think, even as strangers clasped my hands and praised me for being *such a good girl-friend*, was how I felt like I was crawling out of my skin. A week had passed since I'd come out to my mom as trans, since she'd told me I'd *always be her daughter*. I'd tried to explain it to her so many times. Still, when I told her I didn't know what was right to wear to Jason's funeral—I'd gone to my grand-parents' services, but never one for a person my age—she'd told me to wear a black dress with matching heels. "This day is about Lukas and his family," she'd said. "Not your problems."

I'd worn the dress. But even knowing that day wasn't about me, nothing could shake off the red and swirling storm of dysphoria pounding at my temples. It was Ben who finally suggested we get him out of there. When Lukas's father came back downstairs, his eyes red and impossible to meet, he began ushering people out, and we took that as our cue. I grabbed Lukas's hand and pulled him out of the house.

We sat at the long table where the diner served big groups, between the chrome dessert case and the faux 1950s jukebox. The pink-tinted neon lighting reflected eerily off the black we'd worn. Naomi and Debbie whispered in low voices. Ben, Max, and a handful of other football players shuffled uneasily in stiff-fitting suits. I'd ordered fries and a strawberry milkshake, but couldn't bring myself to eat, so I just dipped fries in and out of the ice cream froth. Ben reached over to pat Lukas on the back, then gave me a weird look.

I realized I hadn't spoken since we sat down. *This day is about Lukas*, I reminded myself.

"How're you holding up?" I muttered to Lukas. He'd been super quiet since getting the news about Jason.

"It fucking sucks, it—" Lukas bit his cheek, words tangled. "I don't even know what to say. What to do." He sighed. "I'm just glad you're here with me. You're the one thing in my life that doesn't change."

That stung. And I knew this wasn't the right time or place for this conversation, but my words bubbled out anyway. The weight of being a good girlfriend felt impossible to carry, and I wanted to know if I could ever be anything else to him.

"What if I did?" I whispered back. "I know who everyone wants me to be, and I've been trying to be that person my whole life, but what if that's not me? What if the real me is so different from who everyone knows that you hate hi—the real me?"

"That's impossible," he said, tucking a loose strand of hair behind my ear. Back then, I wore it long. "I love you no matter what. You'll always be my girl."

And, without knowing, he ripped my heart in two.

You'll always be my girl. It sounded so much like my mom's *you'll always be my daughter.*

In that moment I needed something more than boyfriend-girlfriend love from him. I needed something bigger. Something meant for the real me. I needed him to love me more than my body, more than what gossiping assholes would say.

But I couldn't trust he loved me that much. Our relationship had grown from a childish plan to survive high school together, and I was burning that rulebook. Starting over. Lukas existed neck-deep in order and consistency. I couldn't expect him to light that match with me. So, I lit the fuse and pushed him away from the blast.

"Let me out," I said. Lukas's chair was blocking me in, his broad shoulder standing between me and the door. "Move."

On the other side of Lukas, Ben's head snapped up. Max leaned over his French fries, peering in for a better view.

Lukas frowned. "Are you okay?" he asked. But instead of backing away, he leaned in closer. Reaching for my hand.

"You have to let me out," I said, my voice peaking, hated and high. "*Move*, Lukas!" When he didn't, I shoved my chair back, the legs screeching across the linoleum floor, careening into the table behind us.

"Whoa," Lukas said, finally standing up. "Did I do something wrong?" He spoke low and calmly, like he was trying to soothe me. "Are you sick? Do you want me to take you home?"

"I can give you a ride," Naomi offered, gazing up with concerned brown eyes. "If Lukas wants to stay."

"Or a tampon," Debbie added. "You look like you might need one."

"Please." Lukas reached for me, and suddenly his niceness felt like the bone-scouring roar of an open furnace.

"I can't do this anymore, Lukas," I said, and moved to step around him.

"Wait—" And he'd said that name. That one I wanted more than anything to rid myself of.

It hit me like an electric shock. Before I knew it, my hand blurred. A splash. A clatter. Pink bloomed on Lukas's black suit, dripping down to the floor. The color of the roses he always gave me on Valentine's Day. The color of his mouth as it dropped open, disbelieving.

"I want to break up," I said. "You and I—we're *done*." I think Lukas said *what* and then *okay*. I remember his lips moving, but I didn't say anything else. Everything went foggy. My drive home that night is just a blank space in my head.

I hadn't planned to break up with him. But panic and darkness had filled me up and spilled out of me. It didn't matter that I knew Lukas down to his soul, that I knew he loved me in a way that was deep, pure, and real. We didn't fit. Couldn't fit. *If I had asked Lukas if he preferred girl me or real me that day, he'd have picked girl me. Everyone would have picked her. My mom would have picked her. No one wanted me, and it was tearing me apart.*

So I let myself be opened up and remade. I'd thrown my milkshake, yelled in his face, and broken us. But not because I didn't love him.

I broke us because I knew otherwise he'd break *me*. And I was already in crisis.

That night, I went to my mom and told her how close to exploding I felt, like the edge of a cliff had crept up on me. That's how I got through to her. How I was able to set up a new beginning, one I knew Lukas wouldn't want to be part of. *Stupid, infuriating, gorgeous straight cis boy. You don't even know you once held the power to break me.*

I shattered his heart to make room for what I wanted. I'm the one who deserves to be treated like garbage right now. The real me probably disgusts him, like how catching my own soft, unfinished reflection in the mirror disgusts me. He'll never like the person I really am, not even as a friend. I've made it impossible. But saying any of this out loud might destroy me.

"I don't owe you my reasons," I tell Lukas. His spine stiffens. His arm tightens on Naomi's shoulder. "I don't owe you anything. I'm not your girlfriend, and I never was."

The air between us presses tight and cold. Goose bumps prickle down my cheekbones. Naomi bites her lip and looks away awkwardly. Like she's the odd one out, instead of me.

"We dated three years," Lukas says quietly. "Did that entire relationship mean anything to you?"

Three years forcing myself to be something I wasn't. I want to scrub every trace of the girl I'd been from time and space. From my very bones. And Lukas was part of her in a way he'll never be part of me. So why can't he just give up and let the past die?

"It did," I say, and square my jaw, because I want to slam the door shut on this conversation forever. Because my throat is swelling shut, my eyes are brimming, and I refuse to look weak in front of him. "But here's the hard truth. It didn't matter enough."

CHAPTER NINE: LUKAS

"Just over two weeks before the dance," I tell the Homecoming Committee during our Wednesday meeting. Two weeks, two days, three hours, and fourteen minutes, to be precise, but I'll look weird if they find out I've kept a timer. "We need to buy new crowns for the Homecoming Court."

"I'll go to Party City this weekend," Debbie says near my elbow.

We're meeting in the orchestra room, but twice as many students have showed up as I anticipated, and we're packed in tight between the violin lockers and the massive stacked xylophones. "Unless you literally want me to buy you one of real gold."

I laugh, and briefly wonder how much real gold would cost. "It isn't the material that matters. It's what it represents. You know. Me. Winning."

"What if Jeremy wins?" says an underclassman. My knuckles

tighten around my phone at the mention of his name. "We've finalized the ballot. He and Sol Reyes-Garcia are on it. Should we get some extra crowns from the kiddie section? They're both pretty short."

"No one's actually voting for either of them," I say, fighting to keep my breath calm and measured. "We don't have to worry." Sure, some freshmen in the Academic Decathlon group chat were talking about voting for Sol over me, but that has to be a joke. And no one could really want Jeremy up there, with how he's been acting lately.

You didn't matter enough. That's how he sees me. Everything we shared means less than a plastic crown to him.

I'll show him. He'll end up with no crown, no friends, and no me. And while I doubt he'll regret anything—because he wouldn't be setting these fires if he didn't like watching them burn—breaking past his defenses and making him feel even a sliver of shame will be worth it. I need to know I can make him react to me. That I can push past that bitter, obnoxious sarcasm and pull out something real. Sting him like he stung me.

"Jeremy might get some votes," says a spotty junior who ducks my pointed glare. "Some people in my class were really impressed he climbed the flagpole. I mean, not me, Lukas. I'm voting for you. But some people."

"It wasn't nice he hung up Naomi's banner without asking first," says a girl in a Cresswell Cheer sweater. "But what

Philip did was awful. I feel so bad for Jeremy, getting bullied like that."

Some of her friends nod along with her, a tight cluster precariously shoved back below the bassoon racks. Pity votes. But votes all the same. One-third of my Homecoming Committee, with room to grow. *Jeremy is a danger to me. Philip is a threat to everyone.* After Sarika Patel turned Philip down for a date, *someone* sent an anonymous note to the administration saying she had a bomb in her locker, and got the school police called in to search it. Mad as I am at my ex, he doesn't deserve to be Philip's new target.

I drag the conversation back to my agenda. We're supposed to publicize a new dress code the administration released for the Homecoming spirit days. They're clearly still upset over my King Leonidas cosplay from Movie Character Day last year. *Shirts are mandatory for male and female students.* Maybe Sol will come topless.

Monday of Homecoming Week will be the first big event: the canned food sculpture competition, where students build elaborate monuments from donated cans, competing for the favor of the crowd before the cans are sent to the local food pantry. The freshmen only have sixty cans so far. It won't be enough for a sculpture.

"Throwing a great donation drive is tough," I say, sitting down with them as an irate cello player tries to squeeze past us with their massive instrument. "Everyone at this school has a million things on their mind. It's hard to make people focus. Reach out to your class with multiple reminders. Posters, emails, in-person conversations. Putting one announcement on your class website isn't enough."

"You'd think people would care about this more," a freshman mutters. "Everyone at Cresswell cares so much about Homecoming. It should be easier."

"People care about Homecoming because we make it something worth caring about," I say. "It's a celebration of everything our school can build. Yeah, it'll take a while for kids in your class to get into it. But they'll care because you cared first. Because you offered them something so cool it looks effortless. People don't like donating because they expect Homecoming will happen automatically. You've got to push them. Push hard enough, and I promise—this Homecoming will be spectacular." I mean it. Every word. I want this dance to be spectacular. A testimony to the person I'm trying to become. And more.

And it's strange to realize, even without the world pressing down on me, I'd still do this.

Strange to imagine there's a me outside the weights I carry.

The janitor texts saying there's a delivery for the Homecoming Committee at the loading dock they need me to sign for. I excuse myself. As the only eighteen-year-old on the committee, it's my signature they'll need. After the tight, pressing heat and echoing cacophony of the orchestra room, stepping out into the crisp September air feels as refreshing as a Sprite commercial. I'm so glad to be inhaling something other than bow resin and body odor, I don't notice the man unloading the truck until I'm almost on top of him.

Terry Gould is barely twenty-one, but the drawn, pale, pitted planes of his cheeks age him. His blond hair hangs in loose, uneven clumps. Silver flashes in his face and ears as he turns to face me. The ink of a new tattoo lines his neck. *JR May 6th.*

He got ink for my brother. Fury slips down my throat like an intruder's tongue. *I've been too busy picking up the pieces to feel sad.*

Jason's loss hits me in the odd moments and shadows, while sitting in calc and painting the senior class float, catching his face in a hallway photo of past Cresswell valedictorians. An echo in the empty space in my chest. A hole where once my heart had held substance. *He's gone. I'll never see him again.*

I want to be poetic about it. But thinking about him just makes me feel empty, not hurt. There's a hole in my routines where he'd once steal my food and play his music just loud enough to piss me off. A gas-scented smudge on the calendar every May, leaking sadness into my birthday, a date that used to be one of the few things I'd call mine. Somewhere in the tangles of me, I mourn him. But thinking of the standards he left behind just makes me panic, heart flailing like a fish plucked from water. *How can I hold my family together? How can I fill the space left by someone's whole life?* And the biggest, saddest one—that if it had been me in that car and not my brother, everyone in my family would have already moved on.

Of course they would have. They'd have Perfect Jason around to show them the way. I'm not sure why Terry got a tattoo for my brother. They'd been friends since they were kids, sure, but Jason stopped hanging out with him when he left for college. Terry saw the mean, controlling side of my brother no one else did. Years of it. But he also saw the worst side of me.

I know how ugly it gets when I lose control. None of my classmates from second grade wound up at Cresswell, thank god. I'm sure they all remember that meltdown. I do. Miss Brinton, hands tasting of child-safe vanilla soap, reaching for my favorite Batman figure at the end of recess. The snap in my head that ached at things changing. I bit down right below her wedding ring. She'd shook, but I'd been strong, even as an eight-year-old aspiring piranha. The other kids had laughed and screamed as Miss Brinton called for the principal, but it was only Jason's words I remembered.

"Fucking retard," he hissed in my ear as he pulled me off. I hadn't known what that meant. I'd known it was meant to hurt.

Terry hadn't said those words that day. He just stood over my brother's shoulder. I still remember how he'd stared at me, blue eyes wide as I screamed and fought to escape the painful pinch of my brother's grip. Like he knew something was wrong, but wasn't sure what.

I'm still not sure what. I just hate that he knows what happens when I melt down. I hate that he never said anything, left me feeling utterly alone. Even with my brother gone, the memory of that voice lingers.

Be normal, or I'll hurt you.

"Hey, Lukas," he says as I sign the form. Sun glints off the truck's dinged-up side and his silver earrings. "Haven't seen you since summer."

There's a heat behind those innocent words, like how July weather creeps farther into September each year. Some people carry a spark of trouble inside them, and I'm the moth it draws. Before I met Jeremy, Terry was the kid I followed around, watching awed from the sidelines as he cursed at his parents and stole candy from teachers' desks. *A budding Bond villain.* Fascinating because he was everything I wasn't. Because everything he was pulled on something in me too big to understand.

He's trouble, my common sense screams. *You're not kids anymore. Reckless inferno people ruin lives.*

But another part of me wonders what happens between me and Terry when Jason isn't around.

"I've been busy since school started," I say, trying to return the slick July of his tone. I don't think it carries. He knew where to find me if he wanted to talk. "New job?"

He nods. "I do deliveries, wait tables on the side. Taking

some night classes. How are you holding up, with Jason and all? You okay?"

You okay? Two little words are the most complicated question anyone could ask me. "Sure. I guess."

"You're allowed to not be okay, you know. You guys had a complicated relationship."

"Complicated?" I ask, giving him a look.

"Yeah, okay. He was a shit brother to you," Terry amends.

"He was," I say. "But . . . I don't know. It feels disloyal to say it out loud. A good brother would help protect Jason's memory. For the sake of the rest of my family."

"You're a nice guy," Terry says. "But it's okay to be mad. You know, after graduation, Jason went home smelling like weed and your parents lost their shit? He told them he didn't smoke it, that he heard I was dealing and went to talk me out of it. Spun some bullshit story about me, made me sound like the freaking meth kingpin of Bethesda. They called the cops. No charges filed, but my parents kicked me out—over what, two joints we smoked together?"

"Jesus," I say. "I didn't know." But it fits Jason. Pushing other people down was the price he paid for his own perfection. "You still got that tat to commemorate him?" I raise my brows at the ink on his neck.

Terry nods. "We'd started talking again, a few months before the accident. Planning to meet up when he came home for summer." He shrugs. "But we never got to make things right before he passed. Losing a friend, with words left unsaid—it leaves a mark, Lukas. I wanted that mark to be visible to the world. We were good friends before all the bullshit."

"A good friend would have just come around after Jason died instead of making a big show out of his own sadness," I say, rolling my eyes. "I bet you show that to girls you want to sleep with to make them feel sorry for you."

He laughs, raising his hands in surrender. "You're not too far off." Something else wheedles into his voice—a note of wanting, like a student asking a teacher to boost their grade. I don't know where it comes from. "If I had someone like you in my life—if I'd been your friend, instead of Jason's—maybe I'd be a better person."

"You don't need other people to make you better. You can just stop being an ass."

I shoulder the box of T-shirts and march inside, pushing back into the crowded orchestra room, clambering up a locker to stash the box and running late to my next class after I accidentally knock over some oboes climbing down. It's not until then I realize I misread him. He wasn't looking for personality advice. He wanted to make a connection with me.

I shouldn't let that happen. My gut is flashing up red flags quicker than a color guard can toss. Because Terry might not have been dealing back then, but he dropped out of UMD last year for some reason, and with his well-connected family, there's no reason for him to be dropping off packages unless he's done something bad enough to get cut off. Real-world, adult trouble. Not a pool I want to stick my toes into.

But my gut sucks at reading people. Maybe he's reaching out in good faith to the brother of his closest friend. Maybe he's lonely.

He runs circles through my mind the rest of the day. I don't realize I'm chewing on a pencil until it slips between my teeth and I bite the eraser, sending me into a sensory clusterfuck for the next ten minutes. Finally, I type into my history notes, *I have NO REASON to care about Terry Gould.*

After practice, I gulp down the spare sandwich from my lunchbox as I watch the senior class dancers rehearse for the musical sketch. Laurie, our choreographer, assembled a playlist for the Senior Superheroes theme—the classic *Superman* theme, the *Avengers* soundtrack, and the Five for Fighting song about Superman that emo kids like.

"Are we going to run into copyright issues?" she asks as they swirl in circles about the clay of the tennis court. "Using the songs like this?"

I shake my head. "No one will sue a high school."

The musical will be ready on time—but our class T-shirt is another matter. The design team shows me their effort—just Superman's *S* with the word *Seniors* following from it. I nearly choke on my panini. "What? Did they even try?"

"If we change it now, we'll have to schedule a rush printing," the head designer says.

"We have the budget for it," I say, flashing the debit card. "Make something creative. This is our senior year. We have standards." Nothing can be less than perfect where Homecoming and my future are concerned.

After the committees go home, I sit in the backseat of my car and race through a week's worth of homework. I don't make it home until midnight. As I creep through the hall, darting over creaky floorboards, I feel I've pulled off something more daring than my shirtless Spartan cosplay from last year's Homecoming.

My family won't make me talk to them if I'm busy doing homework or anything related to college applications. If I can avoid mentioning Jason—if I can avoid them entirely— maybe I can keep the wounds shut until I'm crowned. And early admissions decisions for the Ivies are announced soon after, in glorious, fat envelopes. I'm so close to feeling my family ring about me and smile. I just need to ignore the pain until the moment I can permanently bind the wound and stop bleeding.

Thursday morning before our next biology test, I track down Sol in the computer lab. "Thanks so much for getting me the answer key," I say. "I've got no time to study with Homecoming and all." I'm lying about the reason I need this. I don't care. Jason would probably be proud of how smoothly I keep my own flaws secret.

They nod, log out of their computer, and log back in using Dr. Coryn's email address and a line of numbers as a password. "She uses her birthdate. She shouldn't, but whatever." The answer key gets loaded into a clean flash drive and pressed into my hand. Clean, anonymous red plastic. "Don't let anyone see it."

"Thanks," I say, dragging warmth into my voice. They're doing me a big favor, and I know they could be expelled if caught. "You're the best. Seriously." I shove it into the bottom of my backpack and turn to leave. But then I stop. "Say, what's up with Jeremy and you? I heard you were running for Homecoming Court together?" I try to sound casual, like I'm not fishing for information.

"It's a queer protest campaign. Pure political anarchism. Don't expect to see me running around in pearls and a polo shirt begging for votes."

I can't imagine them in any outfit that doesn't involve at least three layers of denim, sequins, and leather. "Has he said anything about the breakup?"

"Just that he doesn't want to talk about it. Which I get."

What's there for them to get? Are they seriously taking Jeremy's side in all this? I think back to the heated, angry look on Jeremy's face the other day when he said his reasons are his own. I try a different tactic. "What's up with your campaign? Are you planning any events?"

They smile. "Jeremy is planning to give out free pizza to the whole school Friday. It's supposed to be a student government thing—that's where he's getting the money. He'll set up food stations beneath the posters he's making to promote his antibullying hearing. But he's also using it to talk about his campaign for Homecoming King."

"Awesome idea," I say. Triumphant warmth shoots through my veins. "Hope you have fun."

Jeremy Harkiss, you egotistical asshole. Now you'll get what you deserve. I don't want to ruin Sol's fun—they sound like they're really enjoying themself—but if Jeremy can piss off everyone who's ever cared about him, I can give myself one pass to be a jerk.

Tonight, I'll call every pizza place within fifteen miles, pose as Jeremy's dad, and tell them my shitty kid has been ordering hundreds of dollars of pizza with fake credit cards. No one in town will take his money. The two of us pulled the same prank on Jason a few years ago. He should be expecting it, but he won't. I'm certain he's forgotten every second we spent together, the good and bad alike. I'll get him back in the most delicious way possible. Slicing him up until he has no choice but to remember me and us. *Sorry, but not sorry. My family and future ride on this win. You don't care about destroying that. So I'll destroy you.*

I load the answer key on my laptop, curled up alone against a locker in the hallway, and try to study, but nothing sticks. Math comes easy to me, but biology—especially the way Dr. Coryn teaches it—makes zero sense. I run to another computer lab, a crowded one, and convince Ben to get off his computer so I can print out the answer key. Now I can do what I need—run my finger down the page, whispering the questions and answers under my breath, over and over. It halfway clicks in, and then I'm off to AP Bio, where I all but vomit hastily memorized answers onto the test page.

There's no real way to win. Dr. Coryn asks questions like "Describe the G-protein cascade," and leaves the rest up to us. A ten-point question to sum up a chemical process whole books have been written on. It's never enough to describe what the reaction does—I have to guess which ten factoids she was thinking of when she wrote the question, and regurgitate them all in the right order. Even with Sol's key, my head spins by the time Dr. Coryn collects our work.

She inspects our exams with a sniff, the corkboard pinned with posters and printouts fluttering with her every disappointed huff. "The grades won't be online for a few days, but some of you are scoring awfully high. I've always found it suspicious so many members of Cresswell's football team decided to take my class instead of something more soothing to their concussion-riddled brains."

She eyes me, Ben, and Philip suspiciously. The beehive war helmet of her hair bobs as she nods knowingly at us.

"Can you believe her?" Philip huffs as we leave. "She's discriminating against us because we play football."

Ben rolls his eyes. "Ah, yes, us poor oppressed football players. What's next? Football players being forced to wait in the lunch lines? Football players only getting into in-state colleges?"

"Actually," I add, maneuvering us around a couple making out on the lockers. "People do respect the *futbol* team. They win. Technically, we're playing 'American football.'"

"It should just be 'football,'" Philip fumes.

"Are you not proud of it being American?" Ben says. We high-five as Philip storms away, pushing through knots of students and nearly knocking over nearsighted Mr. McKinney, rolling an ancient projector cart down the hall.

The rush of trolling Philip back quickly evaporates. It feels immature and, worse, ineffectual. This school is my community, the place I'm a leader, instead of a disaster—the place where what I say matters.

I won't let Philip Cross ruin it.

In the locker room that afternoon, as my teammates file out to the field, I corner Philip beside a bench. The high banks of lockers, blue paint flaking off the rusting metal, turn the room into a labyrinth of gym-sock reek. It's easy to trap—to stand tall above—someone who doesn't expect their presence to be challenged.

"I saw what you did to the banner," I say, hands on my hips to casually box him in. "It's all over the internet. What the hell is your problem with Jeremy?"

He shrugs and stands. But he doesn't try to shove past me. "It's fun to see that little freak jump. Say 'oooh, you're a girl,' and boom—fireworks."

Well. As my mom's mom used to say, don't go looking for depth in a mud puddle.

I dig a finger in his chest. "You're going to apologize and pay Naomi for the damages. Then maybe Cresswell will tolerate you until you graduate and get the fuck out. Who goes after an old friend like that?"

"We were never friends," Philip says. "I just liked seeing the crazy shit I could make the little weirdo do. Don't be a fucking social justice warrior, Rivers. It's got to suck knowing you're so bad in bed you turned your girlfriend into a man. Be honest. It's just the two of us. You hate her, don't you?"

"You don't know what you're talking about." I have a right to be mad about how callously Jeremy dumped me. We'd been friends all our lives. He's the only one who knows how I struggled with Jason and my disability. I needed him to lean on. He vanished during the worst moment of my life and came back determined to destroy my world.

But hating Jeremy for being himself—because I've seen the light in him now he's transitioned, seen him alive and angry and moving—hating him for that isn't just cruel, it's pointless. It took all my strength to stop him from breaking Philip's nose. I couldn't hold him back from being himself if I tried.

"Oh my god." He laughs. "You've bought into Harkiss's sob story. God, are you a fucking retard? Man up already."

The sudden descent into trolling slaps me back to the present. I flinch. He doesn't know I'm autistic, doesn't expect it to hit like a hammer—but of course not. All he's trying to do is piss me off and draw me in. I don't want any of the manhood Philip is selling, and I won't play his game. I don't need to.

"I'm not going to fight you," I say. "I'm not getting expelled for you. You're trash, Philip. And if you keep this up, I'll throw you out with the rest of it. Now get up to the field. Tell Coach I'm filling the water bins, because someone on this team has to be responsible."

He turns and walks out, stomping across the bleach-washed tiles.

"Fag!" he spits back over his shoulder. "We all know you two were fucking, Lukas. Did you like it when he stuck his dick up your ass?"

So, you can *remember his pronouns.* But, of course, nothing Philip has said is because he doesn't know what being transgender means, or that he doesn't know the r-word is wrong. He's just saying anything he can think of to inflict pain.

And he's making himself one more item to check off my mental to-do list: *Get rid of Philip Cross.*

Bizarrely, a grin stretches across my face. After everything else I've been through today, it'll be a real pleasure.

CHAPTER TEN: JEREMY

I stalk the entrance to the boys' locker room for fifteen minutes. Slouching on a stack of gym mats near the door, my hood pulled low over my forehead, pretending to fiddle with my phone. No one notices me as the team filters out in uniform, jogging up to the practice fields. *They must be gone by now. It must be empty.* Or it might just be empty enough for no one to care if I scream.

I tell myself to be brave. But in my head, I'm in a dark basement, lips sticky with beer. Brandon Kyle, the quarterback before Ben and Homecoming King of two years ago, grabs my shoulder. *Your boyfriend left you here? Come up to my room. I'll show you what a real man can do.* I tremble, confused and terrified, until Lukas runs up and pulls me away. Brandon's hand never moved farther than my shoulder. But that was all it took to tell me where I stood.

And Philip's stunt with the banner was all it took to remind me.

This is a locker room. Not Brandon's basement, and not a pit of hell. But people get assaulted all over, and the laws don't protect them. The worst Cresswell boys grow up and make laws. I need to get back at Philip, show him there's consequences for humiliating me in public. Chili powder in his gym bag will do nicely. I just need to walk through the door and brave what lies on the other side.

I fiddle with the back of my binder until my fingers grip firm plastic. The four-inch-long knife glimmers as I pull it free, test the edge on my finger, and sheathe it once more. Pepper spray or a rape whistle would be a little more legal, but a knife is clean, masculine power. A talisman of protection. A symbol of the soul every boy like Brandon and Philip wanted to steal away so they could use me.

I'm not anyone's prey, I tell myself, knife gripped in my fist. Just in case. Spine squared, I shoulder the door open and lunge through.

"Oh my god!" Lukas jumps as he sees me. The hose he's using to fill water barrels leaps out of his hand, soaking me down the front before he grabs it back. He takes a second to catch his breath and his eyes lock on my clenched fist. "Is that a knife? What are you doing? You could get expelled!"

"There's worse fates." I hold up a bottle of gourmet chili powder. "Like what Philip will suffer once I get in his locker."

"That's assault." Lukas shuts off the hose and shoves a frustrated hand back through his hair. It's getting long again. Unlike so many cis boys, he uses conditioner, and I can't help thinking about how soft it always was to touch. "You're the future lawyer. You should know that."

"What am I supposed to do? Lie down and take it?" There's something harsh in the way I say that. I wince. It's so unfair of me, when I know lots of people put up with this crap because the alternative is getting hurt worse. When I saw my mom cook my stepdad special meals so he wouldn't shove or pinch me. When even my grandma would go quiet after bringing up my long-dead grandpa's temper. I know resisting Philip is as dangerous as stepping on a snake. I just don't care about my own safety as much as I could. "Sorry. Really. It's just that—"

"It doesn't make you less of a man if you don't fight this battle with Philip," Lukas says. "Put the knife away. You're freaking me out. Where the hell did you get so violent?"

Fear flickers in his darting eyes. This whole time I've wanted Lukas to see me as an equal, and now I've taken it too far. Instead of looking at me like an equal, he's looking at me like I'm a stranger.

I sheathe the blade and slide it back up my shirt. Looking at him is breaking my heart a little, so I step back. The boys' locker room isn't as frightening as I feared. It's a mirror image of the girls' locker room across the hall, albeit more battered and worse-smelling.

"Listen." My voice cracks again. Like a scar across my face. "No one would ever question your masculinity."

"I get it—" Lukas starts.

"No, you don't," I say, shaking my head. "How could you? Even if people *did* question you, that part of you isn't something other people can take away. You have no idea what that feels like, Lukas. It's impossible for you understand how Philip hurt me."

He's quiet for a moment. "Okay. But there's plenty of other shit people *could* say about me. I don't think stabbing people is an answer."

"Because you don't know what it's like!" I shout. My voice peaks. So high, so weak. So incisively true. Because he doesn't know. Because I never told him.

It's just me and him in this room. Alone. Together. And I know, even as I shake dredging up the words, that Lukas won't be mad at me for saying them. I'm the one who can't control his temper. I'm the one who keeps losing it and pushing people away.

"Do you remember Brandon Kyle's back-to-school party? The summer before sophomore year?" I take a deep breath. The shudder runs from my throat to my toes. "We got split up. I was alone in his basement, lost and wasted, and Brandon cornered me. Tried to make me come to his room. He was probably trying to . . . attack me." I can't even say the real word. It feels too heavy. "I know he got farther with other girls. With girls, I mean. It would have been bad. But you came over and got me out of there."

"I remember," he whispers, looking shaken. "I came over, said you were with me, and took you upstairs. You were . . . shaking. But you said you were okay."

Because I wanted to be okay. Because I wanted to be tough, be like the man I didn't know I was trying to be. I wanted to be anything but a target. "Philip was there the whole time. Standing two feet away from me. I kept trying to catch his eye, mouthing, 'Please, get me out of here,' but he just laughed and clapped Brandon Kyle on the back before walking away. And just because I trusted people didn't mean they'd be there for me when I needed them most." *Of course I can't trust people. Who wants to be there for the paranoid boy waving around a knife?*

For all I've fantasized about murdering my enemies, it is only fantasy. I tried to prick my thumb on the knife's tip and failed. I don't know if I could use it to hurt someone. That doesn't matter. The knife is the line in the sand drawn around me. I choose who touches me. I choose what happens to my body. I know it's extreme, but *extreme* is the only word I've got to describe the fear and anger rattling about inside me walking the same halls as Philip Cross with a target on my back. Extreme problems call for everything I can think of to solve them.

I bite my tongue. Taste blood. The salt of tears. "Maybe I'm just a violent fuckhead, too. No better than Philip." I wait for Lukas to agree with me.

But all Lukas says is "No way," and I know he's a better person than I'll ever be. "Philip's trash. You're just messy."

I bite my lip. My face prickles hot, and I don't know if I'm about to cry or smile. I want to throw my arms around him, even though it's the least manly thing imaginable. Even though he's made it clear he's off-limits. He's Naomi's now. "Is that an insult, or a compliment?" I mumble.

"A little bit of both." He smiles. The tightness eases in my chest. "I'll let you work it out yourself." Then he turns serious. "Look, Philip is a loose cannon. He's got to be contained. If Meehan won't act, we'll handle it ourselves—before someone gets hurt. But we'll handle it peacefully."

"Sounds good. I'll tell him he hurt my feelings and ask him to stop. He'll say no and punch me in the face." I roll my eyes. "Is that your plan to become Homecoming King? Think I'll be less devilishly sexy when I'm in a neck brace?"

"Hardly. Showing up with a neck brace will win you votes. Girls love that wounded-bad-boy crap. I'm not even a girl, and I see the appeal." It trips off his tongue in typical Lukas fashion, so I don't know if he understands what he's implying, and before I can overthink it, he says, "Let's take Philip down together. Tomorrow, when we play Silver Spring. Tell Meehan you received an anonymous complaint about the AP Biology cheaters."

"Okay," I say, slowly piecing his plan together. The Code of Conduct punishes cheating with an iron fist. "Genius. But how can we pin it on him?"

Lukas pulls a folder from his backpack and passes it to me. My eyes widen at the test key inside. "You're cheating in AP Bio?" I don't blame him. Dr. Coryn brags her class is so hard 10 percent of students drop out the first quarter. When your teachers take pride in tormenting students, you do what it takes to pass. Freshman year, a senior cheerleader gave me her three-year-old *Romeo and Juliet* essay, and I turned it in for an A. But stealing from teachers is dangerous, especially when colleges are making their final decisions. If Lukas gets caught, his whole future could suffer.

"Why do you care?" Lukas says, lugging the water barrels one-handed onto the cart. His tone is even, but something hurt and angry flashes in his eyes before he looks away. "You dumped me. You threw a milkshake in my face, remember?"

"I'm looking out for you," I say. A half-truth. The real truth coils up below, a whale trapped in polar ice, big and pushing to break free. "I owe you that much, if you're going to help me get rid of Philip."

"I'm helping me," he says. "Philip makes the whole football team look bad. Guys like him and Brandon are the worst things to come out of this school. I don't want college admissions departments to see Cresswell Academy and think about them. Plus, who wouldn't want to vote a hero for Homecoming King?"

His last words are soft. Teasing. Like this is no big deal. But I know Lukas. He doesn't need any bullshit reason to help.

He'll help anyone of any gender who really needs him. It's who he is. A decent person who wants to be good to others.

"Thanks," I say quietly. Holding in my urge to lash out until I can find a deserving target. "Let's take him down."

I've got the whole GSA hanging out in my living room, plus Ben to represent the student government, which is more people than I've had over since before I came out. It's progress, even if I'm not sure I like any of them. Even if I know they're hanging out with me because of what I am, not who I am. I want to be liked and noticed for me, not because of that weird situation with my genitals.

But I'll take what allies I can get. It's not like I had that many friends before I transitioned. I had worshippers, followers, girls who would eat at my feet for a chance to score tips on boutique sales, smoky-eye techniques, single boys. Maybe we could have been closer, if I'd been the person they thought I was. But I've only ever had genuine friendships—where it was safe to share my aches and vulnerability—with Lukas and Naomi.

Now I have Sol. Who doesn't exactly have reason to care about my feelings. "You can't be upset about Lukas dating someone else," they say, draped across my couch. Mom's covered the living room furniture in hand-knitted wool blankets, chunky colorful statement pieces no one actually uses, and they've pulled three over themself. "You dumped him."

"I just said I have no right to be upset," I say. "I just am. Can you listen to me?"

"I will, when you say something new." They roll their eyes. "You've been rambling about Lukas for the last half hour. Like he just ran into Naomi's arms to mess with you. Lukas doesn't take his relationships lightly, okay? The week after you broke up with him, he didn't leave his house once. He sat by the window playing video games and blasting emo music down the block. He hasn't stopped talking about you, either. I could probably write a play-by-play of your ten best dates."

Lukas missed me? My stomach twists. I knead my fingers in my fist, working out small knots. *Even after I came out, he still talked about me?* Or was he just talking about the girl he thought he'd known?

"I still don't understand why you did it, though," Sol says, leaning closer obnoxiously. "Does he have a deep dark secret? Like does he snore really loud, or chew with his mouth open? Does he have a secret baby? That happened to my cousin Lena."

"I had my reasons. Grown-up reasons. I'll tell you when you're a senior." Like I'd ever bare that much of me to anyone. How weak I am. But before I can stop myself, I ask, "Why does Lukas think I did it?"

Ben narrows his eyes. He's sprawled in my favorite beanbag

chair, all leg and muscle spilling free. "Jeremy, didn't you say you weren't interested in Lukas anymore?"

"I'm not interested in *him*," I say. "I'm interested in what he's doing." But Ben's eyebrow stays arched, and I know he's not convinced.

It was all fake. That's what I've been telling people. But what Lukas and I shared wasn't fake. In a world of high-school phonies clambering up the social ladder, he was the only person I could be myself with. Even when I didn't know who I wanted to be. That had meant something.

And I miss it.

"You could ask if he's into boys," Anna says. "There's no shame in asking. If you tell him how you feel—"

"It doesn't matter how I feel about Lukas," I say, and the words grind like glass in my aching throat. I am distinctly aware of Ben on the other side of the room. "He's with Naomi now."

"You could all date each other," Hannah suggests.

"I'm dating Kaytie and Quince," Anna adds. "We all go out to the movies together and then cuddle in Kaytie's basement."

That's the solution for healthy people. I'm not one of them. I'm brimming with enough anger to poison a cheetah. *All the other queers are so . . . sweet. Like that'll save them.* The world wants to devour us whole. I intend to taste bitter going down its throat.

"That sounds nice." Ben rests his chin on his fist thoughtfully.

The beanbag shifts, swallowing him deeper. "How does that work? Are you, like . . . you know, doing it? If you don't mind—"

"What? No!" Anna says. "I think I might be asexual, anyhow, and none of us want to anyway right now."

"That's an option?" Ben says, sounding eager.

I can't deal with these happy, well-adjusted people.

I retreat to the kitchen and grab chips and soda. I half expect the cans of Sprite to boil and explode in my hands.

"Are these all your new friends?" Mom says, voice tense, not looking up from her laptop. Whatever case she's working on this weekend has wound her tighter than a spring. At least, I hope it's a case. I hope she's not twisting herself up to hold in what she might otherwise say to me. "I've never met them before. Do you not still like your old friends?"

"We're fine," I say cautiously, digging through the cupboard balanced on one sock-clad foot. Saying the wrong thing might tip the fragile balance between us. "They're not all new. Ben is Naomi's brother."

"I know. I saw Ms. Guo at heat yoga, and she said you two argued."

I flinch. Mom should know I'm always arguing with friends. Aside from my annual Naomi drama, I spent half of middle school speaking only to Lukas. Debbie and I had nearly split the cheer team apart sophomore year.

But I don't want to tell my mom about this fight. I don't want to listen to her yell at me for being trans when she should be yelling at me for being an asshole. *Grandma would be so upset to see her little girl starting arguments. But she'd probably let a little boy get away with murder.* "We're going to be fine."

"You don't sound fine. You sound upset." She rubs her nose and reaches across the table to light a scented candle. "Remember what I've told you about toxic masculinity and repressing your feelings?"

It's like I can never tell where I stand with her. I hate having to predict how she'll react and fearing consequences if I'm wrong. Coming out to her should have been easy. Grandma had loved her traditional gender norms, but she was two years dead, and Mom was the liberal feminist who donated to Planned Parenthood rallies and cheered when the Supreme Court legalized gay marriage. She wouldn't mind me saying I wanted to transition, right?

But she'd gone white as paper through my mumbled explanation. Knuckles tight on her car keys. "Well, you'll always be my daughter," she said curtly afterward. Like she thought that would reassure me, like that was what I wanted to hear, instead of a right-hook jab to the heart.

After my breakdown at the diner, when I dumped Lukas, I came home and told her I needed to start hormones. She ground her foot on the floor, declared, "You will *not* become something toxic." Like the medicine to make me whole would poison my soul.

And I choked out, "I can't see myself having a future without them."

That scared her. I'd never been depressed before. She'd gone ahead and made me an appointment with a gender identity counselor. But between my dad, who'd dumped her when she got pregnant, and my stepdad, who'd hit me when I was six, Mom didn't have experience with healthy men.

I can still see that moment when I close my eyes. That piece of shit wasn't even tall, wasn't even scary-looking—but by god could he yell. "*Em-ly!*" He'd always leave the *i* out of Mom's name when he shouted, like it wasn't worth the effort. And Mom would shrink, like his words had already cut away a tiny fragment of herself, even before he made one of his ridiculous demands. *Go to the Safeway and get a pre-cooked chicken. It's better than yours. Not Giant, I don't care that it's closer, I hate them, just go.* A baby in a grown man's body with the pent-up anger of a bomb. Mom has good reasons to be uncomfortable around men. Even scared. But I didn't choose to be a guy to spite her.

And I don't know how to tell her I'm not like them without apologizing for being me.

"Naomi and I will work things out," I say, pulling out a bag of Cool Ranch Doritos and holding it to my chest like a shield. We always have, even though this fight feels bigger. Even though I'm pretty sure the last skill Jeremy Harkiss has is conflict resolution. "In the meantime, my new friends and I will do a useful student government project. We're amending the school Code of Conduct to prevent bullying. Tonight, we're making posters to promote our public hearing. I need a lot of manpower to pull it off."

"People power. You need people power. Women can contribute to initiatives, too—and on one like this, women need to contribute."

"I'm not going to forget women exist, Mom." Not when half the world wants to call me one. "And men and women aren't the only people, anyway."

She pauses. "Right." There's a strange stiffness in her voice. Like we're drawing apart from each other. I hate this.

Being a woman—facing sexism in her family, workplace, and relationships—has powerfully shaped my mom's life. She understands the dynamics between cis men and women so well. But I don't think she knows where to fit me in that pattern. I'm scared part of her thinks I've "swapped sides." Betrayed her and everything women have fought generations to gain. Maybe that's me being paranoid, and maybe she doesn't think that deeply at all. But I know she always used to talk about us as two girls, united, against the world, and the more I move away from her idea of us, the more our closeness fades.

I just want her to see we've got more in common than what divides us. I just want to hear her say we're still on the same side.

"That's a sharp design," Connor says as the posters roll off my mom's laser printer, black letters blocked in a smooth Art

Deco font. *Stop Harassment at Cresswell*, they read, and *Help Student Government Prevent Bullying*.

"I tried," I say, immodesty slipping through. "I have an eye for typography." It comes off my lips sounding super gay—or is that just a stereotype? I sort of like thinking I might sound gay. It feels right. I keep an eye on Connor, checking to see if he's caught my signal, if he can tell I'm totally open to flirt. But he just whips out his phone and starts texting, his long thumbs a blur on the screen.

I crawl into Sol's knot of blankets and watch over their shoulder as they set up the inbox. My back starts aching, so I go swap my binder for a sports bra. I wouldn't normally do that where Mom could see me—in case she takes it as a sign I want to go back to being a girl—but these new friends of mine have consecrated a safe space where the old me's ghost isn't welcome. They've only ever known me as Jeremy, as my too-cool, too-wonderful self, and knowing that makes the air fresher to breathe.

"Once we give out the free pizza tomorrow," I muse, "the whole school will know about our plan. They'll feel safe sending us their anonymous stories about the bullying they've faced. From there, we can set up a student government open hearing, discuss the issue, and collect suggestions for change. Then we can submit our formal recommendations to the administration." If we follow the process, if the students take the lead, the alumni won't be able to object. The changes to the Code will be completely student-led.

"You'll get a lot of messages," Sol warns. Their tone grows serious, for once. "Some will be about you. People really hate you. Well, at least one person. You need to be ready to deal with the transphobia, or have someone else read them."

"I can monitor the inbox," Ben says. "Though if people find out I'm the one doing it, they'll probably send me tons of racist and anti-Semitic crap."

"Nope," I say. I won't let Ben expose himself to that, not when I have a plan. "I'll take the hate and use it all. Let it fuel me." Philip will have gotten his comeuppance by then. And once I've amended the Code of Conduct, the other transphobes will shut up. I'll be able to get back to being king of the school. No asterisk, no adjective needed.

We arrive at school early Friday morning and paste up the posters. I skip second period to order pizza, driving my voice low as the other line clicks on pickup. "I need fifty cheese pizzas delivered to Cresswell Academy. We're having a school event—"

"Name?"

"Jeremy Harkiss." It still feels strange on my tongue. Warm and delicious to speak.

"Oh, god. It's that guy." The line clicks and goes dead.

What the hell? I call back. No one picks up. I try the Dominos across town, but they also hang up at the sound of my name.

The third pizza place says my dad is pissed at me for pulling pranks, which feels like a prank itself, since my dad hasn't ever spoken with me.

"No one would let you order pizza?" Ben asks when I convene him and the GSA at lunch. "That's weird."

"Probably transphobia," I grouse.

"Dominos knows you're trans?"

It does sound ridiculous, but I roll with it. "I'm important and famous. What else can I expect?"

Students don't flock to me for free pizza, but I greet everyone who passes my poster with a handshake and smile. "Hi, I'm Jeremy, the student government president, and I'd like to talk to you about the Code of Conduct and bullying." Once I finish my short speech, if they're still paying attention, I toss out, "Hey, I'm also running for Homecoming King."

"You're really desperate for votes," Hannah says.

I shrug. "I'd say I'm excited for them."

Ben laughs, a deep, rich sound I fear my throat will never match. "You're really going to make me choose between you and Lukas, huh? Not fair."

"Seriously," Sol says. "I hang out with Lukas, too."

"I'm not a fair person," I say. Shouldn't they know this about me by now? Shouldn't they have realized why Lukas and Naomi no longer hang out with me? "Votes are anonymous. Tell Lukas you chose him, tell me you chose me, then go vote for me."

Both laugh, but quietly, because I'm asking them to choose

between friends. But I've already chosen between my own soul and the love of my life. My friends can pick a candidate on a ballot. I can't let that bother me when I'm already facing down so much.

If it bothers Lukas, he can save us all some heartbreak and hand over the crown.

After school, I change into my cheer uniform and hop on the bus to the away game. Naomi and the other junior and senior girls still aren't speaking to me, so I sit with Anna and her freshmen, packed three to a seat at the bus's rattly front, and frankly explain how to safely put on a condom. It's clean, being with people who never knew me as a girl, who treat anyone like a god so long as they have the magic word *senior* attached to them. But I miss Naomi, and even Debbie. I miss knowing so clearly where I belong.

Sometimes, I feel like I'm watching my life from the outside. Like I'm haunting myself. I used to feel that way all the time—every breath of me laser-locked on fine-tuning my perfect popular girl guise. It's gotten better. But when we get off the bus at Silver Spring High and Lukas sweeps Naomi into his arms, I'm once more a stranger in my own skin. They look perfect together. I should let them be perfect together. I broke his heart. I ruined her banner. They deserve some happiness after dealing with me, and I can best give it to them by stepping back.

"They're so cute," says a freshman toting a carton of pom-poms. "I love it."

"They won't last past graduation," I snap, hoisting a box of pom-poms on my shoulder and stomping out onto Silver Spring's field. Anger will keep me together. And they can't hear my unfairness, far away and locked up in each other as they are. "He'll cheat on her with the first cute blonde he sees."

"Not Lukas!" said another girl. "He's so nice! Unless . . . Did he ever cheat on you? Is that why you broke up?"

No. He brought me milkshakes when I got my period. He gave me his jacket when I got cold. He was perfect.

"He's a wolf in tight football shorts," I say, nodding gravely.

My phone buzzes in my waistband. I flinch, seeing Lukas's name pop up. Like he knew I was thinking about him, lying to young, impressionable freshmen about him. Thankfully, his text is devoid of feeling.

Lukas Rivers: Don't use the pages. They have Ben's name on them—I printed them from his account. We'll figure out another way.

Shit. He used a school printer.

If the papers are found with Ben's name, Ben will also be charged with breaking the Code of Conduct. *Why the hell did it have to be Ben?* He's done nothing wrong but trust Lukas with his computer login. He's here with me. Helping me.

I know I won't feel safe at Cresswell until Philip knows not to mess with me.

But I don't know if I can throw Ben under the bus to get there.

We parade onto the rolled rubber of Silver Spring's track, warming up with stretches and skips as the humid choke of summer's end leaves our uniforms plastered to our skin. The tight press of my three sports bras leaves me more bruised and breathless than the Cresswell defensive line, which is slammed senseless on Silver Spring's first play. I try not to think about how these guys are big enough to flatten Lukas as we slide into our first set.

With practiced strength, Naomi and her ring of supporters fling me skyward. At the top of my arc, my breath catches. *She could drop me*—but her hands wrap under my shoulders, and she sets me down with less thought than a pom-pom. It's almost worse this way, mattering so little to someone who used to mean the world to me. Will I matter this little to Ben if I betray him tonight? When will I drive away even the GSA's promise of support?

Lukas weaves through the defenders, graceful and quick as ever, Ben's passes dropping into his arms. Naomi closes her eyes when he's tackled, wincing delicately in shared pain. Maybe that's what girlfriends are supposed to do. I can't look away, even when he's wiping grass off his nose. I can't help being drawn by the smack of bodies when another boy pins him to the ground.

You're such a stupid, dirty homosexual, I think with a manic giggle. I almost can't help it. I've always wanted sex, and this testosterone makes it so much worse. I remember him touching me, holding me, the two of us fumbling through things we'd heard about in movies. Sex had only been part of what we'd had, a new and strange part, but it had been important, and I'd liked it. He'd slept over at my house almost twice a week by the end of junior year. Mom scheduled me an IUD, bought him condoms, and let it go.

I miss it. I miss him touching me. I miss how much he cared.

But I can't go back. Not after everything. Not with Naomi on his arm.

I lead my squad through cheers and tosses, smiling as my throat aches and my voice cracks in the megaphone. I hate sounding like a prepubescent boy, and it burns me even more when Philip glances over from where the team is huddled and shoots me a nasty grin and my stomach churns.

When the game begins again, Lukas slides through a defender's grip and scores our first touchdown of the evening. I lead the crowd in chanting for the Cresswell Phoenixes, and under his helmet, I think I catch the flicker of a grin.

He thinks we're working together tonight. His smile warms me from the inside out, but I can't let myself drink it in. I'm too busy worrying about the answer key in my bag, how Lukas asked me not to strike back at Philip if it also means catching Ben in the crossfire. He wants me to wait to find another way.

"Watch it!" Philip shouts. The other cheerleaders duck for cover, but I've been so distracted I don't notice until he barrels into me. His helmet slams into my chest, catching just above my sternum. His elbow jabs into my cheek and eye. I hit the grass hard. Pain radiates up my side as I land on my funny bone and Philip crashes down atop me. For a moment, all the air is squeezed from my lungs.

"Sorry, bro," Philip says, standing. "That ball got away from me." He smirks down at me from above. "Thank god I didn't knock down one of the girls."

"Go get some ice," my coach tells me as Philip jogs back to the field. "Accidents happen."

That wasn't an accident.

I limp off the field toward the golf cart where the trainers keep ice and bandages—then sneak off under the bleachers to where the away teams stashed their bags. In the shadows where the stadium light fractures sideways, Philip's ugly green Go Army backpack sits atop the pile. A prop in a performance. A boy I know I can beat at his own game. And I can't wait for Lukas and me to find another way. I can't trust anyone to put my safety first but me. *Sorry, Ben*, I think as I open the zipper and shove in the stolen papers. *I need to be safe. For me. If Meehan won't protect me, I'll find a way to do it myself.*

Head bowed, I sneak back to the track.

Cresswell loses 27–7, which is . . . expected. Naomi runs onto the field to comfort Lukas. I can't watch. My stomach flips and roils as she cuddles him. I peer through the crowd, looking for Meehan. I need the last piece in my puzzle.

"Hey, dude," Ben says, with his bags already thrown over his shoulder. He offers me the secret football handshake—the one he taught me in the courtyard before Philip ruined my moment of triumph. I perform it perfectly, matching his smile. No one can see my duplicity. They never have. *I'm just as alone as I've always been.* And maybe that's my fault. Just because I've ruined relationships in the past doesn't mean I have to keep messing up forever. I keep letting my ego take over. Make it too much about me and not the people I love.

But how can I let go of my ego? It feels like something that's as essential to me as being a boy. *Hello, I'm Jeremy, my pronouns are he/him, and I'm a massive blowhard.* And how can I work around my anger when anger's the only tool I have to keep me safe?

"Hey." Lukas extends an awkward arm, like he's not sure if we're hugging or shaking hands. I remember smelling him in the locker room and a stupid wave of *yes* nearly wipes my senses clean.

Stupid. So stupid. I can't let him touch me. When he lets go, it'll kill me. And he will let go, because he has Naomi now. He'll always let go.

I sidestep his hand and wave. "Hi, Lukas. You tried hard."

"Is that all you can say?" He smiles. "I scored our only touchdown!"

"Try harder?" I suggest. He rolls his eyes, but he's still smiling. I glance at Naomi, who hovers behind him.

Philip strolls across the field, his backpack loose over his shoulder, and slides into our conversation like a lumbering bear. "Shut up, Harkiss. If you were really a man, you'd be out on that field."

"They banned me from contact sports because I'm too distractingly good-looking." I make eye contact with Principal Meehan, who's chatting with our coach on the sideline. Her eyes flash to my left, and I know she can see Philip looming over my shoulder. All I have to do is give her a pleading look and she's headed in our direction. Part of me wishes Philip would take a swing at me right now, while everyone's watching. Taking a punch would hurt, but it would violate the Code of Conduct and finally get Philip kicked out of school. "Not that I mind. More time to work on my Harvard application."

"Like you even need to try. They'll let anyone in to meet their bullshit 'diversity' goals."

"Actually, they'll let me in because I'm a legacy. Where did your dad go again, UMD?" It's such a douchey, privileged thing to say, and I wouldn't use it against anyone but him. "You couldn't get into an Ivy League if you wanted. Aren't you failing AP Bio?"

His fists tighten.

"It's not my fault Dr. Coryn's out to get all the football players, that stupid b—"

"Excuse me," says Principal Meehan, coming up at his back. "What were you saying about Dr. Coryn?"

Philip freezes. "I—I mean, she's an awful teacher. That's all. If I told my father what she said to us yesterday, he'd pull his donations." He eyes me. I swallow, my spine going cold. The football team watches. I can't back down. "Maybe I should have him pull his donations anyway. This school accommodates freak shows like *it*." The last word is a bullet fired in my direction.

"Excuse me, Philip—" Meehan starts, but I cut her off.

"I'm not an it. I'm a he/him. I did meet someone who used *it* as its pronoun this summer. Goth kid from South Potomac." I pull on a smile. "Though maybe I should apologize to Philip," I say. "I didn't mean to threaten his delicate masculinity and stump him with my existence." I slap him on the back. "Sorry, bro."

With my other hand, I knock the bag off his shoulder. The bottom explodes, splitting and spilling his books and papers across the pavement.

I fight the urge to grip the knife tucked in the side pocket of my backpack. Instead, I kneel and grab the fallen answer key. "Whoa. Principal Meehan?"

She pales as I hand her the papers. "These are the teacher keys. Where'd you get these, Philip?"

Philip turns blotchy red. "I—I've never seen these before!"

"That's pretty convincing," I mutter, biting back a smirk.

"You stole the keys." Meehan reads the watermark atop the page. "And, Ben—you printed them out? Is the whole team using these to cheat?"

"What?" The smile dies on Ben's face. "I didn't . . . I wouldn't ever—"

"Principal Meehan!" Lukas says. "You—you can't . . ."

Oh, shit. For a second I think he's going to tell the truth, rat me out. But then his mouth shuts. His cheeks flush. He turns away.

I'm braver than Lukas. I say nothing, but it's because I don't want to.

This is how victory feels.

Sweet with a toxic edge.

CHAPTER ELEVEN: LUKAS

Two Weeks to Homecoming Kickoff

I say nothing during the bus ride back to Cresswell. Fuming. Hating Jeremy for going through with it when I told him not to, because that's easier than hating myself for not telling Meehan the truth. Because *cheater* looks bad on a college application. Because that'd ruin the whole point of everything I'm fighting for.

I should have just stuck to fighting with Jeremy over Homecoming King. Instead, I tried to do the right thing, to stand up for Jeremy because he's part of the Cresswell community, even if we're nothing to each other anymore. I should have just let Philip drag him down. I can carry a pretty impressive load on my shoulders, but I can't carry Jeremy. He's made it clear he's not my problem.

Ben doesn't return with us—his parents have dragged him home by car, probably shouting at him the whole way for cheating. He hasn't responded to my texted *Hey, man, you okay?* I don't dare text more. I don't want to look guilty.

Coach lectures us on our failures, standing in the aisle so he can look us all in the eye—how our defense wasn't pushing hard enough, how I wasn't anticipating Ben's passes, how none of us were paying enough attention to our surroundings. I don't listen. All of me is caught up in Jeremy's smug smile, the flicker of victory in those green eyes from hell as he tore the team apart.

"We're screwed no matter what the defense does," Max mutters beside me. The linebacker is twiddling his thumbs. "Principal Meehan will probably suspend Ben and Philip from sports. We can't win Homecoming without Ben."

Can't win the Homecoming game. Maybe it's true. Ben and I hold up the team. *But I can win.* I'll carry the football team on my shoulders if I have to.

What matters is that I'm still in the game. I can clean up the damage later.

Back at Cresswell, we disperse. Jeremy's parked his Prius on the edge of the senior lot. I stalk past the cheerleaders and wait for him by his car.

The story he told me about Brandon's party cut me open. Earlier, I was so pissed at myself for never noticing what really happened that night. *He told me that story out of trust. Like I still mattered to him, after everything.*

Naomi texts me she's getting cleaned up in the locker

room. I wait. It takes ten minutes for Jeremy to make it to his car, but it's all worth it when I slide out of the darkness and position myself between him and the door. "How could you?" I ask. Evening wind cuts across my shoulders, tinged with the early earthy scent of fall. Making me wonder what's worth waiting out here for.

"Me?" He yawns. "I wasn't the dumbass who printed the papers on a friend's account."

"I texted you. I *trusted* you."

"Yeah. But none of that was my problem, Rivers." He grins like it's all he knows how to do, green eyes glinting in the low light, carelessly tossing his car keys to himself. But behind his smile is something sour, a guard he refuses to let down. I glare at him—and study him, too, the subtle tightening in his jawline, the sharp angle of his blond buzz cut, the flattened plane of his chest. We lost our virginities together. But I feel like I'm discovering something new when I look at him now. Something that makes my palms sweat and my throat tighten. "You put a tool in my hands, and I used it. What else do you expect from me?" he asks with a smile. I still smell strawberry milkshake in my nightmares.

"You think I would have quit helping you just because one plan didn't work? I may not like you, but I gave you my word that I'd help you deal with Philip." Whatever I've done to make him hate me, he couldn't think I'd break my promise. He couldn't think that little of me.

But then, what do I know? I've missed out on so much.

But after hearing about Brandon, I know I misunderstood so much of his life. Of our relationship. I could have done or said something hurtful without realizing how deep it would strike.

No. I've struggled so long to figure out how people interact, how friendships grow, how to give others what they needed. I'm not an awkward kid anymore.

But I can't control how he sees me. I can't keep anyone from getting hurt. Not Ben. Not Jeremy. And the realization is like ice water poured on my head in a blizzard.

I'm aiming for king. I've never felt so powerless.

Jeremy smiles as my fingers tremble. It sinks into me like a pricking needle. "Did you think I would play nice just because you did me one favor? Take this as a lesson. We're on opposite sides of a war, babe, and no way in hell will you get your crown if you don't realize I'm man enough to pose a threat."

I shove a frustrated hand back through my hair. His own's been cut again, buzzed near flat. I wonder if it feels how I remember. I can't convince myself touching him won't feel like digging my fingers into a live socket.

Would I mind if he electrified me?

"Your definition of masculinity is completely self-destructive. How can you win Homecoming King if you ostracize everyone at school?"

"If you think my plan to win a popularity contest is bad, you should take a closer look at your own plan to pass senior year." His shoulders stiffen. I can tell he aches from binding, can see the flaws in his smile at the corners of his lips. I know he'll break his own bones before yielding a flicker of weakness, and I wonder what I'll find if I crack him open. "Why are you really cheating in AP Bio? I know you care about learning. Let me guess—Coryn isn't letting you take notes on your computer? I heard about her technology policy. You can't learn that way, and you're too stubborn to ask for a disability accommodation plan. Because real men don't admit their weaknesses."

Ouch. It stings, like a poke in a blister, and my good nature wears thin. He knows me too well, and I'm the one who underestimated him. I thought I was doing the right thing, helping him with Philip, but I've got no room in my life to do right for rightness' sake. I'm all eaten up with the promises I've made to others and the weights I've willingly lifted over my own head.

I want us to be popular in high school, Jeremy told me so many years ago, when the world came in simple binaries. Like it was a project we could work on together. And some of it was—figuring out what to wear and who to eat lunch with. Some of it was just a matter of being useful to people. Figuring out where I could stash the pieces of myself to lever me highest up the ladder. Then leaving those fragments behind.

But Jeremy isn't like me. He doesn't root his choices in what other people want and need. Jeremy isn't running because he's mad at me, because he hates me. It's not about anything I've done at all. He wants to show Cresswell he's man enough to take the throne, and he'll kick down anything that gets in his way. Jeremy wants something, and he goes to get it. I'm not sure I've got the energy left in me to want anything at all.

Except to give him the reaction he's provoking. To show him I can also explode.

Fuck you for what you did to Ben. For what you did to me.

I snatch his keys midtoss and fling them off into a field. Silver glints and vanishes. "Want my help finding them?"

He just won't stop smiling. "Of course not. Fuck off, hot stuff."

Heat pounds in my veins as I turn to leave. *His smile. His stupid smile.* The hard, pink quirk of his lip, fixed and focused up at me. My whole body, seized up and ready to surge.

He's got to know he's affecting me like this.

"Lukas!" Naomi ducks out the back of the locker room, changed into a rose-petal-print dress and gladiator sandals, heavy backpack hanging low on one shoulder. "I'm ready to go!"

Even as I take Naomi's hand, I feel his eyes boring into my back all the way to my car.

Mocking me for every moment I thought we could belong together.

The diner sits in the strip mall around the corner from Cresswell's hedge walls. It's windowed on all four sides, with stained chrome jukeboxes and color-your-own paper place mats on every table. The thick booth cushions, that sink deep and creaking when you slide into them, are sticky from decades of spilled beer and soda. The air always smells of sizzling hamburger patties, save for the breakfast rush, when crisping bacon fills it.

It's home, and the burgers are only four dollars each.

"New girl?" the hostess asks as the two of us enter. "She's not your usual, Lukas."

I smile. "Geraldine! This is Naomi."

"You know me." Naomi waves at the old woman. "I come here all the time when school's in."

"You're not Lukas's usual girl. He used to have a short blond. She was funny. Whatever happened to her?"

The two of us exchange awkward, identical grimaces. His truth isn't mine to disclose to a stranger—but he's out to the world, and I don't want him to come in here and get misgendered at the door. How do I handle this?

"He goes by Jeremy now," Naomi says gently. "He's transgender."

"Your girlfriend got a sex change?" Geraldine calls. Loudly. The whole diner turns to look.

"We don't, uh, call it that anymore?" I say, blood pounding in my cheeks. Fighting the urge to duck away as the prickling eyes threaten to overwhelm me. "And he was always my boyfriend, not my girlfriend. My dumb fucking asshole ex-boyfriend."

It's the first time I've called him *my ex-boyfriend* out loud. I want to push Geraldine to use the right words, because I know Jeremy comes here, too—but what I've said feels like it's just as much about me as it is about him. *Mine. He was mine.* And I still want to defend him, despite it serving no purpose at all. A stupid, pointless waste of breath—but I could describe my whole life in those same words.

A ratty blond head pops up from behind the grill. Terry Gould, in a waiter's apron. *Just my luck he works here, too.* If he says something transphobic about Jeremy, I'll call him out. I don't care how awkward it gets.

But Terry doesn't have anything to say about Jeremy. Or Jason. Instead, he's looking at me, his eyes sharp as steak knives.

I duck his gaze and slide into my usual booth.

I expect Naomi will sit across from me, but instead, she slides in beside me, her shoulder touching mine, her vanilla perfume washing strong over me. Sweet, practically. Too sweet. I got Jeremy perfume for Christmas two years ago, and he laughed but never wore it.

Focus on your date, dipshit. I wrap an arm around her and pull her in close. It's nice to feel her cheek rest on my shoulder, even as her perfume tap-dances for my attention. Her spine goes slack, her muscles sag, and I'm holding her up. I wish I could make everyone in my life happy just by reaching out. Being a good boyfriend isn't the sort of thing they let you in the Ivy Leagues for.

"That was awkward," Naomi says. "Do you think I did the right thing?"

"Jeremy will come in here sooner or later. Might as well give them a heads-up so they don't misgender him. What else could you say?"

"I missed my opportunity. I could have said, 'Oh, I'm sorry to tell you, she got eaten by a pack of roving coyotes.' Or, 'Oh, didn't you hear, she got recruited by DARPA to help weaponize bitchiness.'"

"Got a job offer interning for Satan," I suggest. "Went on a volunteer trip to take school supplies *away* from orphans."

"I heard the Harvard admissions essay prompt this year is 'Describe a time you learned from a mistake.' His will be 'I was mean to all my friends and learned not a damn thing.'"

I laugh. "Have you talked to him about it yet?"

She bites her lip and looks away, which is all the answer I need.

"I could text him for you," I say. "If it's too hard for you to reach out. Here, hand me your phone—"

"Um, how about no?" Naomi slides away from me. Looking at me like I just suggested eating both her shoes. "Why are you so invested in that asshole's feelings?"

"Technically, I'm invested in yours. You two have been friends since sophomore year. You're going to be my Home-coming Queen. I want you to be happy." I'm racing to improvise as my own tongue threatens to trip me. To build a rationale beneath my choices. Because I have no reason to care about Jeremy's personal life. I just do.

"I just feel obligated. If I don't drop everything—again—to

make him feel better, I'm a selfish bitch." She purses her lips. Blows a strand of hair off her lipstick. "You can't even imagine the pressure I'm under. With my parents, it's like, there are entire Ivy League schools that aren't good enough to get into. As an Asian kid, I'm allowed Stanford, Caltech, Harvard, MIT, Yale, or Princeton—and even Princeton's pushing it. I have to be perfect—and, I mean, Ben has to be perfect, too, but I'm the daughter. He texted me that Mom yelled at him the whole car ride for cheating in Coryn's class, but she screams at me for small shit like going up a dress size. All I want—all I need—is for Jeremy to show me a fraction of the concern I showed him this summer. And he can't even give me that. And I feel like shit because of what *he* did, which is messed up and gross, and I hate it."

"I get it," I say, and check myself. "I mean, I don't. Not specifically. I feel *so* responsible for Homecoming. Making it perfect. Winning the football game for the alumni. I feel responsible for getting on the court and getting into a school that'll make my family proud. A thousand people want something from me, and it feels like I'm bleeding out into a world that's giving me nothing back."

And I miss Jeremy, too. He's the one person who knows me well enough to see the ache behind the smiles and my stinky mouthguard.

I fumble my way forward. "You're great as you are, Naomi. You don't need to be perfect, and whether your parents understand that or not, I hope you do."

She gives me a sad smile. "Thanks. I needed to hear that. I ... I'm so glad you agreed to give this whole date thing a chance. I needed to talk to someone, and you're one of the nicest guys I know."

"I'm always happy to be there for you, Naomi."

"How is your family? You don't talk about them much."

"They're fine," I say quickly, to shut a door on the topic. I can't say I'm scared of being the only one holding my family together. Jeremy's right about how I'm thinking. *Real men don't admit their weaknesses.* Real men do whatever it takes to fix their problems.

I'm not sure where the borders lie, with girl stuff and guy stuff and everything in between and outside it. If you'd asked me last year, I'd have said there was no real difference between genders—just millennia of stereotyping and traditions—but then Jeremy transitioned, becoming real and alive in a way he's never been before. The difference matters to him. Not because he gets to do guy things—I can't see him dropping cheer for lacrosse or exchanging his Prius for a pickup truck—but because he gets to be himself. *It doesn't matter what gender you are. Until it matters more than anything.*

Until no script the world has given me holds answers.

"How are your college applications going?" I ask Naomi.

"They're going." She sighs. "I've made a color-coded schedule of all the deadlines, put in recommendation requests with every teacher I've had since eighth grade, and drafted two different essays for all the common prompts. But I keep thinking it's not enough."

"Your grades are awesome." She's even acing Dr. Coryn's AP Bio. "I'm sure you'll get in somewhere great."

"I hope so." She winces, eyes wide and anxious. "I want to believe my application is strong enough. But if they put mine next to Jeremy's, all they'll see is a girl who always comes in second place." She bites her lip and changes the subject. "Have you seen the new cheerleading freshmen?"

A girl brings us water and menus. Naomi tells me about the pyramid she and the team are working on for the Homecoming game, with her as one of the bottom supports. One freshman nearly dropped another, and they're all arguing about who to blame. After a minute or two, I decide she feels awkward and is filling space with sound. I do that myself.

Make it interesting. Flip the script. "Not that all this freshman drama isn't fascinating, Naomi, but let's talk details of our homecoming coronation."

She frowns and shifts in her seat. "Sorry. Was that boring?"

Ah. Shit. Have I said something wrong? "What kind of dress are you wearing? I need to match my tie and get you a corsage. Probably something large and flashy, since the girls' crown is so small. It's just a hair clip." I'm blathering now, tossing out whatever pops into my head because I don't know what to say. Dating Jeremy felt so natural and easy. This feels like I'm auditioning for a part at eighth-grade theater camp and I've forgotten all my lines. I stop and take a deep breath. "I'm nervous."

She smiles, a small, nervous gesture that somehow reassures me. "It's navy blue with blue diamonds on the skirt. Anything blue will match. And I get it. You were in a relationship for a long time. But we know each other. We don't have to be, like, a couple on their first date. We can be Lukas and Naomi. On their first date."

What even is that? I feel like I'm drowning. Like I'm a fish who flopped out of water but forgot I had only gills. I don't know what script to follow, and all I can think about is my ex. When what I should be thinking about is the best way to make Naomi happy.

Thankfully, the waiter shows up to take our order. Less thankfully, it's Terry.

It comes back again as he smiles at me, leaning across our chrome-edged plastic table, loose hair spilling from his ponytail. I remember feeling the roots of this in second grade. Memory, thin as a pencil line, flashes through my head. I enter our home office. Terry and Jason are watching some video on the computer, laughing hysterically. Jason turns down the speakers when he sees me.

"Tran and I are playing house," I tell them. "We need people to be the parents. Want to join?"

"You little queer." Jason launches a rubber band at my shoulder. I yelp and rub the spot hard, trying to erase the pain. It stings, a shockwave coursing through my body. I'm used to this from Jason, but I still look to Terry. He'll some-times play with me when my brother isn't watching.

"You can be the dad," I tell him. "I'll be the mom."

He just throws a handful of paper clips. They scatter at my feet. "Fuck off, pussy. We're doing grown-up shit."

I'd been stupid, being drawn to him back then. It had taken me longer than most boys to learn what things I couldn't say.

But Jason isn't here to turn the air toxic. Make me feel I've been pushed into a box so tight I'll never claw out of it. I have nothing to fear from a waiter with long hair and an ear full of hoops. I'm even taller than him now. This scrawny asshole looks like hell has pummeled him and spit him out. My eyes rest on the jagged set of his nose—a souvenir from a hard blow. *I'm trouble*, it says. Not trouble like Jeremy. Adult trouble.

I can't help comparing the two of them. Blonds with a knack for trouble—am I doomed to be forever stalked by the universe's worst personality type?

"Are you here to bother me?" I ask him.

"I'm here to take your order. I could bother you when my shift ends." He eyes me. My spine prickles and my nerves tense as I meet his stare. His eyes are blue, tinted purple by the pink neon lights running above him. Not like Jeremy's mis-chievous green. "I could ruin your day. Ruin your whole life."

"I'm a pretty busy guy," I say, wary, testing. Something unfamiliar stirs on my tongue, electrifying and different like the first time I tried vodka. Slow, sly warmth sneaks into my words. "If you want to ruin my life, I could fit you in next week after the bonfire."

He leans over the table. The neck of his loose T-shirt falls forward, revealing tufts of blond hair around his nipples. One's pierced. I can't stop staring. "Wouldn't your girlfriend mind?" He looks at Naomi.

"She's not my girlfriend," I say reflexively. Naomi winces. "We're just . . . trying?"

"Must be hard," he says, scooping up our menus.

"Not really."

He nods—sympathetically, maybe?—and walks away. Naomi's face turns the color of a bruised plum.

"Sorry about that," I say. "I didn't mean to sound like you're not important to me. I'm sure, like, if you want to use the girlfriend label, we can talk about it. I didn't want to call you my girlfriend without asking."

"Who is that guy to you?" she says.

"He's an old friend." *Jason's friend. Even though I wanted him to be mine.* I don't dare mention Jason and open the family door again. I might let it slip that I'm more angry than sad. That I'm such a mess I can't even mourn correctly.

After a few false starts, I manage to stir the conversation on to teachers we hate. She impersonates her chemistry teacher threatening to staple students to the ceiling, and I dish on my calc teacher showing up to class drunk last week. It's the same Cresswell jokes I can tell in my sleep, worn and easy on my tongue like a favorite sweater. A language I know how to speak, where popularity comes as easily as mastering patterns. *I'm going to lose all this when I go to college.* No matter how fancy the school, leaving here will feel like ripping off a limb. But that doesn't matter if I can throw a Harvard sweatshirt over the stump.

"That was nice," I tell Naomi as we walk to my car. Thick clouds block the night sky, choking the air with the inevitable humid weight of coming rain. "I like spending time with you." And I do. She's relaxing to be around. She doesn't demand that much from me.

"Would have been nicer if you hadn't been flirting with our waiter."

I make myself laugh. "Good one, Naomi."

"I'm not joking." That comes out small and sad. I freeze. *Shit.* I misread her tone. "You were flirting with someone else. In front of me. On our first official date."

"I talk like that to everyone, Naomi."

"Not to me, Lukas. Your whole face lit up when he leaned across the booth. Like fireworks." She sighs. "Maybe this is all my fault. What did I even think would happen, sliding in the middle of your drama with Jeremy? I thought maybe we could work, but now I'm wondering . . . do you even like girls?"

I blink. *Huh?* "Are you asking if I'm gay?" How did she even get that idea? This is me she's talking about, Lukas Rivers, the wide receiver and head of the Homecoming Committee, future Homecoming King, who dated head cheerleaders and—oh. Jeremy.

Should I have questioned my sexuality when he came out? It didn't seem like a big deal. We were over. I heard the news two weeks after the funeral, when I was numb. I read his email to the student body, changed his name in my phone contacts, and went on with my day.

The news had been about him. Not me. I'm still the same person I've always been. Well, I'm an only child now and my family is shattering and my crown is in jeopardy, but some parts of me have to stay static. I'll will myself straight if I have to.

But I know it doesn't work that way.

This isn't fair. None of this is fucking fair. I didn't ask for this. But talking with Terry—flirting with him, whatever— loosened some knot inside me. Some tight, twisting pressure I'd never realized was strangling me until I felt the air rush in. Like the first hit off a joint, an intoxicating gasp that lifts me up and gets me in so much trouble. It doesn't matter who I shared that moment with. It matters that I did it.

Oh, god. I'm almost certainly not straight. And I should have realized that sooner; it should have been obvious. But I've never actually thought about my sexuality. The identity defining me, beyond football, school, and Homecoming, has always been my disability. I've never let myself think I might be something else. Something more.

Something that could mess up everything.

I've never let myself think about who I am and what I want because that means I have to make a choice. Pull something out from inside me when I'm already getting pushed from all sides. When my family needs me to be perfect, Cresswell wants me to be its king, Jeremy wants me just as pissed off, loud, and screaming as he is. So much I need to give, to invest in. To the point there's no space left for my own voice.

Maybe it's better that way. Because I gave Jeremy that answer key just because I wanted to. And I might have ruined my best friend's life.

When I slide in my front door, my parents are still sitting in the dining room. Their plates are heaped high with spaghetti, even though it's past eleven and we've had spaghetti three times this week. The air smells like beer. No one's talking. I feel as nauseated as if I've driven past a dead dog on the highway.

"I saw online you lost the game," Mom says. "Are you okay?"

"Fine," I say carefully, dropping down in a seat. Forcing down a mouthful of undercooked spaghetti so they won't realize I ate without them. "I'm more worried about Homecoming Committee schedules. But the junior class subcommittee finally picked a float blueprint, so we should be back on track." The question *you'll be at the game, right?* knots up inside me. I don't know what I'll do if they say no. I can win if they're not present; I can get into Stanford if they're not watching—but my chest aches at the thought of them missing out on one more moment.

"How's your homework?" Dad looks at me. The wrinkles in

his forehead lace deep, even though he's barely in his forties. "Are you studying? Do you have a test soon?"

"Yes," I say, "and no." This is a lie, but my AP Bio grade is also trapped behind that knot in my throat. Just one more piece of my life threatening to slip out of my grasp. "Have you heard from Nana and Granddad since the restaurant?" What I want to know is if they've moved past the moment where Mom called me Jason, but I don't dare acknowledge the existence of that moment out loud.

"They're fine, but very busy," he says. I'm bad at reading people, but I think this is also a lie. He spoke too fast. Like how he did when I failed speech pathology assessments as a kid and asked him if he was mad after. "Excuse me. I'm going to take a shower."

He marches off. Mom stares at him as he goes. Her head is bowed. Dark circles swim beneath her eyes.

"Don't ask about your grandparents again," she says, and I don't know what to say.

Mom and I clear the dishes. I carry platters to the sink; she dumps the scraps down the disposal. Dad's plate is still mostly full. I notice he was eating off the chipped, hand-painted plate that Jason and I made for Father's Day when he was twelve and I was eight.

Mom takes that plate from my hand, very carefully. She doesn't dump the spaghetti yet. "Lukas," she says, forcing a happy voice, "you've helped enough. Go do your homework."

I know what she means. She wants me gone. But I'm happy to get away. I jog up the stairs as she starts to cry.

Down the hall, my dad's phone beeps urgently on the table outside the bathroom. The tone he's set for my grandmother's messages.

I shouldn't. I really shouldn't. It's such an invasion of privacy, of that bubble of protection my dad has drawn thick about himself. But no one's telling me anything in this house, not anymore. People speak at me, not to me, and the pieces just aren't clicking in my head like they should. And the steam rolling out from under the door says he'll be in there a while longer.

I grab the phone. Unlock it with the year of Jason's birth. Read the whole text chain with my grandparents.

My dad hasn't told us that they've been reaching out all week. Asking when they can next come visit me, inviting my dad to drive down to Virginia and talk, offering to cook all our favorite dishes. Nothing in their words gives away their pain and fear—but I can feel it in the things left unsaid, hanging in the empty spaces. I can see Dad dodging their questions, making up excuses about work and unnamed plans. Sensible reasons adding up to us never spending time together again.

A rush of anger bubbles up inside me. Not sharp and pointed, like my anger at Jeremy. This is a bigger, more suffocating anger. Like a blanket being wadded down my throat. I can't stand the fog of feelings in this house. I can't even let myself miss Jason without wanting to punch his fucking urn. *This is all too big. Too strong. Too bad.*

I have to make it be like it was before Jason crumbled and took our hopes down with him.

You should come to the Cresswell Homecoming Game, I type into the phone. It's not a lie, I tell myself. I'm not impersonating my father. I'm just giving them the grandson they want and need.

And also, maybe, making some small room for me? *If I told them I wasn't straight, they'd probably pretend not to understand me.* Even though last time I went to their house I noticed my nana had three seasons of *Queer Eye* queued up on Netflix. *Okay for television. Not for her grandson.* Especially when she only has one left. We need some common ground that's not swamped or crumbling.

Lukas is going to be crowned Homecoming King, I finish, and hit Send.

None of this is nice of me. None of this is polite, decent, or good. But I need to hold my life together, to find the glue to fill the cracks, to make things as good as—or even better than—they were before. I don't want to lose my family, and Homecoming's the one part of my life it's safe for us to share. I need a victory here more than I've ever needed to win games or scholarships. More than I needed Jeremy to love me.

But just because I need to win doesn't mean I want to.

I don't know if I have the energy to want anything for myself at all.

CHAPTER TWELVE: JEREMY

Saturday afternoon, my mom drops me off at the Metro and I take the red line down to Woodley Park, where the Harvard Society is hosting an open house for potential students. I'm wearing gray dress pants, a crisp white shirt, and a crimson tie I spent a humiliating hour figuring out how to put on. The woman at the entry table still greets me with a "Good morning, ma'am," and I snap, "Sir," my cheeks flaring red a second later, because what sort of asshole runs around demanding people call him sir?

I find my name tag on the table, slip it on, and duck into the cedar-paneled main room. Servers circulate with trays of puff pastry, club members with gold name pins speak in hushed voices, the plush carpet sucking up sound. The dusty bookshelves breathe lineage, and I want to soak some of that up for myself.

"Cresswell Academy?" says a man with a pin, reading my

school off my paper name tag. "One of your classmates is here. Mr. Cross?"

Philip smiles and waves from the punch bowl.

My world flashes red. That *fucker*. What is he doing here? Okay, I knew his rich dad would pay for him to go wherever he wanted—but why does he have to share my stupid preppy Ivy League goal? Can't he at least fixate on Princeton, like all the insufferable douchebags?

Why do we have to be so much alike?

"Hi, Jeremy." Philip says my name like he's allergic to it. But he says it. So, I know it's gotten through to him. "Good to see you. Looks like we'll both be Harvard men together."

Not if I stomp your fucking ass flat first. Vomit roils in the back of my throat. Because there's nothing I can do about him, surrounded by this fancy spinach-puff-and-sparkling-water society. Not if I don't want to jeopardize my admission. And the world I'll be moving into next year is much more of this and much less the halls of Cresswell, where I've scraped together some power.

I have no choice but to be polite to this bastard. But at least I've got the skill of a cheerleader to make it sting.

I don a polite, confused smile and make my move. "You're . . . Paul, right? Peter? I know we go to school together. I tutored you in freshman algebra."

"You took algebra as a freshman?" asks one of the younger alumni, a note of scorn in her voice. Algebra is the lowest-level math class Maryland schools offer in the ninth grade. Among the Ivy-bound DMV elite, there could be no bigger badge of shame than being just normal at math. "What are you planning to major in?"

"Engineering," Philip says. "I like building things. Stuff that lasts."

Phil the builder. I picture him in a hard hat and work jeans—a stupid image, since Philip just wants to be the guy in a suit barking orders at the guys in hard hats, like his dad. "Look upon my works, ye mighty, and despair."

"Exactly," Philip says. "I want to make things. And Harvard will help me do that."

He's almost obsequious. I hope this alumna knows he only acts that way because he wants something from her. Judging by the cool smile on her face as she turns to me, she sees straight through his bullshit. I only hope she doesn't see through mine.

"You know Shelley?" she says.

"Totally! I've read everything he's ever written!"

"What are your top five favorite poems of his?"

Oh, shit. Because, of course, I only know enough of Shelley's poetry to make one reference that makes Philip look dumb for not getting it. "Um. So hard to choose."

"Why do you want to go to Harvard?"

I bite my lip. It's not all that different from the reason I want to be Homecoming King. Because I want to live large and do hard things. Because I want to show the world trans-phobia won't stop me. Because the more being myself upsets people, the more I want to fling myself in their faces.

The GSA would understand, or at least listen to me, if I said that. And it leaves my head strangely shaky to realize I'd rather be back in the club's basement hideout than here. Because here, I don't feel safe expressing my feelings. That I started out wanting the crown because that's what popular boys want, and I want it even more now that the world wants to use my masculinity as a chew toy. To prove to myself and all of them that I am who I say I am. Harvard people don't need to prove themselves. They just arrive.

"Because," I bullshit, "I think an elite institution that champions the liberal arts will best prepare me for leadership in the twenty-first century. And did I mention I'm running for Homecoming King at Cresswell Academy?"

"That's really thoughtful," she says. "And wow! My friend John Bailey went to Cresswell. He was too nerdy to run for the court, though."

The reception blurs into a rhythm of handshakes, introductions, and the same five questions over and over. Artisanal ginger ale sparkling in champagne flutes. Finger sandwiches and mini kebabs dipped in cucumber sauce. I try to keep Philip at arm's length. My stomach crawls whenever he asks if conservatives are still welcome on campus—whenever another rich cis white kid says, *Yeah, it's pretty tough for you there, but you'll fit in fine*, I tell myself it means nothing, that this is DC and people of all political orientations sit at the same table here. But that's not true.

Because if he's welcome at a table, I'm sure as hell not.

I find myself looking for the quiet signals of queerness. A person with green hair and a lip ring. Two girls clustered together in a corner, fingers interwoven but not quite holding on.

I'm going to make myself wanted, I tell myself. *I'm going to make myself royalty.* The thought feels bitter. Almost sick. Another young alumni misgenders me and apologizes. "Sorry. Don't get mad, okay? At Harvard, no one cares if you're trans."

I fake a smile, hating the need to look agreeable and polite. Hating anticipating all the slights and jibes I'll have to swallow to make it in this world when Philip can just walk right in.

This is supposed to be my dream school. But if they don't care I'm trans, they'll never be able to make space for me. Harvard will be one more thing that belongs to the Philips of the world.

If they don't see my transness, my needs, they won't notice if Philip pushes me out into the cold. They might even blame me for getting shut outside.

Monday morning, I enter Cresswell through a shower of confetti.

"Hallie! Hallie—" The boys standing on either side of the hall drop their glittery fists. The guy standing between them lowers his *Hallie, HC?* sign. They've turned this whole alcove into a party, complete with streamers and a giant piñata at the asking boy's feet.

"Jeremy?" he says. "Sorry, I thought you were my girlfriend."

I don't even know who this Hallie is. "You're not quite my type. Too scrawny."

I turn up the stairs toward first period and slam into a boy encased in a Spiderman suit, hanging upside-down over the balcony. He's holding a sign reading *Aisha, be my Mary Jane at HC?*

"Sorry!" he says. "I can barely see in this mask!"

Above him, the balcony creaks under his weight. I roll my eyes and push on down the hall, struggling against the tide of bodies and backpacks toward English class. Something tangles between my ankles. I bang chin-first into a locker.

A boy in a Pinocchio costume, lederhosen and all, is crying on the ground—I've nearly tripped over his extra-long nose. *I'd be lying if I said I didn't want to take you to HC* reads the sign beside him.

"No one finds wooden puppets sexy," I tell him, and prance off to first period.

The week before Homecoming is Asking Week, where boys pull bullshit to impress girls into dancing with them. Like fucking peacocks fanning out their tails. Sometimes it's sweet. Sometimes it's humiliating. Lukas always put together sweet, weeklong scavenger hunts to ask me. I doubt he knows Naomi well enough to do the same for her, and the thought is a thrill of petty joy.

I'm supposed to ask someone. The Homecoming King can't show up without a date.

But dates escape my mind as I arrive to help set up the room for the student government antiharassment forum.

I freeze in the doorway. Ben's already inside, dragging chairs into rows, shoving desks against the wall to make room. He's opened the plastic divider between this classroom and the one next door to give us plenty of space. *Shit.* I had convinced myself I could avoid him until there were other people in the room. That I could avoid what I did to him.

But his eyes snap up and find me. I give a little wave and mutter, "Hey." Guilt already tints my cheeks red.

"Help move furniture," he grunts. I drop my backpack and start pushing desks against the wall. It's quiet aside from the squeak of plastic on linoleum. Too quiet. Normally, I fill every room I'm in with sound, but awkward minutes pass until I think of something innocent to say.

"Pity Debbie isn't working on this with us." I haul another chair into place. My back aches. I bite my lip and try not to show it. "Then again, considering Debbie hates me almost as much as fucking Philip, I should be glad she's not super involved."

"For such a short kid, you've got a pretty long list of enemies. Do you ever think about who your dumbass decisions could hurt? Or do you expect the people around you to put up with your crap forever?" He sighs. "Look, I know I didn't steal an answer key and give it to Philip. I know Lukas is the only person I let use my computer login. And I know you're the one who wants to get back at Philip. So what the hell happened at the game?"

His voice is sharp. Something inside me flinches on instinct. But I'm not the victim here. I know that. I felt so alone last Friday. Scared and frantic after everything that happened with Philip. Isolated and hopeless, seeing Lukas kiss Naomi.

And I took that out on someone who's done nothing but help me get by. That's on me.

I need Ben. I need the GSA. I need all the friends I can get who see me as I am and treat me as me, because the world beyond them is hurtful and unkind. Part of me feels like an ever-detonating bomb, but I'm a person, too, and just because controlling my anger is hard doesn't mean I shouldn't try.

Just because apologizing is hard doesn't mean I don't need to. Especially after what I did to him.

"I fucked up," I say, voice cracking. "I—I was scared Philip would hurt me, and I was scared no one would help me if I asked for it. Because I'm a mess, and I know it, and I just want to be a mess who can protect *himself* on *his* own." I dig hard into the pronouns as I speak, staking my claim. "Lukas printed out the papers from your account and gave them to me. He didn't realize they had your name until after. I knew, but I put them in Philip's bag anyway. It was wrong, and I'm sorry."

Ben sighs again. For a long moment, he's quiet. "Meehan suspended me from the next three football games. She's also making me take an F on that bio test. If I don't get in any more trouble, there won't be a permanent mark on my record. But there could have been. You and Lukas might have screwed up my chances at a top premed school. My parents would *destroy* me if I had to go to a state college."

We have no chance of winning the game without him. Technically, that works in my favor—the court will be crowned win or lose, Lukas will be humiliated as his team flounders, Meehan will have to schmooze our rich alumni without the joy of a victory to smooth stuff over. But this isn't about me and Lukas, about winning or losing. This is about Ben.

"I shouldn't have dragged you into this," I say. "I should have found any other way."

He stares at me for a long time. I look down at my sneakers. Finally, Ben breaks the silence. "Okay. I get it. Don't do it again."

"I won't," I say. "I promise, no matter what. And I won't need to. I think Philip learned his lesson."

And once we've updated the Code of Conduct, I'll be as protected from his words as I am from his fists. Once Meehan accepts the student government's recommended changes, we'll be on the same page about making Cresswell the safe haven it's supposed to be.

But here I am, sitting in the student government room that's supposed to be my throne room, fear crawling up my spine. Telling me the levers of power were never made for my hands. The Homecoming King's crown is too big for my trans head to carry.

"Welcome to Cresswell's first Code of Conduct public hearing in sixty-two years," I say as attendees filter in, standing tall at the head of the room, tapping the list of anonymous emails Sol printed for me. "I'm Jeremy Harkiss, SGA president. I'll be leading this meeting. I'm also running for Homecoming King."

"I'm Ben Guo," Ben says, "the SGA vice president. And I want us to use this forum to talk about how our actions can hurt other people. I've learned a lot about that myself lately."

I smile through the awkwardness tugging at my gut. "So," I say, "who's experienced an act of verbal harassment or other bullying since school began? Be honest. This is a safe space."

Hands go up. Lots of hands. Holy shit. I was expecting two or three people to show up—more like forty or fifty have come, spilling across the double-wide classroom. How has Principal Meehan missed all of this?

Most of what's going on is online. I've seen the vicious rumor-spreading, the slut-shaming and hate that gets smeared across the internet. As one of the most popular girls at Cresswell, I was a target of it once—I'd show the messages to Lukas, and we'd laugh about it. It's never hurt me like I'm realizing it's hurt everyone else in this room. Ever since I transitioned, I've cropped my profile picture so I look like a normal teenage boy—and I've gotten about a tenth of the hate.

I pass around a stuffed phoenix that's supposed to dictate who's currently talking, and soon girls are cuddling it and tearing up. Catcalls in the hallway, groping, older boys staring at their breasts. Along with transphobia and general hate speech, the Code also doesn't cover sexual harassment. As the fifth girl recounts how a teacher made fun of her weight, my fist curls around my pencil until the lead digs into the meat of my hand. I want to hit something. But this problem can't be fixed by a guy getting angry and—as Ben writes on the slip of paper he passes me—*We fucked up. Debbie should be up here leading this with us.*

Debbie's sitting in the front row instead of helping us. I'm pissed at her, but this is bigger than our petty rivalry. I'm not any of my asshole fathers. I know how to pass the mic. I make eye contact and silently plead with her. *Take the stuffed animal. Take the lead.* At last, she grabs the plushie and stands. "I want to talk about the people at this school who hate women. And internalized misogyny."

"The floor recognizes senior Debbie Engle," I said.

"I don't recognize you," she says. "I voted for a female student government president."

It shudders into me like a flash of cold water. I grit my

teeth. "Debbie, come on. Do you really want to misgender me while we're talking about antibullying?"

"I know you're a boy, Jeremy. It's pretty fucking obvious. I wanted a girl to lead student government because she'd understand more of what we go through. Haven't you been listening to the room? Almost all the harassment at Cresswell is guys going after girls. How are you someone who can fix that?"

"You think I don't have the lived experience to understand what girls go through?" Like my grandmother didn't tell me to be quiet when a neighbor boy knocked me down on the sidewalk, to smile at an old cousin when he said I'd grow up pretty. Like I haven't been to hell and back again. I wave my hand over my chest—which I'd never in a million years do unprovoked. "See? Tits. Rather obvious ones, even though I try." I add a theatrical sigh on the end of that sentence. My voice cracks and drops.

Suddenly, I don't mind. I want them to see the ragged lines around the edges of me, the details that don't line up, the voice and the curves and the breasts and the very fine blond hairs on my upper lip. I want to throw the reality of myself in their faces, to make them see me as I really am. The boy parts, the trans parts, the seething parts. I want every inch of me to be worth upholding.

Debbie shakes her head. "But you don't actually give a damn, do you? I mean, you refused to report Brandon Kyle sophomore year."

I wince, that old fear surging back up and clotting my

insides. Is that what this is about? Brandon Kyle had targeted Debbie that year as well. He tripped her in the hallways, groped her in gym class. She'd asked me to join her in reporting him to Meehan, but I'd said no. Even if I hadn't known I was a guy, the shame he'd driven into me had punched deep into my soul. So Debbie had reported him alone. And Meehan hadn't found her word credible enough to punish Brandon.

We sit there for two awkward minutes until the bell rings. And all I can think is maybe I'm even more like a cis guy than I thought, if I don't know what to say next to her. The rest of the group shuffles quietly out of the classroom, but I'm glued to my seat.

Back at my house that evening, the GSA isn't surprised when I tell them what happened. The theme for Wednesday's spirit day is group costumes—you're supposed to get points for coordination and concept—and we've gathered to work out ours and bitch about the people we hate.

"Basic TERFery," Hannah says, pawing through my closet. Piles of fabric spill from bins and out across the floor, sequined swatches of old Halloween costumes and floral blouses I outgrew in seventh grade. High heels and rubber rain boots and all the pieces of a life I'm still not sure I was living.

"Trans-exclusive radical feminists." Anna picks up an old beret and tries it on. "A lot of them are lesbians, unfortunately. They hate trans people because they like to claim they're the most oppressed queers in existence."

That's not quite Debbie. I've worked it out by now. She wanted her fellow cheer girl to stand with her in solidarity against Brandon and help deliver swift feminist judgment to the assholes and assaulters of Cresswell. And there's nothing I'd like to do more. But I can only do it my way, and my way is only the male way.

I don't think that's the explanation Debbie wants to hear.

I pull long blond hairs off an old dress of mine. They don't feel like they came from my body. The dress doesn't feel like mine, either, even though I remember crying when I went into the store to buy it. I'd always hated shopping for myself, even though I'd loved picking out outfits for my fellow cheerleaders. *How did it take me this long to figure out I was trans?* I would die for my menswear collection. I've been sitting atop the outfit I plan to wear to accept the Homecoming crown since mid-August.

I probably should have been working on my Spirit Week costumes since then. I guess I'd just assumed Naomi would make them. Like always.

God, I absolutely suck as a friend. But I can fix that, I remind myself. I can apologize to people I've hurt. I can forge new connections, build them stronger, fight to keep my anger in check. Especially as I'm delving into a community I need, where there's more people I can hurt.

Sol was right. I need friends who understand and welcome my transness. Even if thinking of it sometimes makes me dysphoric. Even if sometimes all I want is to close my eyes and wake up as a cis boy, a normal boy. I felt so invisible at that Harvard reception where everyone danced around my transness like you might ignore a crack in an old dish.

Just because my feelings about my gender are confusing and conflicting doesn't mean I should wish I was cis to make those bastards comfortable.

"What movie characters do we want to dress up as?" Sol says. "Can I suggest *Revolutionary Girl Utena*?"

"Can I remind you not everyone watches anime?" Hannah says. "I don't want to spend my whole day explaining my costume to people."

"Let's do *The Matrix*," I suggest, pulling out my long black pleather coat. I'll sweat like hell in it, but that's the price we pay for fashion. "Most influential trans film?"

"I preferred *Jupiter Ascending*," Connor says, and I chalk up a small victory—the cute guy is actually talking to me. "Have you seen Eddie Redmayne in that movie?"

"I haven't." Eddie's been dead to me since *The Danish Girl*. When I win Homecoming King and the story goes viral and I become superfamous, I'm not selling Hollywood the rights to my story unless they swear to cast a trans actor to play me.

A hot one. Hell, I'll do it myself if they beg enough. "He's cute, though."

Connor shrugs. My bait has missed its mark. How hard is it for me to talk about cute guys with a fellow gay? Why can't I connect with him?

"Kind of sucks the Wachowskis are the only really well-known trans filmmakers," Hannah says. "There aren't even any well-known trans guys in Hollywood."

"Maybe I'll be the first," I say.

"I thought you wanted to be a lawyer like your mom," Anna says.

"Maybe I'll do both. The sky's the limit, right?"

They all look at me like I've grown a second head. I've lived my whole life with the knowledge that people like me aren't welcome in polite society. There's a meme about all trans people working as computer programmers (the ones of us who actually have jobs) and it's true, sort of. We all seem to default to jobs that don't require people to like us as people. Jobs where we can't be fired for looking weird or upsetting people. Like Neo in *The Matrix*.

But I don't intend to let what I am put a cap on my dreams. I won't let fear dictate the terms on which I live my life. There's a reason *The Matrix* exists—people like me are the glitch in the system, the one that reminds them the systems they take for granted are broken.

I grab a set of matching black leather corsets from the closet and toss them at the sisters.

"Why do you even have these?"

"I never throw anything away." I grin as I dig through my stacks of accessories, draping bead chains and floaty scarves about my neck, topping it off with movie-star shades. "I make stuff work."

Connor's brought his fancy camera, so we plunder my closet and put on a photo shoot before the lacy curtains Mom hung up. Black leather and sunglasses, me trying to slick what's left of my hair into a cool wave, Sol draping themself in a dozen thick chokers. "The first nonbinary Homecoming Monarch can dress however they want," they tell me.

Anna tries to walk in stilettos and topples over; Hannah, to my surprise, glides down the hallway in them like a pageant queen. We convince Connor to try on a dress, and I do his makeup, swiping bronze across his eyelids as his lashes flutter below. Someone cranks up music, and Sol leaps up on the bed to sing along into my hairbrush. All the while, the camera clicks away.

I smile and load the photos onto a flash drive. I plan to make them into posters later. My pizza giveaway may have blown up in my face, but these will catch eyes and make people remember my name. Remember that I'm goddamn queer and I'm goddamn doing this. If they vote against me for that, I don't want their support.

Soon we've got outfits for every day of the week, all except Monday, which is traditionally Formal Dress Day. I was planning to wear the tux I bought last year, when Naomi and I were matching Jane Bonds.

"Hey, Mom," I say, leaning over the balcony. "Have you seen my tux?"

"Oh." She's coming in from the garage, dressed in an impeccable pencil-skirt-and-blazer combo. Looking up at me past the chandelier and the sparkling crystals on the ceiling. "I threw it out."

"What?" Am I hearing her wrong? That thing was in good shape. I got it at Goodwill and had only worn it once. I take the stairs two at a time and meet her in the kitchen. But she won't look me in the eye.

"I threw out a lot of your stuff over the summer," Mom says. "I was cleaning."

Oh. It feels like ice water is trickling down my neck. "You didn't 'clean' my Easter dresses," I say. "Not even the ones from when I was five years old."

"I . . . I must have missed them."

No. I know exactly what she was trying to do. She acted like removing Jeremy's clothes would banish an unwanted ghost from her child's body. "If you wanted a straight, cis daughter, you should have dressed me better. Those reds and oranges were autumn colors. I developed gay as a defense mechanism."

My joke falls on straight ears. She shifts her weight, uncomfortable. "I . . . I shouldn't have done it."

"No shit. You're not allowed to hate your own son for existing."

"I'm not mad at you for existing." She laughs, awkwardly brushing loose hair away from her face. I can tell she's nervous. I don't care. "I just had a brief, immature moment. I'm sorry. It was wrong of me. I haven't touched your stuff since."

"You wanted me gone. Erased." I'm still fuming. "What? Did you think that if you fucked with my wardrobe I'd just dry up and go away? Me. Your son." That last word feels like a weapon hurled from my tongue, a neon sign flashing in her face, even though I only want her to love me. I don't want to feel like who I am is a betrayal of her. I just want her to see me as I am, on my terms.

"I'm sorry," she says quietly. "I'll buy you a new tux."

Can you buy me a new mom? I almost say, and bite that back.

I carry that disappointment with me all night, as I design the next round of campaign posters, and all morning, as I print them off and rush to join the GSA. It pokes deep into my spine. *Unwanted.* I look in her eyes and see I'm unwanted, even if she doesn't say that out loud. I don't know what force on earth can make her want me, not after I failed the cardinal rule of being her daughter. *It's unfair. It's so hard to be a daughter even if you are one. I never could have lifted that weight.*

I just want to be wanted as her son. As part of our little, tight-knit family, just the two of us.

It's not like the world's exactly on my side. But just because

I want to try to fix the broken bonds I've scattered doesn't mean I know how.

How do you start persuading your family you belong in it?

Our posters go up in a rainbow flurry, flaming bright over the normal ads for clubs, charity drives, and Homecoming Committees, besides the ones we made for the antibullying forum. The fire marshal will lose his shit if he sees all this paper on the walls. The brightest poster board I can buy, and atop it, photos of me and Sol in black dusters and capes. *Our* Matrix *photos.*

Overturn the old Cresswell, they declare, and *Greetings, comrades*, and *Queers rule the school!* Below it all is my declaration: *Jeremy Harkiss and Sol Reyes-Garcia for Homecoming Court.*

Maybe I'm a disappointment. Maybe I'm not supposed to exist. But I'm me, and I'm fighting.

And the discovery that trans me, boy me, gay me—every part of me—can pull together and fight fire with fire brings a massive, shiny grin to my face.

"How like a boy," Debbie muses as I tack one up over her locker, balancing on a precarious rolling stool I stole from an earth sciences classroom. "Weren't you supposed to be leading Cresswell's new antibullying program?"

"I can do two things at once."

"Can you do two things well?" she says. "Because right

now it feels like you're using updating the Code of Conduct to draw attention to your campaign. Which is fucked up."

I flinch. She's right. I want to be safe from Philip. I want to help the school. But I also want credit for a victory. "Does it matter if I am, Debbie? I benefit, Cresswell benefits. Not everything I do has to be perfectly selfless." All girls—well, everyone with an F marker slapped onto their birth certificate, and trans women, too—are taught they're not allowed to do anything for themselves. That's bullshit.

"This isn't a game, Jeremy. This is about people's lives."

"It's about my life, too." I draw a deep breath, trying not to shout. I don't need more enemies. "I don't think we're on different sides. I think—"

"I think I can't trust you," she says. "Considering you're a traitor who switched over to the boys' side."

Forget this goddamn bullshit. At least Debbie sees me as a guy—just in a way that erases all my experiences. That makes nothing better. I push past her, dart up the stairs, and start slathering the second floor in posters.

She thinks I have no skin in this game anymore. But telling the world who I am doesn't stop truckers from honking at me as I walk to the diner that afternoon. It doesn't stop me from needing to duck into three mini-marts on my way home to find one that sells tampons. It's changed the shape of the target on my back, but it's also made that target bigger.

My transness is part of my masculinity. The way I came to

189

my gender matters, even if it doesn't change what my gender is. I'm not safe from harassment just because I'm male.

And maybe the flip side of that is true, too. Maybe I'm also not less male because I'm trans. Debbie sees one piece of my identity, my mom sees another, but it's all just different pieces of me I need to figure out how to carry. A maze I need to navigate. A minefield.

And so many people want me to walk through it alone.

CHAPTER THIRTEEN: LUKAS

Tuesday came in a tide of rainbow-bright posters, splashed out over the school's walls. Taped onto lockers, pinned above water fountains, suspended at the top of the climbing rope in gym. Flashy stickers, twisted fonts, and photos of Jeremy and Sol in very cool black dusters and capes. *Where the hell do I get myself one of those jackets?* My ex probably blew three hundred bucks on the printing costs. He looks happy, though. Grinning wickedly, green eyes dancing. Like an alien visiting from some planet where everything's okay and fine.

It's feigned confidence. I think. From our argument after the game, I know he's fighting tooth and nail, that he wants this crown so badly he'll even screw over Ben to take it. He's not one of the cis white guys who've swept to victory in a hundred Cresswell Homecomings; he's not just showing up and expecting laurels. But I envy his ability to bluster in, swagger, and demand to be taken seriously. He holds himself tall like nothing can bring him down.

I'm not the only one magnetized by the photos. So's Sol, halfway down the hall. Staring at them with something like reverence.

"You look cool," I say.

They smile. "I look badass. And awesome. Like, I always feel so dysphoric when I look at photos of myself. But Connor's a great photographer, and Jeremy has an awesome costume collection. I love seeing myself as a genderless computer god."

"It's good to have goals," I say, my festering anger at Jeremy blacking out everything else in sight. My family splintered this weekend while he made art projects with his new friends. "I need to do something about this." Jeremy smiled as he blew up Ben's life. Now I'm supposed to let him claim the school walls as his territory?

"Why?" Sol says. "They're awesome."

"For his campaign, yeah. Not mine." I eye them. Skeptically, this time. "You're still on my side, right?"

"Um," they say. "I'm your friend. But I'm not picking sides in your breakup. You and Jeremy are the only ones pushing people to do that. I know it was you who messed up the pizza giveaway, using the tip-off I gave you. You sort of used me."

I wince. Because, yeah, I totally used them. "I'm sorry," I say. But I have one week, three days, thirteen hours, and fifty-one minutes to stake my claim. I have to play this game on my terms, not Jeremy's. "It won't happen again. From now on, I'll stick to just promoting my and Naomi's campaign. Speaking of, you know that rolling cart people use to bring TVs into their classroom?" I say. "It lives in the computer lab, I know. Can I borrow it?"

"For what? Like, an asking or something?"

Asking Week. Naomi. Right. I'm so busy putting together my big campaign event that asking my date to Homecoming in some ostentatious fashion slipped my mind. Worse, I can't just repurpose what I would have done for Jeremy—a week-long scavenger hunt culminating in a massive celebration at the bonfire. A hunt that would have been all about us. Every question, every clue, linking back to our shared history.

What sort of asking would Naomi like? She's spent the past three years in Jeremy's shadow. She enjoys planning big events, but never gets to be at the center of them. She deserves a moment in the spotlight. A chance to shine on her own. The boyfriend she wants me to be would do that for her.

My future may be on fire, but I can pull on a smile and do something nice for her.

"Can you get an email to the whole senior class?"

The email flies out. I ask my classmates for photos and videos of me from the last four years. Ask them to gather in the senior parking lot at lunch on Thursday. Finally, I track down Laurie and beg her to take one period away from the musical sketch to help.

"We have a week and a half until we perform," she snaps, indignant. "The back row still can't even shuffle-ball-change!"

"I'll have Meehan up the time limit on the show so you can have an extra-long ballet solo," I tell her, and that does it.

It may not be sweet and personal, but every girl loves a flash mob.

My AP English Lit teacher lets us use our laptops to take notes. Sitting in the back of her low-light, lavender-scented classroom, I pull up the photos and videos that my classmates have sent me and start splicing them into something epic. Layering Olympic-caliber music in the background. Mentally charting a route through the school. *How can I reach as many people in the building as possible? How can I make them notice my school spirit?* What I'm planning is truly epic, an entry into Cresswell Homecoming legend. I know I can pull it off. I just wish I had the energy to enjoy it.

At practice that afternoon, Coach makes me run drills with Troy, the shaking and scrawny JV quarterback. With Ben suspended, he'll play in the Homecoming game. We sprint back and forth across the rocky practice field, syncing our movements, me trying to stamp the feel of his passes into my muscle memory. I try to encourage the kid, but his hands tremble every time they curl around the football, and I don't know what to say. Things feel off without Ben throwing to me, like

I'm reaching out with fingers I don't have. Like my life has been split down the middle.

It's fine, I tell myself as Coach ends practice with a weary shake of his head. I try to forget the image of Ben at the last bell, dragging himself off to study hall while the rest of us went to the field. *If I'm still on the field, I can make this work. Everyone is counting on me.*

I stay after practice to help the freshmen assemble a skeleton scaffold for their canned food sculpture next week. Since their theme is It's a Mystery, they're building a magnifying glass. It's pathetic compared to the senior sculpture, which is a waist-up bust of Superman, but I give them all the pointers I've got on how to build their cardboard frame.

"We still don't have enough cans," a freshman says, hauling a rusty red wagon of canned peas into the orchestra room. "People are so stingy. I don't know how the school even manages to raise enough money to put on the dance."

"It's the alumni fund's money," I say. My wallet—and the debit card within—feels heavy in my pocket. Full of responsibility laid on me by the elite society I need to push my way into. The people who can get my college application to the top of every pile, the relationships that can mark me out as the best of the best. "It's decent, but the budget's pretty tight. If we run out of money, we can't put on the dance."

"So we can't just buy cans and donate them to ourselves?" he says.

I shake my head. If we allowed that, the competitive rich kids at Cresswell would just buy out the whole contest. "Put in some effort. Effort. *E-F-F-O-R-T.* The *E* is for energy, the *F* is for foresight, the second *F* is for . . ." I trail off, out of any ideas save *need caffeine.* I clap him on the back. "The second *F* is for figuring it out yourself. I don't have the time to write you all a poem."

I buy a Coke from the vending machines and get back to work. After taping together three cardboard braces, calling the bonfire caterers to confirm our drop-off time, and stopping two sophomores from jamming gum into the spit valves of an abandoned saxophone, I meet Sol by my car. They've pulled a tricolored pen from their bag and are fiddling with it. "You took a while," they say. "Practicing your best pickup lines in a mirror?"

"Sorry," I mutter. But how can I explain? That I take everything handed to me and don't push back, don't think about what I want and how I might otherwise reply.

I just deal.

If I keep just dealing, I'll wear out like a pencil after AP exams.

This time, when I get home, Dad's asleep. Mom's out on the porch. I go to ask if there's dinner, and a hot cloud of tobacco smoke washes over me.

She's smoking again.

"Do I need to explain how many people die each year because of those stupid sticks?" I say.

"You do it every time I fall off the wagon." She sighs, leaning across the rail and staring out at the shadowed, tightly fenced backyard. Loose sticks and dead leaves blow across too-long grass. The grill she bought Dad as an anniversary gift lies covered in cobwebs. I make a mental note to clean the yard this weekend. "I know you're worried about my health, but trust me, Lukas, I'm not going anywhere."

I'm not a kid anymore. Have they forgotten that? Maybe they want to keep me young in their heads, since my brother's brief adulthood went up in smoke. Or maybe my autism means they'll always see me as someone they need to care for, even when I'm literally carrying my whole school and family on my shoulders. I don't like either. Ever since the funeral, it's like we've lived in separate worlds.

"Are you excited for the Homecoming game?" I say. "It'll be tough without Ben, but we've still got a shot, and the halftime parade will be amazing." *Notice that I'm building something for you. That I'm still here and you still have someone to hope for.*

Mom takes a long drag on her cigarette. "I love my new job, but it takes a lot of my time. I don't want to promise you I'll make it to the game when I might not."

Her words are soft. I can tell she's trying to cushion the blow. But it still hits hard, and all her platitudes land like lies. *She doesn't want to come to the game.* I could be getting crowned King of England, and she wouldn't show up.

"Ms. Harkiss will be there to watch Jeremy cheer," I say. "She's your friend. You could also hang out with her, if you came." A panicked whine edges my words, and I bite my cheek to ground my racing heart. *Please come.* How could I possibly be doing more to make her proud of me?

"Of course I like watching you play. But I know your father also wants to be there. I'll let him have that one."

"So you're avoiding Dad?" My teeth clench onto the tender skin of my lip. Blood swarms my mouth, a wound only I know is open. "I noticed you had 'marriage counseling' in the den computer's search history—"

"You shouldn't invade my privacy like that, Lukas," she says sternly, cigarette forgotten.

"No one tells me anything!" I shout. Something snaps inside me, like I've pressed too hard on a pencil tip and sheared off the lead. Like I've left wide gray marks on my crisp, clean life. "No one in this house even talks to me. You just sit still and nod at dinner when I talk about my plans for Homecoming. You put it on me to figure out what's going on between the two of you and how to mediate it, and I don't know what to do, I don't, I just don't!" I can push myself harder and harder, I can work until I drop, but if they don't give me enough context I can't course-adjust to help them—

"Don't worry," Mom says. "No matter what happens with your father and me, you're going to be fine. We have all the money saved up for your college tuition—"

"What do you mean? What could happen with Dad and you?"

"It doesn't matter. You'll have the money. You'll be fine."

Since when does having money mean I'm fine? Fine needs to mean I'll have a family to come back to. But screaming *Make your life work! Make it work for me!* will get me nowhere, and I'm not full of fire without Jeremy pushing me. I've never screamed at my parents; I don't know where to start.

"Relax," Mom says. "You're only eighteen." She offers me the packet of cigarettes and her lighter. "Want to destress?"

I stare at them. Horrified. For a second, I think about grabbing them and throwing them off into the woods behind our fence.

Instead, I grab her lighter and march back inside.

I know it's stupid and futile—if she wants to smoke, she can just go buy one at the mini-mart—but the plastic feels smooth and cool in my fingers. In the quiet of my room, I tuck my knees to my chest in my desk chair and rock back and forth, spinning the lighter and staring at the photo of the smiling family that used to be mine.

When the world is falling apart, I'll grab anything as my anchor. I'll unsnap what's broken inside me. I can mend one or two neat breaks in myself. The only thing that would scar me forever is shattering.

But what if my life is more broken than I know? Will any college acceptance letter fix what's wrong between my parents? Jeremy and I made so many amazing memories together, but that didn't stop us from imploding.

Winning might only prolong the day when my world crumbles. Winning might do nothing at all.

On Wednesday, I spend first period texting Debbie under the desk about streamers. My phone counts down: one week, two days, seven hours, fifteen minutes. My chest tightens with each moment that vanishes. The freshmen sent us a blueprint for the Homecoming float they planned to build: a giant Sherlock Holmes head. Cute, but they wanted to go all papier-mâché, and I know from experience Sherlock will topple into two parts if they aren't careful.

I text Stephen, the boy in charge of construction.

Lukas Rivers: You have to build a frame. Not cardboard. Wood and plastic pipes. You've got little over a week until the big parade. Are you sure you want to do something this ambitious? You don't want your build to collapse and then a last-minute struggle to come up with something quick and fast when your original plan falls apart.

Stephen Gibson: Whatever, man. I'm going to try it my way.

His way? I almost text back that I'm the head of the Homecoming Committee, the presumptive Homecoming King, and I was building floats back when he was in elementary school. But maybe I'm not that anymore. Maybe I don't matter.

The school newspaper conducts an opinion poll for the court election: brainchild of Kelsey Miller, who's determined to land a CNN pundit gig before she can legally rent a car. In past years, they've never been accurate—people change their minds, or click the wrong box, or make something up to print a joke in the newspaper. "Chad Blueballs" is projected to win 3 percent of the vote—ahead of Sol, who at least is a real person and a ballot option. So I shouldn't worry. But seeing myself at 36 percent—seeing Jeremy at 44 percent—sends shivers down my spine no projected margin of error can soothe.

I need a reset. Because I'm losing, losing everything, and this is the one thing I can control. Naomi and I can't match this poster game, not when Jeremy's covered every spare surface in school with his grinning face. God, how can he always manage to look unaffected? I remember holding him in my arms as he cried himself to sleep last winter. *I don't know how to be happy, Lukas. I only know how to pretend.*

I'm the only person who ever got to see him cry. Has he stopped hurting?

I hope not, I think, furiously plucking the rubber band twined around my thumb. *I hope he's just as messed up inside as I am right now.*

Thoughts of Jeremy, posters, and victory swirl through my head as I spend lunch driving the sophomore float committee to Home Depot. They want their dragon float to spit actual fire and, since I'm eighteen, I can buy them aerosols to ignite. The Homecoming debit card flashes in my hand as I swipe it over the pad.

"This is going to be sick," says a sophomore boy, flicking his lighter. "Thanks, Lukas. This is going to be the best parade ever!"

I smile in response, but don't feel it. I'm just good at pulling on a smile.

When I return to Cresswell, there's barely five minutes left in lunch. I'm so distracted texting as I rush to the loading deck—more class T-shirts are arriving, and the Committee needs my help carrying them in—that I don't notice Ben until we collide mid-hallway.

"Watch it!" he snaps.

"I'm sorry—" I start. My words come late, absent feeling, and Ben seizes this.

"Pretty weak-ass apology," he grunts. "I know you were the one who printed those answer keys off my account. You could have told Meehan and Coryn the truth. You could have fixed this. Why the hell did you let me take the fall for this?"

Shock sweeps through me, lightning-fast. All I can think is *fix this*, and I drop onto the defensive, like a struck boxer. "Jeremy planted those papers," I insist. I know it means nothing. Jeremy just wanted to throw pepper in Philip's gym shorts. I'm the one who gave him the answer keys, who wanted to help so much that I bit off more than I could chew. "As soon as I realized it was your name on them, I told him not to do it. I tried to stop him—"

"You're stealing from a teacher," he says. "You're cheating to pass AP Bio—a Code of Conduct violation that could get you expelled—and you're throwing your friends under the bus to do it. You. Not Jeremy. You're seriously going to let me go down over one class?"

It's not about the class. It's about giving everyone what they want from me. But I can't give Ben what he wants and needs. The world flickers out of view. I have nothing to say and no way to make this right. Panic surges within me. I need to go somewhere else. I need to be *gone.*

"Lukas!" Ben shouts as I turn my back on him. "You can't just run away from me."

But I can. I can slide deep into myself, shut the world out, and storm away. Breath huffing hard, fists tight, putting as much distance as I can between me and the overwhelming pressure of what I've done. Tight around my forehead like a rubber band. I pass my AP Euro class and keep going, every part of my body held forcibly, artificially still. Through the maze of posters. Feeling Jeremy's mocking eyes on my skin as the hallways clear.

All I can think is I'm just as messed up and hurtful as him. Both of us have put winning Homecoming King and everything it represents above our friends. Above each other. Both of us are hurting people we love. There'll be no peace until one of us takes the crown.

You want to play dirty? The tightness in my head loosens. The thought of ruining Jeremy's day lights something up inside me. I've messed things up with Ben, but I can still be the person—the rival—Jeremy wants me to be. *Explosive.*

My mom's stolen lighter winks hot in my hands.

CHAPTER FOURTEEN: JEREMY

"Jeremy!" Mr. Ewing says when I walk into AP Gov on Wednesday. "I'm excited for your presentation today! It should be quite informational!"

I smile politely. *So glad you're getting something out of my humiliation.*

Han He argues the military should fund biological weapons research, pounding the podium with his fist as he makes his point. Julie Chen presents on commercial fishing bans. Moein Mosleh explains why airline carbon offset initiatives are environmentally unsound. Notes rustle in sweaty grips. Mr. Ewing mutters sympathetically behind his desk. Even with the AC unit blasting from the window beside me, sweat trickles down my neck. If I'm going to build a future for myself as a lawyer, I need to get used to my presence being questioned. I need to practice standing up for myself without losing my cool.

But when Mr. Ewing calls my name—"Jeremy Harkiss, on transgender rights"—and I step up to the podium, I don't feel my anger spike. The class stares at me like I'm an object, not a speaker. I'm almost tempted to scream, just to make them jump. *React.* Show them I have some power, at least the power to make them react.

"I . . . I guess I have to talk about this," I say. It's like I've got fifty cotton balls in my mouth, sucking the moisture and life out of me. My voice cracks. I flinch. "So. Here's why I think I have, uh, civil rights."

"Speak up," Mr. Ewing says.

Sweet secular Jesus or Hermes or whoever, please get me out of here. I'm not religious, but I need a favor. I need an escape. Need to duck the piercing, heavy eyes, each pair seeing how small and oddly shaped I am. *Dear genderfluid Loki, give me answers that aren't screaming or breaking into sobs.*

And maybe the god of mischief is really listening. Because that's when the fire alarm goes off.

We stream out of classrooms, backpacks slung over shoulders, laptops hastily shoved into bags. The maze of students closes tight around me—I can't see over all the assholes around me who have the nerve to be tall. But I do glimpse smoke curling out of a hallway, taste it in the roof of my mouth—this is not a drill. At the end of the hallway I can see ancient ecology club posters, taped three layers thick, declaring *You too can fight climate change!* as they curl and char at the edges.

Suddenly Lukas ducks out of a classroom, fighting with a crackling poster of a smiling Mother Earth. He tosses Gaia's benevolent face in a trash can that immediately goes up in sparks, flinching and wiping his hand across his sweaty face as he darts toward the rest of us. His foot turns on his own shoelace; he skids, cursing, to his knees.

"Move it, Mr. Rivers," says a teacher, giving him an arm up. An absurd giggle escapes me—and dies when I see the little plastic lighter drop out of his pocket.

Weird thing for him to be fidgeting with, I think as we stream into the parking lot. The hot September sun raises sweat on the back of my neck. *He usually uses pens or rubber bands.* But my mind can't go to the obvious place. Not until Mr. Ewing shouts, "Who pulled the alarm? Is this someone's bright idea of a Homecoming asking?"

Sure enough, a clapping crowd rings a freshman couple on the tennis court as the boy shoves a tray of cookies into a girl's hands and she gives him an awkward hug. *How hopelessly heterosexual.* Mr. Ewing storms their way.

I know, deep in my gut, that this isn't about an asking—but it *is* about Homecoming. It's about me.

I press my way to the crowd's edge, where Lukas is standing. From the other side of the building, I see Naomi walking toward us. Her eyes light up when they catch Lukas—*oh no, she doesn't*—and I grab his arm and pull him through the crowd on the tennis courts, into the shade of a tree.

He puts a hand on my wrist, as if to slow me down, but

then doesn't pull. My skin burns where he touches me. Leaves and branches trace sharp shadows on the flat planes of his cheeks. Goose bumps rise from the forest of little hairs down my arm.

"Do you have some kind of vendetta against the ecology club?" I say, trying to keep things light. Like anything could be light when I'm standing close enough to feel his heartbeat.

"Maybe I hate the planet." His grin is all the confirmation I need. "Maybe I've got a secret, evil ex in the eco club, too."

"I can't believe you had the balls to light up their posters and pull the alarm." I can't keep the appreciation from my voice. Lukas is a nice boy, the one you bring home to meet your parents. He's only cheating on his bio homework because his pride leaves him no real choice. "Why?"

"Because I want to win."

How does starting a fire win him votes? Are amateur arsonists a secretly huge demographic at Cresswell? I'm sure he's got something good up his sleeve—he always does—but I can't see it. "You dipshit. Risking this much trouble isn't you."

"How do you know what is and isn't me?" Now his grin has teeth, and it isn't so friendly anymore. My pulse kicks up. "Like you're some expert on my life?"

"We dated three years—"

"And you dumped me on the day of my brother's funeral. You lost the right to act like you understand me." His words come fast and angry. He's not smiling anymore. He's glaring daggers at me, deliberately looking me in the eye. *I hurt him.*

Shame flushes in my cheeks, but I don't look away. Right as he is, I can't let him win.

"I know you're upset," I say. I try to fling it in his face like it's a winning poker hand. It comes out too soft. "What's going on?"

He doesn't say anything for a moment, just looks at me. "Why did you dump me? Was it something I did?"

I freeze. This again?

I refused to spill my guts before the whole football team, the first time he asked. But here, in private, his question doesn't feel so loaded, so accusatory. Instead of angry, he just sounds lost.

"I had to take care of myself this summer," I say roughly. "Coming out was harder than saving myself from drowning. I just didn't have air in my lungs to support you, too." Even the barest admission of my own vulnerability stings. But I need him to know I didn't hurt him on purpose. "I tried to tell you what was going on, when we spoke at the diner after the funeral. But when I asked if you'd still love me if I was . . . different . . . you looked me in the eyes and said I'd always 'be your girl.' And I never was, Lukas."

"You have to know I didn't mean—No. I mean, I can see how that hurt you. I don't even remember saying it." His spine sags. He's leaning closer to me, lips quirked in a rueful frown. "I'm sorry. For that, at least. I chose the wrong words. What I must have meant to say is . . . my feelings don't come with conditions attached. That's all."

He says it like it's simple. Like if he'd just dodged that one phrase, I wouldn't have thrown that milkshake. But it's bigger than that. Bigger than him. I feel the conditions on my mom's love every time she flubs my pronouns. Even now, with her only missing one in five, I still feel like her 80 percent B-kid. *It wasn't your fault, baby. It was mine. All mine.*

Asking for love as a trans person, with the blunt hammer weight that word carries, feels like walking on fragile, cracking ice. Asking for love as the angry mess I am feels like inviting dark water to swallow me whole. Of course I didn't want to test his love for me. I knew it would have a breaking point. I just didn't want to learn where that was.

"Apology accepted," I say, because whatever, he's done the good ally thing. And now we can go forward. I need to get the topic away from "us" before I get distracted. But the tree trunk is at my back, penning me close to him under the dark branches. His breath is hot in the humid air. My skin tingles as he takes a single step forward, his hand within inches of my hip. I *want* him, with a rush there's a jolt of stiffness between my legs that trans forums say can happen on T but that I haven't yet felt around another person. "Are you going to apologize to the eco club for burning their posters?"

"Sure. After I win the crown." He purses his lips, thoughtful, and all I can think about is how it feels to kiss them. "I'm starting to like this whole fighting dirty thing."

I reach for venom. "Go ahead, steal my favorite tactic. That just means you're desperate. You know I'm winning, and it's eating you alive." The words come fast, almost automatic. Like the springy, bouncy pounding of balls off the rackets on the tennis courts behind us. Christ, I thought I'd stop living behind a façade when I transitioned. But I wear another mask now, the kind boys use to hide their true feelings. And even though it fits comfortably, I still know it's there.

When I go back inside the school, the maintenance team is stripping the posters of me and Sol from the walls. Half the hallways already lie bare, lined with wheeled trash cans big enough to ride in.

"Fire marshal called," says the janitor, shoving more of my posters into the trash. At least he's also chucking the *Try Abstinence!* flyers from the '90s along with them. "We've got too many damn posters on the walls. School might burn down if we don't strip 'em."

By the time I sneak off to my car to change for cheer practice at the day's end, not a single poster is left. This was Lukas's plan. No—this was his revenge.

The saddest part is, I still want him. My hand still prickles from when I touched him during the fire drill. I still love him. I opened up to him, showed him my weak points, all to soothe his pain. We fit together like puzzle pieces, my fire and his reason, my energy and his comfortable arms. If the pain of our breakup is a wildfire, our atomic fallout drenching the school and poisoning the lead-up to Homecoming itself, then surely it's a sign. An omen that we belong together.

I want him back. I want us back. Which only proves I'm

too selfish to have him. So much of our relationship was all about me. I picked every restaurant we went to, every trip we took, every song we played on the radio. I kissed him for the first time when we went to a party at my grandmother's house in eighth grade and she said I wasn't feminine enough to have a real boyfriend. Even the day that should have been about him, the worst day of his life, became a backdrop for my drama. Which is something I'm working on, but not something I have any right to demand he stick around for. Every day for weeks after our breakup, I wanted to call him. Beg him to take me back. But he might have said no. Or he might have said yes and messed his life up more.

It doesn't matter now. Lukas Rivers doesn't like boys. And no one likes trans boys.

And even if he did, a mess like me is better off alone.

CHAPTER FIFTEEN: LUKAS

Part one is complete. Reset, obtained. Getting his posters stripped is petty, but my own little AV project—incorporating the new speakers I've bought for the mobile AV cart on my Homecoming debit card—will go off like fireworks. Turn heads. Brand my name into people's minds. Erase the memory of Jeremy and his stupid stunts. Turn awe into votes. Turn votes into a crown and a future.

That evening, huddled over the conductor's podium in the orchestra room, Debbie and I formalize the plans for the Homecoming Week kickoff bonfire: the schedule, instructions for the caterers and volunteers, the playlists, the secret list of designated drivers. By midnight, even Sol has left campus—Jeremy drove them home. *I'm probably the last person they want to see.* Debbie yawns as I walk her to her car. I wait in mine an extra hour, scribbling through my calculus homework, knees shoved against the dashboard, notebooks stacked on my lap.

It's uncomfortable, but by the time I get home, my house is silent and dark. Though cigarette smoke lingers in the halls, especially by my brother's door, I can pretend not to notice. I fall flat in my bed, exhausted but triumphant, because my life is back in balance.

And now I know the truth about Jeremy and the breakup. It's like a ten-ton weight has been lifted off my chest. I said the wrong thing at the wrong time to the last person on earth who needed to hear it. *Always be my girl.* I'd probably picked that scripted reassurance from an old movie, a half-remembered conversation where a hero cheers up his girl-friend after she somehow baked the wrong pie.

Do I even like girls? Like, at all? I think about how close Jeremy and I stood together under that tree this afternoon, his body only inches away from mine. About Naomi calling my name in the distance, and me not wanting to go to her. Jeremy knows who he is and what he wants and broadcasts it louder than a siren in a library. I prefer to keep quiet, hold my secrets safe and closer to my chest. I have too many problems to juggle. If I can still this pressing voice, I can cross at least one issue off my list.

The problem of *me*.

Doubts leak into my dreams that night. I see Naomi, in a blue gown and corsage, holding my hand and waving as

Meehan lowers a crown on my head, with Terry smirking on the sidelines—and then it's Jeremy standing beside me, and I'm throwing blazing posters at him, and he won't stop smiling, not even as his skin ignites.

"It'll take more than this to stop me, Lukas." His burning hands lock around my neck. Pinning us together as the fire spreads. "You fucked up. You made me leave you. You do so much for other people, and you still can't help the ones who matter most."

"I'm sorry!" I shout. "I didn't want to hurt you. I want—" But his hands squeeze the air from my lungs, and I'm voiceless.

Out of words, and burning.

And not wanting him to pull his hands away.

My alarm goes off at seven. My head swims as I dress, grabbing protein bars from the kitchen instead of breakfast. *You know what you did wrong. You apologized. Hopefully, now we can both move forward.* But I don't feel hopeful. I live the morning in a daze, the voices of my teachers little more than distant humming in my ears. My chest feels hollow; the crack in Jeremy's voice when he said *I tried to tell you* plays on loop in my head. Only by lunch have I recovered enough to pull on a smile. I'm about to ask Naomi to the dance, and the future Homecoming King needs to look happy for his queen.

"You'd better donate these to the school when you're done with Homecoming," Laurie says, eyeing the new speakers as I lug them over to senior courtyard, discreetly sliding them beneath the picnic table benches for maximum volume. "I'm doing you a huge favor. Where's your sign?"

My asking sign. Right. I fish around in a trash bin and drag out some poor kid's poster board—likely tossed out after an asking gone wrong. I dart into a nearby classroom, grab a marker from the whiteboard, and scrawl *Naomi, HC?* on the other side.

"Wow," Laurie says when I show her. "I can see how much you care about your new girlfriend, Lukas."

I wince. Even I can pick out the sarcasm in her voice. "I've been really busy with Homecoming Committee." Busy pouring my heart and soul into every vessel I can reach. "The sign slipped my mind. Naomi and I started going out last week. I—"

"You think it'll make her happy to be dating a guy who forgets she exists?"

I feel like she's dug one of her long red fingernails into my gut. Making Naomi happy is another responsibility I carry. Another place I can drop the ball. "I'm doing my best," I say.

And if I'm messing up something else, Laurie doesn't let me know.

The alarm on my phone beeps at 12:15. I step into the senior courtyard. All across the bricks and benches, people turn off alarms on their buzzing phones. Putting down Tupperware containers and soda cans, they stand up and gather in a semicircle around the cheerleaders' lunch table.

And as one, when the opening chorus of "Your Love Is My Drug" rings off the bricks, half my class breaks into dance.

No one in our class has an ounce of the coordination needed to pull this off. Laurie's done her best to keep the choreography simple, but Max trips over his shoelaces and Debbie decides to improvise. Still, two hundred people dance in unison, hands and hips waving to the beat as startled onlookers cheer. I fire a handheld confetti cannon, wade through the mass of bodies, and tuck my arm around Naomi's thin shoulders.

"Will you go to Homecoming with me?" I ask. Her cheer friends snap photos and film us. Behind me, Laurie fires the second confetti cannon. My ears ache. My head spins. But her smile says I'm still on the right track.

"Yes!" Naomi gasps. Her lips brush my cheek. She smiles for the cameras. I flush with triumph, bright and awesome as running home a touchdown pass. The spotlight's on her. I've given her the moment she's always wanted, a moment where she's shining without Jeremy to steal her light. *Even Jason would be impressed at how well his autistic little brother pulled this off.* I'm happy for her, and for me, because it feels like I've finally done everything perfect and *right*.

No one can see another girl's name scrawled on the back of my sign. No one knows I dreamed about Jeremy last night.

But I know. And I search him out. He sits with Ben, neither of them dancing. Only staring in stunned silence. His brow furrows, but not with anger. He's blinking—hard—but not looking away.

Then, with a snap of motion, he shoves his lunch back in his bag and storms into the building.

Like he hates me so much he can't even watch me be happy.

I try to ride the high of Naomi's yes through the rest of the day, as she texts me lists of restaurants for our after-party dinner and notes on who can get vodka for the after-after-party. *It's going to work out. It's going to be okay. Jeremy doesn't matter. You did the right thing and apologized for what you said. Let it lie.*

Committee messages and congratulatory texts fly across my phone screen. The timer spins: one week, one day, five hours, seven minutes until Homecoming kickoff. Everything's lining up in my favor. I need to focus on that and not on Jeremy.

By the time I collect the AV cart from Sol and meet up with the Homecoming Committee outside the orchestra room that afternoon, during the school-wide free period, my heart's racing like I'm braced for a tackle. As soon as my flash drive slips into the port, music pounds inescapably loud.

Jeremy can keep his posters and photo shoots. I have an event. Three mobile flat screens playing video of me and the team, games I've won, victories I've seized. Flashbacks of my life since freshman year form an all-highlights reel. *Everything's a highlight for me.* Images of touchdown catches and summer pool parties and a wild blond girl on my arm. Peppy rock music spilling free down the halls as I push the cart, the senior cheerleaders parading behind me, pom-poms held high, the JV football team tossing candy into the classrooms we pass. Kids stream out of their classrooms to follow us, and the banner we carry is clear. *Lukas and Naomi for Homecoming Court.*

Jeremy doesn't have this, I tell myself as I high-five students, my personal theme song blaring in the background. He'll never have this. This is all me. He's the newcomer at Cresswell. He can't compete against what I've spent all these years building.

I see him when we enter the student government meeting room, taking questions behind a podium, standing on a step stool. His lips shut as I parade in, my escort around me, music drowning out all sounds, videos looped on repeat. Soaking in limelight and turning it back as fire. All eyes go to us. And it's perfect.

You want to play dirty? I think, meeting his eyes deliberately. His face falls. His cheeks flush red. His chest rises and heaves beneath his binder. I grin as the crowd swarms around me and he runs from the room.

It's brilliant. Beautiful. I feel like I'm flying. By the day's end, as I walk the halls and ask people who they're voting for as Homecoming King, not one in ten gives me Jeremy's name. Some freshmen even ask if I'm running unopposed. The way to the crown feels clear and open.

If my life looks solid to everyone around me, then maybe it isn't actually falling apart under my feet.

After football practice, Jeremy and Sol wait by my car. For a heartbeat, I shiver—has Sol told Jeremy about the pizza thing?—but then Jeremy turns on me, his eyes like fire, and he draws a shaking breath.

"If you show that video again—if you post any photos or stills from it—if I hear one more *word* from your fucking campaign that implies I'm less of a man than you—I'll tell the whole school you're autistic."

What? I freeze, heart nearly pounding out of my chest. I'd told him I was ready to fight dirty. But this is a stab in the back. I would have sunk to my knees if they hadn't locked up.

Maybe he didn't enter this race to deliberately hurt me. But now we're two steam engines on the same track, hurtling toward each other with the force of meteors, destined to collide.

He has me. The asshole has me.

"That's low," I say. "Even for you, Jeremy. That's crossing a line."

He laughs. The sound peaks high. His fists tighten, chest hitching as it cuts off the sound, all of him straining to hold back a body fighting against itself. "Like you didn't? Like you didn't cross every line?"

"I don't know what you're taking about!" I slide my hands back through my hair. Frustrated. Needing grounding. The world spins too fast, off balance, and I'm going to fall. "Is this about what I said to you last summer? That phrase I shouldn't have used? I apologized. I didn't mean it. You can still be mad, but that doesn't mean—"

He grabs my shirt and tugs me toward him. Gravel crunches under his shoes. He's stronger than he looks. In the folds of his shirt, new lines of muscle tense and hold me. "Stop fucking with me."

I snort, hard, and lever the foot-plus I have over him into what should be an intimidating height. "You started this, Jeremy. I'm just finishing it."

He stares at me a long time, hard and focused. Water builds in his eyes. At last, he drops my shirt and steps away, stalking back to his car.

One point Lukas.

But it doesn't feel like a win. It feels like I've shattered. A glass dropped on asphalt that no amount of glue and patience can fix. If he goes through with this, he'll tear me open on the school steps and leave my weirdo corpse for the crows.

"You know," Sol says, "I thought Jeremy was just obsessed, competing this hard against you. But he's got a point. You don't deserve to run this school. Fuck off, Lukas. Don't expect the answer keys for tomorrow's bio test, either. Rubbing someone's old presentation in their face is fucked up."

"I didn't—" And I bite myself off before I can say something wrong.

They flip me the bird and climb in Jeremy's car.

And then I realize what about the video made Jeremy threaten me. Made him hate me enough to cross that final line. Because in every video, in every photo I just paraded around school, I'm standing with my arm around a ghost. After apologizing for what I'd said last summer, I went and rubbed those old photos of him into the face of every kid at Cresswell.

CHAPTER SIXTEEN: JEREMY

Fight dirty. That motherfucker. He promised me that, but I didn't realize how far he'd go. I can't even weep my eyes out in the girls' bathroom anymore. I have to cry in my car.

Even as I drive Sol home, my skin prickles, hot, sweaty, and wrong. Endlessly wrong. Not like the girl in those videos. Beautiful, carefree, sexy, loved, and wanted. The girl my grandma had wanted me to grow into. A girl the world could embrace. I know the lie in her eyes, know the pain and pent-up suffering—but I crave how people looked at her. She'd been so easy to love.

Focus, I tell myself. I need to strike back. Now. I've played my dirtiest card. That'll keep Lukas from dragging the old me into this ever again. *The Homecoming kickoff bonfire. Tomorrow night.* Lukas, playing the chivalrous monarch, has volunteered as a designated driver. Wouldn't it be a shame if someone siphoned all the gas from his car? Philip taught me how to do that freshman year. I'm not sure I remember how to do it perfectly. But I'll drink gasoline to punish Lukas.

"Are you okay?" Sol says, rolling down their window.

I rub the last hot, angry tear from my cheek. "No," I say, surprising myself with the honesty. "I trusted Lukas, and he fucked me over. He must have known what those photos would mean. What they'd do to me."

"Maybe not," Sol says. "He's cis, which means he's never going to have the intuition for this stuff that we do. He's going to make mistakes and needs to learn. That doesn't mean you have to teach him if you don't want to."

What I want doesn't matter. Only what I can get. And Lukas has made it clear he doesn't get me, the real me, at all.

I ram my fist down on the steering wheel. The horn blares across the intersection. The man in the car beside me flips me off. I gesture back.

"I never asked for this to be my life!" I shout. "I don't want to teach him, I want him to *know*. I want him and everyone else to know who I am right away, to never get my gender wrong—god!"

"You think you've got it hard?" Sol says. "Try giving a free grammar lesson every time you tell people your pronouns and they don't believe in singular they. Try convincing your literature professor tía that *Latinx* is a real word. At least people know what a fucking *boy* is." They pound their fist on my dashboard. Grin. Do it again. "Fuck!"

Their voice echoes around the car, off the polished

windshield and the bag packed tight with our school stuff. I find myself grinning, buoyed up as my anger flashes and rebounds about. I kept telling myself Sol was weak, nerdy, uncool to let their gender define them, limit them in what they can and can't do. But both of us were just showing Cresswell the side of us we thought would help our queer asses best survive this mess. I've underestimated how much we're alike when they really let go. I've never connected to a friend like this, aside from Lukas, because they're the first friend I've ever made as myself.

"God, I needed that," Sol looks at their hand, which must hurt like hell. "Is Lukas really autistic? Are you really going to tell the whole school?"

I wince. "I shouldn't have said that in front of you." *I shouldn't have said it at all*, I nearly add, but I stop myself. Lukas stabbed me in the back. I should stab him in the heart. Maybe I'm just another toxic male, but if there's a list of guys at Cresswell you can fuck over, I don't want to be on it. I don't feel obligated to play the weak guy because I'm trans. "It wasn't my secret to tell, and it shouldn't be your secret to have to keep."

"I'm not going to say anything. I like Lukas."

And now I feel like an asshole. "Shit, I'm messing all this up. You've been a good friend, and I've dragged you into the crosshairs of my relationship drama. It won't happen again."

They bite their lip, leaving tooth marks in their black lipstick. "I haven't always been a good friend," they say with a shrug.

We pass Lukas's house on the way to Sol's. I try not to look—not at the porch where I had my first beer, or the bedroom window I once climbed out of when his parents came home early. I try not to rub the scar on my knee from when I was ten years old and tripped onto shale while playing tag in his backyard.

I try to forget my ties to him.

"Have a nice evening," Sol says when I drop them off. I nod and take another route back home.

All night, Lukas invades my dreams. My body remembers everywhere he touched me, his hands on my hips, chest, and thighs, his tongue and lips everywhere else, everywhere that mattered. I wake at four a.m., moonlight flooding through my blinds, my thin sheets tossed aside. The protrusion of my breasts under my long T-shirt skids across my world like a car slipping on ice. I tip my head back and pull my blankets higher. I can't bind at night without flattening a lung, but it's almost worth the risk to avoid the crushing pressure of *wrong. My body is wrong.*

Sometimes, in my dreams, I'm cis. I'm as tall as Lukas, my chest as broad and strong as his. I feel whole. Healed. I don't need to fear someone will look at us together and see me as a girl. I can push him, pin him up against the wall. I can tell him to look at me, to see me as I really am, to let me know if that's someone he can love. Sometimes he says no, and I walk away, laughing. *His loss.* Sometimes he says yes, and he forgives me, and the world dissolves into fireworks as we kiss.

But this time, I dream of the body I'm stuck in, of us at the diner, of me screaming at him. Of the moment everything broke down.

"I can't do this anymore, Lukas!"

"Wait—" And he'd said that name. That one I wanted more than anything to rid myself of.

In real life, this was where I'd flung the milkshake. That name had struck me like a slap. I can't let it pass my lips. I can't react with anything but rage.

Now I try something new. To apologize. Make something good out of so much broken bullshit.

"That's not my name. I'm actually a boy, in case you haven't noticed." The words drip with sarcasm and pain. My fists clench so tightly, my nails dig into my palm—but the milkshake doesn't get thrown. "I'm going to tell the whole world, and people are going to lose their shit. Maybe this means things won't work out for us long term. Maybe it means you'll want us to go back to being friends, like when we were kids. But the truth is, I'm Jeremy Harkiss, I use he/him pronouns, and I love you more than anything."

He stumbles. Like I've struck him. I don't know what it means, but through the fog of my dream, I'm reaching for his hand as my alarm goes off.

Right, I tell myself, blinking through the bleary fog of

morning. Pulling on my binder and my most obnoxious orange button-down. *I have gay stuff to do. And Connor, an actually gay guy, to pursue.*

I ripped my heart out of Lukas's hands. I set out to make a new life, a better life, and I have. Now I'm beyond his power to break. I'm going to get a new boyfriend. It doesn't matter that I've barely known Connor a week and can't get a decent conversation out of him. It doesn't matter that all there is between us is me thinking he's cute and him not noticing me. I have to keep moving forward. I have to try something new. Why not him?

I get to Cresswell early and secrete my clues all around the school. I don't know Connor well enough to personalize this scavenger hunt, but Sol gave me a copy of his schedule, and I leave him clues disguised as clever puns. Throughout the morning, I spot him and his brown curls ducking around the school, darting in and out of classrooms, collecting the chocolates I've left for him. I tell Ben and the other football players I've usurped from Lukas's friend group about it at lunch, trying to make it sound like no big deal. But my voice and heart are racing, and I'm terrified they can see how vulnerable I feel.

"Pretty detailed for your first asking," Ben says. "Nice work."

"How does it work, when you're gay?" Max asks. "How do you pick which guy does the asking?"

"I'm being proactive," I say smugly. "One gay does the asking, the other buys the condoms. It's called equality."

"Nice," Max says, nodding sagely, and I tell myself I can do this. So, when I see Naomi and Lukas holding hands in the hallway, I try to make myself think about Connor—just as tall as Lukas, skinnier, always biting his lip. Rust-brown curls long enough to deserve the word *pretty*. Attractive. Watchable. Delectable. I know he likes books and photography and that he can't hear well out of one ear. I don't know what fears and hopes stir the deep current of his soul. *Not like Lukas.*

Maybe all breakups hurt this badly. Maybe it's supposed to be like this. But now I'm starting over with someone better. Having Connor will close up my wounds—and it'll hurt Lukas to know he's replaceable. I want to tear him apart inside.

Maybe Sol is right. A cis boy couldn't have known how those photos would hurt me. But maybe I don't care what a cis boy would have known.

Lashing out at Lukas makes me feel better. And now that we're not together, Lukas is a safe place to put all my rage.

After spending the day scavenger hunting, Connor meets me the night of the bonfire. Fall's starting to creep over the hills behind the school, the woods tinted yellow and red, the air drying out with the scent of musk. Country music blasts from the speakers in someone's car. Logs surround the pyre of old crates, ready to be lit at sunset. Barbecue sizzles on grills, and the eager freshmen queue up for free sandwiches. We cool upperclassmen have brought our own food from the diner.

I bought food for two. I wait in the parking lot as students stream over to the fire—but I'm on the outside by choice this time. Holding my banner and flowers. Ready, waiting, and nervous, but in a good way. *This is how guys feel when they ask someone out. This is a normal experience for a high school boy.* Connor West walks up, holding my last clue, looking confused and adorable.

I offer him flowers.

"There's this dance thing coming up," I say, trying to sound like it doesn't matter either way. He's got a distractingly cute dimple on his chin, and the evening breeze stirs his curls to bouncing. "I thought, if you didn't already have a date, we could go together."

Connor freezes, then shakes his head. "No thanks. I'm gay, remember?"

Oh, god. A fission of dread builds in my chest. *This is it. The worst-case scenario. The absolute worst.* My stupid tongue comes loose, and it just won't stop talking. "So am I. That's why I'm asking you."

"But you—" Confusion flickers in his eyes. Stupid big eyes I tell myself aren't that attractive after all. "I thought . . . Wait, I thought you liked girls. Like, you're a lesbian, right? That's why you cut your hair short and changed your name."

Ice water floods my guts. "No," I stammer out, numb and

too high. "I'm a guy. Who likes guys. That's why I dated Lukas Rivers for three years."

"That's different," he says, like he's tutoring me in calculus. "You can't just decide to be one of us. I mean, it's cool if you want to be an ally and all that, but you'll never, like, live as an actually gay guy. You can date all the men you want just by growing your hair back long, so it's not like you'll ever face homophobia or have real gay sex. In fact, it's sort of creepy that you'd ask me out. Like, am I just a fetish to you?" He finally goes quiet and stares at me with his big, stupid eyes.

Anger spikes in my gut. Not the sore, aching thrum of Lukas—but a punch where Connor struck me. "You could just say no and shut the fuck up." I stomp back down the hill to the ring of benches. Sneakers pumping through long grass, following the scent of smoke through the rising twilight.

This is how it's going to be. This is my life. A dating pool made up of pretty boys who'll never see me as one of them, who'll never let me belong. *The gays like dick. A lot.* I mean, obviously? But it makes me feel like an imposter at being the one thing I know for sure. *I'm a boy. I am. I am.* And I'm trying to understand how the trans part fits into all that, but how can I make peace with myself if the people I like treat me like trash? Every breath I take stings my lungs as the low chorus of laughter rises up the hill. I want to scream, need to scream, need to let this pain out. But I'll only look crazy if I do—or, worse, broken.

"Nice sign," Ben says. Then I shove it into the fire. "Uh, did your ask go well?"

I grunt.

"Harsh luck, man. Better get on it. The Homecoming King can't show up without a date."

No one will vote for me. No one wants me. No one ever will.

It's just a no. Connor has a right to say no. I'm a feminist raised by a single mom; I know people can and should say no. But it's the reason for no that hurts. The idea that everything I could bring on a date—my drive, my humor, my ambition—will always be overshadowed by this body I didn't ask for and can't change.

I will never make them want me. Maybe I'll make them hate me. Maybe I'll make the whole world hate me. Starting with the boy who will never be mine again.

I stick out my chin and march off to Lukas's car.

But Sol stumbles in front of me. They're breathing hard, their face damp with sweat. Checking left and right like a walking cloud of nervous jitters.

"Are people supposed to be drinking at this thing?" they say.

"Yeah. That's the point."

They look scandalized. "But . . . the school sponsors this."

"The school knows we're going to do it anyway. They want us to do it in one place. You don't have to drink if you're not comfortable." I want to get away from here. To run. To drive my keys into the side of Lukas's car and cut my name through the paint and channel every bad feeling into a strike against him. I know it's a bad idea. I know it won't help. I just feel like doing it.

But Sol is my friend. And they clearly need company. There's something adorable about the befuddled look on their face.

I can't run off and start keying Lukas's car. Someone needs to look out for them.

And I need to feel like someone's looking out for me, too. I need a friend. Queer community. And if I need that, I can't just abandon them at a bonfire of drunk upperclassmen.

"It's not that I'm not comfortable," Sol says, even though the sweat beading on their forehead tells a different story. They're still trying to play it cool around me, even though we're friends now. "I just don't know how to drink."

I fish the beers I swiped from my mom's secret fridge out from under my big, comfy sweatshirt and offer one to them. "Want to learn?"

"I don't have a way home. My parents would kill me if I rode with someone who'd been drinking."

I push a second beer into their hands. "Have mine, too. I'll stay sober."

"Okay, I've talked Connor through this bullshit twice already," Sol starts, thirty minutes later, once I've finished telling my pathetic tale. We're sitting together in front of the fire, and through the red and ruby matrix, I spot Philip on the far side of the circle, glaring at me. But I don't want to play his stupid games tonight. I've got all the trouble I can handle. "And he always *says* he gets it, but so many cis gay guys never think twice about their transphobia. They act like they're the most persecuted members of the community and anyone assigned-female-at-birth is an imposter in queer spaces. Connor got upset when a bi girl joined the GSA, because she had a boyfriend. If this keeps up, you, me, and Hannah will need to ask him to leave the club."

"I don't want that," I say miserably. "Like, it feels he should be part of it. Maybe I'm just what he said—some gross imposter, trying to worm my way in somewhere I don't belong. I'm way more of a sweaty, ugly mess than a polished gay on *Queer Eye*."

"Jonathan Van Ness is nonbinary," Sol points out. "Like, it's not possible to have queer spaces that only fit one kind of queerness. Queer identities aren't binary states. There's no such thing as 'imposter queers' because there's no one *right* way to be queer. Does that make sense?"

"A little," I say, though the rejection still stings. "It'll probably feel better tomorrow."

"How long have you liked Connor?"

"I've barely spoken six words to him," I say, shrugging. "He's just the nearest single gay." It's too much to take, watching Lukas and Naomi, hand in hand on the far side of the fire, knowing I don't have that. Fearing I will never have it again.

"Is that the best reason to start a relationship? You don't see me asking out every nonbinary person I come across. It's really not practical, expecting people to get along just because they share a gender or an orientation." They sigh. "I wish it were that easy."

Boy, is that ever true. Most of the older trans guys I've met, both online and in real life, are boring, responsible father figures with lots of cats. All of them have insightful transition advice that involves managing your anger, putting extra care into your close friendships, and a lot of bullshit things mentally healthy people do. None of them understand I'm seeking advice on how to be the obnoxious little shit I am at heart.

"Plus," Sol adds, "the lesbians schismed last year over whether or not I could call myself one of them."

"That sucks," I say. "Any lesbian should be happy to date you. How can two people as attractive as us not have hot dates for Homecoming?"

"Because you're obnoxious," they say. "And I . . . I don't know what I am."

"You're a good friend," I point out. "Like, seriously. Once you get past all the ego and the godlike computer skills."

"Stop." They laugh, but I can see the warmth glittering in their eyes. "Oh my god, stop. I'm having too many feelings." They take a long gulp of beer, and spit and sputter.

Something sad weighs heavy in their eyes, something they want to say but aren't. I know that feeling.

I stuff a fistful of Doritos into my mouth. "How'd you learn you were nonbinary?"

They sigh. "Sometimes I tell cis people this story, where I was three years old and my parents found me crying outside an airport bathroom because I didn't know what room I was supposed to use. But that's not true. I spend a lot of time inside on my computer. I popped over to Tumblr, and things proceeded from there. Nonbinary just feels more comfortable for me. I mean, at least inside me. With the outside world, it's harder. Everyone's idea of a nonbinary person is skinny and white, and my family is super Catholic, and they think it's just a phase or maybe the devil. I can't tell if they're joking about the devil parts."

"That super sucks," I say.

They shrug. "It is what it is."

"When I came out to my cheer coach, she tried to persuade me to be nonbinary first. Used 'they/them' instead of 'he/him.' Like if I spent enough time being 'half' trans, I could get it out of my system." My skin still crawls when I think of it. As if being myself is something I need to get over and done with.

"God, that's bullshit," Sol says, and it makes me glad to hear it. I'm not sure anyone else here would understand how much it hurts. "Gender is stupid. It's like one of those dystopian novels where everyone's assigned to a group at birth and you just have to accept that? Like, how bizarre is that from the outside?"

"Super bizarre," I agree. "It benefits no one, and yet cis people love it. Almost as much as they love blowing stuff up to tell people if their fetus has a dick."

"My cousin in Texas did a gender reveal party where her husband and his buddies were supposed to shoot a balloon full of blue confetti. Only the balloon string broke and it floated out of sight before they could hit it. So they just fired randomly until someone shouted, 'It's a boy!'"

"Provisionally a boy," I say. "That's how it should go. You get a starter gender and can revise as needed."

"You should have to do rotations," they suggest. "Four weeks in each gender, swapping back and forth, until you've experienced every one. Then you make up your mind."

"Much more reasonable," I say. I smile, and for the first time in ages it doesn't feel forced.

I miss Lukas and Naomi, but I'm glad to have someone who understands in a way they can't. Even if that person's a total dork who spends half their time reading comic books in the computer lab—the last person eighth-grade, I-want-to-be-cool Jeremy would ever hang out with. All that feels so shallow now.

I'm glad my world has gotten bigger, not smaller, since I came out. I'm glad some people like me for who I am. I'm glad to have found a community of queer people who like my fire and who welcome me in.

And I'm scared that the next time I inevitably blow up, I'll lose them.

Hours tick by. The flames leap and dance, casting a circle of warmth in the chilling September air. A circle of warmth flickers in my own chest, too. It's nice to relax. Nice to step back from the fury and pressure of it all. Maybe I don't need to ruin Lukas's car tonight. In fact, maybe I should apologize for threatening to reveal his disability to the whole school.

Sol finishes their beers and stretches out across the grass, yawning.

"I need to tell you something," they say. "While I'm feeling this brave. The guilt is eating me alive, man."

"Did you try to hack into the NSA?"

They bite their lip. "That, too. But I haven't really been honest with you, Jeremy. I—fuck, I'll do anything for my friends, okay? But I don't know what to do, since Lukas was such a dick with that video and you're my friend, too, and both of you have totally devoted yourselves to destroying each other, and I feel like I have to pick sides—" They draw a deep, shaking breath. "Lukas asked me to befriend you. To get you involved with the GSA. First, he just wanted to know why you dumped him, but then he asked me about your campaign. That's how he was able to sabotage your pizza giveaway."

Fucking Domino's. Every store within fifteen miles, convinced some twelve-year-old named Jeremy was ordering pizza as a prank. Lukas had called them all. I ball my fists, struggling to keep cool, struggling not to admit that was his slickest move yet in this campaign. "So, whose side are you on now?" *Mine. Please say mine, after what Lukas said to you.*

"Fuck sides. I'm done telling him your secrets, done running back and forth between you, I just—" They hiccup and press their hands to their stomach. I can tell they're reaching for their day-to-day casual swagger. "Are you mad at me? Like, if you are, that's fine. I get it. I can take it. Just tell me."

I close my eyes and see Connor staring at me in confusion. Lukas parading down the hall. Philip growling and primed for violence. And Sol thinks I'll be mad at them for keeping one secret? I mean, I could try. I'm good at getting angry. But that'd just be me shoveling more shit pointlessly onto the nearest person I can reach.

"We're good," I say. "You don't have to take sides in this, okay? Not if you're that uncomfortable." I gently take their beer can and drop it in the trash. "Give me a sec. I'm going to siphon all the gas out of Lukas's car. Then I'll come back and drive you home."

I wander off toward the parking lot, gravel crunching under my feet. Half seething. Half empty. Shivering a little where the evening breeze slides through my sweatshirt. Lukas's car sits at the edge of the darkness, exposed and vulnerable, but I'll need to walk all the way back to the building for tubing, and maybe that's too far. Or maybe I'm just not going far enough.

A gasp of pain comes from the dark trees below, too sharp to miss, a voice I know too well—Lukas.

I turn on my phone flashlight and dart off into the woods, clambering over bracken, pushing through knots of weeds that claw at my sweatshirt and arms. "Lukas?" No response. My heart churns. I push forward, nearly turning my ankle on a rock. My foot throbs. "Lukas!"

At the bottom of the hill, my phone flashes up. I see him, fifty feet back toward the road.

Correction—I see *them*.

Pressed against a tree, the lines of their bodies sharp, clean, long, and intertwined.

It strikes like lightning. A bladed blow that splits my world—and everything I know about it—into befores and afters.

I've been wrong about Lukas. I've been wrong about everything.

CHAPTER SEVENTEEN: LUKAS

One Week to Homecoming Kickoff

The flames crackle high. The marching band parades before the bonfire, blasting the school fight song. The smell of barbecue and whiskey fills my nose. Hundreds of students sing along or toss a Frisbee on the edge of the circle of light or sneak sips of alcohol from tiny bottles hidden up their sleeves. A perfect celebration, and I'm the one who's done it. A triumph one week from Homecoming. I should be basking in the thrill of a good omen.

And all I can think about is how I hurt Jeremy. *Again.*

How had I not noticed it was him in that video? How had I not realized it would hurt him? *Fuck.* Those clips meant nothing to me—that girl I'm hugging might have been some distant cousin or random friend from theater camp. Someone I'd known for a summer and let naturally fade from my mind.

Falling out of love shouldn't be this easy. I remember that time we stayed up until three a.m. to watch a meteor shower on the school's roof, how we cooked hot dogs over a lighter and tried tequila for the first time and mocked each other mercilessly as we spat out liquor beneath the dancing stars. That memory doesn't connect to the girl in the video. It's linked to the boy who flushed anger-hot at the sight of me, who threatened to reveal all my darkest secrets, who will destroy me if I give him half a chance.

It doesn't feel like I've fallen out of anything. More like I've tripped and stumbled into *pain*.

"He hates me," I tell Naomi, wrapping my arms tight around my chest. Like I can hold myself together through sheer force of will. What I really want is to ask her to hug me, but that feels weird. *I never had trouble asking Jeremy when we were together.* But Jeremy dumped me. Everyone is abandoning me. I'd even be glad to see Jason elbowing me in the side when I don't hold eye contact long enough.

"That's tough," Naomi says, not looking up from her phone, blue-white light spiraling up her coiled curls. An app flashes SAT practice questions at her every ten minutes. "That's usually what happens after a breakup."

A girl in a cheer sweatshirt sits on her other side. "Do you have tequila?" she mutters.

"I have Pabst in my bag," Naomi replies. "My cousin got it for me."

"Debbie always has tequila," the girl says, but fishes out a beer anyway and leaves. Naomi's frown lengthens.

"I don't know how to make this better," I say. I've already told her how he reacted to my stupid video. Everything I said and did wrong. "And I need to, Naomi. I can't stop thinking about him, and it makes me want to *scream*."

"So scream," she says. "I get it. For the past three years, I always felt like the sidekick on his TV show. Like, it isn't his fault he won those stupid pageants—those judges probably wouldn't have let an Asian girl get the crown no matter how good I was at waving and hula-hooping—but it still hurt. And it hurt worse this summer, when he didn't even care about me tanking the SAT. The banner only made things worse. What started out as obnoxiously charming is now just obnoxious and mean."

I nod. "How are you feeling about him now?" Maybe there's a simple answer she can give me. How does she want me to feel about him? How can I process him out of my mind, so I can live and breathe and be with Naomi?

"Worried," she sighs. "I feel like he's walking on a tightrope, and the second he loses his balance . . ." She snaps her fingers. "I don't want him to blow up his own life. I miss him. I want us to figure out a way to still be friends. I want him to say he's sorry. And I need him to learn some serious self-control."

"Yeah," I say, and slump forward on my log. "That'd be nice."

There aren't easy answers. You don't stop caring about someone easy as flipping a switch. Naomi hasn't forgotten Jeremy's her friend. I haven't forgotten dating him. But we've got to find our way forward somehow, with or without him.

Because I don't know what to do to bring him back into our lives.

Naomi's phone beeps. She pulls a pillbox from her purse and swallows a tiny tablet. I know I should be glad my new girlfriend's taking birth control, but it makes my neck itch. *Does she expect us to have sex?* I should want it. I'll do it if she asks me. I have an excellent reason to say yes—because I'm supposed to be the kind of guy who sleeps with the Homecoming Queen—and no words at all for why I'd say no.

"Why do we always wind up talking about Jeremy whenever we hang out?" she asks. "Is he the one thing we have in common?"

"We're both attractive overachievers?" I say. She laughs. "Hey, when you spend ninety percent of your waking hours working to get into the Ivy League, a little drama can be refreshing."

"And he sure provides that," Naomi says. "Especially with Philip lurking around."

I wince. The answer key incident hasn't done anything but make him angrier. Now Philip sits on one side of the fire, dropping empty beer cans around his feet. I've been keeping an eye on him, ready to intercede if he takes one step toward Jeremy and Sol. I don't know what I'll do if he makes a move.

"Watch this," Philip says, and grabs a canister from his backpack. He throws lighter fluid on the fire. Sparks hiss and leap. Some of my teammates hoot laughter, but most people swear and jump back from the billowing flames.

"Cut it out," I shout. "You could hurt someone."

"I know what I'm doing, jackass." He lifts the canister again. Ben puts a hand on his arm.

"You're wasted, man. This isn't the right time. Stop."

Philip's brow narrows. If he doesn't like hearing *no* from me, he sure as hell hates hearing it from Ben. "I don't take orders from anyone with a three-inch dick."

"The fuck?" Ben shouts. "Shit, that's so racist—"

"It's a joke!" Philip insists. But his words hover in the air like poison. They sweep in curdling clouds over my skin, acrid as the lingering scent of lighter fluid. Sweat feels slick and all-consuming on the tip of my nose.

"Everyone knows you weren't joking when you trashed my sister's banner," Ben says, stepping in closer. His fists tighten. "Everyone knows you're not joking now. Go home."

I stand, pull on my best copy of Jeremy's pissed-off glare, and crack my knuckles. Philip's eyes flicker from Ben to me. I may be fighting with my best friend, but Philip doesn't know that. And I know, no matter how pissed Ben is at me, having his back in this moment is bigger than any argument. A glimmer of hope lights inside me as we stand shoulder to shoulder. Maybe Ben and I can get past this.

Philip calculates. I see in the set of his jaw the moment he realizes the odds aren't in his favor. He backs away, shouting angrily into his phone as he reaches the road. The fire leaps skyward as he leaves, old wood crates collapsing in on themselves.

I exhale. But not deeply. His ugly words linger in the air, itching like a loose thread. This isn't over.

My phone beeps. A notification from Cresswell's online grading system.

I've failed this week's AP Bio exam.

It's a gut punch. *Stupid, pathetic loser. You think you'll be Homecoming King? You think you can be just as perfect as your brother, when you're inches away from brawling at the bonfire?* I need to escape. If I can't hop on a plane to Mexico, I can do the next best thing.

"Still got that flask?" I ask Max. The linebacker pulls it from his back pocket and offers it to me. I swallow fast-mixed rum and Coke—or something and Coke, whatever he could grab from his parents' basement and Coke. The buzz goes straight to my head. The roar of the world shifts to a manageable hum.

"Lukas!" Naomi says. "You're supposed to drive people home."

"Eight other people signed up as drivers," I say, and toss her my keys. "If we run out, we can use the Homecoming budget to call cars."

Max reaches for his flask. I pretend not to see him and take another sip, metal cool in my fingers, alcohol burning and soothing all the same.

"We want them to see *you* giving rides," she reminds me. "Like a responsible leader. A Homecoming King."

"I'm the *party* king." The alcohol burns my tongue and almost goes down the wrong pipe. I bend double, sputtering, and turn it into a royal bow. It must look incredibly douchey, and I almost apologize. But I take another sip instead.

The party drifts by in a haze. Naomi stares at me like she can stab me with her eyes, and I don't blame her. Jeremy dragged her into his problems, and now I'm dragging her into mine. *I should be a good boyfriend for you. But I don't know if I want to.* So as not to ruin her evening, I move out to the middle of the benches, where the junior float committee is arguing over which version of the *Millennium Falcon* to build atop their sci-fi themed float. Then, after I relieve them of all their whiskey and earn a scornful look, I wander to the bonfire's outer edge.

Dry grass and discarded cups crunch under my feet. The world pounds by, slow and fast. When my feet hit the asphalt of the parking lot, a blur of motion and the sweet smell of pot grab my attention. Terry, dressed in torn jeans and a T-shirt with the diner logo, walking up the hill.

When he gets close, I catch his arm. "You're not supposed to be here." My words slur a little. Stumbling so that I topple onto his arm. He smells like grease on the diner grill—bad for me, but delicious.

"I heard there'd be beer."

"There is. But this is a school event, and you're not a student." I drive the point home. This is a rule, even if it isn't written in any book. "Beer is for students only."

"Would it be okay if I came as your guest?"

I consider. The thought of leading Terry, with his piercings and wild grin, back to my friends feels slightly obscene. *The boy who knows the truth about me and my brother. The boy I might have accidentally flirted with in a diner.* I don't want my messy reality breaking into the ring of benches containing my friends and the image I've made for myself.

But I can't go back over there, either. Because that Lukas isn't real. It's something I made up as a stupid kid, a dream of what I wanted my life to look like. And I'm only just starting to realize how much it costs to keep it going.

"Let's go for a walk," I say instead, and a thrill runs up my spine as he threads his arm through mine.

The woods behind Cresswell rise high around us, cool in evening, heat simmering off the dying leaves, twigs crackling underfoot. The slope of the hill muffles the noise from the bonfire. If not for the occasional flash of headlights from the road, I could imagine we're in the middle of nowhere, with no one to see.

Terry sits on a log—old and rotting—and lights a joint. "Want some?"

I hesitate, sit beside him, and take it. Breathing deep. Sweet, earth, soil, and spice. Not like the crap Debbie passed around at her last party. I can taste his spit on it, too, which, to my stupid surprise, I sort of like. It tastes like sharing a secret.

So I share mine.

"I really hate Jason." I scuff my sneaker in the dirt to

emphasize the point and pass back the joint. "Even though he's dead. Even though he was perfect. Even though I miss him a little." I feel bold. Borrowed smoke puffing out my lungs. Terry can't betray any of this to anyone at Cresswell. It's not like he can tell the principal or my parents that Lukas Rivers is some raging asshole who hates his dead brother's guts. "I'm a horrible person."

"Hell no. You've got a right to be pissed. Jason made his own choices, and they were shitty ones." His fingers trace smoke in curling circles. "He was a dick to you. You were a weird kid who wanted his big brother to like him, and he picked on you because he thought it made him a man."

Oh. A weight I hadn't even known I was carrying dissolves in my stomach, leaving me bubbly and light. I hadn't realized how much I needed someone to say it—that Jason was cruel, that my feelings were valid. *When it comes to bad ways to prove your manhood, running for Homecoming King against your ex is ten times better than bullying a disabled eight-year-old.*

And maybe Jason and Jeremy weren't the only people who hurt me trying to prove themselves. Maybe I'm hurting me, too. "I tell myself if I win Homecoming King, if I get into a good college, I can be just as good as he was. I can pull my family back together. But I'm terrified Jeremy will beat me, and I'm terrified that even if I win, it won't matter—"

I bite my fist to hold in my panicked gasps. I can't break down in front of a stranger.

"Lukas." He turns toward me and runs a thumb along my

cheekbone, brushing off a tear I didn't realize had escaped. His finger is warm and smooth, like the texture of a riverbed rock baked in the sun. "You're already so much better than Jason."

My head's spinning. Fog rolls between my ears. I don't understand this—and then I do.

"At the diner last week," I start, "when you told me to meet you after your shift, was that a joke? Or were you flirting with me?" *Because Naomi thought we were flirting, and I trust her judgment.* I try to make it sound glib, like I don't care, like of course he'd flirt with me because of course everyone alive flirts with me. But I honestly don't know the answer. I can't tell if someone's attracted to me unless they make it clear. If Jeremy hadn't asked me out in eighth grade, I never would have taken the first step on my own. *That's the best part about Jeremy. He's bold. He's exciting.* Balancing out all the unsure and questioning parts of me with his endless fire and drive. Lingering even though he broke my heart.

"Both, kind of?" he says. "I thought there might be some-thing in how you always looked at me. You were only a kid when your brother and I used to hang out at your place, but I thought you were worth a shot. You're cute. And you've grown up from that kid we used to make fun of. Running back, head of the Homecoming Committee. You should be proud of yourself."

I laugh. "I don't even have time to be proud of myself. I spend all my energy trying to be perfect. What if, for once in my life, I want to make stupid, reckless, idiotic choices and have everyone else deal with the consequences?"

"Sounds like you want to rebel." He grins at me. One of his teeth is missing, a flash of darkness at the corner of his mouth. It makes him look dangerous. "Get a piercing or something."

"Yeah? Where should I do it?"

"Get a nose ring. Small enough to be practical, but also pretty."

Pretty? That isn't a Lukas word. Lukas is tall, athletic, good-looking. *Pretty* is for girls complimenting each other's outfits on picture day. But it could be for me. Jeremy shouldn't be the only one who gets to define himself. "Sounds cool. I'm in."

"Sweet." Terry pulls a needle and a small golden hoop from his pocket. *Oh.*

"Right now?"

"Why not?" he asks, grinning again. Through the fog in my head, I think about what an idiot I am for letting everyone but myself decide who I am. I have responsibilities to my family, my friends—but Jason's gone. I'm done letting his memory dictate what I want and what I do. What pieces and parts of myself I bury deep, because I'm scared my flaws will show on my face.

And honestly, I just want to see how it looks.

Terry waves his lighter over the needle. "You can have this one for now. My ex-boyfriend got it for me, but I prefer stainless steel. Gold will look better on you."

"Maybe I'll buy myself one," I say, babbling nervously. "Maybe I'll buy nose rings for the whole senior class. I've got a debit card for thirty thousand dollars, the whole Homecoming budget. They trust me so much at Cresswell. I'm so tired of being the responsible kid. I'd rather have a nose ring." I'm worried this will hurt. I'm saying whatever will run fear into noise.

He touches my face. I'm not sure what I'm expecting, but I don't feel anything but a pinch. Then a rush of blood and snot. Cool metal slides into my skin; I picture Jeremy and that knife he carries, imagining his fingers on my cheek. I gasp, once, and it echoes over the hill, and then all's quiet.

"See?" Terry holds up his phone as a mirror. I don't know what I'm looking for, and it doesn't matter, because it's too dark out here for me to see myself. *I just infected myself with a million different diseases. No wonder I'm failing biology.* "Pretty sexy. Tell me more about this debit card you've got. They seriously trust you with that much money?"

Money's the last thing I want to think about. I feel like I'm falling apart beneath all the weight I carry. I want to pack it up and send it somewhere outside me.

I want to fill myself up, even though there's nothing but empty air here to do it with.

I lean in and wrap an arm around his lower back. I twist my head and hook my tongue into Terry's mouth.

He tastes like beer and cheap weed, like anger and danger. Everything I know I shouldn't have. It speaks to a part of me that's felt empty for so long I almost forgot I wasn't supposed to be numb.

I can't do this, I think, coiling my tongue around his, running my hands through his ratty blond hair. *He's too old. Too much trouble.* But even if this is wrong, it's real. I don't have to pretend for him. I don't have to lie to myself about anything when he's biting my lip and my bloody snot drips down between us.

"Incredible," Terry whispers when we pull apart. "You're fucking excellent. Want to come back to my place? I could give you a ride?"

The hair on the back of my neck stands up. My stomach stirs uncertainly. It takes a few seconds for my emotions to cut through the pot haze and settle into something real. Fear. I'm not ready for what he's offering. I've gotten what I came for. "No, thank you."

And then, because I have to get home and my brain knows home's in the direction of the bonfire, I turn and stumble up the hill. A light in the distance catches my eyes, and I wade into the black.

Time shifts. Seconds slip away. Suddenly I'm lying on my back and I don't know how I got there.

"Lukas?"

The hand on my shoulder is soft. Familiar. The voice, deep and catching, is harder to place.

"It's you." I roll over and vomit across the grass.

Jeremy stands above me, face pale in the halo of his phone

light. His eyes, wide and brilliant, flash green like the ivy of Cresswell's walls. His chapped lips purse. I just know he's going to call me an idiot.

"Thank fuck, you're still breathing." He thumbs my new nose ring. Pain jets through my face. "What the fuck did you do this for?"

"Because of Jason," I say. "And because of you."

"Because of me?"

"Yes," I say, because it's true. Because I never realized how much of a front I put up before I watched him drop his. "I'm tired of trying so hard. It's not working. It's eating me alive." He should understand. Someone has to understand. "You're the only one who doesn't expect that much of me. You only want me to be angry like you."

It's true. We're angry at each other, but I like knowing we're connected. There's something tangled up inside all my desperation, all my pain. *Wanting*. A different kind of wanting than what I felt before. New, hot, and important.

And underneath it all, years and years of friendship and love.

"If you want to try less hard, drop AP Bio. Don't run off into the woods with a stoner. Did you do drugs?"

"Just weed."

"You dumb asshole." He kneels beside me. "You went the wrong direction. You could have frozen to death out here." His hand cups mine. Feeling my pulse. "You're, like, freezing. Here."

He slides off his XXL Cresswell cheer sweatshirt. Beneath is the V-neck T-shirt I got him when we went to see Imagine Dragons in concert. *He still has it. He hasn't thrown out everything I got him.*

"Alcohol lowers your heart rate. It makes your body temperature drop." He shoves the sweatshirt in my face. "Take it. Wear it."

"You're not even wearing a real shirt!" The fabric is so worn and sheer that I can see his sports bra through the cloth. Some small voice in the back of my head says he didn't plan on taking off the sweatshirt, that he's exposing himself to me in more ways than one. He's trusting me with something important, and I should be careful not to drop the ball again.

Jeremy grabs my arms, pulls me upright, and jams the fabric over my head. "This is going on whether you like it or not."

I can't ignore the fire in his words. I let him wrap me in the sweatshirt, force my hands through the openings, breathing in the scent of him. Wood smoke from the bonfire, some unfamiliar cologne, and sweat. *Didn't he buy me that same cologne for Christmas?* Distracted by the smell of him, I barely pay attention as he pulls me up the hill and around the back of the senior parking lot.

"I'm not drunk," he says, tossing me in the passenger side of his Prius. Unlike me, he keeps his car meticulously clean, sprayed with Clorox and air freshener, and I'm scared I'll vomit and mess it all up. "Sol stole all my beer. I'll get you home before I come back for them. Your parents should be asleep by now."

He's covering for me. I smile. "It's weird, knowing you," I say as he drives, warming my hands over the passenger-side heating vents. "As, like . . . two different people. You're not the same person I dated. But you're made of the same parts."

"All the broken pieces."

"The *best* pieces."

"The asshole pieces. I broke your heart on the worst day of your life. I ruined the banner my best friend spent weeks making. I nearly destroyed Ben's college hopes, and I had to walk away from the bonfire so I wouldn't get mad at Sol for spying on me."

"Be mad at me," I mumble. "I'm the one who asked them to."

He makes a choking noise, like bonfire smoke is still coiled in his lungs. "I've already got enough to be mad at you for. I think I might be hitting anger capacity. But I can't stop feeling it. It's like my whole brain is broken. I wish I could be more like you—not just the hot, cis parts, but the part where you always put other people first."

"You think I'm hot?" I whisper. Bloody snot runs down my face. He doesn't answer. "You're not that selfish. You literally just saved my life."

"That's nothing," he snaps. Are those tears in his eyes? Probably from bonfire smoke. "I couldn't let you freeze to death. They'd cancel Homecoming, and all my hard work would be wasted. They wouldn't cancel Homecoming if I died. They'd probably throw a second, bigger, more fun Homecoming. Just to celebrate getting rid of me."

"Jeremy." Teasing warmth creeps back into my voice. I know where we are. This ground feels familiar and safe. "You're not that important."

"Shut up."

"Come on. It's funny. We have fun together. Like, lots and lots of fun. Remember that night we watched the meteor shower?"

"I transitioned. I didn't get amnesia."

"Don't you remember how it used to be?" There's a pleading note in my voice. I hate sounding weak, but this is important. He needs to know how I feel. "I miss it. Honestly. Really. Please say you miss it, too."

"Will it stop you from throwing up on my dashboard?"

"Jeremy. Please." I reach for his hand, but my vision flashes double and my reach falls short. It feels like there's a brick wall between us, built high on the ashes of mistakes and mistrust. "Please tell me you miss me. Please tell me I'm not the only one whose world started crumbling when we broke up."

My eyes are wet. I can't stop tears from rolling out as we drift through familiar streets, all the pain of our breakup fresh and leaking out of me. I didn't cry after the milkshake, when the pain was most fresh. I didn't even cry at Jason's funeral. Everything I feel slips out at the wrong times. Seeing him, the real him, alive and vibrant without me, makes my losses real.

He drags me up the walkway to my house, flips over the

stone rabbit Mom keeps the spare key under, and pulls me through the door. The house lies mercifully silent.

"I'm not taking your clothes off for you," he says, pushing me down in my bed. "Sleep in your muddy jeans. You deserve it." With a grunt, he rolls me on my side. "There. Don't choke on your own vomit. I better run before your parents catch me."

"My parents have their own drama," I breathe, blankets settling heavy over me. "They won't tell anyone at Cresswell you hung out with the loser ex you hate."

He tosses a pillow at my head. I don't have the energy to remove it, and so he sighs and tucks it under my head. "You're pathetic. Honestly." But there's so much warmth in those words, a quiet caring underneath his fire and bluster, and I want to hold it inside me. "And I like the nose ring. I'm glad you finally did something for yourself. You should do what you want more often."

"What if I said I wanted you to stay?"

He freezes in the doorway. Short and spiky-haired, eyes as big as mountains. His shadow reaches toward me, and for a heartbeat, I hope he means to join me in bed.

But his laugh, hard and cutting, slices through my hopes.

"Good one, Lukas," he says. "Kick me while I'm bleeding. For a second, you almost had me convinced you weren't so bad after all."

And then he's gone, and the crush of sleep pulls me under.

Saturday morning goes off like a bomb in my foggy hangover haze.

I kissed my dead brother's old friend, I realize when the painful light of day washes over my pillow. *And he tasted like sweat and weed. I kissed him like nothing else mattered.*

I cheated on Naomi. I didn't know I had that in me. I've never understood the guys on the team who sneak around behind their girlfriends' backs. I still don't. I just had a million things whirling around in my head and so I let Terry pierce my fucking nose.

I knew it was getting harder to pretend my life was in balance. But last night, I tipped the scales so hard they shattered.

It's not until I make it into the shower that I realize I kissed a boy. A boy who I know is a boy. And I asked another boy to sleep with me.

And he left. My room feels ten times colder without him.

Forget Jeremy. You're Lukas Rivers, running back, Homecoming King. What does he matter to you? But the person I'm trying so hard to be for everyone else felt nothing like the one crawling out from inside my skin. I tell myself that winning the crown will make all this uncertainty go away, but the bathroom light winking off the hoop in my nose says otherwise. All my lies are written on me.

I stumble back into my bedroom. My room is grave-quiet, as quiet as Jason's closed one next door. The glittering football and academic decathlon medals over my desk feel like they belong to someone else. My swirling senses feel like they're going to slide out of my head. I need weight, pressure, grounding. Something to hold all the shattered pieces of me together so no one notices my scars are held shut with glue.

I grab a sweatshirt off my floor and pull it on. An unfamiliar scent washes over me. *Jeremy.* A stronger, more immediate scent than I'm used to. Sweat and woods and wood smoke. Like he's declaring his presence in the room he didn't want to stay in. I know I'm to blame for pushing him away. His shirt isn't much of a consolation prize. I wear it anyway.

My laptop whirls as I open it. Smart, sober Lukas of last week gave the Homecoming Committee this morning off. I don't have to be at Cresswell until three p.m. to start hanging the Homecoming banner. My timers and schedules sync neatly. Six days and eight hours until kickoff.

I should work on my college essays, I think, opening a new document. *Tell us about your proudest achievement* is a common prompt, and I should probably start drafting one on *How I won Homecoming King*, but thinking of the upcoming competition just makes my stomach flip.

Let me tell you a story about the love of my life, I type. *And how she turned out not to be a real person.* There. Words. But I don't like the look of *she* on the page. It feels disrespectful.

If we'd still been dating when he came out, I ask myself, *would I have dumped him?* Leaving someone at such a vulnerable time in their life feels beyond cruel, but Jeremy isn't the same person I started dating freshman year. *Neither am I.* Maybe, as he transitioned, things would have ended naturally.

Maybe we'd just be best friends, like we were in elementary and middle school. *He could have hung out with Ben and me. That whole Homecoming thing could have only been a friendly rivalry. I could tell him how torn up I feel about everything, and he'd listen.*

But the thought of us as only friends feels lacking somehow. Wrong.

I don't know how I would have reacted if he'd come out to me last summer. I just know I never wanted anyone to stay with me as much as I wanted him last night.

I close the essay without saving and sneak downstairs for food. Only to find my father waiting in the kitchen.

Shit, I think when I see him at the table, staring down into his tea. Part of me had been hoping we wouldn't speak until at least Homecoming. When I have a crown on my head and his smile is wide with pride. When I shine so bright he and Mom forget all the fighting.

"You texted my mother. From my phone."

I freeze. I crossed a line. A big one.

But no one hands out instruction guides for surviving the breakup of your family. I can't even see where the lines lie until I've broken through them.

"I just wanted to reassure them," I say. "Ever since Jason died, they haven't been welcome in our house, and I don't know why. Are you guys fighting?"

He flinches. "Of course not. Don't talk about it that way."

"What am I supposed to do?" I keep my voice calm, though

my throat is raw from barfing and the room spins a little around me. I'm so tired. "This family is falling apart, and I'm the only one trying to make things be like they were."

"Things are never going back to how they were, Lukas," he says patiently, like I'm still a kid who doesn't get it. Ignoring my anger, for now. "They'll never get better if going back is the first step in that journey."

Okay. I know that. Logically. It isn't like I could bring back the dead. But when my mom's parents died, things went back to normal. When Grandma's cancer won, when Pops fell in the bathtub, Mom cried for a few weeks, Dad held her hand and looked out for her, and things settled. Maybe this is objectively sadder, since Jason was so young. But I want my parents to complete the grieving process. For us to scatter the ashes sitting on the mantel, that suck in our thoughts like a black hole whenever we step into the room, to clean out Jason's room and donate his stuff to charity. We need to take some action so I know that things will heal.

That one day, this won't be so hard.

"You could at least call and say hello," I suggest awkwardly. It feels like the world has flipped over, me advising Dad on how to speak with his own father. "Conversations suck. I had to talk with my ex yesterday. If I can handle Jeremy, I know you can talk to the people who raised you."

"I'm not the son they thought I was. I'm not the husband your mom loves. I'm not the father you and your brother needed me to be." He sighs. "Even talking about my problems with you feels like a failure. A real man would work this out on his own."

I don't know what to say. I don't know how to fix my own mistakes, either. Jason had it easy—he never made many. Me and Jeremy are alike in this—bouncing off each other, making waves, striking everything and everyone we trust. I don't know how long we can continue hurting. I just know I need something to change. Why does it even matter what makes Dad feel like a real man? No one would ever say he wasn't. He's the only one who can tell himself having feelings makes him less.

I swallow, hard, and wrap my arms around my chest. "Maybe you need to take Mom's advice and see a therapist."

Dad doesn't seem to hear me. He rubs his eyes and peers closer at my face. "What's that in your nose?" I flinch. "When did you do that?"

I'm the good son. I lift the burdens even when they crush me. But suddenly, I remember I'm a fraud. The hoop in my nose is a mark of that.

"Does it matter?" I say. "I could have done it weeks ago, and you wouldn't even have noticed."

He winces. I grab some of Mom's yogurt from the fridge and stalk back up to my room. A voice in the back of my mind screams that I was rude, unacceptably so, for snapping at my father. That I'm breaking down like I did in grade school, only this time with harder and messier consequences. With my whole life and future at stake. *How dare I pierce my face? How dare I call out my dad for disappearing on me?*

But I don't go back. I leave the wound between us open and bleeding.

I don't know what more work I can do to fix him. And I'm exhausted from trying.

CHAPTER EIGHTEEN: JEREMY

I saw him kissing Terry in the woods.

I really should have left him there, covered in vomit and leaves. He cheated on Naomi. Worse, he chose a guy who looks like how I would, if I was cis. Seeing Lukas kiss Terry—after throwing those fucking photos in my face, after Connor turned me down—digs like shards of glass in my soul. *He does like boys! Surprise! Small wonder you're so attracted to him!*

It was almost, gut-wrenchingly, perfect. I could deal with the occasional stranger misgendering me if they saw Lukas hold me close. I'd put some distance between me and my old life, so maybe it wouldn't hurt, bringing some pieces of the past forward. Jeremy-and-Lukas—it could work for me. More than work. I could finally smile. Quench the wildfire roiling inside me with the knowledge someone loved me as myself.

But clearly it wouldn't work for Lukas. He's tasted real girls and real boys, and I don't feel like I'm either. I'm nothing but mistakes.

Whatever. If I sit on the Homecoming throne alone, it doesn't matter if no one loves me. I'll still be sitting there.

I want to kill that asshole.

Especially after he asked me to stay. Which had to be a joke. Some prank cis boys grow up playing on each other. *He smiled when he said it.* He couldn't have known that crawling in beside him would put my life in his hands. That the moment he pushed me away and said, *Just kidding*, he'd crush my soul.

I need to strike back. Somehow.

Ms. Guo smiles when I walk into Ben and Naomi's house. I grin when she says, "Hi, Jeremy," like it's just my name and not a foreign weight in her mouth. I exhale. I'm not going to have to justify my existence to her. It's always a toss-up with friends' parents.

"Naomi's out at the store," she continues as I pull off my shoes. "She'll be back in five minutes. Do you want something to drink?"

"Thanks," I say, quickly glancing at the time on my phone. "Actually, I'm here to see Ben." I don't want to be alone with Naomi, especially knowing Lukas cheated on her. I don't know what I'll do about that, but she deserves to hear the truth from him. I know Lukas. He'll come clean.

"He's up in his room, working on his student government project. How are your college applications going? I keep telling your mother she needs to hire this SAT coach I know—"

"Applications are going just peachy." I fake a smile, back out of the room, and run upstairs.

When I slide into Ben's bedroom, he's got a document pulled up on his laptop titled "Code of Conduct Updates." Sol's face is on videochat—their parents don't know they drank at the bonfire, but they did break curfew and got sentenced to their room for the rest of the weekend. Trying to sneak them in the back window when I dropped them at home was *not* a smart idea. They're bummed they can't make it—it's the first time in months they've been invited to hang out with friends on a weekend.

"The current rules protect harassers like Brandon Kyle," they're saying as Ben and I drop down on his bed, in a room so full of sports trophies and Scout camp photos it leaves my heart aching for the boyhood I won't get. "Three girls went to Meehan about him, and she said there wasn't enough proof he'd physically hurt them to equal a Code violation."

Three. I shiver. Would I have been enough to change Meehan's mind? I know she said she wants Cresswell students deciding the standards we hold our peers to, which sounds great on paper, but I hate that we have to do all this work to secure the protection we should already have.

"You told Debbie about this meeting, right?" I say, pulling up a chair to Ben's desk.

He nods. "I texted her. She said she didn't want to come."

"Is she still pissed at me?"

"Uh. She said, 'Tell Jeremy that whatever he's doing won't work.'"

Vote of confidence. "We're supposed to be the leaders of this school. If we can't make this work, who can? So, let's roll up our sleeves and get down to business. Now. Where do we start?"

"What I heard in the forum," Ben says, "is that because the rules are so weak, no one ever gets punished—which discourages people from reporting violations even when they're serious."

"Exactly," Sol says. "No one thinks the administration will help. The old president of the GSA, back in my freshman year, told me I'd only outscored him on a calculus test because me and Ms. Newport were both Latinx. He was also the one who kicked the bisexuals out of the club. He wanted it only to belong to rich cis white gay guys. I wrote up a list of what I wanted him to change to make the club more welcoming, and he ripped it up in front of me. I had to leave until Hannah took over. I never even imagined I could report him."

"Ouch," I say. "Fucking asshole. How can we update the Code of Conduct to cover that?"

We dive into the archaic document, cutting out all references to gentlemen and Christianity. We begin by redefining harassment as targeted behavior, done with the intention of forcing other students out of participating fully in school life; then we draft a section on hate speech, clarifying that it's targeted at historically marginalized groups.

"The historical part is important," Sol says. "We don't want any white kids accusing people of hate speech for calling them out on racist bullshit."

Finally, we get into recommendations for discipline. None of us can really decide on one solid plan for how harassers should be punished. I'm all for zero-tolerance expulsion, but Ben says Meehan will never go for it and Sol adds it could easily be weaponized against people I don't mean for it to hurt. They suggest mandatory counseling, with options for the victims to separate themselves from the harasser—but I'm worried that puts too high a demand on victims. *Philip knows what he's doing is wrong, and all the counseling in the world won't change his mind.* At last, we agree that this is something the administration should handle case by case—but that they need to be transparent about their decision-making processes and justify their choices.

At last, we email Meehan our updated Code, along with our transcript from the meeting and our rationale for how the changes will improve student life. A warm glow builds in my gut as I sprawl back across Ben's bed, weighing all I've accomplished. This is leadership. This is what the students of Cresswell elected me to do. It may be too late to impress Debbie, but I can at least get the rest of them on my side.

I ignore the feeling that there's a wave building over my head, about to crash down.

As I drive to school Monday morning, I fly too fast over a speedbump and something rattles in my passenger side door. I pull over and dig around, feeling beneath the rubber lining of the cupholder.

Lukas's wallet. He must have dropped it when I drove him home after the bonfire. I slip it into my backpack, ignoring how the leather is worn in the exact shape of his hand. Hands that used to cup my cheek when I snuggled against his shoulder. My face tingles at the memory. My heart does a sad lurch sideways.

It's just pre-Homecoming nerves, I tell myself as I park and walk inside. Lukas's Homecoming Committee has strung a thirty-foot-long banner over the school's main double doors, powder blue against red brick. *Welcome, Alumni, to Homecoming Week!* The air is crisp with early fall. It feels like anything can happen. The looming brick building, upper-story towers like eyes, is holding its breath.

I don't have my tux, so I've decided to flip Formal Dress Day—the first of the five spirit days—on its head. I'm wearing pajama bottoms and an oversized T-shirt—I'll kill them with my formal dress skills at the dance; no need to get hasty. As ever, my hair is neatly combed and parted—well, I've shaved it so short it can't do anything else. I don't want people thinking I got out of bed this way.

But people smile and give me thumbs-ups as I enter, crowds parting as I glide into the atrium, so I know it's working.

The voting is live. Any student can log in to the school

website and pick from a long list of choices for the Homecoming Court. Lukas, I hiss through my teeth as I realize, has won the coveted spot at the top of the candidate list for Homecoming King—but I'm right beneath him. Sol, the lone underclassman who stepped forward, has been listed on both the king and queen ballot. I'm not sure if that'll piss them off or crack them up.

It's really happening, I realize as I vote for myself, getting that little frisson of joy down my spine that comes whenever I see my real name on paper. I did it. I walked through hell and back, and now I'm on a fast track to glory. Underclassmen, total strangers, walk up to tell me that I've got their vote. That they loved my posters, that they're grateful I got people talking in my open forum. Even if Lukas sabotaged my free pizza giveaway and rubbed those old photos in their faces, people trust me, trans me, and want to reward me with their vote.

I'm on a high—until I walk out for lunch and run into Lukas by my locker.

That fuckhead stole my idea.

My cheer team crowds around him, a flourish of bright silks and satins; Naomi wears her elegant mermaid gown from last year's Homecoming. He's decided it would be fun to come in loose boxers and a Cresswell cheer sweatshirt—my stolen sweatshirt. He stops dead in his tracks as our eyes meet. That stupid gold hoop still glints in his nostril. I want to rip it free and see him bleed.

"Copycat." He laughs, rolling his eyes.

"I'm not the one who stole the idea to run for Homecoming King." I consider waving his missing wallet in his face, maybe running off to the nearest bathroom and flushing it. The only reason I don't pull it out is because I know he can beat me in a footrace.

"Did your parents like your new face?" I ask. "If you were my son, I wouldn't let you leave the house until you'd either taken it out or gotten six more." Facial piercings is a look you really need to commit to.

"If you were mine, I'd make you do your hair with something other than an electric razor. Are you scared of having to comb it?"

I pause. I'm proud of this hair, and I want to stand up for it—but the warm, slick humor in his voice knocks me off balance. All I can think is *hair* and *razor* and *he's looking at me*. I can't even summon a snappy retort.

With a wink, Lukas pushes past me.

Well. Maybe I'll hang on to his wallet just a little longer.

Naomi pauses as he goes, reaching into the locker next to mine to pull out a book.

"Hey, Jeremy?" she says, biting her lip. "You were the one who drove Lukas home after he got messed up at the bonfire, right?"

I nod. What's she giving me that look for?

"Did you . . . you know. When you brought him home. Did you two hook up?"

"What?" My eyebrows shoot up. I laugh, then bite it back. She looks so serious. "Hell, Naomi, I know you're pissed at me, but I'm not going to steal your Homecoming date just because we're arguing."

"I don't think you'd steal him. I think he might want to go back to you. I think he misses you." She swallows. "I mean, I miss you."

Whoa. I stop dead in my tracks. That's the last thing I ever expected to hear her say. "Are you here to talk to me about you and Lukas, or you and me?"

"All of it, I guess? It's all linked together. I think . . . I think I made a mistake, trying to date Lukas. He's a great guy, but everyone agrees you shouldn't move in on your friends' exes— and now I get why. I feel like I've stepped into the middle of this massive drama."

"Sorry about that," I mutter. I'm almost shocked how quick *sorry* comes out. But if there's any flaw of mine it's easy owning up to, it's my penchant for drama.

"I want things to be all right between us. Lukas and I spent the whole bonfire talking about you, before . . . well, you know. You've always been the person I've come to, with school stuff, cheer stuff, whenever I argued with my mom."

"And I haven't been much help lately," I admit, thinking back to this summer. "The day you got your SAT results . . . I handled that wrong, too. I think I could have made room for both of us to talk about our problems if I'd pulled my head out of my ass. Same thing with the banner. I got all wrapped up in myself, didn't think about you or anything—I'm sorry about that, too. I never meant to hurt you." Now that I've said the first apology, it comes out easier.

"Thanks," she grunts. But her shoulders are still tight with tension. Her brown eyes dart away when I try to make contact. "But . . . shit. Jeremy, it's *really* nice to hear you say sorry, but it's more than that. More than just this summer. I don't want to feel like I'm the only one fighting for our friendship, the only one who cares. I want things to be right between us, but I'm not sure how we can be friends again unless things change. Unless you also want things to change."

My throat tightens. My stomach churns. I don't know if I can do that. Shifting between genders suddenly feels ten times easier than what she asks of me. Being a boy comes naturally to me. Being a good friend is so much harder.

"I'll try," I say. "I . . . I promise."

"Okay," Naomi says quietly, closing her locker and ducking away. I'm left alone, with a lunch box full of cold lasagna and a sinking feeling in my stomach. Like the gulf between us is only stretching wider.

The marching band parades through the hallways at lunch, nearly stepping on me and the GSA as we plot which hairdos we'll wear to the dance. They'll do this every day until the Homecoming game, just as I'll cheer every afternoon. I cut out of seventh period early to change into my cheer uniform for the first of the week's five pep rallies. This time, I'm brave enough to use the right locker room, my knife hidden in my sleeve, just in case. It's nearly abandoned at this time of day, the maze of tall lockers shielding me from sight, though a freshman is weeping in a far corner, and the sound sets my teeth on edge. *I can do this. I'm brave enough. I will pull this off.*

I change, and nothing bad happens. The tightness in my chest loosens a fraction.

Voices ring out near the main doors, a big pack of boys. To stay on the safe side, I duck out the locker room back door into an alley, my bag swinging loose over my shoulder. As I jog around the main building, making my way back to the gym, I cross paths with Terry, unpacking crates at the school loading dock.

"Nice haircut!" he yells. "Haven't seen you around in ages—"

And then he drops my deadname. I wheel around, hands balling into fists, already bracing for fight or flight. That name is a stab in my spine, a high-pitched scream in my ears. A warning that, despite the haircut, clothes, and hormones, everyone is looking at me and seeing her ghost.

"How's being a college dropout working for you, Terry?" I spit, and he stumbles back against the dingy side of his truck. It may not be fair—he doesn't go here anymore; he wouldn't have heard that I transitioned—but fair and sensible can wait until I'm not on fire. "Still hanging around your old high school, I see? Twenty-one, and you still don't have a fucking life?"

"Wow," he says. "You're feisty. I'm just trying to be nice."

He's right. I can't blame Lukas for choosing him. Because

no matter who Lukas likes, girls or boys or anyone else, he couldn't like the hostile, angry, real me. The real me isn't safe for liking.

Burning his wallet outside the boys' locker room tonight will make all of this better. The venom in that thought, almost sulfur, warms me to my core—and fades. I could tell Terry that Lukas begged me to spend the night after the bonfire. Ruin their relationship. *No Naomi, no Terry—looks like we're both going alone to Homecoming.*

But I don't want to drag him down to my level of lonely. I've hurt him enough.

"Give this back to Lukas." I pull the wallet from the bag and stuff it into his hands. "Tell him I don't want to see him or talk to him or answer his texts, but I want him to be happy. I want both of you to be happy." *I want to rip off your skin and wear it as a suit.*

Then I march off to the gym, slamming the door behind me. Because a cheerleader never lets anyone see him cry. I do my routine and call the names of the players. Ben gives me a thumbs-up as I reach him. I skip over the cheer for Philip, though, and the wolflike stare he gives me says he knows. Says he wants to make me regret it.

I'll never regret anything that hurts him.

The canned food sculptures are wheeled across the vinyl floor. Students flank them in ball gowns, suits, and one extremely handsome Edwardian cravat. The seniors' Superman bust is a work of art; I nod appreciatively at his tuna-blue broad shoulders. The juniors tried to build a xenomorph for their sci-fi sculpture, but the result resembles a giant turd. The sophomores' can dragon is at least dragon-shaped, though I don't think their class has a single idea to fit their fantasy theme other than covering everything in dragons. The freshmen stand beside their tiny-but-proud magnifying glass, holding it up as it wobbles.

I parade around the gym, gesturing at each sculpture in turn with my pom-poms as the crowd cheers for their favorites. I flourish at Superman, and a wall of sound slams over me, cheers and crashing, stomping feet. The juniors and sophomores don't even try to match us. By the time I reach the wobbling magnifying glass, a triumphant roar of "Seniors! Seniors!" echoes off the gym roof.

"Victory to the seniors!" Meehan declares at my elbow. Then, quietly, she adds, "Nice job, Jeremy. You're really holding up well under all this attention."

I'm a cheerleader. I thrive on attention. It's my chest and hips I want to hide from the world, not myself. "Thanks. Did you get a chance to read the student government's proposed changes to the Code of Conduct?"

She stiffens. Her voice shifts. Still warm, but . . . strained. Like I've somehow stepped on her foot. "I did. And I'm so proud of you. You drafted it much faster and more thoroughly than I could have imagined."

I exhale. It worked. Everything we've put in will pay off. But . . . "So, you'll sign off on it?"

"I . . . yes, hopefully. I want to run it past the board of trustees, and the legal team will want to make sure it doesn't open us to any liability—"

"Why would having more rules make the school more vulnerable to a lawsuit?" Who does she think might sue Cresswell?

"Trust me, Jeremy. We'll implement the changes. One day. I've just got to push them through a few layers of school bureaucracy, and—"

I grind my sneaker hard against the gym's rubber floor, squeaking as it leaves a dark stain behind. "You said, when I brought up the idea of changes, that you could sign off. Nothing about trustees or lawyers."

"Well. Yes, in theory. But I don't want to make it look like I'm making decisions that favor students like you. A principal has to be a neutral, objective party—I can't take political sides."

I jerk away from her. *Students like you.* My shoulder bumps into the magnifying glass sculpture. In a clatter of tin, cans rain down and strike my head and shoulders. My ears ring. A freshman curses in a squeaky voice.

"I told you to use glue!" Lukas shouts on the sideline, rushing over to sweep the cans back into a pile. Two have burst, spilling black beans across the floor. Meehan sighs and goes to wave down a janitor. The freshmen give me dirty looks from their section of the bleachers. I've likely lost votes over this. I don't care.

Students like me. Doesn't she understand that every day we delay hurts more students? An abstract matter for trustees and lawyers makes all the difference for students here. It's not political to protect kids. There shouldn't be sides.

But I can't dwell on that long, not as my heart does jumping jacks up my airway, not as my lungs threaten to flutter shut. Philip will be coming back for me. How can I fight back when all the power at Cresswell is on his side?

"Jeremy." Lukas corners me as I try to sneak out the back of the gym, blocking my exit with his hands on his hips. A pack of freshmen coming our way pivot and take another door once they see us. "I hate to ask. Really, I do. But I haven't seen my wallet since the bonfire, and I really need it. Did I leave it in your car?"

"I already did you one favor at the bonfire. Don't ask for another." I've got no room for softness left in me now.

"This isn't about me. There's a debit card in there linked to the Homecoming fund. Like, thousands of dollars. If it gets in the wrong hands, we could lose it all. I need that back. Now. Without it, I can't make the final arrangements for the dance. Even if it doesn't get canceled, it'll probably suck."

"And wouldn't that be too bad for you?" I snap. Pushing away that brief, tantalizing closeness from the bonfire. Hammering him with the wrath I can't throw at Meehan. "How would everyone decide to crown you king if you ruined the dance? Well, at least you'd have a chance to get a better wallet.

That fake snakeskin one I bought you in middle school does nothing for your aesthetic."

"You stole my wallet," he says, realization slowly dawning on his face. "You . . . if I lose that money, they'll cancel Homecoming."

His new boyfriend will give him the wallet in an hour or so. Homecoming's in no actual danger. But even though I told Terry I want them to be happy, I grin, because I know that pisses him off. "Maybe I want that."

I shouldn't be snapping at him. It's Meehan I'm pissed at. But Meehan won't listen or act to protect me.

If I have no power at Cresswell, at least I have power to make Lukas sweat.

CHAPTER NINETEEN: LUKAS

My worst nightmare has come true. Not the one about all my pencils snapping during the SAT—the one where my unhinged ex steals my wallet.

I spent the whole weekend looking for it, when I wasn't setting up the gym for the five successive pep rallies. All PE classes will be held out on the fields until Homecoming week is over. Of course, it'll take all week to completely transform the cafeteria for the dance, which is what I work on Monday evening after practice. I have the perfect picture in my head—streamers hanging high above each class's Homecoming mural, gold spray paint covering the dais where the court will sit. *Where I'll sit.* Max and I spend all afternoon building a massive wooden phoenix while fifty volunteers make tissue-paper flowers to cover it. A pizza delivery shows up around sundown, when I'm covered in sweat and the model is covered by flowers. The timer app on my phone swirls down below the four-day mark.

"How are we paying for all this?" Debbie asks me. "Have you taken up stripping, Lukas?" She thumbs the side of her nose.

I sigh. Everyone's been asking about the piercing. People are gossiping about it online. A distressingly high number of those posts theorize I've lost my fucking mind. Only one or two allow that I'm making a fashion statement. When Naomi and I walked around at lunch, just as she's planned, smiling and asking for votes, people happily promised to support her. But eyes flickered to my face before they'd promise me the same. Like one hole and a bit of wire diminishes everything else I've done for this school.

"Everything's fine," I tell Debbie. "I put it against the Homecoming budget. I gave them the card number when I set up the delivery."

The card I still need to get back from Jeremy.

I whip out my phone and text the little asshole.

Lukas Rivers: What will it take to get my wallet back?

Jeremy Harkiss: Suck my dick

Lukas Rivers: Is that an invitation?

I regret hitting Send as soon as my finger smashes down. I might have sent him that when we were together. But I've messed up too many times. He's made it heartbreakingly clear he doesn't want me.

And he doesn't reply.

He's bluffing, I tell myself. *He'll give the wallet back. At least, he'll give back the debit card. He wouldn't actually get the dance canceled. He wouldn't go that far.* But for all I know—for all I know of the person he's become—he's already charged fifty thousand pairs of sunglasses on the damn thing and arranged for all of them to be delivered to my doorstep. Sol doesn't reply, either, when I text them pleading for the answer key for this week's AP Bio test. I tried, last week, to take it on Dr. Coryn's terms. I tried my hardest and got a 32 percent. I need to turn this around so colleges see at least a B on my first quarter report card. A B won't hurt me too badly, once I can put *Homecoming King* on my application. But Sol is still upset over the video thing.

And then I get an idea. A masterstroke of a plan. Leeching worry about the missing debit card fades away.

I'm going to get some answers. I'm going to give everyone at Cresswell what they need. And I'm going to win my throne.

Because everyone in this school agrees Dr. Coryn's AP Bio class absolutely sucks.

Tuesday is Future You, Past You Day. We're supposed to dress like the careers we want—costumes symbolizing our pasts are also allowed, but the senior class, at least, is looking forward. Lots of people wear shirts with tech company logos or university names. A junior who loves marine biology has built themself a life-sized fishbowl. I wear a white T-shirt with a question mark drawn in Sharpie as I take Naomi—in a doctor's coat—out to the diner.

I build up my courage and get us a table by the gumball machine. Terry winks at me as I enter, staring straight past Naomi, whose arm is woven through mine. He's not jealous of her—it's like he doesn't see her at all. He laughs in the bottom of his throat as she orders a salad and I order a BLT. "Girls and salad. Am I right?"

"Don't be an ass," I say, and he shakes his head and ducks back into the kitchen.

In the shelter of the gumball machine, with no milkshake in sight, I find the courage to take Naomi's hand. My heart thuds. *Show her you're a good boyfriend. Say something flirty. Smooth. Confident.* But the façade I've crafted, the mask Jason always pushed me to wear, the perfect straight boyfriend I think she wants from me—I can't hold on. Can't be pulled in one more direction without risking a snap.

"Lukas? What are you doing?"

I realize my fingers are wrapped around her palm like I'm holding a poisonous snake. Frozen that way.

"I like your nail polish," I say, and let go. Terry won't stop staring at me as he brings out the food. Naomi won't stop staring at me as I jam the sandwich in my mouth to avoid talking. Neon lights paint pink lines over my hands as I stare at them and try not to think.

I don't know what I am. I need to know. I need to put a label on myself. I need something to hold on to. I'm attracted to Terry—stupidly so, but attracted. I'm hung up on Jeremy—again, stupidly, because he doesn't want me. Naomi and I make sense. Maybe I'm bisexual. Pansexual. One of the two. Maybe I do like girls. I had crushes on girls in middle school, before Jeremy and I started dating. If I can be attracted to girls, to Naomi, then it doesn't matter who I want, who I kissed in the woods. If my grandparents will dance around me dating a boy and my parents are too caught up in their own drama to care, then what will it matter how I form a family?

Only, it matters to me. Matters more to me than bending every piece of myself to please someone else.

"I don't want to date you," I say, croaking out the words. I'm not sure how to do this. I've never broken up with someone before, and I don't want to be as awful as Jeremy was. "I'm sorry. I'm trying to be gentle—I mean, Jeremy was a real ass when he did this to me. He just was, and it sucks—but I kissed someone else at the bonfire. I'm sorry. You need to know. And you need to know you deserve better."

Her eyes swell with tears.

"I'm sorry," I say. "I'm so—"

"Don't." She holds up a hand to stop me. Lets out an absurd, tiny little laugh. "You don't need to say anything more. I get it, okay? It's fine. It's all fine." Tears streak down her cheeks, running silently through her mascara. I hold out my napkin, offering it up as a tissue. "No, thank you. I've just never felt so embarrassed—"

She slides out of her chair and runs back to the bathroom.

I wince, strangely relieved as the weight of her expectations lifts off me. *Thank god. I don't have to pretend anymore.* I drop a twenty on the table and head back to the grill.

"What's up, Lukas?" Terry flashes his missing tooth as he grins. I flinch and look away, almost stumbling into a family toting birthday balloons. He's trouble. Just because I'm trying to figure out what I want doesn't mean I should chase the guy I want for terrible reasons. But I can push the line one more time. Dr. Coryn and Jeremy, somehow functioning in concert, have left me with no other option.

"I know you do deliveries to Cresswell for your other job," I mumble. "I need to borrow your master key."

"Sure thing, hot stuff. Can you do me a favor in return?"

"What sort of favor?" A warm rumble fills my voice. Maybe I'm not as bad at flirting as I always thought. "I have limits, you know."

"Could you tell me what year you were born? I already tried—I mean, I already know—your birthday's May eighth. I know a lot about your family from Jason, but I never asked this. You're seventeen, right?"

For a second, I wonder why he's asking. Then it comes together. "Don't worry. I'm legal. Eighteen." I roll my eyes.

It's gross he didn't ask if I was of age before kissing me, but I guess neither of us were thinking. "I was born in 2003."

"Damn. Glad to know that." He reaches under the table and pulls out a lanyard. "Go wild. Do whatever you need."

"Thanks," I say, taking it. "I'll get it back to you this afternoon. I'm sure you need it for work."

"Actually, I think I'm going to quit that job. I've come across some money."

"Oh." There's something predatory in his eyes. Something I can't read. "Congrats."

He's still smiling. Naomi's still crying. I leave, because I know my presence is just making things worse. Because I've still got work to do and a need pulling me onward.

Back at Cresswell, the main building is nearly deserted. Shadowy hush fills the hallway, an easy, softer side of the school that blares bright in my daytime hours. I use Terry's key and slide into Dr. Coryn's dark, small corner office. Papers pinned to her corkboard flutter like my heartbeat. I open her desk to find a print copy of the next exam, answers typed in bold font. Quickly, I pull out my phone and take a photo, wincing as the flash goes off. *Victory.* When my classmates realize how much I've done for them, they'll have to give me their votes.

But it doesn't feel like a victory. The question mark on my

shirt feels like an anchor heavy enough to drag me to the bottom of the sea. *What do I want? What am I doing? How can I find balance in a storm of expectations? How can I get Jeremy to give me back my wallet?*

This is Homecoming Week. This is the culmination of years of effort, of everything I've ever worked for and wanted, of me claiming a crown and embarking on a shining journey toward success. To fixing my family and providing for the needs of the people I love.

And I'm running on empty.

CHAPTER TWENTY: JEREMY

At the diner that night, Ben, Sol, and I plan the final push for my campaign. I've sold some of my old earring collection on eBay so I can pay for more printed banners and flyers. The school paper dropped another opinion poll for the court elections. Lukas is surging forward—now at 41 percent to my 44 percent—thanks to the editor banning "Chad Blueballs" as an option. My lead remains, but the poll has a five-point margin of error. I can't afford to get cocky—at least, cockier than I already am.

Sol is also up a few points, which makes me smile. *Hope this election boosts their confidence a little.* They're on two sides of the ballot, meaning the votes for them may be split, but this doesn't seem to bother them.

"I thrive on chaos," they say, dipping a French fry in their milkshake. "I just like knowing I've kicked the ass of the whole concept of gender by pulling this stunt."

"What would you even wear if you won?" Ben says. "A tux or a dress?"

"Probably a leather jacket. Those look good on everyone."

"Even straight people?" Ben questions. "Can I have one?"

"Absolutely not," I say. "At least, not until after I wear mine tomorrow. I got a whole floor-length leather coat for my costume."

"Wasn't your costume today enough of a statement?"

I grin. For my Past You–themed costume, I dressed all in white and fastened an enormous globe of Styrofoam over my head.

"What are you supposed to be?" Ms. Valley said when I entered AP World History.

"My father," I said, almost feeling guilty to make the joke to a lady in her seventies. "Or at least, his biggest contribution to my life."

I was expecting to get formally dress-coded and sent to change. But somehow, she only chuckled. "That's very daring, young man. Very funny."

By the afternoon, I'd realized only girls got dress-coded. If someone didn't get the joke, I just had to explain in my new voice—god, I love the deep and sardonic pitch of it, how it rolls around my throat—and I was golden. A picture of me got seven hundred likes by the afternoon pep rally. Some people dressed up as babies, in diapers and onesies, but I was the only one who went this far. I'm daring, and Cresswell will recognize me with their votes.

As I chow down on my pickle-stuffed diner burger, a red-eyed Naomi slides out from the table near the gumball machine and ducks into the bathroom. Biting his lip awkwardly, Lukas stands and walks to the counter.

Shit. Something's wrong. I get up and follow her to the door. My hand catches the lever and freezes—the *girls'* bathroom. My dysphoria is a tight red knot of *no* in my throat, screaming that, even though I've pissed here a dozen times, this threshold is where I now stop.

"Naomi?" I call through the door. My voice cracks. "Are you okay? What happened?"

Nothing but sniffling.

"Do you want me to murder Lukas for you?" I say. The kiss. Terry. The woods. "Because I'm seriously thinking about it. I know what he did, and I'm glad he didn't lie about the truth." This feels like my responsibility, too. Even with Lukas, people don't fall in love after just a few dates. She's crying because she's been embarrassed. Because, once again, one of her stupid guy friends hasn't thought about her feelings before lowering his head and charging, bighorn-sheep-style, at the dumb thing he wants. "Naomi? Please. Talk to me. I know I haven't been a good friend this year, but I want to be. I want to be here for you."

But she doesn't reply. And after a few minutes, Ben joins us. "You okay, sis?"

"I'm fine," she mutters. "Leave me alone."

I grab Ben's arm. "She's not fine. Listen to her. She's

obviously not fine! We need to do something." I raise my voice. "Naomi! Come on out and we can go pick up those pastel highlighters you love at Staples!"

Ben sighs. "Sometimes girls just need to cry about this stuff. You literally can't fix it all right away."

I'm about to snap, *I know how girls think, dumbass*, when I realize I don't, not quite, not like this. I can only see my own pain and heartbreak through my eyes, and as important as that is to me, my views will never be Naomi's. I want to fix her problems, instead of listen. *How like a guy.*

It's terrible how much that thought cheers me up. I decide to give Naomi some space and cross my fingers that she'll come to me when she's ready.

"Did you make it worse?" Debbie hisses as I pass her table on the way back. The blond wig from her costume—Debbie swears Past Her was Grace Kelly in another life—lies atop her stacks of textbooks. She's ordered a burger, but she's not even touching it.

"I tried to comfort my friend," I say. "Sorry if I'm not always as good at things as you expect me to be. You'll be happy to know Meehan is delaying all changes to the Code of Conduct until, like, a billion lawyers sign off."

"No, that doesn't make me happy. I expected it, though. It's so stupid. She wouldn't have expelled Brandon Kyle if five hundred people had reported him. She spews all this faux-feminist bullshit when it helps her image and won't raise a finger to help the girls at school who need her."

"But I'm the one who betrayed all women, right?" I jab my thumb at my chest. "Me. I'm the problem."

"Oh my god. This isn't about you, Jeremy."

"But it is. I've got just as much at stake here as you do. Not being a girl doesn't protect me from being treated like one—from the worst parts of being treated like one. Both of us are stuck in a system that'll throw us to the wolves if we cause too much trouble."

Her face turns red beyond her cherry lipstick. "What do you want me to say? That fixing Cresswell is impossible because Principal Girl Power values pleasing the rich-boy alumni network over protecting students?"

"Nothing's impossible if we work as a team. We're cheerleaders. We should know that. We can deal with people like Brandon and Philip together." I sigh. "I should have helped you report him, back in sophomore year. I was ashamed, okay? I felt so small and stupid. I just wanted to forget. I thought I could forget. But then Philip came after me, and—"

"Philip." A note of guilt flickers into her voice. She looks away from me. "I . . . You're right. You didn't exactly do all this to get your hands on some shiny male privilege. I thought a girl leading student government would mean someone important at Cresswell would finally listen to me about these problems. But I never tried to listen to you about yours. I'm sorry." She adds, so quiet I can barely hear, "Maybe I was just angry at you because you were safer to be mad at than Meehan."

"I know the feeling," I mutter. "It's not all on you. Ben and I messed up, too. We should have had women involved with writing the resolution and organizing the forum. We all need to listen to each other."

"Yeah, you fucked up." She gives me a small, but genuine, smile. "Friends?"

"Friends." I hug her, one arm around her shoulders, and walk away smiling.

It's a weird world, where Debbie will talk to me and Naomi won't. But I'll take whatever friends I can get.

I can't help build a better Cresswell if I let my anger rule me. Debbie's hurt me, but if she's willing to listen and do better, I can do the same for her. I can put what she said behind me.

It should feel like surrender. Like weakness.

But I don't feel smaller after our hug. For the first time in weeks, I feel my feet rest on solid ground.

When I get home, the whole Cresswell internet swarms with spirit day costumes. I click through the best of them. Mine got some nice attention, and even the comments look favorable—lots of laughing emojis and GIFs, and enough comments about how people think I'm brave and want to vote for me for Homecoming King that I don't have to worry that the laughter is directed at me. *Brave. They think I'm brave.* A word that belongs to tough guys in movies, the sort of guy Philip pretends he is. But my masculinity is equal to his any day. Even without Meehan behind me, he hasn't won yet.

My *Matrix* cosplay comes perfectly together the next day.

Long leather trench coat, cool shades, black leather sweeping down to the floor. The rest of the GSA and I pose for pictures at Sol's house that morning, since we can't bring our toy weapons to school. Naomi and the other cheerleaders outscore us on the morning round of likes, since she's coordinated them all into dressing up as Disney princesses. Still, my costume gives me the confidence I need to sweep into AP Gov Wednesday morning and retake the podium.

"Last week's fire drill interrupted us," Mr. Ewing says. "But I'm happy to have rescheduled Jeremy's presentation on transgender rights for today."

I smile at my teacher. A wide, toothy grin. I'm not sure why he put trans rights on the topic list. But I refuse to give him the performance he craves.

"I'm not going to justify why you should respect me," I say, hopping on the little step stool hidden behind the podium. It doesn't bring me quite level with the mic. Whatever. My voice is a wreck, a disaster, but it's always been strong. "Once my life becomes a topic of argument, I've already lost. I'm going to talk about Homecoming instead. I'm going to defend the idea of having a Homecoming Court."

"You were supposed to work on these speeches for weeks!" Mr. Ewing says. "You can't improvise a whole speech at the last minute."

I shrug. "Watch me." In the back of the classroom, Ben nods in approval. I give him a grateful smile and lean in to the mic.

"Homecoming. Like BlackBerry phones or Rickrolling, it's an outdated tradition thrust upon high schoolers across the country. So why does Cresswell spend all this time, money, and effort electing a Homecoming Court? This school has got *real* problems to deal with. The absence of organic veggies in the cafeteria, our abysmal football record." I pause before going in for the kill. "The fact that a small group of students can harass half the school without consequence."

Mr. Ewing reaches for the mic. "Jeremy," he says. "The assignment was to talk about an important social issue."

I pivot, keeping the mic in my fist. "This is an important social issue. Because it affects all of us. And the truth is, there are plenty of people at Cresswell who want to fix things, who want to make this school safe for everyone. But that doesn't matter. Not when Principal Meehan and our alumni network oppose any change. They're afraid to start arguments over their country club brunches and lose donations from rich old white people who see our school as nothing but a playground for reliving their glory days." At that line, hisses, whispers, and a slow clap rise from the back row.

"That's enough, young la—young man," Mr. Ewing says. "Don't talk about Principal Meehan that way. Show some respect."

"You didn't show me any respect when you put trans rights on the topic list," I say. "When you forced me to stand up here and tell the whole class why I deserve to exist or, worse, listen to anyone argue why I *don't*. Nothing I say could hurt

Meehan or the school administrators. I have no power over them. The only way to have influence in this place is to play by their rules, and they can change the rules whenever they want."

My words come out glib, sarcasm edged hot-red like cinnamon candy. I followed Meehan's instructions to amend the Code of Conduct, trusting that if I did my share of the work, she'd do hers. But she didn't want to change anything. She just wanted me to stop complaining. And if that's what the Cresswell leadership wants most, how will anything get better?

"But that's why we *need* the Homecoming Court," I continue. "Because it's one of the few things at Cresswell where we students get a say. Vote for me, and I'll use the platform of that win to keep applying pressure, to get them to hear us when we say we don't feel safe, we don't deserve to be harassed or disrespected." Beneath the tide of adrenaline I'm riding on, pacing the floor in case Mr. Ewing tries to take the mic again, the promise I'm making feels exhausting. Like I'm committing myself to pushing back, alone, until the day I graduate. But what other choice do I have?

"I thought when I started this campaign," I finish, "it would be enough to make Cresswell forget I was trans. To make you all just see me as another boy. Now I'm wondering why I bothered. Why I felt I needed to distance myself from what—from who I am—to win. Vote for me and vote to put a trans boy on the court. Vote for Philip Cross's worst nightmare. But most of all, vote to change Cresswell in the only way we can." I drop the mic on the podium. Static squeals through the classroom. Everyone claps their hands to their ears. "Sorry. But not sorry. You know."

"Thank you, Jeremy." Mr. Ewing takes back the mic. "Does anyone have any questions?"

"Yeah," says Aninda Sinha, in the first row. "Jeremy, if the system is as messed up as you say it is, how will making you Homecoming King do anything to change it? Won't Principal Meehan just ignore you harder?"

I flinch. Because she's right. I could move mountains, and Meehan could say, *That's nice, but the mountain trustees are upset.* Everything I've been through these past few weeks, everything I've done—making up with Debbie, working with Ben and Sol to fix the outdated Code, trying to handle my rage—seems so small and useless.

"Maybe," I say. "It's just . . . this is the only solution I can think of."

The classroom falls quiet. Ben says, "We've got this," but his words ring hollow in the empty air.

"D minus," Mr. Ewing says. "For going off topic. I sympathize with your points, Jeremy, but you didn't do the assignment as listed."

I nod. Then I slink back to my seat and bury my head in my hands.

It feels like I'm fighting to fix Cresswell all alone. And I'm losing.

I skip out of senior courtyard lunch to stick up our final post-ers. I've got a strict list of guidelines from the fire warden about where I can and can't post things, and I intend to follow them. But this is my final push, and I slam photos of my own lovely face—taken at literally the only angle where I don't feel dys-phoric as fuck—all over the school walls. I'm working on a back hall near the auditorium when Philip corners me. Wear-ing his ROTC uniform as a costume for a second day in a row.

"Hello—" And he deadnames me. Again.

I give him my best smile. The name doesn't really hurt from him. I know he means to cut. When he uses it, it has nothing to do with whether or not I'm passing, whether or not he sees me. It's just another arrow in his quiver. "Actually, it's Neo. Don't you have better things to do with your time than mess with me?"

"You're the one who's messed up. You think meds and sur-gery can turn you into something you're not." He leans in close. "I'm not sure if it was your doctors who pushed you into it or your feminist mom, but someone's got a very sick mind to do this to you."

"It took months of evaluations from doctors to get testos-terone, Philip," I point out. "I wanted this. This is me. Stop listening to the conspiracy theories your buddies feed you and listen to literally *anything* else. Do your parents not even care what you're up to?" Wrong question. Philip's parents made a small fortune off war and violence. They probably don't give a damn what he believes, so long as he can make it sound nice and polite at home. "Stop fantasizing about what you think might be wrong with me and worry about your own shit. *Think*. Why do I piss you off so much?"

He pauses. I hold my breath. I'm not even quite sure what I'm doing, why I'm even trying to reach him. But I want to believe there's some magic combo of words I can unlock to stop him. Like a cheat code in a video game. Like the red wire you snip to defuse a bomb.

Philip's fists tighten. His brow sinks low over his narrowed eyes. "Look at this school. Diversity festivals and after-school clubs to talk about your feelings. There's no space left here for real men. So I'll make room for myself. Whatever it takes."

"You want to know the truth?" I laugh. It's so ridiculous, the force, the devotion in his eyes. How he feels so oppressed simply when the whole world doesn't center him, because he's never known real oppression. "No matter how many people you push down, you still won't feel like a real man."

He flinches. I grin. For a heartbeat, I'm on top of the world, cheeks flushed with victory.

But all my clever words can't talk me out of this one.

Philip lunges forward and punches me in the face.

The world flashes. White. Red. I stumble, ears ringing, sense of gravity gone. The school is floating loose around me, and I'm untethered.

I slam down.

If only my stupid antiharassment project had worked is all I can think as I lie on the floor, blood filling my mouth. If only—

His boot slams into my tailbone. Pain rocks my world. I slide down the hall like a hockey puck, scramble to my feet, and run.

Get away. Get away. The stairs flash before me as my knees jerk up and down, propelling me away. He chases behind, scrambling, breathing hard, heavy and strong. I run like I've never run before, sprinting through abandoned halls, diving blindly for safety—

I hurtle into a bathroom and lock myself in a stall. Pull my feet up onto the toilet, curl into a ball. Waiting. Listening. I hear his footsteps outside, panting—but he doesn't come in.

It's okay. I'm alive. I'm alive. Breathe. This is harder than it should be. I think my nose is broken. Snot and blood dribble down my face. I think of my stepfather, tall and threatening and powerful, laughing over me as I cry.

God, I want to feel powerful. I want the rush my anger gives me, and the certainty lent by my knife that I can keep myself safe. I want to be tall and powerful and cis. *And safe. And safe.* Not like this. Never like this.

When I catch my breath and look down, the blue tulle of a Cinderella dress pokes out beneath the stall divider.

"Naomi?" I slide off the toilet and knock on the stall beside mine. She opens it. Her jaw drops at the sight of my messed-up face.

"Holy *shit*," she mouths, and throws her arms around me. We stand there, lit in the piercing glare of fluorescent lights on tile, holding each other up. Like we should have done from the start.

"I'm getting blood on your dress," I mumble, pulling away.

"Forget the dress—you look like you're literally dying. Who did this?"

I'm glad she asked *who* and not *how*—because if I had room to lie, I might say I'd walked into a door rather than admit another guy had gotten the better of me. "Philip Cross. He—"

My cheeks prickle red as I realize why Naomi is here. Why Philip didn't run in after me. My thoughts, disjointed and panicked, all unspooled and tangled in a muddled mess, kicked in old instinct. I raced into the safety of high school's most ancient haven—the girls' bathroom.

"Fuck off," Naomi says kindly to a pair of freshman girls staring at my bloody nose in horror. "Tell no one about this." She's already texting like crazy on her phone.

"How are you doing?" I ask. It's clear to me that she wasn't just doing her business in here. She was hiding. "Are you okay with the whole Lukas thing?"

"You just got punched. Forget my drama. It's no big deal."

I should want to scream. To yell, cry, and break something. But all that will do is burn up oxygen and leave us both choking. The only thing that will heal our friendship is me showing I care as much about her as she does for me. "I've forgotten you way too many of the times when you needed me. I'm here now. Are you okay?"

"You're seriously saying it's okay for me to vent at you? Right now?"

"Go right ahead." I try to soften my voice, and say it again. I want her to know she really does matter to me. "You can tell me anything. You're my best friend."

"Wow. I don't think you've ever said that to me." Naomi shakes her head, and suddenly she's tearing up and wiping her running eye shadow. I've left a massive red stain on the front of her ball gown. Her blond wig lies skewed. "I don't know if I'm okay. I've spent three years living in your shadow. Sometimes I worried boys only liked me because you were already taken, you know? That people only liked me because I stood next to you. When you came out, I thought that would change. That I'd finally have a chance to shine, that I'd be the one dating Lukas and winning Homecoming Queen and having all that stuff you got easy."

"Girl, I so understand wanting stuff. But none of that came easy to me."

She wipes her eyes. "I know. I just spent so long thinking I'd be happy if I had everything you did. Then I got it. And it sucked, even before it crumbled into a big, humiliating mess. And now I'm, like . . . do I even believe there's something out there that'll make me happy?"

"Um, duh," I say. "You're super smart and one hell of a cheerleader. You're going to be fine. Just don't try to be the old me. That sucked. Like, sucked so badly I had to give up Lukas just so I could let her go, too." I swallow. This next bit makes me look so pathetically weak, but I need to say it. I need to spit out the truth before it crushes me. "Dumping him wasn't an easy choice, Naomi. I had to. But it nearly killed me. I couldn't stand hearing him dump me because I'm a boy. I couldn't keep dragging him into my messes when he has so many of his own."

"I think it's up to Lukas to choose what messes he gets into. He spent every second of our so-called relationship talking about you. He wants to know what he did wrong and how to fix it. I think the two of you need to have a serious conversation—and you need to tell him everything. Including the fact you're still in love with him."

"I'm not!" I insist.

"I saw you glaring daggers whenever he touched me. You two have been a couple since eighth grade. I see the way you look at him, even when you're screaming in his face. Like he's the most important person in the world to you."

Last summer, I wondered if I only loved him so much because I wanted to be him. But that isn't true. Lukas is calm where I'm angry, thoughtful where I'm rash, trusting where I suspect. We balance each other out. Together, we brought Cresswell to its knees and made it kiss our rings. We were a good team, before I ruined everything. Could we have lasted if I hadn't dumped him at his brother's funeral?

It doesn't matter, I tell myself. *Because I did.*

I hate being a fuckup.

I'd hate even more to lose our friendship.

And I hope I can make things right. Make things better.

"I'm scared," I confess. The words leave my throat small, almost shaking—because I'm admitting I'm a coward, the last thing a real man should be—but it's true, and I breathe easier for saying it. "You said you wanted me to change, to be better. But what if I can't? What if I ask Lukas for another chance and ruin it again? What if I wind up with no friends at all? What if I try to be better and it all ends up worse?"

"Jeremy." She rolls her eyes. Even now, after so long, hearing my name—my right name, real name—grounds me. Her phone beeps, a flurry of text messages. "You don't need to get all dramatic. I have faith you'll figure this out." She sends a final text. "If I didn't, I wouldn't have texted the whole squad to come deal with Philip."

She turns to the door.

"Don't go out there," I say, panicked. "He'll hurt you!"

"I'm not going alone." She gives me a brave smile. "We've got this."

Stepping out of the bathroom, I see the entire cheerleading team has gathered in the hall. Ringing Philip in their ball gowns and wigs. Barricading the hallways to the science wing, to the stairs. Arms folded and pissed as hell. Naomi strides out, covered in my blood, utterly magnificent.

"Philip Cross, you will never lay a hand on Jeremy again,"

she says. "You're going to drop out of Cresswell and leave us all alone."

"Make me," he hisses. The circle of cheerleaders steps inward. He flinches backward. The first flicker of fear crosses his brow.

"No one at this school will speak to you. Ever again." Phones are held high, filming this. My own phone buzzes with a link to a live video:

Sol Reyes-Garcia: The whole school is watching! Look!

"Anyone who dares to talk to you will also get the silent treatment," Naomi continues. "Meehan might not expel you, but I can make your life a living hell."

"You think a bunch of loser social justice warriors ignoring me will shut me up?" he scoffs. "I don't even want to associate with you."

But there's a tremor in his voice. And there's a lot of people in the hall. More of us than him.

A whole community. On my side.

Naomi grins. "Goodbye, Philip." Then she grabs my arm and drags me away. The team collapses around me in a wave of tulle.

CHAPTER TWENTY-ONE: LUKAS

Group Day is always challenging, especially when none of your friends are talking to you. Naomi and the cheerleaders are going as Disney princesses. Jeremy and the GSA dressed up like characters from *The Matrix*. Ben and Max are the Ghostbusters—I texted Ben last night, asking if they needed a third, but he apparently prefers giving me the silent treatment to respecting canon.

So, today, I'm groupless. I came to school in a plain white tee and jeans, telling everyone I met it was an ironic costume, that I'd been invited to multiple groups and I dressed up as an Everyman so I could fit them all. It got me some weird looks—some almost pitying—but I forget all about those when I enter AP Bio.

Students flood out of the classroom from last period, hot whispers rising about the test they'd just taken. "Question five was the worst. It made no sense!" At least three of them clap me on the back and mutter, "Thanks, Lukas," as they pass.

"That would have been so much worse without you," says a skinny underclassman girl dressed as a My Little Pony. "Thanks, Lukas. You've got my vote for Homecoming King."

Nose piercing or not, single or not, I'm finally back in the flow of things. People might like Jeremy's boldness, but I'm the one who gets them what they need. Everyone hates Dr. Coryn's stupid tests. Everyone would have been happy to see the answer key when I emailed it out to the whole AP Bio Listserv. Happy to read *Vote Lukas Rivers for Homecoming King* in the email signature.

I'm not stupid. I set up a burner email account to do it, under the username PhoenixFootballFan128. I wrote *A gift from a Cresswell Alum* in the subject line. Hopefully, everyone thinks I've just got a secret admirer. But even if a few people guess it's me, why would they tell? There's no actual proof it's me, and I'm doing them all a favor. I'm just doing the biggest favor for myself.

I sit down at my desk. Everyone in my period files in, their costumes a riot of fabric, glitter, and plug-in LEDs. Coryn passes out the test, a saccharine grin on her face. Glee practically bursts out of her small frame.

I don't think I've ever seen her smile before.

Her questions are incomprehensible as always—with an extra kick of evil, since she wouldn't even cancel her weekly tests for Homecoming. "Describe chlorophyll, ten points."

Gee, what exactly about it? The chemical structure? Its role and tasks? Thanks to Terry, I can scrawl something down. Question five is a doozy—something about how plant neurons are structured—but I just rattle off the list of answers I memorized from the key and hope it works.

"I swear, this class is going to kill me," I say to a girl dressed as Darth Vader as we leave.

She nods, head bobbing behind her mask. "Thanks for getting those keys out. I don't know what I'd do without them."

"I don't know what you're talking about." I flash a knowing grin. "Say, do I have your vote for Homecoming Court?"

Before she can answer, Ben brushes past me, knocking his proton pack into my side and not apologizing. He looks sad. Tired. Coryn made him take the test in the very back of the room and confiscated his cell phone. Philip dropped the class last week and switched into woodshop.

"You okay?" I start, trying to bridge the gap between us. "You look like a wreck—"

"Because I stayed up all night listening to my sister yell on the phone with Debbie." He sighs. "You cheated on her, you cheated on this test—and you told the whole school about it. PhoenixFootballFan128? Come on. It's so obviously you."

"No one can prove it. And no one really understands what is and isn't obviously me." I duck out into the hallway, trying not to step on the tail of a kid dressed as the back half of a donkey. "I'm sorry about Naomi. I didn't mean to hurt her. But I'm not sorry about doing what I have to do to win."

"There's no winning like this, Lukas. Just, like, drop it. Take an incomplete grade and move on with your life."

Where am I supposed to move on to? This is senior year. This is serious. Colleges will look down on me if they see an incomplete grade on my final report card. Without the homecoming crown and the backing of Cresswell alumni, I have nothing that makes me stand out. While my friends go off to Boston, New York, California, I'll be stuck in Maryland. I'll be all alone with nothing but my family's disappointment to keep me company. It'll be fourth grade all over again. Only this time, they don't have Jason to hang their hopes on.

I'm either a champion or a train wreck. There's no room for me to be anything else.

"I'm sorry, Ben. I know all my drama got you in trouble. I shouldn't have blamed what happened with the answer key on Jeremy. It was a dumb, irresponsible decision. But I can't fix it."

"You can," he says. "If you tell Meehan it was you, I could play in the Homecoming game and get my AP Bio grade back up. You can help, but you won't. That's why I voted for Jeremy." Then he walks away.

Ouch. But I let him go. I also want to make things right between us, but apologies will never be enough to fix this without action.

I don't know how to fix this without everything else crumbling around me. I don't know how to get us back on track when I've screwed up so badly.

I skip out of lunch to decorate the gym. Debbie, in her green Princess Merida gown, is ferociously directing freshmen in the art of twisting paper flowers. The giant wooden phoenix has sprouted spirals of blue tissue paper down its wings. I show a couple more volunteers my plan to tack star-shaped strings of lights to the ceiling and pass out staple guns. One of the janitors expresses doubt in my ability to properly manipulate a ladder; I clamber halfway up the wall and begin tacking up hooks for where the four class banners will hang. On the ground, I give a thumbs-up to the kids sketching banners on a massive roll of butcher paper and head out to the loading dock to pick up the tubs of gold paint. The spinning bars on my timer app whirl down. Two days, eight hours, and twenty-eight minutes left. A stressful knot of symmetry.

Terry isn't there, for which I'm weirdly grateful. I kissed him because I needed something from him, but I'd be happy if snatching his master key was the last time we ever spoke. He's not the sort of relationship I need. He won't push me anywhere but off a cliff.

Then, in fifth period, the announcement comes.

"Attention, students of Cresswell High!" The old PA system whines and groans as it crackles to life. No one really uses it—but that's not why the voice talking to us is so sharp and nasal. It's Dr. Coryn, loud and angry, filtered through the speakers and full of rage. "It has come to my attention that half my students cheated on today's AP Biology exam.

I added a fake question as number five on the exam. Only students who read the fake answer key I created could have answered it."

"Robbing a teacher's office is against Cresswell's honor code," Meehan says, cutting in beside her. "Unless the culprit comes forward, we'll cancel all forthcoming Homecoming activities. Up to and including the dance itself."

Canceling the dance. I squeeze the lip of my desk. Tremors seem to invade my hands, flowing into me from the outside until the world is a fizzing mess of sparks. My stomach plunges like a train car dropping free off a track. *It's over. Everything's over.*

I don't pass out. I don't react at all, in ways anyone can see. But inside, I feel the abyss reach up to claim me. Myself, dropping into empty, hopeless darkness, that same place that's eating up my dad. Where no plastic crown or college admission shines bright enough to lead me out.

Everything I've been working on for weeks, everything I've sacrificed and broken my back for—is going up in billowing smoke.

CHAPTER TWENTY-TWO: JEREMY

Debbie drives me and Naomi to the Quick Care Clinic in the strip mall. "I don't want you driving, Jeremy. You might have a concussion, and you drive stupidly fast even when you're not bleeding out your nose."

"You've never said a word about my driving," I snipe as Naomi pushes me into the backseat.

"I would never mock a girl's driving. You're fair game now."

I stick out my tongue. "You could have taken me to the school nurse."

"She would have given you a lollipop and told you to elevate it. Besides, I want you off campus for a few hours while Philip calms down. And I want me off campus for a few hours, too." Debbie fans herself. "I hate that place."

Naomi says nothing the whole ride over, taut with nerves. "We'll go straight to Meehan once we get back to campus," she says, leading me into the building, already planning our counterattack. "She needs to know."

"She won't do anything," Debbie says. "She never does."

"At some point, even she has to take action," Naomi says. "First, though, we need to know Jeremy is okay."

"I'm fine," I insist as other patients stare at our bloody costumes. My voice swivels nasal, high, and awful. I don't want everyone to know what happened. Shame nags me, blood-tinted. What sort of man can't even get his fists up to defend himself? *If I'd just had more warning—next time, next time I'll get him. I'll show I'm just as strong as he is.* I feel like my asshole stepdad as I think it, and the urge for violence does nothing to fix my nose. But it does slap a patch across my aching selfhood. A weapon and a shield. Reliable and close to hand.

I need to be bigger than my anger. But it's hard when I'm only five foot two.

The world's determined to piss me off today. A nice nurse signs us in. Grudgingly, I turn over my still-not-yet-updated driver's license and health insurance card. Scribble black over the "Gender" option on the sign-in sheet they give me.

"It's so nice to see girls taking care of each other," she remarks, and I stiffen. Naomi slides into motion.

"He's a boy," Naomi says. "Everyone can use someone who'll take care of them."

The nurse in the back room, an older woman who shares the pointed gaze of my grandmother, also misgenders me. When I correct her, she rolls her eyes and says, "Do what you want at school, honey, but here we need your real gender to treat you. Now then. Did your boyfriend hit you?"

"Some Nazi fuck at school."

"My, my. Language. What did you do to make this boy hit you?"

"Existed." I feel two feet tall. Choking now. Picturing Philip on fire is all that holds me together. Anger is safe. Maybe it's the last refuge anyone should escape into, but it's a refuge all the same. It keeps these cutting words from entering inside me. Exposing my weaknesses. Every place the world can knock me down.

"You have a broken nose. Might heal a little crooked—"

"I hope so."

"—I'd talk to a plastic surgeon."

"Sorry, first I've got to chop off my tits." I grin at my reflection in the windowpane. My nose is a giant swollen blob. Ugly. Good. If it heals crooked, it'll be one more brick in the wall between my old self and me.

But I can't brick the wall up completely. Coming out of the exam room to see Naomi and Debbie in the waiting room makes me feel calmer and more centered than I have all week. I have a whole team waiting for me, even if I don't deserve them.

I need to weigh their friendship against Philip, against my temper. How much is protecting my ego to feel safe worth if it means I drive off everyone around me?

"I don't believe it," Naomi's muttering. "I don't believe it at all."

"Sorry, cheer family," Debbie says, scrolling through her phone. "Looks like you've both dated a dumbass. Lukas broke into Dr. Coryn's office, stole her answer key, and sent it to the whole AP Bio email list. Asked for their Homecoming Court votes in return."

I laugh. "Good one, Debbie." Lukas may be a little odd sometimes, a little rigid in the plans he makes for himself—but he'd never be so stupid as to rob a teacher's office himself. He's calm. Collected. Even if sometimes I push him harder than I should, we balance out well when we get our shit together. It's why we need each other so much. *Needed.*

"I'm not kidding." She shows me the email. "Never have his babies, okay? I don't need my cheer nieces inheriting this shittery."

My jaw drops.

"We have to get back to Cresswell," I say. "Fast."

I need to get to Lukas before he self-destructs.

CHAPTER TWENTY-THREE: LUKAS

"No one's going to turn you in," says a junior boy, whispering across the aisle at me. "You did us all a favor. Coryn's evil, and that test was evil."

It *was* evil. Teachers need to make their tests accessible, possible, not just exercises in feeling crappy. The students are on my side. I'll have my votes. I'll have my crown.

I try to shake the nagging thought that votes don't matter if Homecoming is canceled. I'll fix this. I have to.

If there's no dance, I'll topple into the abyss. Because I don't know what else keeps me standing.

My AP English teacher puts down her desk phone. "Philip. You're wanted in Meehan's office."

The last cheater. Maybe I can find a way to blame this on him.

The girl sitting next to Philip refuses to move her seat to let him pass. He has to awkwardly slide over the top of a workbench, muttering curses. I let him get in front of me, then scoop up my books. With a whispered "Homecoming Committee emergency," to the teacher, I head off to Principal Meehan's office, boldly prepared to lie my ass off.

Someone has to save this dance. If there was ever a reason to have a Homecoming King, it's a situation like this.

Ben and Philip are already in the office when I arrive, squeezed around the secretary's desk. She pretends to be buried in a spreadsheet as Meehan yells at my classmates.

"—despite being warned, you both violated the Code of Conduct, again—oh, Lukas, thank god. Can you help me?"

"Can you let us have the pep rally?" I say, sliding into their group. "Today's the class banner contest. Everyone's worked so hard painting those darn things."

"First I need answers." She frowns. "I need—oh, god, what now?"

"We need help," Naomi says commandingly, swinging her massive ball gown into the office. Jeremy follows on her heels. For once, he's quiet—then I see his face and realize why.

A massive purple bruise blotches his cheeks, and his nose twists slightly off center. When Philip glares at him, he freezes—but only for a heartbeat. Then he pushes forward to my side.

Oh my god. Philip did this. Philip broke his nose.

"You've got to get him out of here," I whisper to Naomi. "Philip shouldn't be anywhere near him."

"I'm not leaving you alone," Jeremy answers. "I can't let you wreck Homecoming worse than you already have."

"Later, Naomi," Meehan says. "I have real trouble to deal with. Philip, my office, now. I need to know what you know about this loose answer key."

The answer key. Still the answer key. With Jeremy standing right in front of her with his bruised face. I know the Code of Conduct—the line Philip's crossed *should* be enough to get him expelled. But what Philip does doesn't matter if protecting students isn't Meehan's priority.

She will let Jeremy die if she doesn't get the blame for it.

I'm not a violent person. But the hate that bubbles up inside me when I realize this is real and vivid. White as bleached bone. She will never take the steps she needs to. She may have said she'd support Jeremy in his transition, but she won't back that up with action when he needs it most. Philip could target any marginalized student at this school, and she'd let him get away with it, because his dad's a big donor with powerful, rich friends. She may be nice to me, but that's because of all the work I do to win games and put on events. I don't make trouble.

Until now. When I damn well feel like it.

"I need a word, Principal Meehan." I pull on my nicest smile. "Please? I think I can fix this."

Philip pauses. Meehan beckons me to her office. I shoot Naomi and Ben a look over Jeremy's head. *Protect him.* I hope they can read it. I hope they don't hate me so much that they take it out on him. Then I slide into Meehan's office, where her poster of inspirational quotes by women hangs loose over the window, blocking the sun.

I've never read the poster before, but I'm suddenly convinced every woman quoted there was rich and white. A Nancy Reagan quote is framed in block caps.

"Listen, Principal Meehan." I clear my throat and don't sit down in the little, diminishing chair she offers me. My head feels light and floaty. Am I really going to do this? Do I have another choice? Jeremy would have done it already—all ego, all bluster and fire. Rules and patterns hold me up. Hold me together.

Absentmindedly, I thumb the ring through my nose. Meehan frowns. "What were you thinking when you got that done, Lukas? It's so . . ."

Gay? She can't finish that sentence. I smile, like I didn't hear the word she didn't say.

"I stole the answer keys," I say. "Both times. Ben had nothing to do with it."

Her eyebrows arc, and she leans back in her chair.

"It's not because I'm lazy or I don't pay attention in class. Listen to me. Look. I'm autistic, and Dr. Coryn won't let me take notes in the way I need. Maybe I should have asked for special accommodation, but I was . . . scared. Ashamed to admit that I needed to drop the class. I know I did the wrong thing, but AP Bio is designed to make people fail and feel anxious. It's not fair, and you have to change that."

I pause and hold my breath. Swallowing words before I can slip further. Aching, spare, vulnerable, angry. The truth hangs in the air like a live wire, and I hope it sparks something in her. I've given so much to Cresswell. It's my community. More a home than my own house is. Cresswell asks, and I deliver. That has to mean something.

Her eyebrows knit together. Anger writes itself across her face. "Lukas, what have you done?"

"I'm coming clean," I say, even as my stomach drops. "Please. I'll drop out of AP Bio and take an incomplete grade. Just let the dance go on—and clear Ben's record so he can play. He did nothing wrong. It's all on me."

For a moment, I make myself meet her eyes, even though I want to melt into the floor beneath their volcanic-level sizzle. Then her desk phone rings. Meehan wheels to pick it up, snapping, "What?" at the receiver. Then her tone changes. "Oh. Sharon. Sorry. Nice to hear from you."

Sharon. Sharon Carlyle, head of the alumni association events committee. I met her at Homecoming last year, when the old committee leaders introduced us. She administers the account from which the Homecoming budget is drawn.

"What do you mean, overdrawn?" Meehan shoots me another dirty look. "Lukas, did you take any money from the Homecoming budget today? Like, *all of it?*"

"What?" For a moment, I'm not sure I've heard her correctly. How could all the cash in the Homecoming account be missing? "No. I couldn't have. I lost my wallet after the bonfire. It had the card in it."

"Card?" shouts a tinny voice on the far side of the line. "Ashleigh, did you give a student that debit card?"

"I'll call you back, Sharon," Meehan says, and hangs up the phone.

A queasy feeling builds in the base of my stomach, like I've chomped down two boxes of greasy pizza. The empty weight in my back pocket, where my wallet is missing, sucks like a missing tooth. Aren't you supposed to deactivate your credit and debit cards when you lose your wallet? I've never done this before. I'm not sure.

"Lukas. Listen. Do you still have the debit card for the Homecoming fund? Did you share your PIN code with anyone?"

My PIN? No. It's just my birth year. My birth year. Hadn't Terry asked for that? Terry, who knew almost all the other dates that mattered in my family, except that one.

"Terry Gould took the debit card," I say, as it all clicks together. "The guy who does deliveries at the back lot? He stole my wallet and cracked my PIN."

"Christ." Meehan rubs her temples with two fingers. "I thought you were responsible. Easier to trust Lukas Rivers than sign off on paperwork every time the Homecoming Committee needs to buy a can of paint. I should have listened to Sharon and kept the card for myself."

"You weren't supposed to give it to me." At last, I'm reading her right. Seeing the intent beyond the surface of her actions. The alumni wouldn't want a student to have access to that kind of money. They don't even know me. Meehan gave me the money because it was easier. Because she trusted me, and she never will again.

But I don't need her to trust me. And since she hasn't raised a finger to help Jeremy with Philip, I don't even want her to like me.

I just want to make this right with the people who matter to me most.

"Terry had access to the whole school," I say slowly. "He could have stolen it at any time. Maybe even from your desk drawer. We can sort of leave the whole 'you gave me the money' step out of the story we tell the alumni association."

"Are you . . . attempting to blackmail me?"

I bite my lip before I can blurt out, *That's nothing worse than what you did to Jeremy by ignoring him*, and give a careful, neutral shrug.

Meehan stares at me for a long moment, and then rubs her forehead again. "Fine. You're going to apologize to Dr. Coryn and drop the class. You'll take an incomplete for AP Bio and switch into another class; your counselor will be notified. All your computer privileges are revoked, and you'll have lunch detentions for three weeks starting next Monday. But you can still practice with the team, and I'll clear Ben's record, too. Let's put this mess behind us and move on."

I exhale. *Ben's going to be okay.* And I'll have to shut up and take my punishment, but it won't kill me. I can figure out college stuff when the world isn't ending. When I'm crowned. "So the dance is back on?"

"It *would* be. But now we don't even have the eight thousand dollars we would need to cover the building operating costs for an event. I don't think we've got any choice but to cancel the dance for good."

And just like that, the world hits me like a truck. I fold down into a chair. Seconds slip past. No crown. No guiding light. No chance for my family. Nowhere left for me to go.

Nothing feels real until Jeremy's hand curls around my shoulder.

CHAPTER TWENTY-FOUR: JEREMY

Principal Meehan takes one look at my face-wide bloom-ing bruises and rubs hard at her temples. Like her headache is somehow bigger than mine. "What did you do this time, Jeremy?"

"I did nothing," I insist, a denial quick enough even to impress my lawyer mom. "Philip Cross—"

She sighs. "Do I need to speak with him? Am I going to get a call from his father?"

I think it over, then shake my head. Even if I push, what will she do? Call the police? File a report? No one witnessed Philip hitting me. For all I know, he'll say I started some-thing and he only defended himself. We'll wind up as two conflicting reports Meehan will slide into a desk drawer and forget. Brandon Kyle's paperwork is probably still somewhere in this office. Even if I win Homecoming King and get more

attention from her and the alumni, that's not real influence—
that's a wild hope. I'm not sure I can trust her to fix anything.

But I know what I can fix. So I reach out and put a hand
on Lukas's shoulder.

"Hey, Principal Meehan?" I say, once she hangs up. "We
can fix this, okay? Just give us a day. We'll get the money
and save the dance."

She raises a skeptical eyebrow. I quirk mine back in return.
After everything that's gone wrong, she owes me this much.

"Fine. You've got twenty-four hours. Then I pull the plug
and everything's canceled for good."

I lower my voice, trying to be safe and soothing as I take
Lukas's arm. Restraint is hell when I want to start scream-
ing, but it's worth it for him. "Please. You can't fix this here.
Come on."

I drag him out of the office and down the hall. Thank god
it's nearly deserted midperiod. I don't want to have to mow
down freshmen, and I certainly don't want to risk facing
Philip once more.

"Did you give my wallet to Terry?" he asks. "This is serious.
I need to know."

"You left it in my car," I say. "Yeah. I gave it to that shithead."

"Why?" he shouts, pulling at his hair. "What the hell made
you think he could be trusted with money?"

"Because I thought you two were an item!" Are they not?
Something crazy stirs in my chest. Is he single? Someone
that attractive shouldn't be single. And I shouldn't let myself

name the emotion building inside me. I shouldn't call it hope, because hope can be snatched away.

If he takes my hope away, it'll kill me.

He makes a sound that's half giggle, half hack. "Seriously? No offense, but my taste in men isn't *that* terrible."

And now he's got a taste in men. I want to die.

Instead, I lead him farther down the hall, outside across the gravel of the senior parking lot, into the quiet and isolation of my car. The still air and tight spaces help him feel calm. I sit across from him, breathing slow and even, waiting until his eyes refocus on my face. "Jesus Christ, that looks awful. Have you seen a doctor?"

"I see plenty of doctors. They tell me being ugly isn't contagious, so you don't have to worry."

"You're not ugly. You're . . . fine."

"That's a stirring endorsement. You made fun of my hair yesterday."

"That's what guys do to each other. Your hair is . . . fine. Did I hurt your feelings?"

"I'm sensitive about my looks, okay?" I huff. "You didn't hurt me worse than Philip hurt my face."

"Jesus fuck." He throws his arms around me, leaning across the car. A hug. It's cramped with his bulk, but he still manages to get his arms around me. And I let him. I wrap my hands around his wide back, jealous dysphoria writing *want* on my temples and, somehow, subsiding. Toning down my anger. Offering a lifeline I'm afraid to seize.

So much in my body feels wrong. But in this space, with him holding me, everything feels right.

"We need to find Terry," I say, fighting to concentrate past the alluring scent of his deodorant. So familiar. It makes me hungry for a life that isn't outlined in red fury. To smile, to exhale, to exist without the weight of a budding scream in my throat. "Make him give back the money."

We race to the diner. Lukas sweet-talks Terry's address out of the elderly shift manager, and I floor the gas pedal all the way over to a shitty College Park apartment complex, knuckles white on the wheel, not talking. We run up the stairs to Terry's unit. I pound on the door until a disheveled girl with wire-frame glasses and bulky PJs throws it open.

"We're looking for Terry Gould," I say. "Urgently."

She rolls her eyes. "Who the hell wants anything to do with my brother? He's not here, okay? He stole my laptop and bought a plane ticket to live with his loser boyfriend in California." She eyed me. "Please tell me you're not pregnant."

"I'm smart enough to keep his dick fifty feet away from me at all times." I elbow Lukas. "He might be, though."

"I think your brother might have stolen money from our school," Lukas says, ignoring my jab.

"He does that," says the girl. "And I don't need his trouble." She slams the door in our face.

"Right," Lukas says. "I'm broke. Do you have any clue how we can get to California?"

"I've got a car and gas money. But we can't road-trip

cross-country in two days. How much do we need in order to pay the operating fees and save the dance?"

He collapses back against the door. I can feel his breath on my neck when he speaks. "Eight thousand dollars. I've done the math. God, I'm fucked. Everyone at school will know this is on me. There's no way I could fundraise that much, not in twenty-four hours, not without an army—"

"I can get you an army."

"Oh, yeah? And what dumbass thing will you make me do in return?"

Kiss me. Hard. "I want my cheer sweatshirt back."

"Oh," he says. "You sure you don't want something more humiliating? Like, for me to stick my head in a stockade while you laugh and throw rotten fruit?"

"Like our Colonial Williamsburg field trip in fifth grade?" I smile. That was the first time he asked permission before holding my hand. The first time it meant something. I had been the one to stick my head in the stockades. Some kid called me a witch, and Lukas chased them down explaining how witches in history were only really cool women who didn't follow bullshit rules.

It's impossible to be angry when I'm smiling with him. And even with the dance in flames, it's hard to remember why I should be angry at all when I'm looking at him.

Lukas pulls my sweatshirt out of his backpack. *Why's he carrying that around?* I whip out my phone and speed-dial Naomi. "Skip practice. Tell Coach there's an emergency.

Meet me at the diner. Bring the whole team, a binder, paper, pens, and some highlighters." I remember manners past the red and roaring haze in my skull. "Please, please, please."

The threat of canceling Homecoming leaves a fog hanging over Cresswell. Students wander the halls aimless as the pep rally lets out. Afraid. "What's going on?" they ask me and Lukas whenever we pause from frantically texting our moms. "Will there still be a dance?"

"If I have anything to say about it," Lukas growls.

The two of us get a round of applause as we enter the diner. I assume it's all for me, since I'm the one who bravely took a punch to the face and Lukas is the loser who got Homecoming canceled.

"Right," I say, marching up to the head of the table where the cheerleaders and GSA sit. Pink neon light sparkles off the rough-cut fuzz of my hair. I clutch my strawberry milkshake like a judge with a gavel. "This is the part where I apologize—don't get used to it—but I gave Lukas's wallet to a total weirdo, and that's how the Homecoming account got robbed."

"We're both to blame," Lukas says. "And we're both sorry. But the whole school's going to suffer from our fuckups. Homecoming will be canceled. This celebration means so much to so many people. It's about our community, the community that holds us together. The good parts of it, at least. Please. Help us save this dance."

"Are we going to rob a bank?" Sol says. "I was told there'd be a bank robbery."

"Oh no, motherfuckers," I say, pulling out a catalog. "We're going to sell candles. Four thousand of them. In twenty-four hours."

"It's only a hundred and sixty-seven candles per hour," Lukas adds, not helping.

"Who would want that many candles?" Ben says.

"Everyone will," I say. "It's a locally owned business, and it supports a great cause. My mom's bought fifteen candles from them just this month."

Naomi is flipping through the catalog, already jotting notes in her binder, snapping on stickers to mark different sections. She laughs. "I can see why. Did you know she wrote them a testimonial, Jeremy?"

I blink. "What?"

There, in the back of the catalog. A picture of my mom, captioned *Bethesda Resident Emily Harkiss.*

I've always loved Honeyflower Candles! Now that my son's come out and started HRT, he stinks like a garbage dump. I've placed the Lily Iris candles all over his room.

This is the most embarrassing thing I've ever read. But my eyes aren't watering because of that. *My son.* She called me her son. Not in private or because I pushed her to say it. She claimed me in front of the whole world. Like it was nothing.

But it's everything to me.

I'm her son. The thought makes me feel like I'm floating up to the diner's moldy tile ceiling. *She doesn't hate me. She sees me. She sees me.*

"Yeah," I say. "Let's sell some fucking candles."

We cram around the long table and plan.

Philip darts into the rear of the diner; at a nod from Naomi, every sitting student turns their back on him. He starts bothering a knot of freshmen, but none of them crack. The manager tells him he has to buy something or get out. He leaves.

"This sounds good," Ben says when we finish the final draft of our plan. "Impossible, but good."

"Nothing's impossible once you've survived your first month at Cresswell," I say, slurping at my milkshake. "We'll need an early start tomorrow. Everyone, home. Bed. Now."

"What makes you think you can boss us around?" Debbie says. "Like, have you gone mad with male privilege after all?"

She's joking, but it lands badly. After what happened at the clinic, I'm not in the mood for this crap. But I can brush off her remark—until Lukas leans in tight over my shoulder.

"Don't throw that crap at him," he says. "He's had a shitty day."

And with that, he crosses the line, and the red haze begins building around the edges of my world all over again. I could take his niceness in the car. But to defend me in public? "We've all had shitty days, Lukas. I don't need you to ride in on your white steed and sweep me off to your magic castle for protection. I can take care of myself."

"Jeremy," Naomi says. "Lukas is being kind. For once in your life, can't you just let people be nice to you?"

I glare at them both. "Here's the thing: when someone is

nice to me, I assume they're treating me like a girl." The word *girl* hangs in the air, like I've summoned a ghost. "Because I don't deserve kindness from anyone. Not rides home, not the cheer team sticking out their necks to defend me from Philip. I'm an ass. I've been pushing everyone away, butting heads for the hell of it. I dumped Lukas without an explanation, I wasn't there for Naomi after the SATs—"

"Jeremy," Lukas says. "We're cool. We've all made some mistakes. That doesn't mean it's not the real you I care about."

"Seriously," Naomi says. "We stood up to Philip for *you*."

"But . . ." My eyes are watering. *Shit. Shit.* I can't break down here and now. I need to stay calm, collected. Masculine cool-guy Jeremy Harkiss. How can I stay myself if people aren't screaming at me loud enough to make me snap back? I nod and take a deep breath.

"I should get home," I say quickly. "Big day tomorrow, cleaning up all our mistakes." Before anyone can say anything else, I slip out of the booth and head for the door. As I approach my car, I hear footsteps behind me.

"Jeremy. Wait up!" I stop walking, and he runs to catch up, swinging to stand in front of me. "Are you okay?" he asks.

"I'm fine, Lukas," I say. But instead of going back inside, he just stares at me, and the tears I thought had dried up come back. "It's just . . . it's just that the real me is *such* a dick."

Lukas laughs. "You're not even the worst dick I've ever met," he teases. "You should know that. Didn't you catch me making out with Terry at the bonfire?"

"Yeah." My lips tug up into a reluctant smile. "He's awful. You're awful."

"I always said that no one kisses like you and I. Well, now I know why. You always kissed me hard and fast. Like it was a contest and you needed to beat me. You kissed me like a boy, and I kissed you back like one. I've been kissing you, Jeremy, all along."

Lukas's brown eyes are digging into mine now, which almost never happens except when he has something important to say. But I don't know what he's trying to get out. Because I'm finally a real person, for the first time in my life, but I'm not sure I'm a person other people can love. I don't know what happens if I let Lukas back in—I don't even know what he's asking me for—but opening up feels like inviting in disaster.

We could both get hurt worse.

I don't know what to say to him, so I just say good night. Then I slip into my car before the swirling mess of my insides shows on my face. My key grinds against the ignition. The hybrid engine shrieks as I floor it out of the shopping center, head-lights cutting through the cloudy evening dark. Alone. Safe.

Safe from the one thing I want more than anything else in the world. More than crowns, Harvard, fame and fortune. I want to be Lukas's boyfriend. It's the one thing that makes me vulnerable, makes me weak. And it's the one thing I can't have. It's not my gender that matters. It's my temper, my ego, my hair trigger. Just as bad as Philip's. Just as unworthy and unready for a healthy relationship.

He's smart, Lukas. He should know there's no way for us. No future past the fault lines I've punched into our love. I've learned so much, changed so much, grown so much since I started transitioning. For the first time in my life, I'm becoming who I really am.

But I'm not the sort of person who can fix things. I don't even know where I'd start.

CHAPTER TWENTY-FIVE: LUKAS

Thursday, we dress to match our class theme: Senior Super-heroes. I've got a pretty badass Batman costume. Jeremy, of course, outdoes himself in a life-sized Loki cosplay. We meet behind the gym that morning, with boxes and boxes of candle catalogs, each of us avoiding the other's eyes. *Focus. What matters is saving the dance. What matters is saving this for everyone.*

He never hated me. The knowledge makes me feel like I'm floating. At last, I have the truth. *He was scared I'd reject him. Scared I wouldn't love who he really was.* But I've only ever loved the real him, and the more it shines out of him, the deeper I fall.

He didn't refuse to stay after the bonfire because he hates me. Only because he didn't trust that I meant it, that I really wanted him. I need to prove myself to him in the same way he's trying to prove himself to the school.

I can be Cresswell's hero today. Maybe then he'll let me be his.

"Listen," Naomi says, Wonder Woman badge sparkling on her belt, candle catalog open in her hand. She's not quite smiling, but a grim determination blazes off her, and I know I was wrong to jump into dating her when I didn't want to. She's better on her own than with an obnoxious asshole giving her one-third of his attention. "I want a blitz. Cover the whole school. Barge into classrooms, don't take no for an answer. I want every kid at Cresswell ordering five, ten candles. Christmas gifts, presents for relatives they hate, whatever. I know this school. The people here can afford to toss fifty bucks randomly at candles they never plan to use." She pauses. "Don't be dicks to the scholarship students, though."

"Should we work in teams?" Ben suggests. His Superman T-shirt is a bit on the nose, but no one would deny he's earned it, putting up with us.

"We'll cover more ground if we split up," Naomi says. She's drawn a map of the school, colored hallways in highlighter, and assigned each wing a name. "This isn't a horror movie."

"If it was," Jeremy says, "as the blond cheerleader, I'd already be dead."

We split off, spread through the school, and charge into classrooms. People enjoy my Batman voice, even when I'm shoving candle catalogs in their faces and demanding they buy.

"How many have you sold?" Jeremy says as we pass in the

hall, weaving around five hundred freshmen dressed like Sherlock Holmes. "I've sold twenty-four. I cornered a bunch of freshmen and told them they'd ruin Homecoming if they didn't pony up."

"Twenty-eight," I say, mentally adding five purchases of my own to the list. Who needs fifty bucks when I could watch his eyebrows knit together in rage?

"I'm going to beat you," he warns me, face livid red past the burst vessels in his nose.

"I don't mind," I say. "The more you sell, the better our chances."

"We don't have a chance," he tells me, and walks away. I realize too late he's not talking about the dance.

Sol sells five hundred themself. "I invented a new crypto-currency called CandleCoin and gave one away with every candle I sold."

"Is it that easy?" I say.

They nod. "Both to generate the damn things and to get people to buy them. Humans are dumb."

"How rich are you?"

"Let's put it this way, if I don't get a full Caltech scholar-ship, I can pay my own way."

"So, you could just . . . bail us out of this whole mess in a heartbeat."

"I'm not your bank account, Rivers."

I cross paths with Philip when I walk into Madame East's French class. He's sitting in the back of the classroom. No one, not even the teacher, makes eye contact with him. He's not even wearing a costume.

I smile at the other students. "Hi, all. Help me save Homecoming with candles?"

"This is how you raise money?" Philip laughs. "God, you're all such dumbasses. You seriously think this'll work?"

No one in the room flinches. One boy opens his mouth, but the girl beside him grabs his arm and silences him with a look.

"Philip, watch your language," Madame East says, stern. And then she turns to me. "I'll take four candles." Suddenly every kid in class pushes forward to sign the sheet and hand over cash.

"We're still probably fucked," Jeremy says at lunch, his horned tissue-paper crown askew as he tallies the totals. "We need everyone at school to buy some. We need to reach everyone."

"We go big," I say, heart pumping quicker now. Alive with the promise of victory. Of giving something I want to give. Making the dance I want to make. "The seniors have an extra five minutes in their musical this afternoon. Everyone in school will be watching."

"You're planning to perform in the musical?" Jeremy says. "You can't act or dance—"

"I can sing," I say. "Didn't we spend all of middle school singing show tunes in your bathroom?"

He turns scarlet. Between that and the purple of his nose, he's a green away from morphing into a one-man Pride flag.

"And you can dance," I say.

"I can wave pom-poms."

"Oh, no. You're not getting out of this one. Didn't you make a speech last night about how this was all partly your fault?"

"Fine," he says. "I'd hate for Cresswell to know their future Homecoming King sat back and did nothing while his ex saved the dance." All fire and bluster. The flashes of vulnerability he's shown me are hidden now—but I know they're there. I want to find that again. I want to sit in his light, if he would just stop trying to burn me.

The gym feels uneasy, strange, as we gather for that afternoon's pep rally. Bleachers packed with worried faces and nervous, high whispers. The dance is still in danger. The mood in the room hangs on an edge.

Jeremy walks onto the musical stage, the wooden flats I spent hours this weekend nailing together, and collapses the mic stand to match his height. "Afternoon, Cresswell. The cheer team is passing some catalogs and an envelope around the gym. We're selling scented candles to raise money to save the dance. If we can sell eight thousand dollars' worth by the end of the pep rally, Lukas and I will perform a song together onstage. We'll publicly humiliate ourselves in front of the whole school. I know everyone here would love to chip in twenty bucks toward that."

As he walks off and brushes past me, he whispers, "You better make this good."

"I will," I say. For both of us.

Because the only reason he sold more candles than me is that I skipped selling during fifth-period break to make the poster rolled under my arm. One with *Jeremy, HC?* written in big pink glitter letters. I've robbed the art classroom for him. After everything we've been through, what easier way to get us back together than the flashy public asking of his dreams?

The freshmen take the stage. Their musical is called *The Case of the Missing Magnifying Glass*, and it's all about them searching the school grounds for a kid in a mascot costume who stole a magnifying glass. I only know this from reading the script, because their mics malfunction. They've got a pretty hilarious dance routine where all the boys swing their butts in a conga line, and Principal Meehan turns red but decides not to stop them. Our candle order forms snake through the crowd.

The sophomores do a show about a princess rescuing a hapless prince from a dragon, accompanied by way too much Led Zeppelin and the terrible choice of "Fixer Upper" from *Frozen*, of all things. *God, I should have been more critical when reviewing the playlists.* The juniors do better, though. Their space-themed extravaganza has a full orchestra and a live DJ. Dancers whirl in spray-painted black T-shirts. When Jeremy asks the crowd if they liked it, they cheer so loud I'm worried the seniors might actually lose.

Not that it matters. All that matters is ensuring there'll be a dance tomorrow night. All that matters is the fake jewels in the Homecoming crown and the perfect date on my arm.

The lead senior dancers, each draped in a massive cape, take the stage. From the shadows, Naomi gives me a thumbs-up.

We've done it. We've really done it. Pulled together as a community and saved the dance. The whole school, working together to fix something we love.

Maybe I can fix something important, too.

Laurie's lacing up her toe shoes. I meet her eyes and shake my head. "I'm doing the solo. Sorry! Cue the music?"

She runs off to the speakers. The opening bars of the classic *Superman* theme fill the gym. The dancers lift their arms, as if they're about to leap into flight.

And then the theater club pulls back on the wires. And six seniors lift off the ground.

I take Jeremy's hand. "Time to pay up," I say, and pull him forward.

I grab the mic. The opening bars of "Holding Out for a Hero" fill the room. It took some work, finding the gayest possible love song that also fit the theme of the musical. But when I meet Jeremy's eyes, crooning, "Where have all the good men gone?" and watch him turn scarlet, it's a victory sweeter than catching any touchdown pass.

He stands frozen as I push into lyrics about how superhero-caliber boyfriends are just so hard to find. Don't I know it, after Terry—but like the cheerleader he is, he pulls on a smile and whips his pom-poms around in a neat spin. Then he's moving in time with the music as the dancers on wires mime flight—shoulders rolling, hips shaking, head held high.

There's a cold focus to him, a perfect smile, the flip of his head. He knows all eyes are on him, and he gives them a reason to stare.

So, when I finish on "I need a hero," I hope he knows I've already found mine.

The gym cheers as I unroll my poster. Feet drum on bleachers. Shouts ring in my ears. My breath catches. It means something vital, a whole school cheering as a boy asks out another boy. Time slows as I meet Jeremy's eyes. Hoping with every inch of me that the magic of this moment carries through.

"Will you be my Homecoming date?" I say.

He freezes. His chest heaves.

The same face he made when he saw my stupid video.

Cold sweeps me. My stomach drops. I've misread him. I've misread everything.

He wheels around, pom-poms and all, and runs from the stage.

"Jeremy!" I move to follow, but Laurie pushes me back as she takes the stage in her Scarlet Witch leotard.

"Could you not upstage me with your drama?" she says, and leaps onstage as the *Avengers* theme plays.

"We sold all the candles!" Naomi laughs nervously as I pass her. "We met quota and saved the dance. Can we just enjoy this moment?"

"Let him go." Ben, not unkindly, slides between me and the door. Puts a hand on my chest. "That was a lot you just sprung on him. He'll need time and space to think."

"What's there to think about?" I'm as confused and dizzy as the time the Tilt-A-Whirl broke underneath me at the state fair. "I mean—isn't it a yes or no question? Like, you know Jeremy, right? Isn't that how he'd want to be asked?"

"Yes, yes, and yes. But no. No. You heard him yesterday at the diner. He's afraid you're not serious about liking him. And that dance number was a lot of things, but it sure as hell wasn't serious. How'd you even think this was a good idea?"

Because I thought that would be what he wanted. And I read him wrong, obviously. I read people wrong all the time. I've gotten used to laughing it off, to flipping my cluelessness into a joke.

But there's nothing funny about the cold, desperate ache in the bottom of my heart. There's nothing funny in knowing I've hurt him. *Again. Over and over and over.* He's vanished into shadows, like he doesn't want to see me, like he doesn't want to know what I have to say. Even if it's *I love you, I forgive you, I want you just as you are.*

"I just want things to work out," I mutter, knowing it's a dumb hope. I just want the right words to come out of me and fix everything.

But still, I'm at a loss for what to say.

For everyone but me, this evening's football practice is a celebration. We've won. Homecoming will go on. Ben and I are both back on the field, ready to lead the team to victory. But our old rhythm is off. His passes drop from my hands. My feet go left when they should slide right. I can't even get upset—my chest feels empty.

"We're as ready as we'll ever be," Coach says as we finish up. He doesn't sound enthusiastic. "Some more bad news, though. Philip has decided to quit the team. Apparently, he was upset that people weren't speaking to him. I'm disappointed in you, boys."

Ben elbows me. I shrug. *Whatever.* Meehan hates me, and the boy I'm in love with has convinced himself I hate him. Surprisingly, knowing that somewhere an absolute asshole is also suffering makes none of this better.

Twenty-three hours and eighteen minutes until Homecoming kickoff. Tomorrow, I'll show my family that I'm headed toward a glowing future. I'll be crowned king, and college offers will follow, AP Bio or not. Or I'll crash and burn, and head off to a state school, and whatever's building in my family will happen. *I can't let that happen.*

But running over all these problems in my head, for what feels like the ten thousandth time, just leaves them feeling worn and flimsy as tissue paper. I can't keep caring about this forever.

I need to figure out what and who I care about enough to take forward.

Today, I drive home early, running over what happened in that asking-gone-wrong, replaying that memory, forgetting I should hide in my car doing homework to avoid my parents. I've got a full day tomorrow. I need rest. I don't let myself consider that home isn't an easy place to be right now. I walk in the front door expecting sanctuary. I've earned that much. I need that much. I've given so much of myself, for everyone, for my family most of all, and I just need a few hours of unstimulating quiet.

The universe doesn't care what I've earned.

"You're leaving?" Dad says, eyes wide, red, and dry. "Caroline, you can't just go. Twenty-five years together should mean something, god damn it!"

"It should mean something to you, too. You should have put in some real effort. Instead, you're lashing out at everyone around you like a child. Like Lukas when he was younger!"

I flinch at my name, still in the middle of slipping off my shoes. *Is this still how they see me? Don't they know how much I've done to make them happy?*

My father continues. "I'm sorry I've missed those counseling sessions, I should have put in more effort, but I thought—"

"It's not about you," she says. "This is about me. I poured my whole life into you, into our family. I need space. And if I decide not to come back—"

I slam the door. Loudly. Because I've seen the suitcases sitting beside it, lurking in the shadow of Mom's beloved, wilting potted plants.

"Lukas!" They both jump into the hallway together, both

wearing near-identical expressions of guilt and fear, both try-ing to smile.

"It's okay," Dad says. But it isn't.

It's funny, how quickly they move to hide things from me. I don't think it's for my benefit. I think it's because they think, if no one knows how they're falling apart, it's not really hap-pening. If they look perfect, they're still whole and in love.

We're all hiding wounds from each other. All afraid of what people will say if they know. *Jeremy dumped me because he couldn't let me dump him.* I understand his fear now, better than I once did. *You never know how people will react to the truth of you.* If he had to dump me to feel safe enough to be himself, then I can't blame him. He needed to come out as safely as possible.

But he can still come back in. What we have's not perma-nently broken.

I think I know what permanently broken looks like now. Or at least, I know the look of a problem I can't fix. Not with a million colleges and crowns.

"How was your day, sweetheart?" Mom eyes me. "What's that on your nose?"

I look up and meet her eyes. "I'm gay. I thought you should know. Are you getting divorced?"

They go very quiet.

"What?" Mom finally says.

Dad blinks. "Is this about—Jeremy, is this about Jeremy Harkiss?"

"No. It's about me. You know, that kid you forgot you had?" My frustration bubbles over, cold as dry ice. I don't care if what I'm saying makes sense. I need to let this feeling out. Because I'm also part of this family. "There. Now you know." Will they turn back to me now? Realize I'm still here and I need to feel connected to them?

Mom turns on Dad. "This is all your fault. You've made him feel unhappy—"

"You're the one who's trying to walk away!"

I turn and run up to my room. Flicking the light on atop the wall of medals I earned to please them. My duffel bag lies at the bottom of my closet. I sweep my dresser drawers into it, dump in my spare cash from the small box in the back of my sock drawer. *A bomb's gone off. But I'm the only one who feels the blast.*

"I'm going to a friend's house," I tell my parents as I tramp down the stairs, pulling my sneakers back on. "I'll be fine."

They don't respond. They're so caught up in the knot of their own brokenness, they don't even bother to watch me leave.

"I'm really sorry," I tell Naomi when she answers the door. Blood rushes to my face. *I tried to make you happy and made everything worse instead.* I've apologized, she's accepted it, but things will still be awkward between us for a good while. "I need to talk to your brother. I need a place to crash for the night." *And, like, the foreseeable future?*

She purses her lips. "What's wrong?"

"My parents are getting divorced," I mutter, keeping it short, trying not to let anything too embarrassing slip out. "And I don't have any other real friends." Even after everything, that truth stings to admit.

She turns aside. "Ben! This is your problem!"

My best friend bounds down the front steps. I can't bring myself to meet his eyes as I mutter, "I'm so, so sorry I didn't do the right thing earlier. I was afraid. But I'm not afraid now. I told Meehan it was me."

"I know," he says awkwardly. "I mean, she told me I could go back to practice, so I assumed you'd stepped up."

"Oh. Okay. I mean, I just wanted to clear the air and, like, say I'm sorry?" It feels like there's a wet towel twisted up in the back of my throat. I need to concentrate to push out every word before my brain locks me down. But I stumble through. It's important.

He sighs. "Come on in. I can't let you sleep in your car."

I duck through the door and kick off my shoes. My squirming guts note that he hasn't actually accepted my apology.

"My parents could still work things out," I tell him as I drop my duffel on the floor of his room. His trophies cast long shadows on the floor. "Like, tomorrow, maybe they'll come to the game. Maybe I've got enough votes to win this thing. They'll see that and realize we're still a family and we can all support each other. Then I'll get into Harvard, and they'll throw a big party, and—"

"I'm sorry, Lukas," Ben says. "But you do realize there's no chance in hell that's what happens, right? Like, this is all way bigger than you. It's not your responsibility. What happens between them is . . . what happens."

"Yeah," I say, sagging back on my sleeping bag. "You're right. I . . . It's out of my control."

I want to. I want to believe that caring hard enough can fix things. That if I rip myself open and present my beating heart to the world on a platter, everything from there will work out okay. *Easier to give pieces of yourself to others than the words you can't find.* But it's not working. I'm not making anything better. I'm just hurting myself.

"Can I talk to you about something?" I ask Ben. "I just . . . need to get out everything I've been struggling with."

"Go for it," he says, and waves me forward.

And so, I tell him. Everything I told Meehan. Everything I've held back.

"It made me feel weird when you made fun of my underwear drawer for being too organized," I say, and though it feels lame, it's true. "Could you, like, not?"

"Yeah. Sure." He scratches the back of his neck where he sits in his computer chair, clearly uncomfortable. "You're not going to use autism to get yourself off for lying to Meehan about the first test, right?"

I wince. "God, no. That was me being an ass. Everything

this past month, everything since Jeremy and I started running against each other for Homecoming King, has been me being an ass. I wanted that fucking title because I thought it would get me into a fancy college and make my family feel better about losing him. But I can't fix all our problems. I'm just breaking myself and pushing my friends away. I'm sorry. I'm really, really sorry."

The words don't feel right. I'm not intoning enough; I'm not meeting his eyes. But I mean it. I really fucking mean it.

"Okay," Ben says. "I . . . I get it. You were dealing with an asshole, and you had to move fast. Just . . . next time you need help, let me know. Work with me. Not against me."

"Okay," I say. "I . . . yeah. I can do that. Sorry. Again." What words come in the space that opens next? How do you move a friendship forward past something this big, awkward, and awful?

We're both quiet. Ben checks his text messages, then says, "What's going on with you and Jeremy? That music number was . . . I think the word I'm looking for is homoerotic? What's up with that?"

"Oh, that. I think I'm in love with him," I say. The words feel daring, dangerous, weighted somehow in a way they never would have if I said, *I think I'm in love with her.* But they feel right. "I don't know how it works, because he's kind of infuriating. But every time I get mad at him, I can't stop thinking about how amazing he is. How I like every part of him, even his anger. I don't know how I'll convince him I really do like him, because he's convinced himself he's unlovable. But I really do think I'm in love with him."

"Are you going to tell him that?" Ben says. "I don't think this is the sort of relationship problem you can fix with a flashy Homecoming asking. Like, normally I think Jeremy would eat that shit up, but he's not in a good place right now. You've got to have that painful conversation with him and explain what's going on in your head. Not with Meehan, not your parents, not me. Him."

"Yeah, but . . . what if I explain everything I've been through, and everything going on in my head, and he laughs at me?" A musical number is one thing. I'm an expert at putting on a show. But he didn't stay the night of the bonfire. He could always walk away again.

"That might happen, dude. You can't control how he reacts. But if you're this serious about him, isn't it worth the risk?"

All my carefully laid plans have crumbled. Win or lose, the outcome of the court election won't solve any of my problems. I'm not who I thought I was. I'm not straight, and odds are, I'll have to cheer on my ex as he crowns himself Homecoming King, tell him I'm still in love with him, and then go to the dance alone as he dumps me a second time.

In short, I guess I'm kind of a loser. But I can still hope my family will pull back together. And there are good people on my side. Ben and maybe Naomi, both of them who never hesitate reaching out to someone who needs help. And I'll be a lot happier if I can add Jeremy to that list.

I write an email to the anonymous reports inbox. He'll check this, even if he's already blocked my number on his phone. *I'm sorry for what happened at the diner and during the musical number. I shouldn't have made this so public, or turned it into a massive stunt. But I really do care about you, and I think we'll both be better off if we can just talk about the breakup and how we feel about it. Can you meet me in the cafeteria tomorrow during final period? When everyone's getting ready for the game?*

I hit Send and cross my fingers. If I'm lucky, he'll come. Maybe alone and in private, he'll even listen.

CHAPTER TWENTY-SIX: JEREMY

Eleven Hours to Homecoming Kickoff

The final day of Spirit Week is School Colors Day. We're all supposed to find the most elaborate way to wear Cresswell's blue and gold. At first, when I had my costume idea, I was terrified—because it was so flashy, so goddamn pretty, that I feared everyone would look at me in it and see a girl.

But when Naomi makes the final strokes of makeup—washing a mask of blue paint and gold glitter over my eyes—and I strap the elaborate tailpiece to my back, I can't stop winking in the mirror as I strut across my clothing-strewn bedroom. I see myself. I see the obstacle in everyone's path, the one everyone must notice. Gold stiletto sandals, royal-blue shorts and T-shirt, and an enormous spray of gold and blue plumes fanning out from my spine.

I need Cresswell to see me as a boy. But I also need them to see me shining. See me gay, and trans, and in their faces. Choose me as Homecoming King, and choose every piece of me besides. I hope it'll give me the leverage to keep pushing Meehan for change, but it might only make me feel wanted. Still. That would be enough. Something I could build on.

My mom freezes as I come downstairs in the full outfit. Naomi slides past her and out the door, but she's too busy staring at me to even make room on the stairs. "What's that?"

"My costume for the spirit day."

"But it's so . . . colorful. Girly. Are you . . ."

Not a girl. Never again. "I'm gay!" I blurt out, the words like matchsticks on my tongue. Echoing around the staircase, off the faux crystals of our atrium chandelier. God, it shouldn't be that hard. She said in the catalog I was her son. She should understand.

But just because she knows I'm a boy doesn't mean she knows what to do with me.

"Oh." Mom blinks. "I thought you were transgender?"

She still doesn't get it. I have a right to be upset, I guess. But I have friends like Sol who understand me and friends like Naomi who'll support me when I need them most. I'm tired of being upset with my mom over what she can't give me. I need to live in what we can have.

"I'm both," I say, and tell myself to sound calm. "People can be both. Don't you know I'm still in love with Lukas?"

"But . . . you broke up with Lukas."

"Because I couldn't trust him to still want to be with me, after I came out." I bite my lip and try to fish up something to joke about, to lessen the pain, but find nothing. It's like

I've run out of gas. Broken down on the emotional highway, lined with feelings I can only withstand if I speed past them at a hundred miles per hour.

What am I supposed to do? Lukas went up before the whole school and sang me a gay anthem. Looking into my eyes, even though it cost him, because he needed me to hear what he had to say. Hinting that I might have been wrong. That we might have a future. Asking me to the dance.

And I couldn't make myself say yes. I couldn't let myself believe in him, in us. So many people have let me down.

I drop down on the bottom stair. Mom sits beside me and strokes my hair. It feels different than when my hair was long; it still feels good. "Oh, honey. Why wouldn't he still love you?"

"I felt like you didn't." The truth slips out. "The way you reacted. How you didn't let me transition until I was completely collapsing. If you wouldn't love me, how could anyone else?"

"I love you. I do." She swallows hard, deep in her throat. "I won't lie and say this hasn't been hard for me. But I want you to be happy, Jeremy. You're going to work all this out, and I'll be here for you as you do."

It's hard for me, too, I want to shout, but I also don't want to cry and mess up my makeup. I guess this is something I can carry along. We're in a better place than where we were, and I can talk to her about my problems. Not complete victory, but a win.

I don't know if Lukas loves me or not. I don't know if me and Mom will ever feel seamless. But I'm going to go get my fucking crown. I've earned it. And I'm hoping, somehow, when I'm crowned, the whole school cheers along.

"We've got a long day ahead of us," Naomi says as I drive us to Cresswell. "Counting Homecoming after-parties, I doubt I'll get home until two a.m. If I even get home at all."

"Do you have a date?" I say.

"No. I'll just dance with every boy who's brave enough to ask. Do you think Lukas will ask you again?"

"I don't want to talk about Lukas."

"I think he means it. I really think he still loves you. Like, when we tried to go out, all he could talk about was you."

What if? What if? That question runs through my head, a record stuck on repeat. *What if it's true?* I keep my eyes open for him all day—rushing through classes that are bullshit because no one likes them anyway, as Mr. Ewing compliments me on my latest AP Gov test score and tells me I'll make a good lawyer one day. *What if he'd say yes to me? What if he really loves me?* All through the day, students step out of my path as I walk the halls in a blaze of gold and blue, gasping at my audacity, admiring my feathers. All I can think about is Lukas. Singing his heart out yesterday. Reaching out after I'd done everything in my power to push him away.

I'll talk to him at the game, I decide. *I'll ask him what he means and if he has feelings for me.*

Before the pep rally, when I head to the locker room to change into my cheer uniform—right before I pull my knife out of my binder—I fire up the anonymous inbox. And I see the note.

I read it, and my heart drops.

He wants to talk. Alone. To see if we can work things out. Everything I've dreamed of, everything I'm scared of—is he scared in the same way?

He can't possibly mean it, I tell myself. But my feet take over and carry me to the cafeteria all the same. I can't help it. That asshole's like a magnet, sucking me into a black hole of stupid feelings.

And that asking. That was a lot of feeling to put into a prank.

Maybe. Maybe.

I'm stupid.

Maybe.

When I enter the cafeteria, it's near dark. Streamers weave in shadowy silence from the ceiling. Wires wrap around the half-assembled DJ booth. But in a crack of sunlight, I see lights swinging free.

"Lukas?" I shout, anger outpacing my sense, my peacock tail gathering dust on the floor. "You said you wanted to talk, asshole. I'm here. Let's talk."

The delicate strands dangle loose from their nails. The banners lie torn. The tissue-paper phoenix is missing half the gold foil down its side. Flowers lie on the floor of the cafeteria, shredded paper flames stomped by boot prints. And Philip stands in the middle of it all, torn paper knotted in his fists.

"Your boyfriend isn't here," he spits. "It's just you and me."

"He . . . He asked me to come." My voice cracks high. I'd smack myself in the face if I dared take my eyes off him. *Lukas doesn't love me. Lukas doesn't care if I live or die. And my feelings for him are nothing but a weakness that exposes me to danger.* The words feel feeble. My cheeks burn. I'm on literal fire. Turns out, I'm not out of anger. It's not something you can run out of. If you reach into the abyss of your feelings, if you dig, you'll strike it rich with an infinite supply.

Philip must have written that note. No one likes me. I should have expected that. I'm an ass, an out-of-control, testosterone-fueled monster in the making. My own school won't protect me. Lukas didn't want to meet me. Lukas didn't care. And Philip only cares enough to fuck with me.

I've been stupid to come. But I won't show weakness now I'm here.

I think I'll just turn and burn this whole school to the ground.

CHAPTER TWENTY-SEVEN: LUKAS

Thirty Minutes to Homecoming Kickoff

Friday afternoon comes hot and glaring. The timer app on my phone is down into the hours. When the bell rings on final period, I draw a shaky breath and jog off to the cafeteria, which we just finished decorating this morning. Three weeks of effort, and now everything's in place. This evening's Homecoming Dance will be the best Cresswell has ever seen. But nothing will be right if I'm dancing alone.

Maybe I shouldn't be chasing him. But I'm also chasing down this thing in his head that says he's unlovable. I want to show him I'll always be there for him. That he doesn't need to be afraid. *Please*, I think, planning clumsy words in my head. *Please open up for me.*

But when I enter the cafeteria, all my words fall away.

My kingdom. Months of planning, weeks of building. Almost completely ruined. Lights cut off their strings, tablecloths shredded, the orange phoenix missing half its feathers.

It's like a part of me has been shredded. Order torn open like my chest. I run my hands fast back though my hair, a scream beyond frustration building in my throat—then I catch movement and freeze.

Philip, straddling the wooden bird's neck, his hands full of paper. Jeremy, at its base, fingers fumbling with the bottom hem of his shirt.

"You know you could get expelled over this, right?" Jeremy says coldly. *Too cold. What's wrong with him?*

"I'm leaving anyway," Philip says. "I'm wasting my time at a school where no one talks to me. Dad says there's schools in Virginia where I'll get the respect I deserve."

"Buying respect with your dad's money and name?" Jeremy whistles. "And you say I'm not a real man?"

Don't provoke him! The world runs slow, like honey trapped in a jar. I step toward them. My tongue feels numb in my mouth.

Philip climbs off the phoenix and takes a step toward Jeremy. "What's your problem, freak? Are you really going to fight me over a few paper flowers?"

"As a matter of fact," Jeremy says, balling his fists, "I think the flowers look dumb. But Lukas worked hard on this dance. I won't let you destroy everything he cares about."

A wave of happy stupidity boils up from the pit of my stomach. *Oh my god, I am so in love with this idiot.* But my brain fizzes at the thought of seeing all my hard work ruined, all my passion shredded, my kingdom brought low. If Jeremy hits him, Philip will happily press charges. Meehan—and the world—will take Philip's side in this. She won't hesitate to expel Jeremy for violating the Code of Conduct, even as she protects Philip from the same. His future will crumble out from underneath him.

Which is exactly what Philip wants to happen. Why he's doing this right now.

I can live if my kingdom crumbles. It's just one dance, no matter how much weight I've put on it, and tomorrow it'll be gone. But I'll still have a future. And I want a future with Jeremy in it.

I can't go with the flow and let this happen. I need to tell him this is a bad idea.

My tongue slides free. "Jeremy!" I shout. "He's not worth it."

Jeremy doesn't look at me or give any sign he's heard. Philip laughs. "Hey, Lukas. Come to back up your freak girlfriend? Is he not man enough to fight me himself? Needs you to do it?"

I step forward, holding up my hands. Trying not to get too close. Lines of taut violence mark the space between them, a web of energy that'll snap like a spring if I dare too much. "Jeremy, I'm not going to fight him. Neither should you. Listen to me." *Please, please, please actually listen.* "The law is on his side, the school is on his side, and he knows it. Even if you win the fight, it'll be his victory in the end. You'll go to jail. Not college."

"What about the dance?"

"Fuck the dance," I say. "You're more important. Listen to me. I need you to know—"

Philip shouts and lunges at Jeremy. Jeremy ducks under the swing, though, and Philip's sneakers slide on the cafeteria floor. His ankle twists viciously as he slams into the wall and collapses, cursing and grabbing at his leg.

Jeremy grabs a metal folding chair off a rack. Muscles roll in his shoulders as he hoists it over his head. Towering over Philip, for once.

"Okay, motherfucker," he says. "You wanted my attention? You got it."

"Don't!" I shout. He doesn't even turn. My hand flashes for my pocket—*grab phone, call Meehan, call police*. I can't stand by and do nothing as Jeremy brings that down on his head. *He's fucked if the administration sees this. His future is over.* But I've done everything I can think of to pull Jeremy back from the brink of self-destruction. Maybe this is just who he is. Six foot six of anger packed in five foot two. I should let him blow up and salvage what I can. Jeremy was never what I pictured for myself, for my life at Cresswell, for my future. He blew in out of nowhere, knocked my life sideways, and grinned as he left me floundering.

And he can't claim the crown tonight if he's arrested.

"You wouldn't dare!" Philip's voice peaks. He tries to stand. His ankle seizes. "My father—"

"Isn't here to protect you." Jeremy feigns a blow, laughing as Philip cringes. "Come on. Take it like a real man."

Something glints at the hem of his shirt. His knife, sliding loose from the sheath where he's strapped it in. *Idiot keeps bringing it to school.* But he hasn't pulled it out. Of course not. He's not a monster. Not a maniac. He's scared and fighting like the devil himself to look strong. Because Jeremy's anger isn't meant to hurt people, even when it does. He's protecting himself. Cutting people away and cutting into his own skin, too.

I finally understand him, and it might be too late. If he lashes out now, he'll cut away every last line that keeps him tethered.

He needs to see there's another way to be safe. That I care about and value him. That I see him.

That even though he wants me to let him explode, I won't. Because I want something from him, too, and he isn't the only one who gets a say in what happens between us.

I take my finger from the emergency button and shove the phone back into my pocket. Then I do the only thing I can think of. To show him who he'll really hurt if he goes through with this.

I slide between them and lift my hands high.

CHAPTER TWENTY-EIGHT:
JEREMY

I could actually murder this guy.

Nothing has ever tasted so sweet. I'm surfing the tide of my own anger, lifted on the wave of red energy. It may be toxic, but it's the toxic bits in life that taste best. It's seeing Philip skitter back against the wall, seeing his eyes widen and start to water. A cafeteria chair in the wrong hands, and I'm all-powerful. Every taunt he's thrown my way, every word that leveled our friendship, every lie and blow. I've escalated it with a flick of my wrist.

It's excellent. And Lukas ruins it all by stepping between us.

"Move," I say through clenched teeth, "and let me take out the trash."

"It's not worth throwing away your future," Lukas says, his gaze patient and laser-focused on me. His voice is quiet, so quiet, but it's working its way through me. Invading and overthrowing my better senses. He should be angry. Should be screaming. He's put weeks of effort into planning this dance, into turning the Cresswell cafeteria into a kingdom worthy of his imagination. Instead, he's focused on me. Because I'm the angry, screaming one. "Our future. It's our future you're breaking here. It's us."

"What future?" I hiss, sweat rolling down my forehead. Philip tries to skitter sideways. I feint a jab his way, steel winking in the cafeteria lights. Lukas doesn't move. *Idiot.* I taste salt down my throat, hear the ocean pounding against my ears. I'm a force of nature in this heartbeat, a colossal, crashing wave. Ready to shatter everything beneath me. *Everything.* My new friendships with the GSA. The reforged alliance of me, Naomi, and Debbie. *Naomi's scared I can't control myself.* And maybe she's right. Maybe I can't be the sort of friend she wants and needs. All my friends have given me, all they've done for me, has never been enough to slake my desire to burn.

"I love you. I do. I'm sorry I made a show out of it yesterday. I should have told you how I felt without the backup dancers. You're amazing, and we can have anything we want. But you can't go down this path."

"Maybe I'll flatten you when I'm done with Philip," I say. Because now I'm pissed. Every word he speaks cuts into my anger, filing its edges dull. I need my anger to keep moving. I need its power to push me forward.

Maybe I'll push forward through him.

I take one step. My hand is shaky now. My eyes blur with tears. But I won't back down. I can't. I've summoned all the strength I've got, and if I don't use it, I know it could slip away forever.

But Lukas has a strength of his own. "If I could reach into your head and convince you that you're worth it, I would. But I can't. All I can do is show you how I feel, show you what I'd give up for you. All I can do is live like I love you and hope that pulls you through. Tonight is not the night you self-destruct. And if I can help you not blow up today, maybe I can help us last long enough to get somewhere where people like Philip don't matter."

He's an idiot, I think, my heart pounding so hard it drowns out all the world. Standing here. Endangering himself for me. Like some noble fool. Like he wants to save me.

Like he believes I can be saved. Like he believes in me.

Like he loves me more than anything. In every way I need. In every way that matters.

And so many people do. Coming out earned me Philip's attention, but it also linked me so much deeper with everyone around me. Showed me what parts of myself I had to work on. Showed me that, when the school administration and powers that be won't protect me, my friends will, even when it means taking a risk.

I can't hurt Philip without destroying everything my community has built. And the man I want to be isn't so selfish as to go up in flames when it burns everyone around him.

I can take Lukas's hand or slip under the tide. I can drown or keep struggling to swim, figuring myself out one painful, dragging stroke at a time. *It hurts. Like needles in my stomach and holes in my chest.*

But I can hurt with his hand in mine. And we can pull each other forward. Build a better place together, no matter what stands in our way.

I dart forward, twisting around Lukas. He grabs for my collar, but being short and quick finally gets me somewhere. Nothing lies between Philip and me but the bludgeon of my chair.

"You're an asshole," I say, enjoying his flicker of fear. I know why he's doing this. Because I represent something new, something unpredictable. My existence means all the little boxes he stands tall on are crumbling into ash. Every second I breathe is a blow against his power. "Even freshman year, you always brought the worst parts of me to the surface."

He knows this. He's the one who's scared. Not me.

"We're going to leave." I watch him as I grab Lukas's hand and tug him back to the door. I fling down the chair. It clatters at his feet. "You can stay here, trash the dance, do whatever you want, Philip. But you can't follow. We're going to go get our crowns. You can stay here and mope in the ruins of an empire that only exists inside your head."

Philip's mouth drops. I don't take my eyes from him as we back away. Lukas's hand shoves open the cafeteria door. Sunlight spills into the room.

"Fucking fags!" Philip shouts. He crawls forward, scrambling on his good leg, and grabs the chair. My eyes narrow. He falters. Turns and slams the folding chair into the neck of the papier-mâché phoenix. It buckles.

Lukas pulls me into the light. Nothing that matters has been broken.

We shove the door shut and leave him in the dark. Both of us, leaning with our backs to the cafeteria door. Breathing hard. The trace of a smile dancing around his lips as he looks at me.

"Well," Lukas says. "That was fun." He reaches up behind me and tucks my knife more securely up in its sheath. His hand brushes my hip as he pulls away. My breath catches. "Glad you didn't pull that out. For a second, I worried you were a murderer or something."

"I'm definitely something," I murmur weakly. My heart still hammers in my ears at a million miles per hour. The world swims back into focus, and my feet feel unsteady as I step forward. I buckle.

"It's okay." Lukas catches me and pulls me close, his arm warm around my shoulders. "You didn't do it. You're okay."

"I don't ever want to be that angry ever again," I mutter into his collar. "It—it hurts. I want to feel better. Positive. Happy. I want to be a better person for you and all my friends. Better than who he is. The sort of friend who deserves all the faith you put in me."

Because I've never been as alone, as vulnerable, as I feared I was. I just didn't know how to find the people who were really on my side until I learned how to be on theirs.

"Then put the anger aside." He squeezes my hand. "I have faith in you. Now, go get changed. The game's starting soon. Ben and I need you to cheer us on."

I run off to change, then sprint up to the field. Pope Pius, our opponents this evening, are exactly as pathetic at football as we'd hoped. The worst team in the district and the second-worst team, head to head—but I lift my pom-poms high and scream as Ben throws Lukas the first touchdown pass. Naomi flings me atop the human pyramid as my mom waves proudly from the bleachers. Sol and the rest of the GSA cheer as Lukas sprints down the field, a blaze of blue and gold. Then, just before halftime, Lukas leaves the bench to embrace his grandparents, who walk up the pitch hand in hand.

And the anger isn't burning me. It lies off to the sidelines, put away in a box of its own. Maybe I can leave it there.

"Nice flip," Naomi says, helping me down after a toss. Sweat glitters on her forehead, dazzling under the stadium lights.

"I couldn't have done it without you," I say. "Any of it."

Halftime arrives in a clash of cymbals. The marching band takes the field in a clatter of trumpets and drumbeats. Wind whips the lingering humidity from the air. The floats parade around the track as the losers from Pope Pius groan in the guest bleachers: the freshmen's flatbed full of question marks, the sophomores' dragon with a roaring papier-mâché head that falls off halfway around the ring, the juniors' *Millennium Falcon* with speakers blasting the *Star Wars* theme, and the two senior floats—one for the Avengers and one for the Justice League.

My breath catches. It's time. It's time for everything.

"Hello, Cresswell!" Principal Meehan takes the microphone and strides out onto the field. "Time to announce the members of the Homecoming Court!"

"Here it goes," Ben says, walking over to me. Lukas leaves his grandparents and comes to stand with us.

"May the best man win?" Lukas says, shaking my hand.

"Is that your concession speech?" I say, grinning. He looks hurt. I sigh. *You asshole. Stop being so prickly for once. Stop trying to drive him away.* "I mean, thanks. It was a good fight."

And in some way, I can't help feeling we both won. We survived. We're here together. We learned how to take care of each other, and that our friends will take care of us.

I don't need a crown to know people support me. I've seen it with my own two eyes.

"Homecoming Queen: Naomi Guo!"

The bleachers erupt in cheers. The marching band rattles out a triumphant drum solo. I clap until my wrists ache.

"Homecoming King . . ."

I hold my breath. Lukas smiles at me.

No matter what happens, I've won. We've won.

Meehan clears her throat. Rubs her eyes a few times. Like she can't imagine what she's seeing.

"Sol Reyes-Garcia?"

And the bleachers explode into confused applause as Sol steps down, glittering in a rhinestone-bedazzled tuxedo, and curtsies before the waiting crowd.

CHAPTER TWENTY-NINE: LUKAS

Homecoming Dance

I'm wandering the cafeteria in a daze. I mean, a lot of people are. The banners have been ripped and shredded. Philip beheaded the phoenix with a chair. Posters from the science classrooms have been hastily taped over the word *Fag* drawn in Sharpie on the wall. The school police officers mutter in low voices, tallying the damage.

"How did this happen?" Debbie says.

I shrug. "At least the DJ equipment still works. And, hey, we've got snacks."

Naomi and Sol sit on the dented thrones on the stage, dazzling in rhinestones and tulle, chatting to each other. "Good game," I mouth at the sophomore, and they wink, the crown slipping forward on their brow. At least they seem to be having a nice time. The DJ has started the evening with Kesha, which isn't a bad choice, but maybe not how I want things to go.

The timer on my phone has run out. My kingdom lies in ruins. My crown went to a geeky sophomore. Neither of my parents have shown up, even though Mom said she'd let Dad come. And it doesn't bother me as much as I thought it would.

Because for all that the world pushes on me to be a perfect son, a perfect football player, a perfect person, I can push back. Carve out a space where my needs are in balance with everyone else's. Salvage shining moments and string them together into a life worth living.

And I can start doing that right now.

"Put on something slow," I tell the DJ, and hand over my last twenty bucks.

A slow, crooning song fills the room.

A hand takes mine. It belongs to a short blond boy with a swollen nose and a flashy paisley tie worn over a pink shirt. My white shirt and blue tie feel rather plain next to him, but I'm used to feeling that way. He loves being the center of attention, and I'm happy to let him.

"Can I have this dance?" Jeremy asks, disco lights swimming up and over the pale hollow of his neck. "As a peace offering?"

He doesn't mean it as just a peace offering. There's only two ways to settle the war between us. Both terrify me. One means changing everything I assumed about myself and my future.

But the other means walking away from him, and I can't lose him again.

I pull his hand to my hip.

"You can have this dance," I say as he leans into me, "as the love of my life."

"Please. You're only eighteen. Those feelings could change."

I laugh. "Don't talk to me about things changing. I know things change. Everything's changed this year. I only love you more."

"I hate you," he says, and kisses me.

We slide back together smoothly, easily, and it's like all the weights I am carrying lift free. His warm breath on my lips, his tongue pushing through, his hands tangled in my hair. I can feel his heart race in time with mine, his bound breasts pressing hard against my chest, the new brush of blond stubble on his upper lip. *All heat and wanting. Nothing left on the field.*

And I know he can take anything I could throw at him. I know I don't have to be gentle. I know we fit.

"I love you," he mumbles when at last he pulls away, his voice a deep thrum on my chest, welcome and perfect. "There. You've got my whole heart in your hands. Don't drop it."

From the dais, Naomi and Sol cheer us on. Ben and Max clap by the punch bowl. Meehan shouts, "No PDA!"

"Homophobe," Jeremy mutters, and I grab his hands so he can't punch anyone. I'm really glad I get to do that.

"There's someone I want you to meet," I say, and pull him along.

My grandparents, holding hands, wait by the wall. Their smiles, I know, are genuine. They probably won't accept what's really going on between me and Jeremy, but I want to be honest. Be clear with my family about my own life as I try in my own way to make them proud.

I want to build my own relationship with them. A balance, where I'm not giving over every part of me. And if they don't like the truth, I'm surrounded by people who do.

"Hi," I say, holding his hand tight. "I know tonight wasn't what you expected. But I want you to know I'm okay, and I'm happy. And I want you to meet the reason why." I take a deep breath. I can't believe I get to say this. I want to savor this first time, even though my gut says I'll never get tired of this. "This is Jeremy Harkiss. My boyfriend."

EPILOGUE: JEREMY

After

When I woke up in Lukas's arms the morning after the dance—and crawled across his chest to grab my phone off my nightstand—the video of Sol's coronation had two hundred thousand impressions. *Trans Latinx kid crowned Homecoming monarch by supportive classmates!!!*

In the end, Lukas and I were footnotes in their story. Two assholes with egos bigger than one school could hold. Two aching, broken hearts that felt painful enough to eclipse the whole world, but that only really mattered to us, our families, and our friends. Our pain didn't make us special.

But that was okay, because it meant our pain didn't define us, either.

We could just be ourselves. In love and happy to be so.

Cresswell produced a second viral video that evening. Max escorted Philip into the locker room to remove his gear before he got kicked off campus. He'd filmed while

Philip had opened his locker to find a hissing—but otherwise benign—black rat snake inside. Philip had run away, screaming. *MarineBoy faces danger!!!* made an online sensation. I hoped his future fellow West Point cadets would find ways to sneak snakes into his bags.

Anyway, Max let me keep it as a pet.

Lukas's grandparents—well, Lukas thinks they don't quite understand I'm a boy now, and I think they do understand but just really wish he could be dating a girl. They still aren't great about my name and pronouns, but I can let that be. For a while, at least. Just because I protect my own queerness by throwing it in people's faces doesn't mean Lukas has to do the same.

▷

"Are you pissed at me?" Sol asks when we catch up at the diner a few days later, munching on a burger topped with milkshake foam. "I know the crown meant a lot to you. I just . . . I hated knowing that, no matter which of you won, one of you would be devastated. You'd freak out that Cresswell didn't think you were manly enough, or Lukas would break down because his life was ruined. And after putting up all our posters, I felt like I really had a shot. So I didn't start campaigning until pretty late, but I asked all the underclassmen to vote for me. You and Lukas split the upperclassmen vote pretty neatly down the middle. It was wide open."

"You wanted us both devastated."

"I wanted to win. And I figured you two would console each other if you lost."

They're right. "If I'd been sitting up with the court, I wouldn't have danced with Lukas."

"And you two—"

"Are perfect together. Madly in love. Nothing could come between us."

"Aren't his parents getting divorced?"

I shrug. "I said we're perfect together, not that life is perfect." But I don't need it to be. The Cresswell administration may have failed to protect me from Philip, but my friends pulled me through. The community we've built can hold us together, no *perfect* required. "Why have you and Naomi started hanging out? I didn't think you had much in common."

"We do," they say, in a weird but mysterious way that convinces me they're hiding something.

But I don't push. I don't need to. People can have stories they don't want to share with the world yet. People are allowed to have secrets.

"Sol," I say, "you set up the web poll. Which one of us came in second?"

They wink over their milkshake. "My secret. Now all three of us have to stay friends, since I'm the only one who knows the truth."

There's worry in their voice. I tuck an arm around their shoulder. "We're friends indeed, Your Majesty."

My name change paperwork comes through the week I'm supposed to send in my college application, which I'm glad of. I write my essay on the lessons I've learned as a boy on the cheer team and don't mention my transition. Not because I'm ashamed of who I am, but because I want there to be more to my story moving forward—and because I don't know if there's a Philip in the Harvard admissions office. He's gone from Cresswell now, but not from my thoughts. I'm impatient for my scrub goatee to fill out, to finally get to my top surgery, but I'll always be slight and vulnerable to the world's eyes.

I can handle that. I know, in Lukas's eyes, I'm everything.

After the last game of the season, I hang up my pom-poms for good in the storage shed. Tears fill my eyes as I walk off the field for the very last time. *Goodbye, cheer self. Goodbye, pep rallies and pyramids and belonging to the crowds. Hello, big, scary, awesome, post-Cresswell future.*

He's waiting for me by my car. Holds my face in his hands and kisses my forehead, anchoring me against the world.

"I can't wait for our next big adventure," he says. The setting sun glints off the three new gold hoops in his ear as he smiles at me.

Everything's an adventure from here.

ACKNOWLEDGMENTS

I am so incredibly thrilled to see *May the Best Man Win* finally make it into the world! It takes a village to make a book, and it wouldn't be in your hands without the hard work and encouragement of many people—Kaitlyn Johnson, my agent, who always goes above and beyond to fight for me; Mekisha Telfer, my editor, who brilliantly and insightfully untangled this story to find its heart; and Tara Gilbert, who told me I simply had to write it.

I'm forever grateful to my critique group, the #Dragon-Hatchlings, for helping me develop my craft while protecting my sanity in this wild publishing world! Briston Brooks, who brought me in and always pushes me to be better; Alexandra Overy for her keen insight and wicked humor; Tiffany Elmer for her leadership and guidance; and more—Annemarie Pettinato, Esme Symes Smith, Jessica Bibi Cooper, Rosey Waters, Fallon DeMornay, Kindra Pring, and every author who's taken part in this journey. Another shout-out to the wonderful authors I've met online who've provided support, advice, and friendship—Kelly Quindlen, Cassandra Farrin, Laura Weymouth, Tasha Suri, Rebecca Thorne, Rebecca

Podos, Becky Albertalli, Kat Enright, Julian Winters, Rebecca Mix, Saundra Mitchell, Ray Stoeve, Cory McCarthy, A.-M. McLemore, K. M. Szpara, Isaac Fitzgerald, Kacen Callender, Naseem Jamnia, Sophie Gonzales, and more.

And I would be nowhere without my incredible real-life found family: Aster, who has always been my rock; Kitty, who never hesitates to give me a much-needed dose of reality; Layne, a wonderful book-and-movie buddy; Ally and A.J., an unstoppable wonder-duo; Charlene, with her incredible love for queer life; and Carrie, who loves queer life but also the Steelers.

I've been lucky to receive excellent advice on navigating the publishing world from Jennifer De Chiara, Marie Lamba, Roseanne Wells, and Whitley Abell. A special shout-out to Print Run Podcast, my favorite publishing-adjacent podcast, and to Saritza Hernandez, for her invaluable input. I'd also like to thank the MCPG production team, including Jennifer Healey, Starr Baer, and John Nora, and the publicity team, Mary Van Akin and Cynthia Lliguichuzhca.

Finally, I'd like to thank all the booksellers, librarians, and teachers who brought this book to its audience, all the brave transgender activists who've changed this world, and all my readers, for opening the page. As so many of us grapple with the upheaval in our world, I still believe community, friendship, and teamwork can prevail where authority falls short. Communities have the power to protect one another, and I am very deeply lucky in my own.